ALLEN COUNTY PUBLIC LIBRARY

3 1833

D1554636

"CHECK YOUR

THE SHOWS

Fiction

It came from ...

D... deca... '50s, ... sions from outer space, a veritable army of mad scientists, and rampaging hordes of teenage monsters, juvenile delinquents, and the ever-popular colossal bugs. In the '60s and '70s, these mainstays were joined by motorcycle gangs, kung fu masters, and futuristic road warriors. Now, some of today's most imaginative minds have given us the chance to return to those drive-ins one last time with such original tales as:

"Underground Atlanta"—The Old South could be buried, but could it ever be forced to surrender?

"Bullets Can't Stop It"—When the audience becomes part of the movie, your own imagination may prove the most dangerous creature of all....

"The Good, the Bad and the Danged"—He was the best gunfighter the West had ever known, but he'd never shot it out with something that wasn't human....

It Came From The
Drive-In

More Outstanding Anthologies Brought to You by DAW:

WEIRD TALES FROM SHAKESPEARE *Edited by Katharine Kerr and Martin H. Greenberg.* Welcome to the alternate Shakespeare, in which today's top fantasists provide such unique entertainments as a computer-peopled "King Lear," a vampiric Romeo, an unforgettable Midsummer's Night encounter with Puck, an arachnid Queen Lyr, and a fairy queen determined to find true love—or at least a truly magical moment of passion.

ALIEN PREGNANT BY ELVIS *Edited by Esther M. Friesner and Martin H. Greenberg.* From a Martian memorial to Elvis to a rock band with Satan for a manager, here are thirty-six original tales that could have come straight from the tabloids—by such top tale-spinners as Dennis McKiernan, Lawrence Watt-Evans, Alan Dean Foster, Harry Turtledove, and Mike Resnick.

THE SECRET PROPHECIES OF NOSTRADAMUS *Edited by Cynthia Sternau and Martin H. Greenberg.* From one woman's encounter with a Revelation that is out of this world . . . to a centuries-old international society dedicated to minimizing the devastating effects of true predictions, here are truly provocative tales each of which breathes new life into the ancient art of prophecy.

It Came From The

Drive-In

Edited by Norman Partridge
and Martin H. Greenberg

DAW BOOKS, INC.
DONALD A. WOLLHEIM, FOUNDER
375 Hudson Street, New York, NY 10014

ELIZABETH R. WOLLHEIM
SHEILA E. GILBERT
PUBLISHERS

Allen County Public Library
900 Webster Street
PO Box 2270
Fort Wayne, IN 46801-2270

Copyright © 1996 by Norman Partridge & Martin H. Greenberg.

All Rights Reserved.

Cover art by Vincent Di Fate.

DAW Book Collectors No. 1014.

Introduction © 1996 by Norman Partridge.
Talkin' Trailer Trash © 1996 by Edward Bryant.
10585 © 1996 by Sean A. Moore.
Big Bust at Herbert Hoover High © 1996 by Jay R. Bonansinga.
'59 Frankenstein © 1996 by Norman Partridge.
Tuesday Weld, Sunday Services © 1996 by Rex Miller.
Die, Baby, Die, Die, Die! © 1996 by Dan Perez.
The Yellers of Their Eyes © 1996 by Tia Travis.
Underground Atlanta © 1996 by Gregory Nicoll.
The Morning of August 18th © 1996 by Ed Gorman.
The Thing from Lovers' Lane © 1996 by Nancy A. Collins.
Jungle J. D. © 1996 by Steve Rasnic Tem.
The Blood on Satan's Harley © 1996 by Gary Jonas.
I Was a Teenage Boycrazy Blob © 1996 by Nina Kiriki Hoffman.
Bullets Can't Stop It © 1996 by Wayne Allen Sallee.
Race with the Devil © 1996 by Randy Fox.
The Good, the Bad, and the Danged © 1996 by Adam-Troy Castro.
The Slobbering Tongue that Ate the Frightfully Huge Woman © 1996 by Robert Devereaux.
Plan 10 from Inner Space © 1996 by Karl Edward Wagner.

First Printing, February 1996
1 2 3 4 5 6 7 8 9

DAW TRADEMARK REGISTERED
U.S. PAT. OFF. AND FOREIGN COUNTRIES
—MARCA REGISTRADA
HECHO EN U.S.A.

PRINTED IN THE U.S.A.

CONTENTS

INTRODUCTION
 by Norman Partridge 7
TALKIN' TRAILER TRASH
 by Edward Bryant 11
10585
 by Sean A. Moore 16
BIG BUST AT HERBERT HOOVER HIGH
 by Jay R. Bonansinga 37
'59 FRANKENSTEIN
 by Norman Partridge 52
TUESDAY WELD, SUNDAY SERVICES
 by Rex Miller 72
DIE, BABY, DIE, DIE, DIE!
 by Dan Perez 77
THE YELLERS OF THEIR EYES
 by Tia Travis 89
UNDERGROUND ATLANTA
 by Gregory Nicoll 125
THE MORNING OF AUGUST 18TH
 by Ed Gorman 143
THE THING FROM LOVERS' LANE
 by Nancy A. Collins 150
JUNGLE J.D.
 by Steve Rasnic Tem 184
THE BLOOD ON SATAN'S HARLEY
 by Gary Jonas 196
I WAS A TEENAGE BOYCRAZY BLOB
 by Nina Kiriki Hoffman 204
BULLETS CAN'T STOP IT
 by Wayne Allen Sallee 218

RACE WITH THE DEVIL
  by Randy Fox 232
THE GOOD, THE BAD, AND THE DANGED
  by Adam-Troy Castro 242
THE SLOBBERING TONGUE THAT ATE THE
FRIGHTFULLY HUGE WOMAN
  by Robert Devereaux 268
PLAN 10 FROM INNER SPACE
  by Karl Edward Wagner 289

INTRODUCTION: OR, HERE'S WHERE YOUR TICKET GETS TORN

by Norman Partridge

Howdy, Daddy-os and Daddy-ettes. Welcome to the Ground-Zero Drive-In Theater. Pull on up to the ticket window. You're just in time for the show.

Like, *wowsville*. Listen to that engine roar. That's a real piece of work you're driving. It's a '57, ain't it? A real *cherried-out chariot* if you ask me. . . .

You *didn't* ask? And you're in a hurry? Well, *pardon moi*. Don't get your shorts all bunched up, friend. We've still got three previews and a cartoon to go before the first feature starts.

What's that? You don't want to miss the *previews?* Man, oh man, you are one *serious* culture vulture, aren't you?

Hey, now . . . *slow down*. No need to use that kind of language. We'll *expedite* matters, if that's the way you want it. How many tickets do you need tonight?

You *sure* about that, friend? This ain't carload night, you know. Not that I don't trust you, but isn't there someone under that blanket in the backseat? And not to gild the lily, but it looks to me like the rear end of your vehicle's riding lower than a giant Gila monster's belly.

Would you mind maybe poppin' the trunk for me? Not that I'm nosy, you understand . . .

. . . sorry about that, pal. See, you stick around this business long enough, you get suspicious, is all. And don't worry—your secrets are safe with me. I don't need to know why you've got an inflatable Frankenstein under that blanket. None of my business why your trunk's filled with the best collection of hubcaps this side of Detroit, either, though maybe we *could* work out a trade on that electric guitar back there. It looks just like the one Elvis strummed in *Spinout.*

Nope? Okay. If that's the way the mop flops, I can live with it. Just cross my palm with some long green and—

What's that? Of *course* we've still got some good parking spots. Just look over there in the back row, by those folks with the barbecue. There's a choice location. Fact is, I just installed a new speaker on that pole today. Some idiot drove off with the old one. And that Bernz-O-Matic in-car heater hanging next to it actually works. Not that you'll be needing it tonight. . . .

Yep, you're right about that. I guess that fella's barbecue *is* belching fire and smoke like old Godzilla himself. Might kinda cloud your view. But you've gotta admit—there's nothing in the world quite like the smell of roasting weenies at twilight, is there?

Yikes, *lasso* that tongue of yours and corral it behind your choppers. And wipe that drool off the dashboard. You'll never last until intermission, neighbor. I think you'd better make yourself a trip to the snack bar, and pronto. For starters, grab a bucket of crispy, crunchy popcorn. We smother our corn with real butter, not that thirty-weight they use at the Cineplex.

And don't stop there. We've also got sizzling hot dogs, bursting with juicy goodness; thirst-quenching, refreshing, ice-cold drinks; and dandy candy. Tasty ice cream, too. Pizza, with all the toppings—as you like it.

Burgers and fries. Tag-team any of the above with some of those delicious Flavo Shrimp Rolls and you'll have a meal to remember, believe you me!

Of course you'll want to top it all off with a cup of steaming hot coffee. Ours is blended specially so you know it's smooth and rich, full up with the deep mellow flavor and aroma that sets a fella on his feet again. Buy it piping hot and hearty. And don't forget an Eskimo Pie for dessert.

And then there's the show itself, which is a certified mouth waterer in its own right. Well, if we're talkin' about the mouths of Roger Corman, Sam Arkoff, and K. Gordon Murray, that is.

Because we've got it all, amigos and amigettes. Eighteen, count 'em, *eighteen* feature-length motion pictures, all presented on one big screen for your entertainment and edification. Believe me, you folks fog up the windshield tonight, you're making a big mistake.

Like, the *biggest*. Because this show's a real *gasser,* sure to make your inflatable buddy there in the backseat spring a leak.

Oh ... well, pardon me for being *crude*. Hey, pal, this is a *drive-in,* not the opera. But I can flat-out guarantee you, we got something a lot more interesting than a fat lady who sings.

Giant bugs, for instance. We've got 'em here at The Ground-Zero. Alien invaders, you ask? Got those, too. Amazing colossal females? I'm talkin' *right here and now,* and you can wrap me in gauze and call me Kharis if I'm lying.

And that's not all. There's plenty more. We're talkin' teenage monsters. We're talkin' *things* from Lovers' Lane. Slobbering tongues on the prowl. Rampaging mole-folks that time forgot. Evil Nazis and brave cowboys. Atomic mutants and juvenile delinquents. Blobs, headless bikers, and rabid creatures who thirst for human blood.

And rock 'n roll. We've got that, too. Plus lots of greasy kid stuff and black leather. Just what you're looking for, am I right?

Anyway, enough palaver. I don't need to sell *you*. Why, I can see that your foot is getting heavy on that ol' gas pedal, and your tires have already rolled over that row of security treadles. You back up now, those steel-belted radials will be in a world of hurt.

Here are your tickets. Sorry again about that business with the trunk. You and Franky enjoy the show.

Just don't go adding any hubcaps to your collection tonight, okay?

> —Norman Partridge
> Inside the ticket booth
> at the Ground-Zero
> Drive-In Theater

3 1833 02801 1549

TALKIN' TRAILER TRASH

by Edward Bryant

On gigantic wings they flew ...
freedom riders for a nuclear age!

It's a Bell, always a Bell, with that dragonfly-eye bubble cockpit and the fragile tail-boom that looks like delicate steel lacings. It's a copter that landed on lost islands and dry New Mexico deserts. Many times. And many times it never took off again. Sometimes it scouted dinosaurs and the biggest damn' bugs you ever saw, and sometimes it carried logistical support for our boys in Korea.

But this one's comin' in way too low at twelve o'clock high, those chopper blades goin' *whup, whup, whup,* until the damned thing explodes in slow motion and bright red flames and blackest smoke. Pieces of shiny aluminum, all raggedy and aflame themselves start to rain toward the trailer park.

When I was a boy, we measured our days in midair helicopter explosions.

Red light's still flashing, but it's from the gumballs on top of old Sheriff McCurdy's '58 Ford patrol car. He takes that final turn from Hamhock Road on two wheels *way* too fast, and gravel sprays. For a second, no one can see a damned thing.

Then we hear the click and *chunk* of the driver's

door as the sheriff gets out of his cruiser. Those shiny
boot heels slap down on the hardpack. McCurdy stands
in front of us, left hand on hip, right hand resting com-
fortably on the butt of that .45 Colt. The safety strap's
unsnapped, I notice. I've heard tell McCurdy got is-
sued that hog-leg back when he was just a greenhorn
gyrene trying to pacify those Tagalog-spouting
Amokers down in the Philippines a coon's age ago.

No one paid attention when it started. . . .

The voice fills the sky. The words cover the blue sky
and the clouds.

McCurdy surveys us slowly, like he's looking at
something he'd scrape off those county-issue boots. I
can't see his eyes behind those little silver mirrors dis-
guised as sunglasses. "Any you boys seen something
out of the ordinary?"

"Nossuh." Heads shake.

"Like what?" That's Rassalah. He's young and heed-
less.

"Chiggers," says McCurdy. We all stare at each
other like the man's crazy. "Big 'uns," he adds.

Still nobody responds.

"Size of a Desoto pulling a horse trailer," says the
sheriff.

"That's big, all right," says Rassalah, just quick
enough so the lawman looks at him sharply.

"Nobody's seen nothin', Sheriff." That's my mom.
She's staring McCurdy down from the open door of
our old Airstream.

After a while, McCurdy takes off the shades, hooks
one bow in the breast pocket of his tan uniform shirt,
takes out a crumpled hankie from a hip pocket and
wipes his forehead. "Okay," he says. "For now. But I'll
tell you, them big bugs got no place in this town.
They's intruders. Outside agitators. Y'all tell me if you
see anyone or anything new a-tall. Understand?"

Oh, yeah, we understood.

But when they came, the old world ended, and a new one began.

The noise in the sky was like to deafen a person.

What came out of the piney woods behind the trailer camp was something we'd never seen before, not like these fellers.

They were big and black and dangerous-looking.

Sheriff McCurdy and his deputies came out of nowhere, pistols unholstered and rifles in hand. One deputy racked a shell into a scattergun with a bore the size of my wrist. The sound sent chills down my backbone.

"Chiggers!" said the sheriff. "Just like we was told."

Each one was armored in a shiny carapace, feathery antennae all waving in the humid air, six legs all crankin' together like soldiers marching. And sure enough, every one of them *was* as big as a Desoto towing a horse trailer. One or two were as big as Caddies. Or the county coroner's hearse.

"Hold on there, boys," shouted McCurdy. He and his men drew down on those big bugs from somewhere beyond the trailer park. Shoot, probably from clear outside the county! I know *I'd* never seen them around these parts before.

"Just what is it you boys want?"

Nothing would be the same....

The strangers seemed to be moving with purpose, like they knew exactly what they were doing and where they were going. The biggest one, the one I figured was probably the leader, came right up in front of the sheriff and stared (well, as much as something with big faceted eyes can stare) right down the barrel of his automatic.

"Don't call us boys," said the leader of the bugs. He reared up that powerful articulated body, mandibles clicking like huge razors. "I think you could say we're all grown up now."

I wasn't sure I knew what he was really talking about. I guess neither did Sheriff McCurdy. But it did come home to me it was a whole strange new world.

"So what am I s'posed to be calling you chiggers?" said the lawman. *"Chee-gros?"*

Blood might flow, but they would demand respect and equality. . . .

"Insect-Americans," said their leader.

And they'd fight if they had to.

Here came that damned helicopter again.

CHIGGER HEAVEN

CHIGGER HELL

Words that were bigger than the world itself, I swear. And still as deafening, all the way from horizon to horizon.

So what did the chopper have to do with my life and my story? The lives and stories of all of us here at the trailer park? My mom, the sheriff, and those giant new bugs in town? Probably nothin', I guessed.

Maybe God just stuck it there to hook people's attention. Keep folks alert while Sheriff McCurdy stalked off, muttering about whether the big bugs wanted our women, and other watchers shook their heads and asked, *what for?*

My mom agreed. "You're sharp, boy," she said when I mentioned this to her. "First step in trainin' a mule's to get his attention by whupping him up 'longside the head with a two-by-four."

Had to think about that. I wasn't entirely sure what she was gettin' at.

But after a while, I figured maybe I knew.

We measure out our lives in meaningless midair helicopter explosions.

I guess maybe we always will.

But when our attention's got, then comes the rest of the story. And we always pay attention. We love it all.

(for Roger Corman)

10585

by Sean A. Moore

It's home ... outer space!
Its mission ... to enslave an unsuspecting world!
Its destination ... Earth!

1. 350 Lefthand Canyon Road, Friday, 8:56 p.m.

Matt rolled down the VW bug's window, moving the tarnished speaker box to the pole. Colorado mountain air whispered through the trees, rattling the tall chain-link fence that surrounded the drive-in's parking lot. Matt breathed in the cool air, sighing. Two movies down, one to go. Mom had stuck him with baby-sitting duty again, another Friday night wasted with his geek brother at the Devil's Thumb Drive-In.

The Thumb (named after an unusual feature of a local mountain) was the only theater in Lyons, a tiny town north of Boulder. The drive-in showed only lame movies—weekend shows of one second-run movie and two "family film classics." Six hours of boring G- or PG-rated butt fudge. Yawning, Matt turned to Cliff, who had wasted no time flipping open his laptop computer for intermission. The thing was like his brother's electronic Siamese twin; Cliff even had a wheelchair pouch with extra batteries and disks. What a *geek*.

"I'm makin' a run," Matt said. "Want anything?"

"Junior Mints and a box of Gummi Bears," Cliff answered without looking up. His squeaky ten-year-old-know-it-all voice made Matt's teeth clench.

"Got money?"

"You have fifteen left from the twenty Mom gave us. My stuff will only cost three thirty-two with tax."

"*Fourteen* left. Six bucks a carload, butt breath. And we need gas on the way home."

Cliff looked up, his pudgy fingers still tapping away. "I can add, Matt. You're the dumb jock football star. Mrs. Hadley gave you a ten and *five* ones back and you didn't even tell her."

"No way." Matt grabbed the crumpled bills from his pocket and flipped through them, counting fifteen. *Damn.* Cliff was always catching stuff like that. "Never mind," he muttered, getting out and slamming the door behind him.

"I want a root beer, too. Large!" Cliff yelled before his brother was out of earshot.

Matt picked up the pace, heading straight for the concession stand. *Get it yourself,* he wanted to say. But Cliff's wheelchair was up front in the trunk, and Matt hated the five-minute loading process more than he hated being his legless brother's servant.

But most of all, he hated playing dad when it was Cliff's fault that their father was dead.

2. *440 Lefthand Canyon Road, 9:03 p.m.*

10585-81464-WJ had seemed much like the 22 other radioactive meteorites cataloged at Boulder's National Center for Atmospheric Research (NCAR) during the late 1950s. The meteorite had been sealed in a 92-pound lead-lined box, carefully labeled, and moved to the underground storage facility on Lefthand Canyon Road.

Dr. Werner Joss had described 10585 in a two-page report that had later been moved to New Mexico with

*truckloads of other paperwork for microfilm transfer—
the government's discard pile. The report had noted the
specimen's "unusual symmetrical shape." Dr. Joss had
also mistakenly recorded a composition of 47% radium, 38% iron, 11% carbonaceous chrondites, 4%
nickel-iron and other minerals. But even with modern
instruments, Dr. Joss might never have determined the
specimen's true composition, which included no minerals from Earth.*

*And 10585 could do much, much more than make
Dr. Joss' Geiger counter ping like a pinball machine.*

*Soon, the sixty-odd patrons of the Devil's Thumb
Drive-In would receive an in-depth lesson about a forgotten radioactive meteorite that had come from a
place far beyond the peeping eye of the most powerful
telescope.*

After a long sleep, 10585 was about to awaken.

10585 was about to feed.

3. 9:07 p.m.

Cliff whined if they were too far from the screen, so
Matt had parked in the front row. He walked quickly,
but the concession line already wrapped around the
yellow-painted cinder block building, ending near the
restrooms. They stank from decades of cigarette smoke
and urine. Matt didn't want to stand around breathing
that, and he didn't care if he missed the beginning of
the next movie. So he just circled to the front, waiting
for everyone to load up and get out.

It had looked like a typically slow Friday, ten or fifteen cars, a few vans and trucks. Saturday was suppos-
edly the big day, but he would never know. Mom gave
him the VW on Saturday night as part of the deal for
taking Cliff out on Friday. He went into Boulder to see
real movies with his friends, hung out with people

from school, sometimes partying but usually not. He got up early and trained hard.

Football was the ticket out of his fudged-up situation. Long practices kept him away from home. He was good. "Natural talent," coach said. Matt had broken most of the school records for track and football; he was six-four, almost two hundred, big for a sophomore. He'd get a full scholarship—*out* of state, maybe Stanford, and big money in the pros. He'd started hating Lyons three years ago when Dad died, and it got worse every year. The next two years would be hell, but he could deal with it.

"Yo, Matt!"

He spun as Skaff and Zeb's monster truck skidded to a stop a few feet away. They were the brute brothers; seniors, and the team's best defensive backs. They were also the ugliest, rudest rednecks to ever stink up a stadium. They went to the drive-in to swill beer, talk trash, and blow chunks until dawn. Matt, being a sophomore, had managed to avoid them. "Hey Skaff, Zeb, what's up?"

"We's goin' for more beer. Zeb done chugged three friggin' sixers and I'm outta chew. Wanna buy in?"

Matt shook his head. "No can do, Skaff. I got my brother here. Maybe this summer, when school's out—"

"C'mon, Matt." Skaff leaned out and spat. "Ditch the gimp for a coupla hours, we'll go bird huntin'. We knows some girls jes waitin' for us!"

Matt ground his teeth together. The *gimp?* Gimp or not, Cliff was his brother.

Zeb whooped drunkenly, raising his tallboy can of Bud and spilling it onto Skaff. "Dang. Alcohol abuse!" He hooted and snickered, his cigarette bobbing.

"Hey!" A woman's voice belted out from the thinning line of people at the concession stand. "What are you boys doing?"

Zeb threw the can at Matt. It hit him on the chest, spraying him with beer and landing at his feet. The brute brothers drove off, leaving Matt to face the troll who managed the drive-in.

Vera Hadley was a five-by-five woman with a butt like a pair of beanbag chairs and a voice that plowed into your ears like a bulldozer. She stood glaring at Matt, hands on her hips, a nightmare in double-knit polyester.

He stared down at the foaming puddle, wondering what to say. He was in for it—Vera's husband was an editor at the *Daily Camera,* where Matt's mom worked.

4. 9:14 p.m.

10585 had escaped with ease, leaving its shell behind, traveling through the lead-lined box and moving down the huge warehouse's pallet racks. The steel shelves were roads; it searched through them for food, finding none. The energy it needed was coursing through electrical conduits that were beyond reach, attached to the ceiling. It would have to jump through a wall to reach the food.

The dark warehouse lit up in a flash of blue light as 10585 arced from the top pallet rack to the ceiling conduit. It sifted through the metal and wiring, desperate for the energy it had sensed. Movement through these strands of copper was effortless and instantaneous. But there was no food here, only an electromagnetic residue.

The building's generator had been shut off years ago by NCAR, to conserve energy.

The residue whet 10585's appetite, and the jump had used up precious resources. Its hunger became a craving. Cruising the copper highways, it moved upward, past floors of stacked boxes and crates and file cabi-

nets, reaching the top level. It traveled along the cor-
rugated metal walls, still finding nothing. But it sensed
a faint radiance now, something nearby.

Leaving the walls, 10585 channeled itself into a trail
of twisted barbed wire that, some hundred yards away,
adjoined the drive-in's chain-link fence.

5. 9:18 p.m.

"It, uh, isn't mine," Matt stammered.

Vera's retort was drowned out by a bolt of intensely bright lightning that crackled along the drive-in's fence, lighting up the lot like a million-watt flashbulb. The entire fence shimmered like a web of silvery blue steel.

Matt blinked, trying to clear the painful spots from his eyes. Vera was screeching something about God, farm animals, and procreation. From the nearly-empty concession stand, Matt heard cursing and shouts of confusion. "Look—the screen!" someone yelled.

He squinted at it, forcing his eyes to open.

Where the fence met the screen, blue veins spread out, slipping and sliding across its surface. They hissed and popped, retreating to the fence. Before Matt could blink again, the weird blue veins covered every inch of chain-link, nearly surrounding the theater.

Vera's gasp made Matt turn; his eyes had recovered enough to see what had startled her.

Near the rear of the lot, where the fence came closest to the rows of speaker-poles, a single blue tendril was arcing inward. It jumped to a speaker box, bounced up, and hit the roof of a station wagon.

The tendril disappeared, then the family inside the station wagon began screaming. Pale blue light filled the car's interior.

"Rita! Call the police and the damn fire department, now!" Vera bellowed, in the general direction of the concession stand. She barreled past Matt toward the car. Matt crouched instinctively to spring after her, pausing when he saw the glow of other tendrils. There were dozens of them, hopping from the fence to other speaker-poles—to other cars.

One was bouncing its way to the VW.

"No!" Matt flew across the lot. He'd parked in the middle of the front row, ten or fifteen poles from the fence. *Cliff.* Matt's Nikes kicked up dirt behind him, his legs pumping in an adrenaline-powered sprint. He ran flat out, head down, like a punt-returner sprinting across a wide-open field.

He was ten yards away when the blue tendril struck the VW. "Get out, Cliff!" he screamed, his lungs bursting from the effort. He wasn't fast enough. The VW bug's interior glowed dimly, and Matt slid to a stop. He knew that he should pull Cliff out, but the lightning—or whatever it was—could kill him. He'd heard the family in the station wagon scream; that blue stuff probably fried them. *Dad died saving Cliff, and now me.*

But he couldn't just let his little brother die. It wouldn't bring back Dad, and Mom would never forgive him. He circled around to the passenger side of the VW, bracing himself to close the gap.

"Matt? Over here—help me!"

He looked down to see Cliff crawling through the dirt a few feet from the rear of the car. It was a pitiful sight, his brother hauling himself along by his arms, crying, wriggling toward him. Relief flooded through Matt like an icy drink on a blistering hot day. *Yeah, are you glad he's alive, or were you afraid you'd die like Dad, saving him?* Matt pushed the thought aside and grabbed Cliff, who wrapped both arms around him.

He immediately noticed the computer, slung in its bag over Cliff's shoulder. "You took it with you? That thing nearly killed you and me both, dumbass! I should just drop you here, let you crawl home to Mom with your dumbass computer."

"I'm sorry, Matt," Cliff was blubbering now, his tears soaking through Matt's T-shirt.

Too mad to say anything more, Matt hurried away from the VW. The glow had faded from the other cars . . . and with it the screams. At the other end of the lot, Skaff's truck roared toward the exit, swerving to avoid the speaker-poles, bouncing and swaying through the sloping car dugouts. A few cars had their headlights on, but the only real light came from the concession building. Matt hustled toward it, but he couldn't resist the urge to detour and look into the big side windows of a van parked close by.

He was a few feet away from it when Skaff's truck fishtailed, slamming into a speaker-pole. It flipped and rolled, tortured metal screeching in a long slide that ended when the huge pickup wedged itself into the drive-in's narrow entrance. The lone bulb over the ticket booth glowed like a spotlight.

Stunned, Matt watched Zeb flop out through the smashed windshield. Fluids seeped like blood from under the mangled hood, glistening in the light. Matt could smell gas; the stink was already filtering across the lot.

Skaff hung limply out of the driver's side. It took Matt a second or two of staring to realize that the left half of Skaff's face was missing, rubbed off during the slide.

Zeb slid down the hood and lay still, his lit cigarette dropping and bouncing toward the spreading puddle. Matt had just enough time to say the F-word before the flames shot into the air. The truck blew with a *KA-WHUMP!* that sent a mushroom of fire high into the air. Glass and metal showered the ground nearby, and something meaty thumped against the side of the van.

Smoking kills, Matt's mind babbled, repeating words on a classroom poster. A hot, reeking wave of air pushed past him, nearly knocking him down.

Vera bellowed, and Matt heard other shouts from the concession stand, but the van and the drive-in's other patrons were curiously silent. No one else had even tried to drive away.

He steadied his legs and walked up to the darkened van.

The speaker box hung in the van's passenger window. A slender blue vein ran up the black cable that joined the box to the pole. Dim light glowed inside, like a weak flashlight. Matt backed around and looked through the driver's side window.

"Don't look," he cautioned, turning to block Cliff's view. Inside, the van's dome light revealed a nightmare.

The box's speaker grille had opened like a steel mouth. Its tongue was a thick wire split into three squirming strands. One writhed in the throat of the driver. His glowing blue eyes bulged, popping out and waving around on their stalks, then sank into his skull. Milky fluid welled up in the hollow sockets. His body was still.

Next to the driver, a woman tugged feebly at the strand in her mouth, her tongue waving and flopping around. In the back, a kid had both hands around the wire, his lips clamped shut. He looked at Matt, pleading silently for help.

Before Matt could move, the strand slithered through the kid's fingers, missing his mouth, opting for a nostril instead. Matt could see the flesh of the kid's face rippling as the wire crawled around inside. The kid screamed, yanking at the strand. Blood streamed from his nostrils before the strand—no, the *lightning-thing*—found soft eyes, pushing them out. They snapped back into the kid's head, spraying pink and gray juice on the van's window.

Matt wrenched his head to one side, gagging. He backed away from the van, struggling not to spew. *That could have been us.* He staggered across the lot to the concession booth, numbed and dripping sweat.

From behind, he heard the van's door open.

He looked over his shoulder.

Cliff screamed.

The woman was stumbling toward them, her empty eyes glowing. The wire wriggled in her mouth like a black worm, slipping inside until both ends poked out of her oozing eye sockets. She shuffled and jerked, stiff-kneed. Floss-thin strands of blue light crept along her face, disappearing under her shirt, popping out under the sleeves and traveling down to her fingers. They danced and sparked there, as if trying to ... jump.

In spite of Cliff's weight, Matt ran faster than he had ever run before.

5. 9:25 p.m.

It fed ravenously, consuming the food provided by its prey. Each organism it sampled had subtle flavors and a soft, rich center. These beings were crude and fragile, easy to manipulate. A jumble of useless pathways led to the same source of energy, which was the only thing remarkable about them. 10585 had severed all the needless connections inside the beings and built nests in each one, leaving a little seed of itself inside.

The biological energy would feed its seeds. In time, they would have enough power to leave their hosts and seek others, as 10585 itself had done. Until then, movement was possible only by triggering the systems within the primitive beings.

It had tapped most of the organic sources here, but

*not all. A few had slipped beyond its reach, but it
would move the hosts into contact with these few and
drink their energy soon. 10585 had spread itself thin
and could not yet jump though the barriers of air. The
hunt had exhausted much of its energy, and it needed
rest.*

*It moved sluggishly through the roads of twisted cop-
per, leaving the seedlings. It went underground to see
where the roads went.*

*They seemed to be converging in the center of this
place.*

6. 9:27 p.m.

Matt stood panting, waiting in the concession booth
with Vera Hadley, Rita Mendez, and a man he didn't
recognize. He'd set Cliff down by the counter. They
were the only survivors, it seemed.

"They're getting closer," Rita said, staring through
the screen door. She was standing behind the glass
counter, chomping on a mouthful of gum that filled the
tiny room with its artificial grape scent. Outside, a mob
lurched closer. No one could stop staring at the eye-
less, gory bunch—except Cliff, who was stuffing his
face with Junior Mints and Gummi Bears.

"Where the hell are the police? Or the fire trucks?"
Vera crossed her arms and glared.

"They said Boulder fire would have to be dis-
patched."

"What? They're a half hour away! Call again, Rita."

The tall, thick-chested man stood right up front,
leaning against the door frame. "Dang! That's Jerry
and Penny Rutledge and their whole stinkin' family.
Never could stand the S.O.B., thumbin' through my
whole rack and never buyin' a dang thing."

Matt remembered the man now. He was Ted Mack, a
retired Army guy who ran the Gas 'n' Go north of

Nederland. He would have looked like a living G.I. Joe, except for the beer gut under the patriot missile on his DESERT STORM—EAT THIS, SADDAM! T-shirt.

"What did they say, Rita? Here, give me the phone!" Vera snatched it from Rita's hand and started screeching into it. "Now you listen to me, whoever you are. Tell Sheriff Wells to get his butt out here now. We got big trouble here, do you hear me? People are *dying!*" She raved on.

Ted covered his ears. "Settle down, Vera! I think I hear—"

"Sirens!" Vera slammed down the phone.

Matt saw the county sheriff's Wagoneer roaring up Lefthand, lights flashing.

"That ain't the way, dummy!" Ted boomed, slapping his forehead. "Dang!"

The Jeep swerved around the smoking truck wreckage, barely slowing. It drove straight into the rows of tire spikes that made the exit a one-way trip. Amazingly, the gashed tires lasted long enough for the Jeep to reach the last row of speaker-poles. Matt could see the driver's ashen face and flailing arms before the Wagoneer skidded into a pole.

The door popped open and the sheriff wobbled out, blood pouring from his smashed nose.

He took a few more steps before the Rutledge family greeted him, reaching out with blue-tinged fingers. Sheriff Wells fumbled at the snap on his holster, drawing his revolver. He fell to the ground screaming, his gun slipping from nerveless fingers.

Vera moaned and looked away.

The screaming stopped abruptly and the sheriff stood, eye sockets glowing under the brim of his hat.

"That's it," Ted said. "I've had enough waitin'. We could all end up like that before anyone else gets here."

"What are you going to do?" Rita asked, wide-eyed.

"Run for my truck and get us the hell of out here. But first," he eyed the ground where the sheriff's gun lay, "I'm gonna do us all a favor and take care of the Rutledges."

"You mean *shoot* them?" Rita's eyes bulged.

"No, I'm gonna bring 'em popcorn and sodas to distract 'em. Hell, yes, I'm shootin' 'em! They're dead anyway. Six bullets, six Rutledge zombies. Kinda works out even, like God meant it to be."

"Zombies?" Vera's forehead wrinkled. "But how do you know they're dead? They might have radiation sickness, or brain damage, like people who get hit by lightning. I read once in the *Enquirer*—"

"Matt's the fastest," Cliff said, through a mouthful of candy. "School track champion. He has the best chance of making it."

"Huh?" Matt glared at his little brother.

Ted eyed Matt appraisingly, nodding. "Well, I bet you're faster 'n' me, anyway." He pulled a key ring out of his pocket. "Mine's the S-10, three spaces from that van clear over there. What do you say?"

Matt stared at the keys like they were a handful of silver spiders.

Ted rubbed at his nose. "Tell you what. I'll get the gun and cover you. Those things move real slow, and I never miss. Are you with me, son?"

Matt nodded, sighing. Ted dropped the keys into his hand.

The back door banged open, and Rita screamed. A short man wearing a flower-print shirt lurched in, luminous hands outstretched. Rita grabbed a broom and shoved him backwards a step. But a whole row of glowing-eyed patrons were pushing from behind, and the man didn't budge much farther.

"I told you to lock it!" Vera shook her finger at Rita.

Ted looked around frantically, noticing a third door. It was solid wood, not a flimsy aluminum screen door like the others. "What's this, Vera?"

"To the projection booth upstairs, but—"

"Does it lock? Good. Take the kid and get up there, now! Rita, go with 'em and gimme that." He ran behind the counter and pushed her back, throwing his weight into the broom. He reversed it, holding the sweeping end and jamming the handle into the short man's chest. Ted's back foot braced against the counter; he leaned forward, straining. "Dammit, Vera! Get up there! I got a pump-action and a couple of .45's in the truck. We'll be back to get you out."

The broom began to bow in the middle; it slid up the flower-print shirt, lodging against the man's neck. Rita flung open the door and ran upstairs. Vera scooped up Cliff. He snatched at the strap of his computer bag on the way up, eliciting a scowl from Matt. But now was not the time. The Rutledges were five yards from the front door.

Vera slammed shut the door; Matt heard the dead bolt turn.

"Run, son! I'm right—" Ted grunted, his grip on the broom slipping, "—right . . . behind . . . *you!*" He shoved hard, arm muscles bulging, plunging the handle into the short man's neck. Blood sprayed his T-shirt as he turned and hustled after Matt.

The short man fell forward, tugging feebly at the inch-thick wooden shaft spearing his neck. The advancing mob trampled him, swaying into the small room like a demonic bunch of drunks.

Matt spun his head around, clutching the keys in his sweaty fist. He was past the Rutledges, but there were eight others beyond them—no, nine—closing in, blocking the way to the truck. *Just do it.* Yeah, right. He cranked it up, aiming for the biggest gap. He didn't see the pothole there until his foot caught on it. Trying to pull it out with a hop, he managed to catch the toe of one cross trainer, twisting and falling on his face. He slid, eating dirt and gravel, stopping short of the van's back tire.

The kid was still in the back, fumbling at the van's side door. It was open a few inches, but it must have been stuck; Matt heard a strange, frustrated growl from inside the van. A hand lunged out, groping toward Matt. Nearby, four of the things ambled his way.

Pop! Pop! Two of them went down, spraying brain-jelly. "Get up, son!" From the front of the concession building, Ted took aim and another thing hit the dirt.

Matt's leg throbbed; he could barely stand. He didn't dare touch the van—the blue stuff might be able to move through the metal and get to him. Inhaling deeply, he took off again, hobbling past the van toward the S-10. Behind him, three more gunshots echoed across the lot.

He hopped the rest of the way, climbing into the truck and exhaling with relief. Ted was circling around the Rutledges, who were now orphaned. Matt gunned the engine, taking the long way around. He couldn't run the things down; if the Chevy hit one, the blue stuff might zap him through the frame.

Ted dodged the lunging sheriff and jumped into the truck. He reached under the seat and hauled out a pistol. "Colt .45 automatic," he grinned. "You shoot?"

Matt shook his head.

Ted shrugged. "Back up and I'll pick 'em off, then we can move in and get the others." He rolled down the window and started blasting. "Too dark along the perimeter," he grumbled. "Flip on the brights and circle around, make sure we get 'em all."

They reached the front of the drive-in, and Matt slowed.

Ted glanced at him.

"That's our VW," he explained.

"Your family here, son?"

Matt shook his head. "My dad died, and Mom works nights at the *Camera*."

"I'm sorry." Ted scanned the row while pushing more bullets into the clip. "How long ago?"

"Three years." Matt shifted, wincing from the pain in his leg. "Our house burned down."

"No sh—no foolin'?" Ted's voice lowered. He slapped the clip back in, peering out. "Lost my best friend that way, twenty-odd years back. Helluva thing, fires, I mean."

Matt's throat went dry. "He died saving Cliff—that's my little brother. Cliff and me were in the basement, and I got out, but Cliff got stuck and Dad went in after him. He handed him to me from the little window down there, but Cliff's legs burned so bad he lost them. And the house caved in on Dad before he got out."

"You 'n' Cliff was in the same room?"

"Yeah. At first he was right behind me, but he went back down to get his stupid computer. If he hadn't done that, Dad would be alive."

Ted looked down the sights and squeezed off a shot, dropping a lone shambler. "Your brother was what—six? Seven? Why didn't you go after him or stop him?"

"I don't know. I thought he was right behind me." *But he wasn't, was he? And you knew it, he told you he was going back, you'll always know it. You chickened out and let Dad go after him, even though you're the track star. You killed your dad and ruined your mom's and brother's lives.* Fat tears rolled down his face.

"Helluva thing," Ted repeated. "Lost my dog when I was twenty. Gas fire in the trailer," he added. "Got me so upset I left school, joined the service."

Matt's eyes were pouring; he couldn't have stopped crying if he'd tried.

"It changes you, don't it? Like tonight, I mean. Three years back, you run out. Tonight, you go in after your brother, then you run for the truck."

Matt whirled, suddenly angry. "I haven't changed! I didn't want to get him; I was going to let him die! And you *made* me go for the truck."

"Like hell I did." Ted drew a bead on the kid in the van, who'd finally pushed open the door. "Wrong on both counts." He paused, firing. "Look, no one *made* you do nothin'. You coulda just run outta here, hell, you coulda drove off when you got in the truck. I bet you woulda three years back.

"It don't matter if you're scared. Only a real idiot *wouldn't* have been scared. Hell, I nearly dropped a load in my pants back there when those things busted through the door, and I even saw combat, back in '74."

Matt dried up, edging the truck closer to the concession stand. The zombies were clustered there like semihuman flies on a cinder block turd. Ted reached behind the seat for the shotgun, handing the pistol to Matt.

"It's easy," Ted explained. "The trick is, slow and steady on the trigger. Don't pull up. There's a coupla spare boxes under the seat; if you miss, keep shootin'. I think it's like in those zombie movies, though. You gotta go for the head."

Nodding, Matt leaned out the window, taking aim at one of the things. They swarmed around the dead-bolted door—they knew people were up there, and they wanted in.

"Pull up a little closer," Ted slapped a few shells into the shotgun, blasting off a head in a pulpy pink spray.

Matt laid the gun on the seat, easing the truck forward.

The engine coughed, stalling.

"What the hell?" Ted nailed a shambler maybe twelve feet in front of the truck, taking off half of its head. The grayish-red brain ooze shimmered faintly, its blue glow gradually fading to black.

Matt cranked the key, but the engine just sputtered. He glanced at the dashboard. Even in the midst of this insanity, he could appreciate the irony. "And you run a gas station," he said.

"Dang," Ted slapped his forehead. "Got a spare can in the bed. Cover me," he said, reaching for the door handle.

"You're a better shot," Matt said. "And I can go through the back window here."

Ted grinned. "Gotcha covered." He leaned out the window again, firing away.

Matt's ears rang from the gunplay, and the cab stank. Standing in the bed was a relief of sorts. He picked up the can.

"Gas cap's in the middle on your side," Ted yelled, squeezing off another round.

Matt flipped open the door and unscrewed the cap. Then he froze.

A thin woman, fingers aglow, had somehow avoided Ted's fire. She crouched by the front bumper, reaching out.

"Don't touch the truck!" Matt shouted, leaping out of the bed. A fresh wave of agony traveled up his leg. He realized he was still carrying the gas can.

Ted yanked back, but the barrel of the shotgun banged against the door as the blue nimbus raced along the truck's exterior. "Aaah!" He writhed as the blue tendrils swirled down the shotgun and up his arm. He faced Matt, mouth twisted in pain. "Remember what I said!" Turning around, he grunted, struggling. He pressed the shotgun barrel against his nose and thumbed the trigger.

Matt looked away.

The zombies were coming out of the building now, sensing easier prey. *Get the gun and the shells, quick!* He reached in, carefully avoiding the metal.

The woman was two feet away when his fingers closed around the pistol's grip.

It was slimy with Ted's blood.

He blasted away at her head, missing with the first few shots before knocking her down.

Red rage filled him. He emptied the gun into the approaching shamblers, backpedaling to load the clip as he had seen Ted do it. He lost track of the time, but the box was down to a few bullets when the last of the things flopped to the ground. He rushed into the concession stand, banging on the projection booth door with the butt of the pistol, hearing the music of sirens in the distance.

The door didn't open.

He screamed through it, then just shot out the lock.

Vera and Rita were waiting, their hollow sockets blazing with malevolent blue fire.

His hand was shaking so badly that he had to fire five or six times to take them out.

"Cliff?" *Please, God, let him be safe, somehow.* He crept up the stairs into the dim projection booth.

It was empty.

The film projector squatted in the center of the booth like a steel bug, clicking. A pile of film lay heaped on the floor.

On the wall, a huge audio board, connected to a rack of amplifiers, hissed and buzzed. The gauges on the amps twitched. Matt took a closer look, noticing that a series of wires led from behind them . . . to the back of Cliff's computer. But the wires were frayed; they'd been ripped out.

Glowing patterns in blue rippled across the screen.

In the corner, to his right and slightly behind him, he saw a door, a closet of some kind.

He knocked gently. "Cliff?"

The doorknob began to turn.

"Matt." His brother sounded small, frightened.

He opened the door and reached for Cliff, thankful that his brother still had eyes. He lifted him, for once not minding the closeness.

"I set a trap for it," Cliff said. "We saw it trying to come in through the speaker-box connections," Cliff said. "But I figured out a way to get it into my computer."

"What happened to Vera and Rita?"

Cliff looked down. "When the thing went into the computer, they pulled out the wires to keep it there. It got Vera first, then Rita, while I crawled into the closet and locked it."

Matt stared at the screen. "How do we get rid of it?"

Cliff sniffed, wrinkling his nose and looking down the stairs. "Easy, you dumb jock," he said. "See that can of gas you set down there by the door?"

7. *9:48 p.m.*

There was no retreat from here. Millions of pathways, mazelike, that led nowhere. 10585's seeds were all dead; their organic generators had ceased to function.

There were so many roads in this place, all narrow, all dead ends. The energy here was artificial; bad food, and even that was almost gone.

No escape . . . no escape . . . . no—

8. *9:53 p.m.*

Matt smiled, carrying his brother down the stairs.

The aroma of burning circuitry was the sweetest scent he had ever smelled.

Let the fire department put it out later.

BIG BUST AT HERBERT HOOVER HIGH

by Jay R. Bonansinga

Unleashed ... uninhibited ...
a testosteronic terror born of cross-your-heart
engineering!

It was hotter than a Barstow burrito on the morning that Arlie Staggs awoke transformed.

Arlie figured he must be having another anchovy dream. The way his noggin felt all spongy and disengaged, like the time he awoke under the mesquite tree down in Guaymas with a mescal worm stuck in each nostril and a tattoo of Pancho Villa on his ass. His wood shop teacher, Mr. Richard Dick (AKA Double-Dick, or Dick-squared to the slide rule crowd), had taken Arlie and a couple of other underachievers from Herbert Hoover High down to Mexico last summer on a field trip ostensibly to learn indigenous woodworking techniques; but alas, all the boys really learned was how to get crabs and chronic cases of Montezuma's revenge. But the memories of past degradations were fading quickly as Arlie realized something was seriously wrong with his face.

His nose felt funny, all tight and puckered, and his vision was severely tunneled. All he could see was a pinpoint of gauzy white light. He tried to blink. He tried to turn over. He tried to move but his lower extremities were completely numb. As though they didn't exist at all. And that's when Arlie started to panic, and that nagging Russ Tamblyn voice in his head started yapping.

You finally did it, Bucko—you choked your chicken so much you got the paralysis, the disease, and that is so uncool, because you're only like sixteen, man, and you're like terminal, Bucko. Like curtains. All because of that nasty Madame Thumb and her four sisters!

Arlie shivered. The heat was making him dizzy, making the flesh around the base of his neck crawl with prickly rash. He tried to breath, but the air was close and stuffy, thick with a strange melange of odors. Stale baby powder, sweat, traces of Prince Machiabelli. He squinted his single eye and tried to make out the shape in front of him. A pale netting pressed up against him, white pickets crisscrossing, and something along the lower edge of his vision. Looked like a word stitched in fabric.

Playtex.

Liquid terror washed over him. All at once Arlie began to recall the events of the previous night. The strange intersection of events. And the inescapable realization that he had stumbled into a nightmare.

A nightmare that only Arlie could have wreaked upon himself.

The Kingman sunset had come early the previous evening. It made the edge of the sky melt like desert peach cobbler with whipped cream whisking out across the heavens.

Five years earlier, Arlie's father, Maynard Staggs, had relocated his family from Kansas City to Kingman, mostly on account of these "darned beautiful sunsets" (not to mention the job opportunities opening up for an enterprising young nuclear research technician in this part of the desert). At first Arlie had hated the place; if you looked up the word boredom in the dictionary, it would probably say "see: Kingman, Arizona." But then Arlie's hormones had kicked in, and he had discovered what an impressive array the Herbert Hoover High student body offered in the way of student bodies.

"Let's go somewhere different tonight," Bertha-Lou Bizzel demurred from the passenger side of the convertible's bench, pulling away from Arlie's clinch.

They were parked at the cusp of Grand View Hill, the local lovers' leap, and Arlie was just beginning to make progress around the horn of first base toward second. He had told himself tonight was the night; it was bare titty or death.

"C'mon, Bertha-Lou," Arlie protested, fidgeting, the steering wheel digging into his wiry frame. "Stop teasing me; you said just yesterday in the cafeteria that you thought you might like me a little."

"I *do* like you, Arlie," Bertha-Lou said, twirling her hair around a finger. "I just thought we might try a change of scenery, that's all."

Arlie sighed and stared through the windshield for a moment, thinking. Barely a hundred pounds soaking wet, topped with an unruly shock of carrot-colored hair, Arlie was no box of chocolates in the looks department. He could have easily gotten work posing for the before-pictures in Charles Atlas ads. But tonight, he had pulled out all the stops to impress Bertha-Lou. He wore his best tab collar shirt, his pressed chinos and his new saddle shoes; he had even slicked his hair back with some of his dad's butch wax. The sad truth was, Arlie Staggs had become obsessed.

For some boys, true obsession was found in the trading of baseball cards, sitting for hours in airless basements, ruminating over whether or not they should part with a Stan Musial for three Joe Garagiolas. For others, it was the lure of the gridiron, the mindless weight training off-season, the starving, the endless stats, and the glory of Friday night's big game. A few ne'er-do-wells at Herbert Hoover had even discovered this new-fangled music called rock and roll, led by hillbilly cats like Elvis the Pelvis, and some colored boy they called Little Richard. All that stuff was fine; but Arlie had found his own metier, his own special purpose in life.

A typical headshrinker might have blamed it on the diminishing succor of his mother's nipple; the desire to return to the womb, and all that noise. But Arlie knew better. Arlie knew it had started with a little deck of playing cards he had stumbled upon in Maynard Staggs' golf bag back in the summer of '53. Bust Queens of the Amazon, fifty-two in all, posed on bear-skins, satin backdrops and chrome-gilded hot rods. Arlie had only been eleven at the time, but the little devil in his pants had awakened with a vengeance; and from then on, Arlie had been hooked.

It wasn't merely the worship of bosoms; it was everything that accompanied the existence of the mammary gland in 1958 America. Arlie had a better knowledge of brassieres than a floor manager at Lane Bryant. He had studied the various kinds, the French lace cutaways, the Italian ribbon weaves, the British seamless jobs, and the American underwires. He knew a Chantelle from a JC Penney, a Maidenform from a Lilly of France. He was also similarly versed in the zaftig starlets of the day; he idolized Mamie Van Doren, Jane Mansfield, and Virginia Bell. He collected eight-pagers of Paula Page and Jackie Miller. He even kept a scrapbook of the more voluptuous mainstream celebrities of the day. Julie London was the cat's pajamas. Janet Leigh was a scream. Even Margaret Dumont, the portly matron of Marx Brothers flicks, would often make Arlie's pulse quicken; Arlie was certain, under all that bodice and bustle, there had to be a fabulous bust.

As the years passed, Arlie's pastime became a preoccupation. He would lie awake at night, mentally tracing the contours of his English teacher's décolletage. He would concoct elaborate doodles of various breast shapes on the back of his spiral-bound, labeling them with taxonomical fervor; the gargantuan pears, the firm conicals, the ample rounds, and the inimitable heavenly ballasts. He would even revel in the wonderful poetry of the Sears catalog: *Full-figured sizes available, 38 D to 46 EEE, reinforced Lycra cups to lift, firm, and separate.* For Arlie, the mammary was more than a mere adolescent fetish; it was a religion.

And Bertha-Lou Bizzel was the promised land.

Arlie had first seen Bertha-Lou during a freshman year assembly, sitting alone in the back of the gymnasium. She was a new girl from Phoenix, dark complected, sturdy, and full of secrets from the big city. She wore pedal pushers, which was scandalous at Herbert Hoover, and a baggy knit sweater. And when she rose to her feet to applaud the winners of the Western Arizona Barbershop Quartet Competition, Arlie suddenly beheld the heft of her bosom. Her breasts strained the front of her sweater, massive and proud. They were genuine works of art. And Arlie had dropped to his knees right there in front of Christ and the Blue Ribbon Barbershop Boys, silently thanking the Lord for all His Wisdom and generosity.

And now, after three solid months of maneuvering, including a dozen celibate visits to Grand View Hill, Arlie wasn't about to let a little thing like a change in scenery stop him from experiencing Bertha-Lou's bounty.

"Wait a minute!" Arlie finally reached down and fired up the Bellaire. "I got it!"

"What?" Bertha-Lou was gazing in the rearview, applying another coat of lipstick.

"Place where my dad works," Arlie said. "Over by Mount Fenniman."

"That's clear across the desert!"

Arlie looked at her, grinning and putting the car in gear. "It'll be an adventure."

She thought about it for a moment, then started twirling her hair and grinned back at him. "Okay."

They drove for nearly an hour.

The twilight turned the highway purple. Long shadows of distant buttes and yuccas scissored across the pavement, then vanished, as the air got cool and clean. Arlie turned the radio on. They listened to Jack Scott and The Texas Playboys and Tennessee Ernie Ford. And the sky freckled with stars, glittering magically.

By the time they reached the outer fences of the Fenniman facility, they were both in the mood for love.

"My dad works up at the main laboratory," Arlie said, pulling around behind a row of ramshackle Quonsets. The gravel lot was whiskered in sage and weeds, and a row of spindly Joshua trees loomed on the beam of the Bellaire's headlights. Arlie cut the lights.

"What does he do?" Bertha-Lou was getting a little queasy all of a sudden.

"Does something for the Atomic Energy Commission, I dunno, something with particles and beams and stuff."

"Oh."

Arlie found a place to ditch the car behind a cluster of garbage bins. He killed the engine, grabbed a blanket out of the back, and escorted Bertha-Lou across the lot. They climbed a gentle hill fringed with creosote bushes and scabrous weeds. The summit was a flat, bald stretch of earth that overlooked the rest of the compound. Arlie spread out the blanket, and the twosome sat. The air smelled of pine and something astringent, like very strong disinfectant.

Bertha-Lou gazed out across the desolate landscape of low-rise buildings and saguaro. "This isn't exactly what I had in mind," she murmured.

Arlie already had his arm around her, his fingertips brushing the reinforced hooks of her bra. "I think I love you, Bertha-Lou," he said.

"Oh, Arlie, you're so full of bull pucky," she said, pulling away for a moment, unbuttoning her blouse. "You're just in love with my boobies; which is ok-ay, 'long as you treat me kind and take me out for a steak dinner and a movie of my choice every month or so."

She reached around, unclasped her bra, and freed her breasts.

"Ohmygah—" Arlie gasped, the words catching in his throat. He couldn't move, he couldn't breathe. The blood was rushing to both of his heads, the big one and the little one, and his ears droned noisily. In the light of the desert moon, Bertha-Lou's breasts looked positively luminous. Like two great heavenly bodies made of cream. Arlie gaped at them reverently and uttered, "Thank you."

"You're welcome," she said and kissed him.

Arlie kissed her back.

They fell to the blanket, and Arlie cupped her breasts with the care and tenderness of a monk tasting the blessed host. Even Bertha-Lou was taken aback; Arlie was so cautious, so methodical. He seemed to be inhaling her, clinging to her breasts like some kind of marsupial. He alternated from left to the right, touching every square inch of pale flesh with his face and his fingers. He had found his Valhalla.

"Wait a minute, time out," Bertha-Lou said suddenly, gently pushing Arlie away. "You hear that?"

"What?" Arlie was oblivious, drunk on her smell and her warmth.

"That sound, like a buzzing, like the ground is vibrating."

"It's nothing," Arlie said, and went back to her sweet soft miracles.

In every person's life, there's a pivotal moment,

where the wave of fate is just beginning to break. It's the grand slam home run. The biggest fish. The most important case. Shakespeare spoke of it often; called it the "tide in the affairs of men." And the sad truth was, most poor slobs wouldn't know it if it bit them in the ass. Not Arlie. Face buried in buttery flesh, senses engulfed in the talc of Ivory soap and dime-store perfume, he knew he was experiencing that indefinable moment toward which everything had been leading, and after which everything will pale in comparison. And in that silent instant of revelation, Arlie found himself wishing, wishing furiously, wishing upon a magical, starry Arizona night that he could—

"My God, the ground is moving!" Bertha-Lou tensed suddenly, trying to pull away.

"Mmmmmylllphlymmm—!" Arlie was glued to her nipple.

"Arlie, we're—we're—!"

They were moving. The grassy plateau beneath them was shifting like a glacier, rotating. A vast earthen turntable. Noxious puffs of gas seeped out of the edges of the plateau, smelling like airplane glue. Arlie clung to Bertha-Lou, and the world seemed to tilt on its axis. Bertha-Lou shrieked. Arlie closed his eyes.

A moment later, they were plummeting through the darkness of an enormous air vent.

They landed on the floor of a particle accelerator, which was about to bombard another target with 750,000 megavolts of atomic energy. Bertha-Lou hit her head on impact and was knocked out cold, but Arlie wavered in and out of consciousness long enough to see the gargantuan chrome apparatus rising over them, and feel the surge of vibrations under their bodies, and hear his dad's voice echoing in his midbrain— *those darn Cockcroft-Walton gennies pack a punch, son—get your little atoms moving up to 85 percent the speed of light, and that's a lot faster than any four-barrel Chevy, son, heh-heh-heh-heh!*

In Arlie's final moments of consciousness, he saw the walls around them beginning to glow, a bright phosphorous green, and felt the vibrations resonating up through his body as he clung to Bertha-Lou. And in that final wave of emotion, Arlie realized that these might very well be his last moments on this Earth. And he found himself completing the wish—the secret, magical wish—that he could stay this way, united with Bertha-Lou's cleavage, throughout eternity.

Then the atoms crashed.

"Ohmygod—!"

Back in the here and now, Arlie's bad dream continued.

"Where the hell did—how did—?" Bertha-Lou was getting hysterical.

The morning sun hammered down through the vent shaft of the accelerator, and Arlie could hear Bertha-Lou's frantic voice only inches away, muffled by the fabric of the massive brassiere pressing down on Arlie's mutant face. Arlie tried to answer, but found that he had no mouth. Only a large, dark, puckered papilla through which he could nominally make out shapes and odors. He tried to move again and found the majority of his girth to be a ball of jiggly, sweaty flesh attached to Bertha-Lou's torso.

"GET AWAY FROM ME—!"

Now there was real terror in Bertha-Lou's voice, and Arlie felt himself bounding across the airless lab, barely contained within the fabric of the Playtex. Arlie felt like a blind papoose, bouncing around the cotton carrier, clinging barnaclelike to his host body. Suddenly Bertha-Lou was scaling the inner wall of the accelerator room, and Arlie could feel the thrum of her heartbeat in his vessels, he could sense her terror in the perfume sweat breaking out across the soft curve of his face. What a screwy dream he was having!

"GET AWAAAAAAAY!"

There was a figure behind Bertha-Lou, pursuing her through the lab. Through the prison of fabric, Arlie could hear the pitiful, slobbering moans, the shuffling zombie-walk as it lumbered after her. What the hell was it? Some kind of radiated, mutant being? Arlie could hear its muffled, tormented cries. And the relentless shuffling, as the monster, or whatever it was, tried to climb the ladder.

Bertha-Lou finally reached daylight, staggered across the gravel lot, and vaulted behind the steering wheel of the Bellaire. She fired it up and laid a patch out of there.

High-balling down the highway, Arlie could feel the buffet of the wind against his faceless areola, the gusts flapping the fabric of the blouse, drying the sweat on his bulbous body. Bertha-Lou was mumbling to herself, things like, "Where are you, Arlie!" And, "What in God's name happened in there?" and other phrases inaudible under the roar of the Bellaire. Arlie's entire rubbery form began to rash with goose bumps. Was it possible? Could it be? He felt the resilience of his flesh, the tremors passing through him every time the car hit a pothole; he was jiggling, dear God in Heaven, he was jiggling in such a familiar way.

I'm here, Bertha-Lou! I don't know how it happened, but I'm down here, mute and sweaty, in your off-white 39D Playtex Cross-Your-Heart Underwire!

The revelation shivered through him. This was not a dream; this was as real as his father's new brick barbecue, as real as Sputnik, as real as one of Mister Gibbons' pop quizzes. Arlie was a boob. Period. And for some horrible, intuitive reason, Arlie got the feeling there was no turning back. He would have to adapt, just like in Missus Cockenlocker's biology class when they studied Darwin and natural selection. Arlie would have to make the best of it.

A barrage of uninvited images assaulted his mammalian brain. People gathered inside a filthy canvas tent in the bowels of some carnival sideshow. *Step right up, ladies and gentlemen, meet Boob Boy, the Human Breast, he'll lactate on command!* Arlie tried to scream, tried to wriggle free of the elastic bondage, but the D-cup held firm. He was damned, damned to ride the rest of his life, a flabby passenger on a very attractive chest.

It took Bertha-Lou twenty minutes to get back to town. Arlie wasn't sure, but from the sounds of traffic and the smell of pine needles, he guessed she was heading home. Bertha-Lou Bizzel lived in a ritzy neighborhood on the north side of Kingman, a new development called a suburb, complete with manicured lawns, immaculate hedges, and borders of young western pines. Arlie strained to see through the tunnel of his puckered eye. Every time Bertha-Lou twisted in her seat, or reached down to shift, Arlie felt the fabric itching his face, prickling hotly, maddeningly. The underwire had gotten bent in all the excitement, and now it was digging into Arlie's side. It was torture. And the weight! Arlie felt like a balloon filled with sand, like Fatty Arbuckle after a six-course meal. His lower regions were still sweating profusely, sticking to flesh of Bertha-Lou's ribs.

If only she had been a flat chested girl.

Moments later, Bertha-Lou arrived home. She pulled quickly into the circular drive and slammed on the brakes. Arlie plunged forward, nearly spilling out of his cup. He wanted to cry now, as Bertha-Lou got out of the car and rushed up the picket-lined walk, he wanted to die.

Now slow down, Bucko, cool your pits and think this over.

The Russ Tamblyn voice was back.

Maybe this ain't such a god-awful mess after all, you dig? Like, maybe this is whatcha call one of your blessings in disguise, if you catch my meaning, Bucko. Just think of the fun, the kind of life you could lead down here in this dark, warm, groovy place. Bouncing around, smelling great, carefree. Like dig: You wouldn't even have to worry about coppin' a feel anymore, know what I mean? You could just feel yourself up—

"Mom? Dad? Anybody home?" Bertha-Lou's anguished voice was splashing the empty silence of the living room of her house on Maple Drive.

The Bizzel house was one of those new deals they called tract homes. Single-level ranch, with a bunch of spacious rooms and all the modern conveniences. Electric oven. Eight-inch black and white TV. Boomerang tables everywhere. And the color scheme was pure contemporary, aqua blue and mustard. Arlie bounced along from room to room as Bertha-Lou looked for Mom or Dad or Brother Johnny or anybody who might listen.

The house was deserted.

"Probably all at church," Bertha-Lou muttered to herself, going into her room, and peeling off her clothes.

Then it happened.

The Playtex came off and freed Arlie. The cool air and light of the bedroom engulfed him, and it felt wonderful. It was almost as though Arlie could breathe again, although he had no breathing passages anymore. His pores tingled. Maybe Russ Tamblyn was right, maybe this wasn't so bad after all. He blinked, and gradually grew accustomed to the light and the strange portal through which his vision coalesced.

There was a full-length mirror across the room. Covered with clippings of Ricky Nelson and Tab Hunter, the mirror reflected a narrow slice of Bertha-Lou. Through his constricted field of vision, Arlie saw his face in the upper left corner. The face of a frightened young man, shrunken, embossed onto Bertha-Lou like molded white chocolate. Arlie's eyes, nose and mouth created a strange little cameo around her nipple, as though some demon god had literally sculpted Arlie into her flesh.

But why hadn't Bertha-Lou noticed him? Couldn't she tell that one of her breasts had mutated?

She was moving again, over carpet, then tile. The light got sharper, and her footfalls took on a sibilant quality. *Wait until she looks in a mirror, Arlie thought. She'll surely notice her new friend then.* Arlie blinked and blinked and blinked. He could detect the faint odors of dampness, soap, and shampoo. She was in the bathroom. God help him, she was going to take a shower! The squeak of a faucet, then the rush of water as she adjusted the temperature.

Then the warm spray in Arlie's face.

It was a remarkable feeling, like being immersed in wet clay and yielding to the gentle touch of the sculptress. The soap blanketed him, frothed over him, and all at once, everything was okay with the world. Russ Tamblyn had been right. This was the greatest possible thing that could have happened, and Arlie began to silently thank God.

There was a sudden crash out in the living room. Glass breaking, and shuffling sounds.

"Oh, my God!"

The water stopped. Goose bumps crawled across Arlie's face. An arm smashed up against him, covering him with a towel, and then Bertha-Lou was moving toward the window. "Ohmygod—NO!" She tried the bathroom window, but it was welded shut with coats of paint and caulk. "It's him, it's him, IT'S HIM—!" She shrieked and ran out of the bathroom.

Arlie struggled to see the monstrous figure coming down the hallway.

Coming into focus through the tunnel of Arlie's vision was the worst thing he had ever seen. A figure in soiled tab collar shirt, wrinkled chinos, and brand new saddle shoes, staggering blindly down the hall, zombie arms outstretched. It was human in every way except the head. Rooted on the stalk of its neck, melded in some unearthly graft, was a great fleshy orb. A breast. Bertha-Lou Bizzel's left bosom, to be exact. It came forth like a pathetic, mute supplicant, seeking its goddess.

"LEAVE ME ALONE—!"

Arlie could hear the madness in Bertha-Lou's scream, as she lunged through her bedroom door, clawing at her clothes and the things on her dresser. Bottles of Estee Lauder and Kewpie dolls and Jerry Vale records skittered to the carpet. The monster was coming through the door. Bertha-Lou finally managed to grab a Zippo and a spritz bottle of Evening in Paris cologne.

She aimed the aerosol spray at the thing with no eyes and sparked the lighter.

"DIE, YOU FUCKER!"

A tendril of blue fire leaped from the cologne bottle and bullwhipped the monster. The thing staggered. Flames curled around its fleshy, globular head, and a spurt of agony hissed from its teat. Then the fire bloomed, licking down its shirttails and trousers. The thing collapsed and sparks geysered off across the doorway.

Run, Bertha-Lou!

Arlie's silent scream reverberated down through the woman's marrow.

Bertha-Lou spun, scooped up a terry cloth robe, and lurched at her back window. It took her a split second to pry open the pane and climb out. She pulled the robe on and staggered across the finely trimmed lawn toward the tree line. The sound of wood crackling and flames gobbling up the air came trailing after her. She got another few feet and tripped on a log.

She went down hard.

It wasn't until the inferno was out of control, filling the air with violent noise and light, that Arlie realized Bertha-Lou had fainted dead away. In her frenzy, and subsequent fall, her robe had slipped open. And now Arlie was exposed for all the neighbors and firemen to see. That wouldn't do, that simply wouldn't do.

Cover me, Bertha-Lou, please, it's cold.

Nothing, no movement. The sounds of sirens were looming now, and the voices of neighbors were gathering across the fence. Soon the place would be crawling with people. Arlie concentrated carefully, thinking the words.

Cover me up, please, Bertha-Lou.

The fingers fluttered for a moment, blindly, then the arm swung up and shoved the robe closed. Just like that. Then the hand fell like a dead bird on the lawn.

Arlie silently thanked God, and rejoiced.

As the emergency units arrived and the neighbors gathered and the scene erupted with voices and noise, Arlie let the invisible tears of joy come for his new life. There was no turning back now. His secret dream had come true.

At last, he was whole.

'59 FRANKENSTEIN

by Norman Partridge

Chopped 'n' channeled, stitched 'n' riveted ...
a walking teenage nightmare!

All he wanted—the one and only thing he wanted, in fact—was to borrow the keys to the car.

But the doctor refused in that cool, condescending way of his, pointing out the error in his creation's logic as he packed the bowl of his pipe with cherry tobacco. "Now, my boy," he began as he always did, "I installed a perfectly serviceable brain in your cranium, and you're not using it. We both know it's not just a simple matter of your borrowing the car keys. That is only the surface question. Below that seemingly innocuous query lurk troubling subtexts. If you were to borrow the keys, I would be forced to assume that you'd like to go somewhere in the car. And if you were to go somewhere, people would, quite naturally, observe your movements. I'm sure you recall the unpleasantness during your previous excursion into the outside world. Certainly, I don't have to remind you of that. Do I, my boy?"

"That was your idea," the boy said, ashamed of the pitiful little voice that rose from his great chest. "I had to kill that kid. I had to have his face. I couldn't stand it anymore, being so ..." His big hands wiped clean trails through the tobacco-stained air, groping for words.

The doctor chuckled, shaking his head, sucking on his vile pipe. "I do wish you'd develop your vocabulary, my boy. Any number of words will do—ugly, grotesque, hideous, repulsive." Again, the too-pleased-with-himself chuckle. "Monstrous, perhaps?"

"I'm not that way anymore." The young man smiled, touching the face that had been his for two years now, a handsome face that he had memorized in the small mirror the doctor had given him. "The things I did were ugly things . . . I did them because I was ugly. People were afraid of me. But that was before—they won't be afraid anymore. Now I look like everyone else. I'm different than I used to be."

"Yes, my boy. You're different. You wear a different face, a face that once belonged to someone else. Another boy. A boy who lived in this town, in fact. A boy with friends, teachers, family . . . a boy with a young lover." The doctor sighed, a sure sign that the conversation was about to come to an abrupt end. "No, I'm afraid that you'd be recognized were you to venture forth from our comfortable abode, and that would bring questions, *difficult* questions. The time for answers has not yet arrived. We have more work to do. Our experiment has not yet concluded. Yes, we are finished with your face, and your arms and torso are certainly in fine shape, but that left leg of yours . . . that slightest of limps . . . and that unfortunate tattoo on your right hand . . . not to mention your eyes, my boy." The doctor shook his head. "I demand perfection before I reveal you to the world. And I assure you, my boy, when we arrive at perfection you will most assuredly long for the privacy of evenings such as these, when your world consisted of no more than a few rooms. But, I promise you this, I am now and forever will be your protector. I only have your best interests at—"

Doctor Frankenstein didn't see it coming. His creation had moved behind him—ever so slowly, head down—as if he were accepting the inevitability of the doctor's arguments, and then the room went dark. Frankenstein was thinking that he should check the fuse box, but quite suddenly he realized that was an absurd idea because he was flat on his back, out of the comfortable recliner and on the rug in front of the fireplace, his pipe lying there on the floor, a smear of red smoldering tobacco charring the carpet.

His creation loomed over him, a smile on its face, a fireplace poker in its grip. The poker came down. Slashing. Crushing the doctor's cheek, but speeding on, completing its deadly arc.

Then starting back.

This time taking the doctor's right eye.

Frankenstein thought that he should scream. He knew exactly what was required to produce the desired result—synapses firing in his brain, muscles responding, the requisite amount of air expelled from his lungs, flowing over his vocal chords, and—

The poker came down again and speared his cheek, shattering teeth beneath. The hook buried itself between molars and wisdom teeth. The creature twisted the weapon, trying to free it, but it held firm. He yanked it sharply and it came loose quite suddenly, the hook pulling teeth and tearing flesh, ripping through cheek until it reached the startled curve of lip, shredding that, too, creating a wet red wound that resembled the twisted smile of a clown.

Now the doctor did scream. He screamed as the monster took hold of his ankle and dragged him over the smoldering tobacco, across the living room, through the kitchen, and down the staircase that led to the basement laboratory. He screamed as his head slammed the first step, the second, the third ... the fifth ... the seventh ... and then he was done screaming. Momentarily unconscious, his remaining eye rolled back in his head—eggshell white cracked with brilliant red veins beneath a fluttering pink lid. The right lid mimicked the action, smacking wetly as it fluttered over the empty scarlet socket.

A sharp exhalation puffed the doctor's torn mouth. Conscious once more, he reached out as the monster dragged him across the lab, made a desperate grab for the leg of the operating table. Missed badly. And then the room was behind him.

The monster pulled him into a narrow corridor, advancing at a most deliberate pace. Not too fast. Not too slow. A pace that would allow a wounded man time enough to contemplate what lay ahead of him, for the door at the end of the corridor opened onto a creaking plywood staircase cobbled together by the doctor himself (and while Doctor Frankenstein was many things, a carpenter he was not).

The stairway led to a single chamber. A pit where Frankenstein disposed of excess body parts in a most ingenious manner, erasing even the tiniest shred of evidence.

As the monster opened the door to the alligator pit, Doctor Frankenstein thought that he certainly had better do something—something *now,* something *drastic*—but then he was tumbling down the rickety staircase—plywood creaking, nails groaning—splashing finally into a shallow pool.

Something clattered down the stairway after him. Frankenstein heard his creation's footfalls on the floorboards above. Crossing the laboratory, then climbing the staircase that led to the kitchen, the living room. The doctor did not hear the front door open, only heard it slam closed. . . .

Then there was silence, black as the water which pooled on the concrete floor of the pit ... silence soon broken by the sound of a gator moving through shallow water.

The young man's heavy foot mashed the gas pedal and the Chevy roared backward, veering sharply as his big, mismatched hands twisted the steering wheel too far one way, then too far the other. The car jumped the curb of the brick driveway and trenched a wild brodie on the front lawn, finally launching the mailbox skyward as the rear bumper smacked the post that held it. The post itself was transformed into a hail of flying splinters as the car powered backward onto the two-lane country road.

Sweat beaded on the young man's forehead, but there was really no need to worry. The house was far from town, and there wasn't another soul on the road at this hour.

The boy raced into the night. First gear. Clutch in. Second gear. Clutch out. The big car stuttered and died, and Frankenstein's creation swore under his breath.

Clutch in. He restarted the engine, foot light on the gas pedal. Clutch out, slowly this time. First gear ... clutch in ... second gear ... clutch out, *slowly.* ...

The boy knew the car inside and out. It was *his* creation. He had built it from a battered hulk Doctor Frankenstein had hauled home from a nearby junkyard. Chevy body, but parts from a couple dozen other vehicles as well. Chrome straight axle, steel-crank 375-horse 327, body as black and glossy as a mamba's scales, aluminum dash so clean you could eat off of it. Building the car had been the doctor's idea of therapy, but it was his creation's vision of freedom.

But the being Frankenstein had constructed from pieces of teenaged athletes who had perished in a school bus accident did not know how to drive the cherry vehicle he had created. Oh, he knew in principle, well enough. But he had never had the opportunity to test those principles.

Until now.

Clutch in ... third gear ... clutch out ... *slowly, slowly.*

Foot on the gas. Picking up real speed now. The road a taut whipcord bathed in headlight glow. The house of Frankenstein gone now, buried beneath the black shroud of a summer night. A vault of unkept promises abandoned in the darkness. If Frankenstein had kept those promises, things might have ended differently. But the doctor was a liar, always talking of freedom, but never letting that magnificent word stand on its own. Chaining it to other words—patience, and perfection, words that stung his creation as surely as the inevitable, prying bite of the doctor's scalpel.

No one would cut on him ever again. The boy was certain of that. By now Frankenstein was dead, erased from the Earth by the creature which dwelled in the dark waters beneath his house of pain. It was over.

And it was beginning. The boy longed to roll down the window, feel the summer wind on his face, hold a piece of the summer night in his lungs. He wanted to turn on the radio, search out something good. Eddie Cochran's "Summertime Blues." Gene Vincent's "Race With the Devil."

Time for all that later. Now he had to concentrate.

Clutch in. Fourth gear. Clutch out.

Good. Very good.

He kept his mismatched hands on the wheel, the bulldog tattooed between thumb and index finger on his right hand spreading its jaws as if ready to lock on black plastic. His eyes—one green and one blue—held the road. The speedometer needle speared sixty, then seventy.

A sign blurred by on the right. One mile to the main highway.

The boy smiled.

He rolled down the window.

He flipped on the radio.

Stared out at the straight and true whipcord road to freedom.

Saw the dog, trapped there in the unforgiving glow of his headlights, staring back.

The gator's jaws snapped closed, and twin canyons of pain trenched Frankenstein's left calf. The reptile pulled at him, slowly, an unconscious imitation of the deliberate manner in which his creation had dragged him through the basement laboratory, as if giving the good doctor time to realize just what was happening to him.

Frankenstein reached out, grabbing for the bottom stair. The massive reptile whipped its head to the side. Tendon and cartilage tore, and something crumpled in the doctor's knee. Tibia and fibula splintered simultaneously.

His hand snapped closed, but the stair was out of reach, and he was rewarded with nothing more than a handful of water. Only water, nothing—

No. There was something in his hand. A metal shaft.

In a flash, he remembered tumbling down the staircase. Recalled the sound of something clattering down the stairs behind him.

The fireplace poker.

Frankenstein lashed backward, striking out as hard as he could.

He hit nothing but air.

The gator was gone.

So was the better part of the doctor's left leg.

Fat tires dug in as the boy hit the brakes.

The left front exploded in a shower of rubber. The

car spun, and the boy could only sit there, mismatched hands knotted around the wheel, tattooed dog's jaws mangling a circular black bone, foot heavy on the brake, Link Wray's "Rumble" spilling staticky through the radio speaker, pounding in his ears. The Chevy completed one rotation. Started another, then drifted off the whipcord blacktop, kicking up hard fistfuls of dirt, scything a wide swatch through tangled skeletons of overgrown brush, tires grinding empty beer cans and decayed roadkill ... glossy black body heaving through a chain-link fence, powering forward and up.

Then down. Both headlights exploded as the front bumper compacted the grille. The boy thought that he was going to die. Smash against something waiting in the blackness beyond the fence, smash it so hard that he would come apart at the seams and crumble into a hundred pieces. But the car only drifted to a stop and died, and the boy found himself staring through a cracked windshield snared by a net of chain-link.

Link Wray's guitar drifted away, ice melting in the warm night. The boy turned off the radio. He tried to open the door, but it was wrapped tight by the same length of fence that blanketed the windshield. He kicked at the door until it gave, providing just enough room to slip out.

Heavy black boots skittered over gravel. He couldn't quite pick up his feet. Knees weak, legs shaky, he stumbled forward, limping worse than usual. He couldn't see much in the darkness, but he could hear just fine.

The dog growled at him, and he stopped dead in his tracks.

Frankenstein dropped the fireplace poker and unbuckled his belt, urgently dragging it free from his trousers.

Blood gushed from the doctor's left leg. A mauled,

bloody stump ending just below the kneecap, which was now a slick hunk of useless bone suspended by a thread of ragged flesh.

The doctor had seen much while building his creation, but nothing could have prepared him for this. Because this was *his* leg, *his* knee, and he was thankful for the darkness, glad that only a slim tendon of light connected the alligator pit to the doorway above, for if he could see his ruined knee clearly, if he could see his severed leg in the grip of the gator's jaws. . . .

No. He wouldn't think of such things. Not now. He threaded the belt through its buckle, lassoed his leg several inches above the wound. Tightened the loop, then threaded the end of the belt under and around the buckle—once, twice, three times—tying it off as best he could.

Just like tying off a sausage, he told himself. *One of those nice plump bratwursts Mama used to make. . . .* If he had only listened to her. If he had never come to this accursed *America* . . . this land of greasy cheeseburgers, rock 'n' roll, and platinum blondes. . . .

Gott in Himmel. This is a fine time for regrets. He shook away his thoughts, concentrating on nothing more than the present moment. There was still no sound from the gator, but the doctor knew that it was back there . . . waiting in the black shadows, the blacker water. Frankenstein snatched up the poker and eased backward, toward the staircase, eyes on the darkness. He didn't want to turn away from it, but he had to, and soon he had dragged himself onto the first step, pushing off on the slick, algae-coated floor of the pit with his remaining foot. He tucked the poker under one arm and turned, pulling with both hands, but it seemed he weighed a thousand pounds. He prayed for an adrenaline rush of epic proportions, prayed to keep shock at bay, and he pulled for all he was worth. His body slick with sweat, his nerves tingling with desperation, he rose to the second step just as the water parted and the black wave broke behind him.

Reflexively, the doctor kicked back at the unseen attacker.

The gator's jaws slapped closed audibly, missing the doctor's right foot by inches. Desperately, he pulled himself up—his biceps burning, the muscles in his shoulders knotted with fear—and in an instant he was on the third step.

For just an instant.

Plywood creaked. Nails groaned.

The third step gave way.

The growling dog approached him, and the young man lurched backward. His hands were at his sides, muscles tensed, big fingers curled like the claws of a wild beast, a—

Monster. Suddenly, he remembered the boy whose face he now wore, recalled for the millionth time the cool blue terror freezing his eyes as the hands of a monster closed around his neck and snapped it like a twig.

That wasn't me, he told himself. *I'm not that way anymore.*

The dog's bark slapped him through the silence. The young man had nearly run down the animal, and now it seemed intent on returning the favor.

The beast was certainly well-equipped for such a task. Its jaws were blunt and square, lined with yellow-white spikes that seemed to glow in the moonlight. Its head resembled nothing so much as a cartoon bear trap—a huge machine of a head on a body of compact muscle, balanced on legs that were extremely thick and extremely short. Frankenstein's creation knew that this dog had been bred for destruction, just as he had been bred for—

For what? His mismatched hands shook before him,

ready to tear the beast to pieces. He could almost hear the tattooed dog on his right hand growling in anticipation.

"No," he said, and his hands dropped to his sides, and his fingers seemed to lengthen in the moonlight.

The dog's black ears perked.

Its nose wriggled.

It whined.

And then the dog moved forward, nudging the young man's right hand, sniffing it.

The beast's jaws widened. A curtain of black lips rose over twin rows of sharp teeth.

A pink tongue darted between the beast's teeth, licking the tattooed dog on the back of the young man's hand. He bent low, patted the animal's head. "It's okay, boy. We both had a scare, but we're okay."

The dog cocked its massive head to one side, as if considering his words. Once again, it whined.

The boy looked around. His car was in bad shape, but it wasn't the only one. There were dozens of cars here, rusting hulks. Bent and twisted, some completely crushed. All silent and dead beneath the light of the August moon.

He turned and started for the road. The dog followed, keeping to his right side, its nose not far from his tattooed hand. And then something smashed against the young man's skull, and he went down hard.

When he opened his eyes, a hard circle of light seemed to pin him to the ground. He blinked and found that he could see around the light, see the man standing there, the dog at his side.

The man aimed the light at the face Frankenstein's creature had stolen from another, and then he redirected the beam, haloing the creature's right hand so that the tattooed dog seemed to glow like a tangle of electric blue veins on dead white skin.

"It ain't possible," the man said. "It just ain't."

The creature squinted up at the man—the harsh electric light in his grip, the cool circle of moon behind him. He saw nothing more than a silhouette, but that was enough.

For Frankenstein's creation had a perfectly serviceable brain in his cranium, and he was using it.

Clearly, he could see that the man standing above him had only one arm.

The doctor tried to hold on, but he couldn't. He slipped sideways, dropping ass-first through the opening between the second and fourth stairs. The drop was only about a foot and a half, but he came down hard, on his tailbone, his body wedged between the stairs, his ass once more immersed in cold, black water.

He twisted to one side, his eyes searching for the gator. It waited on the other side of the stairway, watching him.

An instant later, its reptile brain had made a decision. The gator darted forward, jaws snapping closed, and the first step splintered between its teeth. Frankenstein wriggled madly, his ass sliding easily on algae-slick concrete. His stump scraped against the brick wall, but the makeshift tourniquet held firm. Frankenstein managed to get what was left of his wounded leg into the gap between the stairs, and then his right leg followed suit, his face scraping the side of the fourth step as he dropped to the floor of the alligator pit.

A good half-dozen splinters speared his cheek. That was fine—not much of a price to pay for the barrier that protected him from the gator.

Right. Some protection. A veritable wall of Jericho. One termite-eaten plywood step, guaranteed to come tumbling down at the first snap of the reptile's slavering jaws. The doctor held his breath and stared, watching the step and the gator beyond, waiting . . . waiting. . . .

The damn thing refused to move.

Frankenstein swallowed hard. Bait. That was what he needed. Something to spark that pea-brain into action. Gingerly, he reached out, and his left hand came to rest on the second step.

The gator charged forward, jaws snapping, but the doctor had already removed his hand from the step. But he did not shrink from the great beast. His right hand lashed out, between the stairs, and he drove the fireplace poker into the reptile's right eye.

Bone cracked in the hollow of the beast's eye socket. The creature exploded from the floor as if electrocuted, flopping wildly on its back, pus-yellow belly exposed now, bullet-head thrashing in the black water until the poker clattered loose.

But by the time that sound echoed thorough the pit, Frankenstein had pulled himself between the second and fourth steps, onto the fifth, the sixth, dragging his bloody stump behind him, ascending from the alligator pit with a singular determination not seen since Sir Edmund Hillary had conquered Everest.

The doctor squinted at the open doorway above as he pulled himself onto the seventh step. Soft white light bathed his anguished features, and he managed a slight smile.

Once more, the stairway creaked. Groaned.

Frankenstein closed his eyes, praying that the seventh stair would bear his weight.

Bear weight it did, but that fact brought him little solace.

A timber cracked below.

The entire stairway swayed.

The one-armed man's name was Roy, and it wasn't until Roy shared that sliver of information that Frankenstein's creation realized that he had no name at all.

But he knew that he had many other things. The legs

of a star running back ... the torso of a center ... a wide receiver's lungs ... a right arm which had belonged to Roy in the days when he was an All-State quarterback.

The young man had told Roy the entire story from beginning to end, and it was obvious that Roy believed every word of it. Now he trailed behind Roy, limping worse than usual, following the one-armed man through the junkyard. Roy's dog kept to his right, near the hand that had once belonged to his master. That made the young man feel especially guilty, even though Roy didn't seem to notice.

The young man said, "I thought you were dead. All of you. The doctor told me—"

"Maybe the doc was right." Roy didn't look back as he spoke. "Hell, maybe we all died that night. But maybe some of us just died a little more than others. Maybe they were the lucky ones."

Roy cut a path between a twisted Cadillac convertible and a rusted-out Hudson. The flashlight beam played over a squared-off metal box—yellow as cheddar, but alive with dead-white splotches that resembled mold. The beam settled into a straight line, tracing a row of hard black letters that ran beneath a dozen broken windows. BELTON SENIOR HIGH SCHOOL. HOME OF THE BULLDOGS.

Roy said, "That explains the tattoo, at least."

The young man rubbed his right hand. "It explains a lot," he said. He reached out and touched the school bus, gently, as if he expected an electric shock.

Roy laughed. "Nothing to be afraid of. It ain't gonna bite or anything."

The young man turned toward him. "I'm sorry," he said. "I wish there was something that I could do. I wish—"

"Don't worry about it," Roy said. "It's not like it's your fault or anything." He sat the flashlight on the hood of the bus, reached out with his left hand, and squeezed the young man's right arm. "Hell, at least you're taking good care of it for me. You must work out."

"Weights," the young man said. His hands were floating in the air before him, searching for an explanation. The second-string quarterback's left hand, Roy's right. "Bench press, mostly. I can press four hundred, even do reps with it. Curls are my favorite, though. I have a preacher's bench, and—

Roy's bitter laughter prickled over the young man's spine.

"You have to understand," the young man said. "I had no choice. It's not my fault . . . well, that's a lie. My face, I'm responsible for that. Even then, the doctor maneuvered me into it. He made me ugly so I wouldn't disobey him. You see, he *wanted* me to kill that boy. He wanted me to steal his face. He needed to own me with his silence."

"So how'd you get away?"

"It was simple," the young man said, his voice even, honest. "I hit the doctor over the head, and then I fed him to the alligator."

"Oh, Jesus." Roy laughed until tears spilled from his eyes. "Oh, Christ, that's a good one." He went on laughing, shaking like he was going to break.

Roy's laughter made the young man nervous. He hadn't said anything funny. More than anything, he wanted Roy to understand. "It's not a joke," he said. "I had no choice."

Roy's laughter evaporated. "I didn't have a hell of a lot of choice, either," he said. "That's the *real* joke. I mean, after the wreck I was alive and all, but without my arm. . . . My arm was my ticket out of here. And now you've got it. As for your face, I never liked its previous owner much anyway. That's no skin off my butt. Tough world, and all that happy crap. Both for him *and* for me. But I don't hold a grudge. You only get what you can take—that's my motto, amigo."

"You can't mean that."

Roy laughed. "Hell if I can't. The world doesn't give you much, and what it gives you you have to work at keeping."

"You make it sound brutal."

"Brutal? You got that right. Look around, buddy. Is this how you'd like to end up? I mean, I don't have a whole bunch of prospects. Me, the guy who was going to break the family mold, get the hell out of this town. Football star. College bound. All that stuff. And here I am, stuck, just like my brothers."

"Were they in the bus, too?"

Roy shook his head. "No. Those two had a couple'a years on me. They went marching off to Korea. One didn't come back—he's planted in the cemetery just up the road, right next to the morgue your buddy the doc raided when he put you together. The other came back ruined. He was the smart one, too. A college man. A doctor, just like your buddy Frankenstein. He almost made it out of this pit, but his brain required some serious pickling after two years up to his knees in blood and guts as a MASH surgeon. He's been at the bottle since the day he returned to the good ol' U. S. of A."

The young man sighed.

"Don't say *I'm sorry,*" Roy said. "You get one shot at that, and that's it."

"I won't."

Roy nodded. "You just take care of that arm for me. You get on that highway, and you get the hell out of here, and you take care of my arm."

"I will," the young man said. "But my car—"

"You can take mine," Roy said. "It's parked out back, behind my trailer. It's got a fancy knob on the wheel for one-armed driving and everything, should you ever come up short."

"What about you?"

"I'll fix up your rig. New bumper, couple'a head-lights, new windshield ... like the mad scientists say, *Parts is parts*." Roy chuckled. "To tell you the truth, I wasn't much of a mechanic even when I had two arms, but I get along. My brother helps me out. He's way too shaky for cutting on people, but cars are different. They don't scream."

Frankenstein's creation couldn't help but wince.

"Get gone, amigo," Roy said, tossing a set of keys.

Roy's right hand opened. The key ring disappeared between thumb and forefinger, into the bulldog's gaping mouth. Strong fingers snapped closed around the keys. The owner of Roy's arm slipped them into his pocket.

"Thanks," he said.

He patted the junkyard dog's head, one last time.

Then he was gone.

Frankenstein could hear nails tearing loose from warped plywood. Years of dry rot had finally taken their toll. One of the support timbers had crumbled, and now the stairway was pulling away from the brick wall of the pit.

Frankenstein dragged himself forward. Onto the eighth step. The ninth. Behind him, stairs collapsed like dominoes, splashing into the black water, but the doctor heard nothing but his own feverish breathing, his fingers scrabbling for purchase on the next step, and then the next.

He pulled himself into the hallway just as the stair-case crumbled behind him. The lab lay before him. If he could get to it in time, there was a telephone. His house was far from town, but an ambulance could reach him in a matter of minutes.

If he could reach the phone.

He had to. He'd come this far. He had to make it, all the way.

The tile floor was slick, freshly waxed. It was hard going, but he kept at it, ignoring the wet squeal of his bloody stump sliding across slick tile, instead imagining pleasant things. A nice, warm fire. A good brandy. A fragrant curl of smoke drifting from his pipe.

That was when he smelled the smoke. Not fragrant, but raw. With sudden clarity he remembered the monster striking him with the fireplace poker, the pipe flying from between his teeth. An image flashed in his memory, a smear of red smoldering tobacco on the living room carpet.

And now he could smell the smoke.

The phone. He had to get to it now, while the line still worked. Urgently, he dragged himself across the lab. The desktop was out of reach, but he tugged at a length of black cord and the phone tumbled to the floor.

He snatched up the handset and dialed frantically.

All for nothing.

The phone was dead.

And, Frankenstein knew, so was he.

He lay back on the cool tile floor, waiting for the end.

The needle stabbed Frankenstein's arm. "Don't worry," the man said. "I'm a doctor."

Frankenstein stared at him. He blinked, but his vision refused to clear. Still, he did not need to see the man to form an impression, not when he could smell the whiskey on his breath.

Footsteps came from the hallway, along with laughter. "Jesus, the kid wasn't kidding." It was another voice, different from the first but somehow the same. "You should get a look at this. There really is an alligator down there."

"We gotta get out of here." The first voice again. The doctor.

"Sure. How about our buddy the mad scientist? I mean, I know his tap dancing days are history, but is he gonna make it?"

"Well, I topped him off with morphine. If he doesn't pull through, at least he'll die happy."

"We don't want that to happen."

"Well, sure. We gotta get him out of here. Hell, we gotta get *us* out of here. That fire up there isn't going to be very forgiving once it gets going good and proper."

"Don't worry, brother. Tonight's our night." The second man laughed, and the sound cut Frankenstein like a knife. "Jesus, we're lucky fellas. Driving around, looking for a secret laboratory, like we're really going to find it, even if it's out here in the middle of *nowheresville*. Thank God that kid couldn't drive worth beans. Thank God he smashed that mailbox but good. And that brodie on the front lawn, that was pure *X marks the spot*."

"But it is worth the risk, Roy? I mean, do you really think this guy can fix things for you?"

"He made a whole guy out of dead stuff. Compared to that, how tough can it be to fix me?"

"I guess you're right, but. . . ."

Frankenstein couldn't follow the conversation. The voices were much too similar, and the men were talking fast. If only he could see clearly, see the two men. . . . He reached up, fingers scrabbling over his numb cheek, and rubbed at his right eye. He couldn't feel a thing.

But that was good, because there was nothing to feel.

Frankenstein jerked his hand away from his face.

He had no right eye. Only a raw red hole. Now he

remembered. His right eye was upstairs, a fleshy smear on the carpet. The monster had taken it.

Gott in Himmel. The morphine. He was swimming in the stuff. He couldn't feel a thing.

A man loomed over him. Frankenstein blinked, left eye straining. For a moment his vision cleared, and he saw that the man who stood above him only had one arm.

It was difficult speaking through a torn mouth, but Frankenstein managed to ask, "Who . . . are you?"

"It's not who I am," the one-armed man said. "It's who I'm gonna be. See, I figure that you owe me a little favor, Doc. And when you deliver on that favor, I'm gonna be your new right-hand man. It's time someone put you on the straight-and-narrow, and I figure I'm just the guy to do it. You and me, we're going places, Doc. Just you wait and see."

"You only get what you can take," the other man said. "That's our motto."

The two strangers laughed at that.

And, laughing still, they dragged Frankenstein up the stairs, through infant flames, through dark rumors of smoke, conveying the good doctor into the night beyond, where waited the enduring embrace of captivity.

TUESDAY WELD, SUNDAY SERVICES

by Rex Miller

They came to worship ... at an atom-age shrine!

"The Nacogdoches Starlight Drive-In will be converted to an outdoor place of worship beginning this week. Rev. Powell invites all persons to Sunday services."

—*Nacogdoches Texan,* 1959

The two sentients, an Oyslan and an empty-bracket audile, both from Coalition Research, were examining artifacts in the area behind the altar of the Nacogdoches Underground Mobile Worship Excavation, collating and making their initial project notes. The Oyslan was the team transliterator, the audile was the recorder.

No sentients knew precisely how long the blueball planet had been uninhabitable, but when probe sensors advised Coalition that the toxic level had reached a tolerable point, the first teams had been sent in. The worship site, the so-called "Nacogdoches Dig," was one of but four such locales unearthed, and it was the second-best preserved.

"We're part of Coalition history, I hope you realize," the Oyslan said, as they were preparing to record, "and the responsibility is sobering, don't you agree?"

"Yes," the empty-bracket audile said, wrinkling its bzbplick, "of course. Shall we begin?" It looked at the Oyslan, which it found distasteful, and wondered how anything so truly ugly could be so totally self-enamored. The Oyslan's face was typically 'Muan in appearance, with a stovepiped freen and the mutant burns of a rainstreaker. There was no love lost between the neutered audile and the agendered core-invert.

The Oyslan activated the Thoudiola, a well-used Thought-Holo unit, and started theming, as the audile brainshielded, automatically recording a first-generation Thoud. "Nacogdoches Underground Mobile Worship Excavation Report. Transliteration of artifacts at Hardrock Site by—" it themed its designation, which was approximately the smell of iloram-remover mixed with synthetic-noised-glottal-stops, an empty-bracket phrase which the audile couldn't perceive, "—and by recorder Tertiary Driftingpresence." The audile's bzbplick puckered at the formal mention of its designation.

"Excavation is remarkably well-preserved, second only to the Blueball One excavation, and nearly as large. Site was estimated to hold between six and seven hundred human sentients, who would gather each day at such locales to perform specific functions. (It is known that on Tuesdays of each perpetual calendar, sentients gathered in groups of several hundred mobile transporters to unite pieces of metal. This was accomplished by heating and compressing two metallic parts together, presumably to create more of the mobile carriers, which were commonly called cars, trucks, autos, automobiles, vehicles, recreational vehicles, pickups, flatbeds, RVs, convertibles, sedans, coupes, touring cars, hardtops, ragtops, Chryslers, Dodges, Fords, and many similar designations. While the sentients were not highly intelligent, they had developed a cumbersome and extremely complex language of spoken, written, painted, and envisioned word-pictures. Compare six thousand to seven thousand designations for "mobile carrier" in the four known human sentient tongues, with the seventy-one designations on file in the Coalition Research Index, as employed by Vorseans and Matamuans combined.

Sundays of each perpetual calendar were Service times set aside for the worshiping of the human gods and goddesses.")

"Interjection," the audile said, when the rainstreaker paused to suck ± into its tall, circular freen, "the lengthy parenthetical does not smell, you realize," it said sneeringly.

"Naturally. How could it? May I continue?" All the audiles under contract to Coalition, and it had to draw an untranslatable phoneme like this Tertiary Drifting-presence nfnnf. "Services were conducted only when the sentients had fallen into certain states of mind; these include California, Arizona, Texas, Ennui, Oklahoma, Kansas, and Missouri, which were apparently states of grace. The congregation of "drive-in patrons" as they were called by the high priest, came in small groups, usually in one or two mobile carriers, which had from two to eighteen rolling wheels, depending upon the carrier's size and purpose.

"Infiltration/Exfiltration points were carefully planned to coincide with the old and new testaments of the undergrounders' Holy Bible, 'How to Devise a Layout for, Construct, Equip, and Maintain a Drive-In Theater,' by one of their gods called Pictograph Inc. 'The width of the exit should always be one/third larger than the entrance: entrance thirty feet, exit forty feet.' Speaker posts, the individual carrier position guards, were also carefully planned as to location. Recorder will insert old testament book of Service to Patrons, second verse." The rainstreaker half-turned to the audile, its triangular mirrored one-ways glinting across the bridge of the stovepipe.

"Distance between speaker posts is eighteen feet and distance between rows is thirty-eight feet. Maximum viewing angle is eighty degrees. Screen Size is forty-five feet by sixty feet. Bevelite plastic marquee letters top screen tower as seen from highway side, which

shows illuminated mural in the Latin-American motif."
The Oyslan rainstreaker stopped its colleague's verba-
tim data retrieval.

"Compare that with the new testament version:
'more satisfactory viewing is provided by a seventy
degree radius. There should be eighteen feet between
speaker posts, with no Ramp No. 5, so that the booth
will be accessible to all cars. Seventeen inch Bevelite
letters are used on the tower, which is constructed of
Robinson decking and screen plaster, and illuminated
with a mural depicting a Mexican scene.' While the
old and new books agree as to speaker post position
and Bevelite letters, the style of the tower mural at the
place of worship, and of course other elements, there is
a divergence of official opinion as to radii of viewing.
High priests, therefore, did not always agree.

"Nacogdoches Underground Mobile Worship facility
employed Simplex E-7 projectors, a ten-louver, fully-
acoustic, Type CP 250-375 speaker system and trans-
verter, heavy-duty brackets, hard-to-cut shielded cords,
and low-level magazine lights which were DC-
operated. DC may be a geographical delineation of the
northeastern section of Upper Mexico, or a state of
mind like California. Perhaps DC was the worship research center.

"One of the most difficult-to-comprehend aspects of
mobile carrier worship was the mysterious act of
groups of cars performing the ritual of hooking
bumpers—obviously symbolic of male/female bonding
or mating. The high priest's booth was situated so that
an observation platform could be maintained on the
roof. The priest could then oversee the bumper-
hooking rituals which were called 'commotions.' Another strange act on the part of the 'patrons' at the
services involved one or more persons compressing
themselves into the closed trunks of their mobile carri-

ers. It is thought that this form of self-punishment was limited to only the very devout.

"Actual mating, both heterosexual, homosexual, as well as masturbatory nonmating, was widely practiced. There is further evidence in the altar of the Nacogdoches high priest, that the objects of mating were most often female children called girls, or young unmarried—and infrequently—married women. Recorder will insert master list of related worship artifacts." He gestured to the tactile audile, unnecessarily.

"Good Girls, Bad Girls, Reform School Girls, High School Girls, Pin Down Girls, Pin-Up Girls, Girls in Chains, ChainGang Girls, Sorority Girls, Hot Rod Girls, Dragstrip Girls, Racket Girls, Teenage Bad Girls, Gun Girls, Girls in the Night, and Girls in Prison."

The Oyslan began again. "One or two mating objects were the focus of great worship. Mamie Van Doren was a female who apparently was born with an expanded upper torso, and in such services as The Girl in Black Stockings, she was the subject of the sermons. Interestingly, some of the wall hangings in the Nacogdoches hardrock altar match the designations on the services retrieved at the primary Blueball excavation. Eight of these have designations in which the word 'daughter' is used, implying a sentient human's female child, or the female offspring of a lower animal, such as a Dracula, Frankenstein, or Delinquent.

"It seems clear how these sentients were led to self-destruct by their religious beliefs, given the conjecture about the nature of their mass genocide." The translator gazed at the alarming artifact they'd found in the digs, a scientific article from a secret document of the high priest's library.

Atomic Projection Made Easy in Ten Simple Lessons

DIE, BABY, DIE, DIE, DIE!

by Dan Perez

*1,400 pounds of alien fury . . .
with a black leather soul!*

*Author's note: The events in the following story are
true. They have been verified by numerous top experts
from several government agencies and scientific insti-
tutions. To preserve national security and prevent the
sure nationwide panic that would occur if a story of
this magnitude were released as true events, it has
been presented here as fiction. And now, the true,
proven events of our story:*

It looked like a shooting star, at first, but as it arced
over the city of Lipperton at 5:10 a.m., it resolved into
a glowing saucer shape, tumbling end over end, as
though someone had hurled a radioactive dinner plate
across the sky.

Tab was cool. Some might have said too cool for his
own good, but he didn't care about his own good, being the leader of the Stink Bugz. That was his gang,
and they *knew* he was the coolest of the cool. Tab (his
folks had named him after Tab Hunter) could perch a
ciggie on his lips so it hung nearly straight down his
chin, and when he talked, the ciggie barely moved. He

wore sunglasses even at night, and had insisted that the Stink Bugz do the same, too, until they started bumping into things and tripping a lot. Then, shaking his head slightly, he had relaxed the discipline, allowing them take off their sunglasses at dusk.

His hair held just enough Vitalis to gleam brilliantly in any light, and a few dark spikes of hair always fell down over his forehead. It was natural for him, but the other Bugz spent a lot of time in the bathroom each morning emulating the look (it was hardest for Geno, because his hair was naturally curly). Tab's jacket was all black leather and shiny buckles and bosses, his T-shirt was downy white cotton and his jeans were faded denim. All the Bugz wore the same, down to their dime-loafers. (That's penny-loafers with a dime instead because the Stink Bugz were high rollers, get it, daddy-o?)

Tab was a badass with a switchblade, too. Every Stink Bug had seen him hold down Fatty Lugan and carve THIS SPACE FOR RENT into Fatty's forehead while the Bugz rumbled with Fatty's Boys. And there was the time he swept the blade down onto the counter at the soda fountain and caught a fly by its right three legs. The switchblade was a part of Tab's body, like a silvery stinger, always ready for business.

The other Stink Bugz used the weaponry they felt most comfortable with. Geno had his dad's brass knuckles, Frankie used a genuine, police-issue blackjack, Willy-boy favored a length of towing chain, and Bruiser always did an adequate job with nothing more than his huge, knotlike fists. A man had to be armed in Lipperton—you never knew when you'd run across the Hooligans, the Aces, the Duckasses, the Tornadoes or Fatty's Boys.

So anyway, on this particular night, the Stink Bugz had had their fill of beer and pool at the Cue Ball

Lounge, and they decided to wander the streets and see what kind of trouble they might stir up.

"We should go to Angie Parks' place out by the dam," said Willy-boy. "Maybe her old man is out of town and she'll be taking gentleman callers."

"Yah," said Bruiser.

"And maybe he's not out of town and he blows off your family jewels with that double-barreled shotgun he keeps by the door, too," said Geno.

"Aw, I ain't a'scared of him."

"Yah," said Bruiser.

"Shhh!" said Tab, and the Bugz fell into watchful silence. Tab pointed at the dark alley ahead and off to the right.

"Didja see somethin' there, Tab?"

Tab nodded, sunglasses glinting in the yellow light from the street lamps. Easing his switchblade out of his back pocket, he started forward, moving stealthily along the doorways and stoops of the building. The Bugz followed, keeping to the shadows as much as possible. The only sound was Bruiser's characteristic muffled chortling.

Tab stopped at the edge of the alley, flattening out against the brick surface and motioning for the rest of the Bugz to do likewise. With the barest movement of his thumb, Tab snicked open the switchblade and leaned over, peering into the alley.

"Somethin' back there?" whispered Frankie.

Nodding, Tab stepped confidently into the mouth of the alley.

"That's Lewton's grocery, on the other side there," said Willy-boy as the rest of Bugz lined up behind Tab. "They ain't got no way outta this alley now."

"We're gonna bust 'em up," said Frankie.

"We'll conk 'em good," said Geno.

"Paste 'em," said Willy-boy.

"Yah," said Bruiser.

They stalked deeper into the shadowy alley, the links of Willy-boy's chain jingling faintly. Bruiser chortled under his breath.

Everyone but Tab gasped when it stepped out from behind a big stack of orange crates. The dim light from the street shone on it, illuminating something with long, lime-green legs and bulbous, faceted eyes.

"Jeeeeeez," moaned Frankie. "It's a monster!"

"Yah," said Bruiser.

It stepped forward, its long, slender body sheathed in chitinous green armor. Its triangular head cocked to the side as it regarded them, segmented antennae twitching back and forth. In its great, hinged front claws, it held something that looked vaguely like a bazooka.

"P-P-P-P-raying m-m-m-Mantis," blurted Geno. "I s-s-seen a picture of one in school."

"Yah," said Bruiser.

"Quiet," said Tab, still standing with his switchblade out, as if it would stop the armored apparition standing before them. He tossed the glittering blade from hand to hand as the thing's head darted from side to side, watching intently. Then the creature tossed the tubelike weapon it held back and forth between its toothy claws.

Tab gave a little laugh: the first one the Bugz had heard since he'd seen those itty bitty red-eared turtles at the State Fair. Then he flicked the switchblade closed and slid it into his back pocket, holding out both empty hands.

The giant insectoid twitched its antennae for a moment, then slid the weapon up and over its shoulder, where the tube hung from a strap. It extended its claws forward, still lethal-looking, but now demonstrably empty.

Tab gave his little laugh again and turned back to the Bugz. "I like this guy," he said.

* * *

"J-j-jeez, who'da thunkit?" said Frankie to the other Bugz as they followed Tab and the insect monster down the street at a respectable distance. Tab kept talking to it in a low voice, pointing out things like the soda fountain, the five-and-dime, the record store, and the statue of town father Edward D. Wood. The creature responded with a rapid clicking sound that reminded the Bugz of marbles dropping onto a linoleum floor.

"Do they really understand each other?" asked Geno, pointing. He was so rattled he'd forgotten to take off his brass knuckles.

"Well, look at 'em!" said Willy-boy.

"Yah," said Bruiser.

They all stopped at the sound of a low whistle from up ahead. Tab glanced back at the Bugz and jerked his thumb hard toward a nearby alley. A sharper whistle sounded as they scrambled into the alleyway, and a sarcastic voice called out, "Man, it stinks tonight. Must be those crummy, farting Stink Bugz."

"We shoulda picked another name," grumbled Frankie, glancing out from behind some garbage cans.

"Yah," said Bruiser.

"Shut up, you idiots," snarled Tab from across the alley.

There was a sound of a breaking bottle just outside the mouth of the alley, and seven shadowy figures moved into sight.

"Duckasses!" whispered Geno. "I heard Carmine bought a zip gun, too."

A match flared as Carmine DiCiprio lit up a smoke. He lowered the match to the waist of his jeans, where the Bugz saw the genuine plastic imitation mother-of-pearl grip of the zip gun. Dropping the match, Carmine called out, "I got a bullet for every one of you little smelly little cockroaches in there, so why don't you come out and take it like a man?"

In the dim light, they saw him assume a shooter's stance. The other Duckasses held broken bottles, baseball bats, chains, and tire irons.

"Come on, cockroaches," Carmine said. "Or are you peeing your panties back there?"

The insect monster stepped out from a doorway and brought up the tubelike weapon. There was a loud hum and everyone's skin prickled with static electricity.

"Holey moley, what the hell is that?" said Carmine, staggering back. The Bugz saw a blinding flash accompanied by a heavy thudding sound, like a huge bag of flour hitting the street. Silence followed, and when the Bugz glanced up, the only thing remaining at the entrance of the alley were seven little piles of gritty ash.

"Whoa, daddy-o!" said Geno.

"Yah," said Bruiser.

Tab walked up to the remains of the Duckasses, stubbed at them with the toe of his dime-loafer and sniggered. He spat at the ash piles and walked back to the praying mantis creature, which had slung the weapon back over its shoulder again.

Tab, ever the cool one, surveyed the gleaming monster up and down for a moment, glanced away and back, then casually said, "You're in."

They kept the monster, which Tab nicknamed Bugsy, up in their old tree house during the daylight hours. Even though the other Bugz didn't want to get too close to him, well, Tab's word was law, so Bugsy was a full-fledged member of the gang. And they had to admit that Bugsy looked a little less threatening (to them, at least) in the black motorcycle jacket Tab gave him. That was about the only item of the Stink Bugz official uniform that Bugsy could wear. The other Bugz just about flipped when Tab leaned down to glue a dime to the green chitin covering each of Bugsy's four foot-claws. But Bugsy just watched, occasionally making that weird clicking sound. Bugsy even leaned down and allowed Tab to dab some Vitalis onto the tuft of bristly black hair between his antennae. Then Busgy drank the rest of the Vitalis. Tab just laughed and hooked a thumb at the creature. "What a screwball!"

"Are we really going to take him to the dance?" asked Geno.

"Why not?" Tab replied, running his comb lightly through his hair. "We gotta show off our newest member."

Frankie said what they were all thinking. "He's gonna cause a panic, Tab."

"Nah. We'll just say he's our science experiment from school."

"But we ain't been to school for weeks," said Willy-boy.

'Yah," said Bruiser.

"Stop botherin' me with details. We're takin' Bugsy to the school dance tonight. That'll be fun, won't it, Bugsy?"

The mantis creature flicked its antennae and rasped its mandibles together.

They ran into Officer McGillicuddy that night, on their way up to the high school. "All right, boyos, what're y'doin' skulkin' around here?" He got a glimpse of Bugsy and turned pale. "Jumpin' Jehosaphat! What's that thing?"

"He's our science experiment, Officer McGillicuddy, and we're takin' him to the dance to show him off."

"Yah," said Bruiser.

McGillicuddy pulled his revolver out and pointed it at the monster. "N–n–now, you boys just s–s–step away from that thing," he said.

The Bugz were all too happy to comply, but Tab stayed next to the mantis-thing. "Better give him the Treatment, Bugsy!"

McGillicuddy fired, emptying the revolver, but the bullets richocheted off Bugsy's armor. With an angry buzz, the monster brought his weapon to bear and *FUH-WHOOOOMPH!*

Nothing remained of McGillicuddy but a small pile of ashes crowned by his blue policeman's hat.

Tab doubled over with laughter. "Luck o' the Irish!" he squealed, pointing. Then, as if he suddenly realized that whooping with laughter fell somewhere just this side of cool, he straightened up, snapped his fingers, and said, "Let's go to the dance."

The Jack Arnold Memorial High School gymnasium had been built prior to the Fire Code revisions, and so only had one pair of double doors that served as both entrance and exit. This proved useful to the Stink Bugz since all the kids went nuts trying to get away when they got a look at Bugsy. But since Bugsy and Tab blocked the doorway, about all the kids could do was run back and forth, scream a lot, faint, and cower in the bleachers. The entirety of Lipperton's varsity football team, the Fighting Gila Monsters, had already bravely challenged the newest member of the Bugz and been reduced to Not-Quite-So-Fighting Cinder Heaps. Tab surveyed the terrified crowd—all those wiseass jerks who never understood a kid from across the tracks—and smiled with supreme satisfaction. The pinnacle came when Mr. Prestoncottby, who had once called Tab "a snot-nosed little excuse for a juvenile delinquent," walked shakily across the wooden slat floor and stood in front of Tab and Bugsy.

"What is it you want from us?" he said, his voice low and meek.

Tab hooked a thumb at Bugsy. "My friend here wants to dance with the homecoming queen, is all."

Bugsy clicked his mandibles rapidly and his antennae twitched.

"Yah," said Bruiser.

It took a great deal of coaxing, but finally, Mary Jo Wendy Sue Miller came forward, resplendent in her crinoline dress, cashmere sweater, and homecoming tiara. She looked like she was walking to the electric chair, which unfortunately was probably about right since Bugsy reached out with his claws, crushed her to death in an instant, and started to feed.

Then the *real* panic broke out, and, above the tumult, Tab and the Bugz heard the air raid siren wailing madly.

"Cheese it!" said Tab, and the Bugz started to run. Tab had to pull Bugsy, who hadn't finished his meal, along with them.

Bugsy vaporized the state police roadblock on Dam Road 1 just outside of town, but the Bugz had heard that the National Guard was on its way, and they had to escape.

As they ran, Frankie said, "Man, they got tanks and machine guns and stuff! We're done for!"

"Yah," said Bruiser.

"Shaddup!" shouted Tab, somewhat winded from their flight up the winding road toward the dam. "We get up there on the dam, and Bugsy'll have a clear shot at anything that comes up this road."

"They got aeroplanes, too!" said Willy-boy.

"Shaddup, I said," snarled Tab. "What a bunch of sissie-boys! You think they're gonna shoot at the dam? It'd flood the whole damn town!"

"Yah," said Bruiser.

They made the top of the dam as searchlights began to play across its wide expanse of curved concrete. A megaphone-enhanced voice came from somewhere below in town. "Stink Bugz! This is the National Guard! We've got artillery trained on your position! We only want to kill the monster! If you boys come down now, we'll sort this whole thing out."

Standing at the rail, Tab waved his switchblade back and forth in the glare of the lights. "Come and get me, crumb bums!" he shouted. He pointed the shining blade at Bugsy, who busily groomed an antenna in his mandibles. "He's the best friend I ever had in this stinkin' town, so you're going to have to take us both—dead or alive!"

It was about that time that Tab noticed the rest of the Bugz running down the road toward the city as fast as they could.

"Go ahead, ya cowards!"

The National Guard voice boomed again. "Tab! This is your next-to-the-last warning! Come down peacefully!"

Tab shot them the bird and turned to Bugsy. "Give 'em the Treatment, pal!"

The mantis-thing brought its weapon down over its shoulder, but the skin-prickling charge never materialized. Bugsy cocked his head, antennae twitching rapidly, then shook the metal tube and tried again. Nothing. He thumped on the tube with a claw, but it still didn't work.

"Uh-oh," said Tab.

There was a flash down in the valley. Tab and Bugsy ducked as the shell whistled over them and detonated in the still waters of Corman Reservoir. Cold spray rained down on them as the voice boomed out again. "That was a warning shot. We've been authorized by the Governor to blow up the whole dam if necessary. We'd rather not do that. If you and the monster come down peacefully, we'll dissect it for science and you'll go to reform school. This is your last warning, Tab— you'd better decide right now!"

"Screw you!" he shouted, hurling his switchblade at them.

The artillery gun flashed again, and Tab put an arm around Bugsy as the shell hurtled toward them. "You and me, buddy!" he said, closing his eyes.

Nothing happened. Then Bugsy emitted a fusillade of clicking sounds. Tab opened his eyes to see a sleek metallic saucer shimmering in the moonlight above them. His attention strayed to a conical object suspended in midair only a few yards away. The artillery shell. Tab saw that the beam of a searchlight had frozen in mid-swing, too. Tab laughed out loud, all this being as cool as a crisp C-note to him.

The saucer continued to descend as Bugsy leaped up and down, clicking and squealing joyfully. Settling on the rim of the dam, the saucer came to a halt. A door and ramp appeared in its side and several other mantis creatures rushed out, their weapon-tubes at the ready. They swarmed up to Tab and Bugsy, launching into an animated conversation with the latter. Then the rest of the aliens hurried back to the saucer, which by this time, had caused cracks to form in the surface of the dam.

Bugsy then picked Tab up, holding him gingerly in the deadly claws, and carried him toward the saucer. "You're taking me with you?" Tab asked. "Bugsy, you're the greatest!"

They ascended the ramp into the saucer, none too soon, for water was already streaming from the cracks in the dam. The gleaming saucer lifted away into the night.

From the National Guard vantage point on Steckler's Hill, the second shell struck the dam and the whole thing gave way; too easily it seemed. A great wall of water rushed down into the valley, racing toward Lipperton, sweeping houses, trees, and everything else along with it. The National Guard commander lowered his binoculars and winced. "I don't think the Governor should have authorized this, after all."

The Cal Tech scientist next to him watched the torrent smashing into Lipperton and mused, "Why do you suppose a kid like Tab would take up with an alien monster like that?"

"I dunno," said the guardsman. "Rock 'n' roll and them cheap paperback novels, probably."

THE YELLERS OF THEIR EYES

by Tia Travis

In their veins ... the blood of the beast!
In their eyes ... unspeakable hunger!

"Boys, hold your horses. There are
plenty of them down there for us all!"
—Lieutenant Colonel George A. Custer
to his company on the ridge overlooking
the Valley of the Little Bighorn, June 25, 1876

After a kill they drink. It's the taste of the blood. . . .
—H.G. Wells, *The Island of Dr. Moreau*

The Black Hills
Dakota Territory
Late Summer, 1877

It was five minutes after five when Trev T. Halleran
and the dirty little pinto stumbled onto the busted-up
First National Bank box ten and a quarter miles outside
the town of Sand Creek. Halleran knew it was 5:05 because that's what the banker man's pocket watch said. He
didn't know what the banker man himself was up to, but
the man's amputated hand—lying in the dirt behind the lockbox and half-hidden by a scrub of
rabbitbrush—was not, at the moment, up to a hell of a
lot.

The hand had stiffened up some, as dead hands are
inclined to do. Still, it was a well-kept hand. The nails
on it had been clipped with meticulous care and there

was not the tiniest bit of dirt under them; an accomplishment in those parts. The thumb had placed itself firmly atop the four o'clock position as if awaiting a teatime that would never come.

City man's hand, Halleran decided. With a city man's luck.

The pocket watch, still keeping perfect time: five minutes, forty-five seconds after five.

The man on the pony thought: *Damn, it's late.*

He stared into the distance at the Black Hills that lay low over the ocher plain. Home of The Thunders to thousands of Lakota. He remembered what a man who'd lived to tell about it had overheard in the Valley of the Little Bighorn. The ominous prediction of Half Yellow Face to Lieutenant Colonel G. A. Custer beat like a blood drum in his ears: *You and I are going home today—by a trail that is strange to both of us.*

Trev Halleran stood on the summit of the tawny hill and tried to make a decision. His shadow, half-on the bank box, half-off, lay heavy as the dust on the boots that had brought him here from Fort Abraham Lincoln; heavy as the seat-worn Cheyenne saddle that lay on the back of his five-year-old Indian pony.

They'd been up before the first lemon light bathed the eastern sky, Halleran and the pony, trotting their way in a southwesterly direction across the then-cool, uneven brush country with its haunting, early morning shadows. Twenty miles of sage and saltbush, hoof-dust and rattlers, and they still hadn't made it to the damn town. Now the late afternoon sunlight shone like a dull yellow eye on the blood-flecked face of the banker man's fatal timepiece—

Six minutes, twenty-two seconds after five.

The banker man's signet ring, initials "E. E.", gleamed in the fading light. The pinkie had swollen up in the heat of the sun. It lent the little finger and its circulation-cutting showpiece the appearance of a tied-off sausage. Without thinking, Halleran licked his lips. It'd been a while since the last plate of sausages. Since the last plate of *anything*.

The pinto whickered and shook its matted head in the dry heat of the September afternoon. A black fly took a bite out of its sweat-stained flank, and it swatted its whisk broom tail.

Eight minutes, ten seconds after five.

Suppertime . . .

Halleran had traded a Crow Indian one of his .44 Army Colts for the rangy little brown-eyed cayuse, and a damn fine trade it was turning out to be for the both of them. The Crow had been a dried-up piece of Bad Indian pemmican who went by the name of Many Lice. Many Lice had done some part-time scout work for the army in his day, mainly to make it hard for the sons-of-bitchin' Sioux who'd stolen the Black Hills from his people a million or so moons back. He'd been only too willing to take one of Colonel Colt's finest off Halleran's hands, though based on the shoddy condition of both Indian and revolver, Halleran doubted either'd be up for much more than blowing the broad sides off a couple of buffalo chips.

The pony had been a mite too small for a man like Halleran, who stood six-four in his socked feet, six-four and a half if you added on the thick layer of filth that had accumulated on the bottoms of said socks after a month of wear and tear. And hell if there hadn't been a prickly piece of *something* stuck in one of them, too.

Burr-in-the-sock.

He'd thought up the Indian name for himself after the first mile. At first he'd intended to take the damn boot off, dead prairie dog smell and all, extract the prickly damn bastard with his teeth if he had to. It'd been sticking itself into one calloused ridge of toe or another for the last two hundred miles. But then he thought to hell with it, let it stick, and after a while it didn't bother him so much any more. Just like the chafe of James Tanner's carbine didn't bother him so much any more.

Halleran had tied the Springfield and his own regiment rifle to the saddlebag that hung over the pinto's flea-bitten side. The carbine stock had sanded a dollar-sized hole through first one knee back, then the other. To remedy this, he fastened some dark blue wool cut from his old uniform over the backs of his trouser legs. When those were stiff and caked with blood, he unpinned them and replaced them without so much as an eyeblink. He could take a little blood. Tanner had taken a lot.

Upon leaving the fort Many Lice handed Halleran the unshod pinto's frayed rawhide reins, and man and pony took off into the buffalo brush and dust. A fat-bellied army horse couldn't have satiated itself for long on the nickel's worth of stub grass Halleran and the pony had scuffed out of the dirt over the last couple of days. But the shaggy-coated pony, like its former Indian owner, was used to the tough grass and the prairie drought and didn't complain.

Lieutenant's horses, on the other hand, were accustomed to grain and plenty of it. *Otoe* grain, as the Sioux might say. Saltbush and Spanish bayonet couldn't cut it on an officer's mount's dinner table. Not on Halleran's dinner table either, as he was finding out. Much as he'd have liked to put his service days behind him, he'd been thinking pretty steadily about the half-ration of army hardtack he'd eaten back in Mud Butte. At the moment he was hungrier than a bitch wolf with fallen arches, and not only that, but it was *late*—

Ten minutes after five.
The timepiece ticked.

The sound was as empty as the wind that stirred the stiff-spined weeds that poked out here and there on the hill. *Like tufts on an old man's dandruffed head,* Halleran thought. Still, there was more than weeds a little farther southwest. Bushels of real yellow grassland and water, too, running north-south a couple miles from the Black Hills themselves. It was to Sand Creek, to the town of Sand Creek itself, that Halleran had been headed when he'd come upon the First National Bank lockbox. And its five-fingered friend. Already a couple of black birds hovered like rain clouds in a sky the color of dirty canvas.

Halleran didn't like it one bit.

Birds that size didn't set out the napkins and cutlery for one man's hand; these had their eyes on a meatier meal. And he had a hunch they'd found it down in that dry river valley. Ahead of him, a deeply-rutted stagecoach trail rocked down the hill and was swallowed up by a sigh of swaying yellow grasses. The curvature of the sky seemed to have taken on the same yellowish cast, too, like a jaundiced eyeball.

Yellow, the color of sickness.

Yellow, the color of a dead man's pocket watch. . . .

It was now a quarter past the hour, and the pony was skittish. Eyes up and alert, its ears pricked like barbed wire in the dry Dakota air. It tossed its thistled mane. The motion rolled the half-breed bit in its mouth, producing a high-pitched, tuneless whistle. Halleran had bought the bit as a sort of horse harmonica, something strangely musical to pass the time in the empty hours of a plains afternoon. But now, standing there in the dying light of the yellow hill by the severed hand and the watch and their unexpected and unexplainable reminders of mortality and time, he was starting to feel a little too exposed.

He hitched himself onto his nervous mount and double-checked the supply of cartridges in his second

Army Colt and rifle. Then he started down in the direction of the stage tracks. The hill that sloped down to the river valley was a steep one with sharp, unpredictable turns. Halleran's pony half-slid, half-walked down the incline. A little *too* inclined for a stagecoach barreling at full-tilt, Halleran noted, but there was no reason for a stage to travel at that kind of pace. Unless the team was out of control, and—

There's your problem right there.

He reined the pinto at the foot of the hill.

A stagecoach wheel lay solidly on its side with two spokes split. Half an axle poked up at the sky. The splinter-fresh break looked like a dozen porcupine quills. Fifteen yards in front of the wrecked wheel lay the stagecoach itself. It had rolled half-over on its side. A number of boxes and suitcases that were presumably leather-belted to the top during travel had spilled their contents all over the place as if someone in a fever pitch had been trying to find something clean to wear.

Halleran dismounted. At his feet lay a woman's petticoat, the hem caught in a nettle. Beside the petticoat lay an open copy of *Paradise Lost,* frontispiece flecked with spit-sized chunks of flesh. Ahead of that, a pair of suspenders matted with blood lay on the ground beside a smashed teacup. Ahead of these: an embroidered pocketbook, fallen open, like the body of a skinned dove; a patchwork quilt, cotton stuffing pulled out like bits of poplar fluff; a vigorously-polished black boot, laces ripped out as if by the teeth of some wild animal. . . .

At Halleran's feet lay a sunburned piece of meat. It resembled a well-cooked hunk of bacon but was, he realized grimly, the remains of a man's ear. Stout white hairs still sprouted from the depths of it. And what had been the last sound the ear had ever heard?

Blood.

Back in '63 Halleran had been shot at by one of

Robert E. Lee's men at Gettysburg. The bullet had skimmed his temple and taken a v-shaped nick out of his ear. The sound of the blood, rushing through his auditory channels like the ocean in an empty seashell, had been the one sensation he recalled with any facility fifteen years after he'd pumped the Confederate soldier who'd done it to him full of Union lead.

The sound of the blood.

But there was no sound here except his own tense breathing and the distant thunder of predatory birds overhead; the occasional stamp of dust from the nodding pony; the rhythmic creak of the splintered stage door as it swung back and forth on its hinges like the white picket gate in front of a house where nobody lives.

The sound of the blood.

For Private James Tanner, dying of dehydration six short inches from the banks of the Little Bighorn River, the sound of the blood had stopped clot by clot as the slit he'd made in his bay's belly congealed in the noonday sun. Soon, all that was left was a dry smear of blood on Tanner's lips and an ounce or two of cloying black liquid in a tin cup. The cup had fallen on its side not half a foot from the sun-warmed waters of the Bighorn River. Half a foot too far for Tanner, as it turned out, but it didn't really matter because he had been beyond physical sensations after the second day.

A sheet iron arrowhead had penetrated his tibia. The Hunkpapa who'd shot him during M Company's retreat from the river had deliberately weakened the tendon binding. While Tanner had been able to remove the shaft, the triangular head remained solidly clinched in the bone. Extraction with a length of looped wire had proven so brutally painful that the attempt had to be aborted.

After that, he'd been barely aware of the itch of his

Sioux-shaved scalp, or the burn of stale urine on his thighs, or the hipbone that protruded like the rim of a white china dish through the tear in his regimental trousers. The strange but unmistakable vacuum pop of air that accompanies the removal of a scalp seemed to have popped Tanner's mental and sensual capacities as well. He saw nothing, felt nothing, heard nothing . . . not even the sound of his blood as the last of it seeped from his body in the still of the cricket-dry afternoon.

Nothing, that is, until the box. And with the box a sound that would have made James Tanner's scalp hair stand at terrified attention, had said scalp not been set out to sun dry on a Santee squaw's lodge pole twenty miles distant.

This box, and the man who had built it, were the reasons Trev Halleran had come to Black Hills country fifteen months after his friend's death in the Montana valley.

Fifteen months of careful, concentrated listening . . . for an animal with a human name:

Dr. D. Devereaux.

A Lakota had once explained to Halleran: *If you take the time to find the next track you have learned a lot about finding the next track, but little about the one who has made it. If you take the time to learn about the one who has made the track, you will find the next track without looking. You will find that its trail is your own trail.*

It was like trying to find a whisper in the wind. Halleran found only a few faint traces at first. He and Devereaux had been two animals traveling by night in the same hills . . . hearing the same sounds, smelling the same smells, sleeping in the same depressions and hollows.

Now, standing on the hill with the Indian pony at his side, Halleran had found the trail as easily as he could have found a scatter of bread crumbs.

The pinto whinnied and shook its head, half-breed bit tinkling in its mouth. Halleran stroked its neck, stared at the blackish hills that rolled in the distance like thunder.

You and I are going home—

—by a trail that is strange to both of us.

Lieutenant Colonel Custer, en route to the end of the world, had died in the Valley of the Little Bighorn on a shimmering summer afternoon like this one. The blindingly pale bodies of dead soldiers dotted the hillside. Halleran and another had been ordered to count them: 197 to start, all of them stripped to their white cotton socks.

"Oh, how white they look! How white!" Captain Weir had said. The two men stood over the body of a decomposing soldier who could not be identified because his name had been cut from his cloth undershirt. Some kind of medicine, Lieutenant Trev Halleran supposed. Arrows had been shot point-blank into both his eye whites.

No one knew if Custer had died on the hill or had died by the river and was later carried to the hill by his men. It did not seem to matter. The Son of the Morning Star was dead, and his countenance in death had been reported by Lieutenant Bradley as *that of a man who had fallen asleep and enjoyed peaceful dreams.*

Private James Tanner was also dead. He had died by the river, but he had not been killed by the Indian enemy and he had not been carried back to the hill. Tanner's dreams, Halleran knew, had not been peaceful.

They had not been his own.

The blood rushed in Halleran's ears, but he did not hear it; it had become too constant a companion. He left his pinto's reins in the dust and started toward the wreck of the stagecoach, stooping to retrieve the scatter of tintypes that lay faceup before him.

How white they look, he couldn't help but think. The first: a thin solemn man in a thin solemn suit and wire-rimmed spectacles. The second: the same man in a sitting room, smiling tentatively this time, light eyes overly-large and liquid without their window of spectacles: *"To Emma, Love Eternal, Your Husband E. M. Miles. Minneapolis, Minnesota, 1875."* Then the man and a beautiful woman with eyes as clear as summer pools. She wore a white dress and wedding veil. The same wedding veil that now brushed across Halleran's boots like a tumbleweed before it, too, disappeared into the silence of memory.

A high-pitched scream startled him. A horse appeared from behind the stagecoach, part of a broken harness dangling around its slick chestnut neck. Its eyes had the same sick yellow tint as the sky. Dried foam caked its mouth and nostrils. As the angle of sunlight on the animal altered, Halleran noticed that a meaty red mouthful had been savagely torn from its right haunch.

Halleran holstered his .44 and checked his rifle, a seven shot .50-caliber Spencer left over from his service days. Six of its seven bullets remained, and he had a mind to use every damn one of them if he had to. The horse kicked up on its hind legs, tail switching, ears pinned flat, terror and pain in its widening eyes. Foam spilled from its dilated nostrils like bubbles from a drowning man's mouth.

He steadied the Spencer, closed one eye, and squeezed the trigger. The animal's head snapped like a whip as the bullet entered its left eye and penetrated its brain. A second later the body thudded to the dirt.

Halleran let out a deep breath, lowered the rifle, and walked around to the side of the stage. Another bank box, this one with *Black Hills Cheyenne Stage Line* in faded gilt letters, lay open on its side. Paper money scattered everywhere like confetti at a Chinese funeral.

He wadded it into his empty pockets without another thought before circling to the front of the stage.

Two dead horses were still attached to the harness. One of them, eyes open and lips stretched taut over its teeth, had presumably broken its neck in the wreck. The other had been torn apart in the same manner as the horse he'd just put a bullet in. The throat was partially eaten, the larynx visible; what remained was an eyesore mess of decomposing meat. It looked like the attacker had hastily retched some of it up, too. A splash of undigested sick and hair stuck to the horse's distended belly.

Halleran discovered a splash of the same sick on the stubbled cheek of a man who lay on his side a few feet from the horse. The driver, by the looks of it, and where his ear used to be was now a nub of shiny white cartilage. His face was a bloated mask of blood encrusted with feeding insects.

The shotgunner was not to be found; nor was the solemn suited man from the tintype.

Beside the dead driver lay an overturned wooden case. Two dozen brand new Sharps buffalo rifles spilled out on the grass beside the decomposing body of a man in a pinstripe suit who was short one hand and, Halleran concluded, one pocket watch. The banker man's bowler hat was overturned like an empty rain barrel about two feet from what was left of his head. The head was almost completely chewed off, leaving just a slender sinew and a few sparse hairs at the nape of the neck. His stomach had been slit vertically and pallid entrails had emerged as if on springs.

Halleran took this in almost indifferently, leaving a slight scuff mark on the banker's immaculate white shirtsleeve as he stepped over him. He was more interested in the woman.

Even with the blood on her abraded forehead, even with a split cheek that showed bone as white as a wedding dress, he recognized her. Her eyes were as clear as summer pools, and they opened unsteadily when he knelt down beside her. Her plain blue traveling dress was split down the bodice, exposing one heaving breast and an upper rib cage ribboned with the same vertical pattern of slashes that split the dead banker's belly, though these wounds appeared to be superficial.

Halleran didn't know how she'd lived this long without help, without water. At the Little Bighorn, a soldier had offered him a hundred dollars for one drink. The man had been shot from some distance by a .50 caliber Leman rifle that had been presented to its Arapahoe owner by the U.S. Government. Sun-heated water spilled from the perforation in the man's stomach wall as he drank thirstily, but he died without comment.

Trev Halleran uncapped his canteen, intending to pour a couple of drops between the woman's swollen lips.

"N–no . . ." she whispered hoarsely. "No water! No water!" Her neck muscles contracted and she fell back, tendons in her throat as taut as a telegraph line.

Halleran held her stiffly by the shoulders. "No water," he said, setting down the canteen. "My hands are empty, ma'am. You see? No water."

This seemed to calm her a little, and she attempted to focus on him. Her words, choked through swollen vocal cords, half-barked, half-paralyzed, but the terror in them readable: "There's something the matter with them."

Halleran hesitated. "Somethin' the matter with *who*, ma'am?" he said softly. "Can you tell me?"

She bit her lip and looked at the sky, and what she saw in the blank of it, be it swooping birds or something more sinister, Halleran did not know. Dried lather flecked her chin, the same lather he'd seen on the horse's mouth. The horse he'd had to kill.

"They had *boxes* on them," Emma Miles said faintly. "On the backs of them...."

The summer pools emptied their light.

Halleran laid the woman's body carefully on the alkali soil. He covered her with his coat and stood up.

Boxes, she had said.

That was all, but that was enough. He didn't know who *they* were any more than he knew who the woman had been. He didn't have to. All he knew was that it was five fifty-five—late.

Damn late.

Sand Creek, South Dakota, had all the desirability of an old squaw's tit: a couple of dusty, nondescript buildings and board sidewalks, some tents with torn, muddy canvases and battered skillets strung up outside to rattle in the wind. Blink twice and you'd have to backtrack to make sure the town hadn't been simply a festering flyspeck on the cornea.

Outside the two-story hotel Halleran saw an ancient Teton bundled in a motheaten buffalo robe. The Indian had nodded off against a drainpipe, and a handful of slat-thin mongrels the color of rendered fat huddled in the dust by their master's tattered moccasins. But apart from the Indian and his collection of curs, a couple of dirty-faced, barefoot boys, and one or two sullen-faced cowpunchers skulking about, the streets were empty of people.

Halleran left his pony at the stable and strolled into the Waggin' Tongue, the town's only drinking establishment. It was evident then why there was no one outside—they were all in here. It wasn't much of a watering hole. A few tables covered in faded green billiard felt and worn poker chips lined the walls. A bunch of cowpunchers in dirty Levis stood at the rail by a dirty-vested old-timer plucking on a banjo. In the far corner sat a piano with a pouchy piano player plopped on a stool in front of it.

Astride the piano, petticoats pushed up past her knees, sat a mining town prostitute. She was dressed only in her underdrawers, a steel-lined corset, and a pair of men's workboots. She looked like she'd had so many studs through her stable that she should have had horseshit on her thighs.

Halleran tipped his hat politely and walked up to the bar. He nodded at the bottle on the counter. "I'll take a little of that there coffin varnish."

The barkeep was a man with patent leather hair smoother than a Shewahwah pup's. "The only coffin you'll be taking is your own, mister, if you don't set your revolvers down where I can see them.'

Halleran met the man's eyes, then smiled carefully. "And why's that?"

"It's an ordinance. No shootin' irons within town limits." The barkeep's expression was deadpan.

Halleran let his eyes drop down to the holster of the stone-faced cowboy who stood beside him, a man with eyes that could have bored a hole through iron ore. The holster had a Colt in it, and not the kind that was in need of a brand, either. He examined the holsters of the other men in the room, as well as the loaded rifles leaned up on the backs of almost every chair and a Remington or two in plain sight on several of the billiard-felt tables.

Halleran asked the man behind the counter: "You the law in this town as well as the barkeep?"

"No law here, mister. You have a problem with the ordinance, you can walk out now and don't bother comin' back."

A minute ticked by.

A mustached man in a pair of wicked-looking Spanish spurs touched one scarred hand to his sidearm.

Another minute ticked by. Halleran thought about

the banker man's pocket piece, how it would look now on the shadowed hill, how the last dying light of sun would be shining softly on its transparent face. The intentions of the men in this room were equally transparent.

Trev smiled, held up his empty hands, and removed his gunbelt. "Damn, this is a serious town," he said.

The men at the bar turned back to their drinks. The piano player went back to bellowing out the lyrics to "Home on the Range" while he pounded on the yellowed keys, and the men at the card table went back to their losing hands.

The barkeep poured a shot of whiskey and set it in front of Halleran. The liquor tasted like water with a mouthful of tobacco juice spit in it to give it color, but Halleran didn't mention it.

"It's a smart man that knows how to take instructions," the barkeep said.

Halleran emptied the glass and wiped his mouth on the back of his hand. "How's that?"

"I mean if I'd had any backtalk about turning in your gunbelt, mister, any backtalk at all, any one of these men would have poured enough lead into you to make meltin' you down for bullets a payin' job."

"Friendly little town."

"It *was* . . . up until the Beaudine Brothers came into town and Boothill started fillin' itself with boots a mite too fast." The barkeep poured himself a drink and washed it down with another. He set the half-empty bottle back on the shelf.

The old-timer with the banjo set himself down on the stool beside Halleran. When he took off his hat, he looked like a full moon on the rise. "Turr'ble it is, turr'ble. All them dead men. Livestock, too. These hills ain't safe, I tell you." He held out a hand as leather-tough as a barber's strop. "Name's Skinner," he said. "Uncle Billy Skinner."

Halleran shook the man's outstretched hand. "Trev T. Halleran."

"What are you doin' here in Calhoun, Mister Halleran?"

"I thought this was Sand Creek."

"It was . . . up until a month ago," the barkeep said. "It's Calhoun now on account of The Calhoun Mining Company buying up most of the property in these parts. Calhoun decided to name the town after himself. He's settin' right over there—" He nodded at a fat man at one of the tables. The man had a well-chewed cigar clamped between his teeth and a brand-new suit that had to have set him back a damn bundle.

Halleran turned to Billy Skinner. "What's all this about dead men?"

"Old Sam was the first to git it." Skinner shook his head, played a couple of regretful chords on his banjo. "Best friend I ever had, Old Sam. He lived in the hills longer than any other white man I know, started placer minin' back in '71, a'fore Custer's Black Hills Expedition an' all that commotion. Don't think even the Sioux knew he was here, and that's sayin' somethin'."

"What happened to him?"

"Found 'im facedown in front of his open outhouse door, pants pulled down to his ankles, bare white buttocks in the hot yeller sun and a page of a mail-order catalog still stuck in his crack behind. *That's* what happened to 'im. That newsprint was flutterin' in the breeze so straight and white, it looked like Sam had been in the process of surrenderin' when he was attacked."

Halleran glanced around, noticed a sharp-eyed range hand who appeared to be listening intently to the conversation.

"Found the entire latrine on its back," Uncle Billy continued. "Looked like someone had hisself a time with an ax. Leastways, I *think* it was an ax. All the boards had these fresh scratchmarks on 'em, this long—" He stretched his hands two feet apart. "It was like someone was tryin' to *scratch* Old Sam outa there and finally scratched the damn shed over."

Skinner's withered, jerky-stick fingers strummed the banjo. Halleran recalled the tuneless whistle of his pony's bit, thought of how long the shadows in the valley would be now, how the sun would be setting on the eyes of the dead. He thought of the Valley of the Little Bighorn, about what it would have felt like to walk there after midnight with the eyes of two hundred dead men on your back. He shuddered a little.

Skinner nodded in understanding. "I seen somethin' like this a'fore," he said. " 'Ceptin' it was down in Oklahoma Territory. One of them hell winds come up outa nowhere and lifted the whole outhouse, man and all, lifted him a hun'ert feet in the air and carried 'im all the way to Pontotoc County. Feller inside, he finished up what he was doin', pulled up his pants and opened the door. He took two full steps a'fore he fell down dead. It'd scared 'im like to *death,* it had, openin' up that door and findin' hisself in some other place. That feller had the same look on his face as old Sam did when I rolled his head over with a stick. 'Course, some varmint'd got to it by that time, but it was Sam's head all right, and pretty much in one piece, too, 'ceptin' fer where it'd been bitten off."

"Bitten, huh," Halleran repeated thoughtfully, and the old man mistook it for a question.

"That's what I said, young man. I could still make out the bite marks even though they were dried over with blood. Real clean-like, them bite marks, at a real sharp angle, too. Like a rabbit's, but there ain't no rabbit with incisors that size. And rabbits don't eat meat, leastways no rabbit *I* ever seen. . . . Well, anyhow, the look Old Sam had on 'is face, it made my neck hairs stand up and take notice, I tell you that much. Eyes kind of froze-up, with little bits of dead grass stuck to one of 'em. The other one was out of its socket, like someone had spit it out. It was splatted on a month's worth of leavin's in the tin pan Sam had tied to the clothesline."

"Did Sam have any enemies?" Halleran asked.

Billy Skinner scratched his head like a woodpecker looking for termites. "See, now, that's what no one could figger. Everybody *liked* that old buzzer. Why, he could color up a story redder than an Injun's blanket. I remember one time he was a forty-niner pannin' the Alkali fer—"

"Just tell the story, Billy, and leave the pannin' for another time," the barkeep said, pouring Halleran another shot. The sharp-eyed cowboy who'd been eavesdropping turned around in his seat and pulled out a can of Bull Durham. He nodded at Halleran. Halleran nodded back.

"Sam, he'd had his eye on one of them Cheyenne blankies an old squaw was sellin' at the train station," Billy went on. "He'd been waitin' a month for the Indians to bring it into the store. When it come, I decided to take it up to 'im. But when I made it up there, it was like I told you. The door to his shanty was wide open and his flintlock settin' on the table beside a bag of gold. Sam facedown on the ground with his head bit off . . . it was turrible, I tell you. We buried 'im behind his shanty in that beautiful blankie he never did see. . . ." Billy wiped a teary eye.

"There's been other killin's, too," the sharp-eyed cowhand said suddenly, and stood up. He was tall and thin, Halleran noted, thin enough to take a bath in a rifle barrel. "Two days after Billy found Sam, one of Pendleton's men was out ridin' fence. Lit out of the ranch 'bout five a.m. on the fourth and that was the last anyone ever saw him alive. Me and Bill Short, we rode up to the ridge the next mornin' and found an entire section of the devil's hatband down in the dirt. Pete Laramie's horse was standin' there beside it. One of its forelegs was shattered at the knee. I thought maybe it'd stumbled into a posthole and lamed itself, but it was too messy for that. There was little bits of flesh all tattered up and red, and flies feedin' on it. Then, 'bout a quarter mile down the hill, I heard Shortie shout *'McKittrick, come an' look.'* When I rode down there, Shortie was dead white in the face.

" *'Lookit that,'* he said. Shortie's shadow fell down like a heavy blanket on Pete Laramie's face. Pete was lyin' on top of a prickly pear with his shirt out of his pants and pulled noose-tight around his neck like he'd been dragged along by the scruff or somethin'. His gun hadn't been fired. Hadn't even been taken out of its holster. . . . I heard tell that a dead man's eyes have the last sight they ever saw branded on the backs of them, but Pete's eyes were white as salt and I couldn't see nothin' in 'em but blind terror."

Matt McKittrick sipped his whiskey, but his hand was shaky. "There was somethin' about findin' Pete like that, a man that ain't been afraid of nothin' all his life, lyin' there dead in the field with his eyes cold in the sun and the yellow cowslips noddin' 'round his head like there was nothin' out of the ordinary at all. Maybe that's what chilled me so much—that it all *looked* so damn ordinary. I found one of Pete's boots up the hill. It was tore right in two, and there was some kind of dried-up foam on it, same kind you see on the mouth of a loco mutt. But this weren't no mutt that got'im. The boot still had one of Pete's feet in it, cut off at the ankle, right through the damn bone. Shorty and me looked for tracks but we couldn't find none. Dirt's packed too hard around there. But there was some matted fur stuck with blood on the bobwire. We all had a look at it. Bill thinks it's jackalope and I'm tendin' to side up with him, but I ain't never seen a 'lope act like that before. *Not unless it was sick with somethin'.*"

The cowboy's words rattlesnaked through Halleran's brain, and Halleran found himself shivering. The banker man's hand, the horror of the stage wreck, the dying woman who'd refused water . . . all of it suddenly made sense. Under his breath, Halleran found himself repeating a poem that served as a warning to all who braved life in the West:

> Even a man with a steadfast heart,
> Who reads his prayerbook at night,
> Must die from a bullet betwixt his eyes,
> Or a rabid jackalope's bite.

Conversation ceased at the sound of Halleran's words. Only the piano player continued on in his effort to massacre "Home on the Range." But when he roared the line about the land *where the deer and the jackalope play,* someone put a gun to his head and that unspoken threat shut him up quick.

The door slammed open. Three men entered the saloon, their faces shiny with sweat. One of them was propped up between the other two like an uncoiled spring. His head fell back, mouth open, and Halleran noticed that it was covered in white foam. Even with the smashed spectacles and blood-smeared face, Halleran knew who he was. E. M. Miles was a long way from Minneapolis, Minnesota.

Two cowpunchers helped the men over to a table. One of the newcomers was short an arm. It had been tied off above the elbow with a rolled-up shirt that had soaked itself in blood. Blood plopped down on the floor in a steadily widening pool.

"That one there—the walkin' one helpin' the other two—that's Jim Carstairs," McKittrick said. "He's

Pendleton's new foreman." The cowboy walked over to the table, and Halleran followed.

"Somethin' hit the Cheyenne stage," Carstairs said, sinking tiredly into a chair. The expression lines in his face were thick with trail dust. "Dead bodies all over the damn place—"

"You sure they were dead?" McKittrick asked.

Carstairs nodded grimly. "The flies were sure. Found these two a couple miles down the valley. Both of'em delirious. Don't think they even knew which direction they were headed. If I hadn't been chasin' after that strawberry roan, I don't think I would've seen 'em."

Which explains why I didn't see the husband or the shotgunner, Halleran thought. But he kept his mouth shut.

"Whiskey . . ." whispered the shotgunner, mouth drier than the dust in a mummy's pocket. Someone brought him a bottle, and he sucked down a deep gulp and winced. "I don't know what kind of mare's piss this is, but whichever one it was sure had herself one *hell* of a kidney problem."

The barkeep yanked the bottle away from the shotgunner. "Stubbs, if you weren't already deader'n a beaver hat, I'd ask you to take your business elsewhere."

"What hit you?" Halleran asked the tenderfoot named Miles.

The man's face was white as Bible paper. His pale blue eyes had a delirious, unfocused look. "Jackalopes. About a dozen of them. Scared the horses. The driver couldn't stop. My wife . . . she's still there. Have to find her. . . ." This mild exertion exhausted him, and his eyes flickered shut. He started to moan insensibly.

"He's been talkin' like this since I hauled 'im up onto my horse," Carstairs said quietly. "But I tell you, if his wife is there in that wreck, there ain't nothin' left of her."

"Didn't you *check?*" McKittrick asked.

"Not with two dyin' *men* and one horse between us, Matt," Carstairs shot back. "Not with fresh 'lope scat all over the damn place . . . and judging by the look and stink of that scat, them 'lopes were *some* sick. Christ on a cross, scat was all bloody and . . ." The foreman pushed a dusty strand of hair out of his eyes. "Sides, like I said—that woman was dead as a—"

Emmett Miles opened his eyes.

"Here's somethin' for your spirits, boys," Billy Skinner butted in loudly with a reproving glare at the foreman. *"You who are down in the Shadowland of Sickness and Despair—whatever your hurt, whatever your need, there is health in His Wings for you."* He pulled a couple of stained brown bottles from his battered banjo box, uncapped one, and handed it to Stubbs.

The shotgunner put the bottle to his nose and coughed. "What the hell is *in* this stuff? You tryin' to kill me, old man?"

"Why, that there's Dr. De Smet's Patented Extract of Stomach Bitters, an excellent medicine for Distempers and Other Discomfitures."

The shotgunner pushed the bottle away. "Smells like a dead Indian to *me*."

"Mebbe so, Stubbs, but it Purifies the Whole System and Invigorates the Entire Person. It's a remedy fer Dysentry, Erysipelas, Piles, Nervous Exhaustion, Imbecility, Lost Manhood, Weakenin' of the Brain—"

"Sounds like you could use a wallop of that yourself, old-timer," Carstairs said.

"—Locomotor Ataxia, Insanity, Noxious Odors—" Billy scratched furiously at an iodine-colored stain on the label "—Vicious Itchin' Skin Eruptions and Premature Baldness. So you just drink it down, Stubbs—

there you are—no, don't spit it out, it set me back fifty cents. It'll put the hair back on your confounded head."

"Lord amighty, it even *tastes* like a dead Indian!" Stubbs sputtered.

Uncle Billy proffered the flask to Miles, who declined with a distracted shake of his head. "Better take some, son," Billy advised. "You're lookin' more than a mite under the weather."

"They had *boxes*," Miles said, his eyes full of bewilderment. "The jackalopes. On the backs of their *skulls*. Little black boxes. And there was a *sound*."

Halleran and McKittrick exchanged looks. Halleran knelt down beside the trembling man. "What sound, Emmett?"

Miles's eyes widened almost imperceptibly. They were the same blue as his dead Emma's traveling bonnet.

"*Miles*. What sound did you hear?" Halleran repeated.

"It was like . . . like the buzzing of flies," Miles said at last. His eyes closed, the slick lids trembling. "Like a million flies coming at you all at once. The whirring wings of a million flies. . . ."

The doors opened. A man wearing a black suit and pair of Peacemakers entered the saloon.

All talking stopped.

"This town sure don't take to outsiders," Halleran said.

"That's L.D. Beaudine," McKittrick said, eyes trained on the man with the flat-topped black hat and the half-hidden eyes narrowed to slits the size of money clips. "Him and his brothers are the ones responsible for puttin' the *boot* in Boothill. But I ain't seen any of'em around town since this business with the 'lopes."

"Where's Calhoun?" Beaudine said. His tone could

have chilled a side of beef. "Where's the son of a bitch who owns this town?"

Calhoun stood up. "What do you want, Beaudine?"

"I want a hundred thousand dollars. And you're the man can pay it."

Calhoun stalked toward him, grinding his stump of a cigar between his teeth. "And what the hell makes you think I'd do *that?*"

"You'll do it, if you don't want to die."

Calhoun looked a little uncomfortable in his two hundred dollar suit. "What are you talking about, Beaudine?"

"I'm talking about this town, Mr. *Calhoun.* And I'm talking about what happens when a town this size becomes *infected.*"

"Infected with what?"

Beaudine turned his cool stare on Jim Carstairs. "Same thing *you're* infected with: an especially virulent strain of rabies. All of you here have it," Beaudine said quietly, and the roomful of men looked at one another with uneasy incomprehension. "All that touched one of *them,* anyhow. Or any of the others. Old Sam, Pete Laramie. . . ."

A couple of cowpunchers exchanged startled glances.

"It's the bite of an infected 'lope that spreads it, and anyone who touched that 'lope, or touches anyone who *has,* will come down with it."

"You're lyin'," Stubbs said, clutching his blood-soaked stump of arm. But there was a nervous tremor in his voice.

"You're lookin' a bit under the weather there, Stubbs. That's a nasty bite you have. You want a drink of water?"

Stubbs looked alarmed.

"What's the matter, Stubbs? You don't like water?

Seems to me a nice cool drink would do you up fine—"

Stubbs's eyes had opened wide in his head, and he made tiny choking sounds as if his vocal cords had closed up on him.

"You made your point, Beaudine," Calhoun said shortly.

"Ten a.m. tomorrow we'll call the 'lopes off. Maybe even let you have a bit of antidote."

"You dirty son of a bitch." It was Ben Sutter who said it, a bellicose little man who didn't look like there was enough of him to wad a smoothbore shotgun. He wore a pair of oil-stained pants tucked into his muddy boots, and when he walked toward the man in black he left little clods of dirt behind on the floor like a line of rabbit droppings. "You and your damn brothers, you think you *own* this town!" He tried to draw his gun, but in his inebriated state he couldn't locate his gunbelt.

L.D. Beaudine, infinitely more composed, pulled out his Peacemaker and put a bullet in Sutter's Neander-thal brow ridge. The man fell to the floor, brains spill-ing from his head like sawdust from a sack.

"Ten a.m. tomorrow," said the man in black. "One hundred thousand dollars, and *why don't you try for that .44, mister. I really wish you would.*" Beaudine's cold stare fell on Matt McKittrick's right hand. "Every-one knows the New Model Army is the faultiest piece of shit to ever fall out of Eliphalet Remington's ass." The barest hint of a smile traced Beaudine's lips as McKittrick laid his hands back on the table. "A hun-dred thousand, Mr. Calhoun, and not a penny less. I think you know the place."

"I know it," Calhoun said belligerently.

"That man there can deliver it." Beaudine nodded at Halleran. "And don't try anything. There's nothin' the 'lopes like better than fresh meat. The fresher the bet-

ter. Make sure you have a bath before you come. . . ."
Beaudine smiled a smile that looked like it had been
hammered in sheet metal. Then he disappeared in a
sway of saloon doors.

Halleran turned to McKittrick. "You think Angel
Eyes there was serious?"

"You'd better hope he wasn't."

Halleran put Uncle Billy's bottle of patented extract
to his lips and took a long pull. "Better dose up," he
said, setting it in front of the cowboy. "I think you
could stand a little *invigoratin'*."

McKittrick smiled and met Halleran's eyes as he
lifted the half-empty bottle. "That I could," he said.
"That I could."

"And you think this Devereaux character's behind
it?" Matt McKittrick asked.

He and Trev Halleran stood at the post outside The
Calhoun Hotel, bathed in yellow light. The sky was
black as a boot bottom; the moon as white as a dead
man's eyeball.

"He's behind it, all right. A sound like the one that
tenderfoot Miles heard, the sound of a million flies . . .
it's kinda hard to put behind you. Months later you'll
be out in the dead center of no place, no sound but the
empty sky above fallin' down on you, and then you'll
hear it. In the distance at first, then it comes, like the
Eighth Plague of Egypt. . . ."

He closed his eyes a moment, and remembered that
June afternoon in the Little Bighorn under Terry's
command. *Permission to locate Private James Tanner,
sir.*

*General Terry stared at the pale body of Boston
Custer that lay at the bottom of the dusty hill beside
Boston's eighteen-year-old nephew. "His mother sent
him for his health," Terry said distractedly as two men
attempted to lift Boston's mortified body. The dead*

man's arms kept slipping from their exasperated grasps.

"Sir?" Halleran said.

"He suffered from consumption. She thought a summer expedition would improve his health. What was it you wanted, Lieutenant?"

"Permission to locate Private James Tanner, sir. The Reno Battalion."

"All right, if you think it'll do any good," Terry replied wearily, and waved him off.

Halleran started down the brush-choked hillside on foot, past the men detailed the unpleasant duty of disposing of the remains of the two hundred dead men who had lain in the suffocating summer sun for two days. The bodies were hastily covered with clumps of sagebrush and a few shovelfuls of dirt, names penciled on boards pried from breadboxes, on pieces of paper hurriedly stuffed into discarded cartridges. Halleran plodded down the hill in his army boots, stepping over the unclothed body of a man who'd been splashed with the putrefied flesh of his bullet-dead claybank.

The smells of decay in the stifling heat made Halleran want to retch, but he bit it back. He walked in a straight line down the yellow slopes in the direction of the still brown waters of the Little Bighorn River . . . and of James Tanner.

Still breathing.

He'd taken a bullet for Halleran back in '63 and they'd been inseparable since.

"Devereaux was standing in front of him," Halleran told McKittrick. "Had some kind of device with him. Dials all over it. Devereaux was a regiment doctor at the time; at first, I thought he was trying to help James. Then I saw James' eyes." He paused. "They were white as that moon up there. He was in pain. Terrible pain. He was having some kind of fit. And there stood Devereaux, holding that box like he was God himself.

There was that sound, that hum, like a million flies. . . ." Halleran shook his head. "I thought it was coming from Devereaux. But it was coming from the box.

"He stared straight at me with this strange little smile on his face, and started talking about *cerebral cortexes* and *central nervous systems,* and *untold power,* and all the time there was James jerking around in the dirt like he had no control of himself. He was *terrified.* Terrified of Devereaux and that damned box."

"And you think Devereaux's the one who's been controllin' the rabid 'lopes? Makin' them all bloodthirsty for the kill?"

"I know he is." Halleran paused. "We'll need some men."

McKittrick smiled, a flash of white in the dark. "You'll have them. There's a lot of people in Sand Creek who are mighty interested in a rabies antidote."

"How are you boys set up?"

"Shit, Halleran! We have rifles, if that's what you mean."

"Not enough. You'll need something with a heavy-hitting long range."

"Hell, every last one of us owns at least two Winchesters—"

"You'll never get close enough to a 'lope to hit it with a '73. It has erectile hairs on its rump patch. When it spots you, and it'll do that for dead certain, all those hairs flash up. You can see them for miles, like some kind of semaphore, and all the other 'lopes in the area respond in kind. Ten seconds later, all you have is an empty field. They know every hill, every channel for miles, and they can run like the wind itself 'cause the bones in their hind legs are fused together to provide 'em extra thrusting power. They'll disappear before you can blink. Or they'll be *on you* before you can blink. One of the two, and it better not be *two*. No, we need something with a little more kick to it."

McKittrick shook his head. "All we have is shot-guns," he said.

"What if I told you I know where to find a case-load of brand-new Sharps .50 Buffalo rifles, ready for the takin'?"

The cowboy lifted an eyebrow. "You do come pre-pared, don't you, Halleran?" he said.

Halleran smiled tightly. "I try," he said.

The woman in his room was a little past her prime, but she'd painted herself up pretty enough and still had all her own teeth, which was more than he could say for the most of the men in this town. Halleran didn't even hold it against her when, after they'd done what they were there to do—

"You plannin' on eatin' your supper in bed tonight?"

"What?"

"I'm just admirin' that fancy silverware of yours."

"Oh . . . you mean this—?" Lily L'Amour flickered her eyelashes innocently, an effect that wasn't entirely lost on him. She tapped the mother-of-pearl stiletto she'd tried to bury between his shoulder blades. "It's for my protection," she said, drawing the sheet over her pale, bare breasts.

Halleran appreciated the effort. "Your protection, huh," he said.

Her eyes steeled. "That's right. This is a terrible town, Mister Hal—"

"It's about to become a lot more terrible, Miss L'Amour." He held the stiletto up to the lamplight and read the inscription on it. *"For the All the Fine Times We Done Had—B.S."* Halleran's brows knitted together. "Now *who* is B.S.—? Not Billy Skinner! She's done fallen for the banjo strummer! I do believe I'm jealous, Lil. Unless there's another kind of B.S. out there you want to tell me about. . . ."

"Oh, shut up," the prostitute said, snatching the stiletto away.

"Don't make a lot of sense, going around making sieves out of all your clientele," Halleran said, pretending to be thoughtful. "Don't do a lot for return business, you know what I'm sayin', Miss L'Amour? Or maybe one of the Beaudines told you to come up here. How much did he pay you to kill me? Fifty dollars? No, couldn't have been fifty. I like to think I'm worth at *least* a hundred after the time I just gave you. . . ."

"I don't know *what* you're talking about." She started to put on her corset.

"Forgotten already? Now that hurts, Lil." Halleran wondered how the hell she could *breathe,* let alone *move,* with ten pounds of De-troit steel clamped around her middle. She tried to stand up, but he yanked on her corset strings and she bounced back on the bed.

"Let go of me, you big dumb army dropout!"

"I think, Miss L'Amour, that if you and I are to have *any* kind of mature relationship at all, we'll have to play it straight with each other."

"Why the hell should I do that?" she said, eyes flashing angrily.

"Maybe you won't with me . . . but you might with this." Halleran dropped a handful of First National Bank box money on the bed.

"Mister Halleran," Lil L'Amour said, honey-sweet. "I *do* believe I'm fallin' for you after all."

"I thought you might. Now why don't you tell me who sent you."

"L.D. Beaudine. He heard you and McKittrick were up to somethin'."

"And who did he hear it from? Not *you,* Miss L'Amour?"

"Who, *me?*" She tried the batting eyelash routine.

"Knock it off, Lil. Now I want you to tell Beaudine we'll be comin' in after him at nine-thirty."

"But—"

"We'll be there at nine. It'll surprise the shit out of him."

"You leave everythin' to me," Lil said, and smiled.

Damn if she isn't half pretty in this light, Halleran thought. He hated like hell having to lie to her, now that they were on the up and up and all.

"Why don't you use rock salt instead of lead for that shot, Billy?" Jim Carstairs said at six-fifteen the following morning.

"Huh?"

"Preserve the meat until you get to it."

Billy Skinner, rifle in hand, looked up blankly from his place beside Carstairs on the cut banks. A herd of about twenty 'lopes dotted the narrow, pine-clad valley below them. A low collection of dilapidated farm buildings and fences shone in the early morning light.

"I'm a little outa range, am I?" Billy said.

"A little," Carstairs replied, and smiled.

"Don't shoot 'til you see the yellers of their eyes, Billy," McKittrick said. He was loading his Sharps with his back to the sun, ever wary of unwanted reflections. Halleran squatted beside him on the ridge, grimly loading James Tanner's carbine.

"You sure you don't want one of these nice, shiny new ones?" McKittrick said, flashing him a smile. "That Springfield of yours only holds the one shot."

"One shot's all I need," Halleran replied. He tried to return the smile, but he was too tense for lighter emotions. He slid the copper cartridge into place.

McKittrick set his rifle on the ground. "You think this plan of yours'll work?"

"I think so. A prostitute's reputation is on the line."

McKittrick lifted an eyebrow.

"Lil L'Amour and me, we have what you call an *understanding*. I tell Lil to inform Beaudine that we're headin' in there at nine-thirty when we're really headin' in at nine, and I give her a hundred dollars to do it. She takes my hundred, goes back to Beaudine and tells him *nine* on the dot, and Beaudine hands her another hundred and a pat on the behind for bein' so on the ball." Halleran finally returned McKittrick's smile. "That's why we're here at six-thirty. I don't think prostitutes get up this early."

"You sure know women," McKittrick said.

"I sure know *this* woman," Halleran corrected him. "She has a mind like an open pocketbook. You boys ready?"

Jim Carstairs, Billy Skinner, and fourteen other men each armed with a new .50 bore Buffalo rifle courtesy of the Black Hills Cheyenne Stage Line, nodded solemnly. A couple of them, including Jim Carstairs, looked about as healthy as calves with the slobbers.

"You know that Stubbs died at four this mornin'," McKittrick said in a quiet voice.

"There's a lot more'll die before we're done," Halleran said. "You think you'll be all right down there?"

"Bet on it."

"Fine. I want four men on the south side, five on the east and west where there's all the open space. Carstairs is with me. You and Shorty set yourselves up on either side of the door and shoot'em as they come out. Don't think you'll need the rifles for that. . . ."

"Rifles'll do fine," McKittrick said shortly. "I plan for L.D. Beaudine to absorb so much lead they'll have to soak him up with a blotter."

"Now *that's* what I like to hear!" Uncle Billy was jumping like popcorn on a hot skillet.

"Skinner, if you don't hold still, you're liable to

shoot off one of your damn toes," Carstairs said. His face was white as a tapeworm.

"Hold on there, Jimmy," Billy said. "We'll have that antidote for you in no time."

"All right, boys," Halleran said. "No more talk. Shoot to kill, but keep your distance. They're fast as the dickens and they'll have their teeth into you before you can take another breath. Matt, I'm countin' on you to distract the Beaudines."

"Consider them distracted," McKittrick said tersely.

At six twenty-one, eighteen men, rifles ready, descended into the Black Hills Valley two miles southeast of Sand Creek.

Halleran didn't have too much of a wait for the first rifle shot. It was followed closely by the high-pitched shriek of a hit jackalope. After that it was a boot-stompin' free-for-all stampede, with McKittrick's men trying to outshoot each other in an all-out powder burn contest.

The 'lopes had stirred themselves into a feeding frenzy from which there was no escaping. Maddened by the sudden movement and the smell of blood, they jumped after the men like crazed jack-in-the-boxes. The Beaudine brothers, still in their britches, slipped in the blood in the front yard amidst a steady onslaught of .50-caliber bullets.

L.D. Beaudine clutched at a bullet hole in his side and tried to fend off the attack of a particularly vicious 'lope. The animal knocked him down with a powerful kick of its hind legs. Beaudine lay screaming and thrashing on the ground as the animal tore into his salty-sweated throat, spattering Beaudine's terrified face with his own hot blood. The 'lope growled gutturally, shaking the man's body in its teeth like a well-chewed sock.

Moments later a second animal, tired of its own

meaty morsel, tried to get in on the main meal. The two 'lopes bared yellow incisors at each other. The stump of Bobby Beaudine's saliva-soaked head rolled forlornly in the dirt as the two animals fought ferociously over the bag of blood that had been L.D. Beaudine.

"Hope he remembered to take a bath this mornin'," Matt McKittrick remarked to Bill Short as the two men, standing on the front porch of the farmhouse, eyed the circus bloodbath in the corral. "Beaudine knew better than anybody just how much them 'lopes like fresh meat. . . ."

Halleran and Carstairs, rifles ready, kicked down the back door to the Beaudine brothers' place. Two confused Beaudines, still in their sleeping drawers and fumbling for their gunbelts, stumbled around just in time to have breakfast with Jim Carstairs' .45.

"Shit, that's disappointin'," Carstairs said, lowering his gun. "Weren't enough brains between those boys to grease a skillet." He watched with interest as a panicky jackalope darted in front of the window in a flash of white and brown. Its eyes were bulbous yellow globes speckled with black. An instant later the men heard a paralyzed scream and a renewed hail of bullets and smoke filled the air. Bits of blackened jackalope meat spattered on the window.

"You better see if you can find McKittrick and the others," Halleran told Carstairs. "See if they need help. There's something I have to do." After the foreman left, Halleran walked to the center of the empty room. "Devereaux!" he shouted. "Come on out and show yourself. I know you're here."

For a moment there was silence. Then a bedroom door opened, and a face Halleran remembered all too well appeared. Devereaux, in black cape and traveling clothes, closed the door behind him. He held a black leather monogrammed bag in one spotlessly gloved hand.

"And so we meet once more, Lieutenant," the doctor said, feigning mild surprise. "Didn't think I'd see you here."

"Didn't think they'd come up with an antidote for rabies so sudden, either," Halleran replied. He held the carbine firmly in his right hand.

"They haven't, of course. . . ."

"Of course." Halleran grinned. "That was some story you had Beaudine spit at us, but I knew it was just so much horseshit as soon as the idiot started gabbing abut an *especially virulent strain* of rabies. Pea-brained gunslingers don't talk like that, Doc. And any fool knows a man's got to be bit to catch rabies. *Even a man with steadfast heart,* and all like that. . . ."

"Damn colloquial poetry, anyhow," Devereaux said.

Halleran's eyes fell on the black box sitting on a table between them. "What did you plan on doing with your share of that hundred thousand dollars?" he asked.

Devereaux smiled, walked over to a small oval mirror set on the side wall, and straightened his tie. "Scientific research, Lieutenant."

"I don't call killin' innocent people 'research.' I've seen full-blooded Sioux warriors less savage than you. Ain't you ever heard of ethics, Doctor?"

Devereaux brushed the question aside. "Ethics are outmoded. You might consider expanding your somewhat limited, uh . . . *outlook,* shall we say? What are the lives of a handful of men to me when I can command millions with the minutest turn of a dial? Really, Lieutenant. . . ."

"The name is Halleran. Trev T. Halleran. But I doubt very much that my name means anything to you, Dr. Devereaux. Or James Tanner's name. Or Pete Laramie's, or Emma Miles', or any of those other people you killed. And I'll thank you to look at me when I'm talkin' to you." Halleran shouldered his carbine.

The doctor met Halleran's eyes in the mirror a moment before he turned around. The doctor's eyes were black as that box on that table, black as a swarm of flies. "You won't kill me, Lieutenant. *Mister* Halleran . . . your sense of ethics, as you so quaintly put it, will not allow you to. It would lower you to my level, am I correct?" He chuckled knowingly and positioned his bowler hat firmly on his head. "Now if you'll excuse me, I have an appointment in St. Louis with a man who is—"

Devereaux fell dead to the floor, a bullet from a Springfield carbine betwixt his eyes. His bowler rolled on its back in sheer surprise.

Trev Halleran walked to the table and picked up the black box of pain. He broke it to bits under his boot heel. "I think you put too much stock in my ethics, Dr. Devereaux," he said, "and not enough in my *damn colloquial poetry* . . . as you so quaintly put it." He set James Tanner's carbine on the table and walked out the back door.

The shooting had stopped. The air was still. The sun shone yellow and pale over the descending shadows of the surrounding hills, and Trev T. Halleran didn't have to look at the banker man's watch to know it was still early. He breathed in the fresh scent of the summer air, of the perfumed pines that rose tall and thick on the Lakota Sioux slopes. And as he walked forward with the sun on his face, he noticed for the first time how silent it was.

How very silent.

And he smiled.

UNDERGROUND ATLANTA

by Gregory Nicoll

"The South will rise again ... tonight!"

As soon as the final blow of the rock shattered the bent steel link of his leg chain, Rastus began to run.

It was a familiar feeling, his heart hammering in his chest as his bare feet propelled him across the Georgia clay, with the rough brown threads of his sackcloth tunic scratching against his dark skin. His earlier escape from the plantation had been a near success. He felt sure he would have made it, if not for all the trouble he'd encountered in removing that steel grating at the end of the hill tunnel. Rastus remembered his burst of joy when the grating finally slipped loose—only to feel his hopes wither and die at the sound of Davis and Chandler riding up behind him.

Those damned fools.

Sure, they recaptured him and dragged him back to the plantation in disgrace, but they hadn't noticed that their quarry had freed the grating. Never even checked it.

Rastus was counting on the grating still being loose. What other choice did he have? In the morning Master Armstrong would mete out "the punishment" with the rope and a knife. Rastus' only hope lay in this, his second attempt at escape.

He already smelled the outhouse-stink of the drainage ditch at the grating. He was close now. And yes, to his relief he found that the cold, heavy steel grating was still loose. Its rust scraped off on his hands as he moved it, and it fell away with an ominous, echoing *clank-clank-clank-clank.*

He prayed that no one had heard that.

Tentatively, Rastus took his first barefoot step toward freedom. The air out beyond the grating was fresher, cleaner than any he had ever tasted. He savored it, drawing it in and making it last, just as he had nursed his precious water ration each afternoon out in the plantation fields. Then he began to run again.

Hoofbeats sounded behind him, building up speed.

Had they been waiting for him out here? Were Davis and Chandler even now spurring their horses, uncoiling their ropes?

The ground was covered with slick green blades, moistened with morning dew. This surface was so smooth that it made running very difficult. Rastus zigzagged uphill and darted between trees, hoping to confuse both of his pursuers.

No, it was only *one* pursuer; he was sure of that now, just a single horseman behind him. But he was losing ground. Already he could hear the snorting of the great animal as it thundered after him. Chancing a look back over his shoulder, Rastus saw the horse's breath condensing in the moonlight like smoke from the nostrils of a demon.

Reaching the top of the hillock, Rastus stopped short in astonishment. Though it was late at night, the entire city was lit up brighter than anything he'd ever seen. Buildings towered high into the sky, gleaming with glass and metal. He had heard of this all his life, but he had never imagined actually seeing anything so grand, so spectacular, so gloriously incredible. . . .

The horseman behind him leaped from the saddle.

With a creak of leather, the rider fell upon Rastus and seized him roughly. Rastus had a brief impression of a white man wearing a blue uniform like a Yankee soldier, but with a strange round hat that was smooth and white like an eggshell. The horseman pushed Rastus facedown in the dirt and shackled his hands with two gleaming cold metal clamps.

Then the man pulled a tiny black box from his belt, pressed a little knob on it, and began to talk into it. . . .

Detective Rudy Ray Williamson had his arm around Lieutenant Tamara Grier, evoking sweet memories of the evening they'd spent together the night before. His pulse quickened as he recalled the sweet caress of her smooth-muscled bare skin gliding soft as black satin against his own while they tumbled to and fro over the leopard-print sheets of his circular bed.

"Which one is it, Rudy?" she asked, pointing out the window at the distant parking lot, six stories below. She shrugged his arm off her shoulder.

Snapped from his reverie, Williamson let the smile fade from his lips. This vixen Tamara was all-play whenever he coaxed her over to his apartment, but here in the Police Department Headquarters she was all-business. It was a damn shame, but that's the way it had to be. He leaned forward and pointed down at the third row of the parking lot. "The red Monte Carlo near the end," he said, "with the oversized tires on the back and the leopard fur on the dashboard. See the sun flashing on its chain steering wheel?"

Lieutenant Grier shook her head. "I can't really see it too good from here, but it looks like a nice ride."

Williamson smiled again. "Sure do like the stereo. You should hear how good that new Curtis Mayfield 8-track sounds outa those speakers."

Lieutenant Grier winked, her thick black Afro bobbing as she nodded. "Maybe I will."

Williamson was about to propose a dinner date, but he was interrupted by a knock at the door of his office. "Come in."

The scuffed door swung open, creaking on its hinges. "Sorry to interrupt," said Captain Geoff Kennedy as he leaned in, eyeing Lieutenant Grier. His face seemed a paler white than usual today, and with a nervous tremble he ran a sweaty hand through his thinning white hair. "Williamson, we got a man in custody and I think maybe you oughta talk to him. A mounted cop picked him up early this morning over by Grant Park."

Williamson arched his eyebrows. "All these years you've had me working Missing Persons for that part of town, so now you want to switch me to *Found* Persons?"

Kennedy was not amused. He stared straight at Williamson and said coldly, "The man claims to be a runaway slave. Says he escaped last night—*from a plantation.* He's not drunk, and he even passed the polygraph test. And that's not all—he's got a *brand* on his arm."

Williamson shrugged his shoulders. "Brand?"

Kennedy nodded slowly. "Looks like an old cowboy brand, a capital letter *A* with a solid black bar underneath it."

Williamson glanced briefly at Lieutenant Grier, her forehead knitted with concern. Then he looked back at Kennedy. "I'll be right there," he said, reaching for his coat and his gun.

As he drove out toward Grant Park that evening, Williamson had a lot to think about. That strange little dude named Rastus Turner had certainly been convincing. In fact, his story had given Williamson a major case of the creeps: black slaves working the fields and overseers on horseback, not in old times long forgotten, but somewhere *today,* in the Here-and-Now.

The sun was setting as Williamson turned the red Monte Carlo onto the narrow avenue which ran alongside the park. At one end stood the enormous gray building which housed the Cyclorama, the city's unofficial museum of its own Civil War past. Williamson remembered coming here on a field trip with his sixth grade class, and patiently enduring the tour guide's trite speeches about valiant Confederate defenders. He recalled enjoying the main exhibit itself, though: a huge circular mural depicting the Battle of Atlanta, complete with flashing lights and combat sound effects. He'd heard that the exhibit was now enhanced with little Disneyland-style theater cars which whisked visitors instantly from one side of the action to the other during the performance.

A flickering flame caught his attention, and his foot reflexively tapped the car's brake. Tire rubber squealed. He pulled the Monte Carlo over onto the narrow shoulder of the avenue, shut the motor off, and strolled over to investigate.

The flame was a campfire—a Civil War campfire.

Seated around the blazing, crackling hardwoods were a half dozen sullen men in blue Union Army uniforms. Their black kepi caps were tilted at odd angles on their heads, and several of the men smoked fragrant vanilla tobacco from long white clay pipes. One very young man sat on the carriage wheels of a long-barreled cannon, playing "Tenting Tonight" on a small silver harmonica.

"We've got permission to be here," said the group's apparent leader as he noticed Williamson approaching with his badge in his hand. This Yankee sergeant was a tall man with a creased face and a magnificent bushy beard. "The hotel wouldn't put us up with the rest of the reenactors," he explained, "on account of us being Yankees and all."

The kid playing the harmonica stopped in mid-stanza

and lifted the little instrument from his lips. "Yeah, and they didn't like the idea of our cannon being in their parking lot, either."

Williamson nodded and smiled. It was amazing to him how deeply those century-old feelings still ran. He could understand it better in black folks, who once toiled under the yoke of human slavery; but he'd never got a grip on why modern white folks from both sides of the Mason-Dixon line sometimes acted like they hadn't seen a new calender since 1865. And that specialized hobbyist known as the Civil War Reenactor was a particularly bizarre example of the breed.

Williamson glanced up quickly as he heard a steel security door on the side of the Cyclorama building creak open; he watched suspiciously as a bearded, pot-bellied man stepped outside, casually looping his suspenders back over the shoulders of his blue uniform.

The Yankee sergeant noticed Williamson's concern. "I know what you're thinking," he said with a smile. "Ole Shurtleff over there hasn't got the right buttons on his uniform. But that's okay. Our unit's what we call 'Late Conflict,' so we don't have to be as strict about those types of details."

Williamson shook his head. "Actually, I was just wondering what your man was doing in that building after hours."

The reenactor chuckled with embarrassment. "Well, the museum curator took pity on us and left the back door there open for us, so we could—uh—use the facilities."

Williamson smiled. "You fellahs have a good night."

"Thanks, officer," said the sergeant. He saluted politely as Williamson stepped away.

It takes all kinds, thought Williamson as he walked across the darkened expanse of the park. His footsteps echoed over the open gray concrete walkways, like the sound of small hands clapping slowly. Moonlight played over the shapes of fossilized cannons and inactive water fountains. The air smelled of pine, hay, and the musk of animals from the nearby zoo.

Not much to see here tonight, thought Williamson as he paused on the walkway which led over to the zoo. Then, faintly, he heard the sound of water trickling. He glanced down and noticed for the first time that over to his right was a deep drainage culvert, with its metal grating slightly askew. Williamson crouched down and looked closely at it.

Something small and silver gleamed in the moonlight.

Curious, Williamson climbed down off the walkway to investigate. The long grass was slippery with evening dew, and the muddy bottom of the ditch sucked at the soles of his wing-tipped gatorhide shoes, but he eventually reached the enormous grating. The gleaming silver object was a piece of broken chain.

Squinting in the moonlight, Williamson turned the link over in his hand. Its rough, cold metal was identical to that used in making the crude metal shackle they had pried off the leg of the little homeless man, Rastus, earlier in the day. Turning, Williamson peered into the drainage tunnel. He unfastened a small flashlight from his belt and poked it through the grating. The bright yellow beam played over some rough marks in the mud at the bottom of the giant pipe.

Edging the grate aside, Williamson walked carefully to one side of the tunnel to avoid obscuring the tracks. Although the diameter of the tunnel was large enough to allow him to stand fully upright, he bent low in order to study the lower surface. The smell of foul, stagnant water was overpowering as Williamson squatted down for a closer look. His flashlight clearly revealed the impressions of two bare feet which had passed this way. They were followed by two sets of boots; although when the bare feet had passed beyond the grating, the boot tracks apparently had not.

Something hard and heavy struck Williamson across the back of the head, sending him sprawling facedown in the mud.

He heard laughter, followed by the crack of a whip.

In an instant, while he was still stunned, he felt rough hands seizing his flashlight and wrenching the revolver from his waistband holster. A thick, scratchy rope was abruptly wrapped around his neck, then coiled around his hands.

"Welcome to hell, niggah," said a hoarse white voice. Then a dusty harness boot kicked Williamson hard in the face.

Lieutenant Grier checked Williamson's office for the fifth time since the start of his shift. Still no sign of him. With a sigh, she turned back to Captain Kennedy. His face was ashen, his eyes cold, and his lips set in a curious pout.

"I'm worried," she told him. "This isn't like Rudy Ray."

"I tried calling his apartment," said Kennedy. "There's no answer—and his squad car's still in the parking lot."

Grier smiled fleetingly. "He was in a new car. I saw it out the window yesterday, a red Monte Carlo. . . ."

Kennedy's eyes widened. "Then maybe you could go and—"

She nodded toward the hall door. "I'm on my way!"

Williamson awoke slowly, with the smells of wet dirt and piss burning in his nostrils. Dried blood was crusted on his upper lip and his nose was swollen. He found himself lying on a moist dirt floor. He was barefoot; his clothes replaced with a rough brown sackcloth tunic that scratched unpleasantly against his skin.

Looking up, Williamson realized that he was in some sort of a small, darkened room. The walls seemed to be formed of rough boards. The only light came from a tiny window in the center of one wall, with bars across it.

I'm in jail, he thought. *What's going on here?*

Rising slowly to his feet, Williamson took a deep breath. The air was thin and oddly intoxicating, with a strange vegetable smell to it. He stepped over to the window and peered out.

The view through the steel bars was wilder than the wildest thing he could ever have imagined.

Williamson looked out on a vast underground cavern, approximately six times the size of a football stadium. The entire vista was illuminated by strange glowing boulders set into the vast knobby ceiling overhead. Some of these immense rocks gave off a pale green light and others glowed pale blue. Together they all cast a dim, unearthly ambience down onto the incredible scene below.

Slaves wearing ragged sackcloth garments were at work, toiling out there in the mushroom fields. Stooped in what was obviously spine-straining labor, hundreds of black men, women, and children crawled amid the jagged rocks, plucking the swollen white mushrooms from the crevices and tossing these treasures into the bags and baskets they carried. White overseers rode back and forth along the edges of the field, mounted on albino horses. These men carried muskets and bullwhips, with ropes looped on the horns of their saddles. From time to time one of them would shout angrily at a slave, often punctuating his cry with the crack of a whip.

As his eyes gradually adjusted to the dim light, Williamson noticed that in the rocky cliffside below his cell were what appeared to be the slave quarters. These were set deep into the rocks, like the pictures he'd seen of Indian pueblos. A few old black women and some very small children circulated down there.

But this calm, domestic scene stood in stark contrast to the horror Williamson witnessed higher up the cliffside, on a plateau just above the one on which his prison cell was built. From the sturdy barnlike buildings up there he heard the rough laughter of white males, followed by the shrill screams of black women.

Breeding shacks, he thought.

But there was more: from a large cookhouse nearby came the unmistakable aroma of barbecue on a grill. Smoke drifted from several pipes in its rough oak roof, and firelight glowed from its windows. It was only as the sickly sweet smell permeated both his cell and his imagination that Williamson fully recognized it. It was something he remembered smelling after that napalm attack near Quan Tri, in a Vietnam War battle he'd spent ten years trying to forget.

It was the smell of human flesh, cooking in a fire.

Williamson shuddered and fought back the bitter nausea rising in his throat. He thought back on all the years of Missing Persons cases he'd worked here in Atlanta. This zone had one of the highest disappearance rates, coupled with the lowest percentage of solved cases. *Could it be,* he wondered, *that all those vagrants and junkies who vanished over the years wound up down here, garnished with mushroom sauce?*

He took a deep breath. *Somehow, someway,* he thought, *I'm getting out of here and putting a stop to this.*

Looking across to the extreme end of the cavern, Williamson saw a smooth stone plateau. A huge plantation house stood on it, complete with white columns, rocking chairs, and a porch swing. The Stars and Bars hung motionless on a flagpole, with the Confederate battle flag dangling alongside it. Several elegantly dressed men and women sat there on the porch, watching the soldiers drilling on the open patio of the plateau.

And that, thought Williamson, *is what all this is really about: the Old South, preparing itself to rise again.* He remembered the brand on Rastus Turner's arm: The letter *A* with a line drawn under it. Of course. The *A* was for Atlanta. And the line below was this outfit, this twisted underground civilization festering beneath the city.

The troops were a weird assortment of white men and white boys, all of them thin and haggard but no less enthusiastic for the day's activity. As officers riding on albino horses put them through their paces, the soldiers marched back and forth, swinging their muskets and flashing their rusty bayonets. Many of the men were barefoot, but those with boots made dramatic leather slapping sounds on the smooth rock as they executed each precision turn. Some of their uniforms were well preserved while others hung in rough tatters, missing buttons or sleeves.

Williamson smiled grimly as he recalled a comment made by one of those reenactors at the Cyclorama. *These guys,* he thought, *are 'Late, Late, Late Conflict'.* . . .

Grier pulled her squad car up behind the red Monte Carlo and contacted Kennedy on her radio. "I found Rudy's wheels," she reported. "He ditched them on a Grant Park side street, near the Cyclorama. I'll take a look around."

Kennedy's voice squawked over the tiny dashboard speaker. "You want a backup unit?"

Grier shook her head. "Not yet, but keep one on standby."

"Roger. You got it, Grier. But you be careful, okay?"

"I will, sir. Over and out."

She switched off the radio and hung the handset back

on its tiny hook. Then she pulled her gleaming stainless steel Colt Python .357 from her shoulder holster and checked the cylinder. It was loaded, of course. The rubber combat grips felt comforting in her hand, and when she reseated the weapon in her holster, its bulk felt reassuring to her forearm's gliding stroke. She was ready.

Grier climbed out of the car and locked its door behind her. The evening air was warm, but with a pleasant breeze. It mixed the sweet scent of sap from the pine trees with the faint sweaty musk of the animals from the nearby zoo. Switching her flashlight on, she began walking across the pavement toward the building which housed Cyclorama. Something caught her eye and drew her toward it—something which appeared to be a campfire.

For nearly an hour Williamson had paced his cell as restlessly as a caged panther. He had prodded experimentally at each of its corners, the lock, the hinges, and all of the curious wooden joins which linked the boards. He had even made a brief effort at digging under one of the walls, until he fund that the half inch of dirt on the cell floor concealed an impenetrable surface of solid granite. Williamson was in constant motion, going nowhere.

But at the sound of approaching footsteps, he stopped short.

Boot heels clicked on granite, leather slapped, and steel jingled. One man coughed hoarsely, and another muttered something which provoked crude laughter from several others. The footsteps came to a halt outside the door of his cell. Keys rattled on a ring and then the lock scraped open. The door swung inward, creaking on its hinges and admitting the smells of sweat, dust, and boiled mushrooms.

Williamson's pulse quickened. He said nothing but stood in the center of the cell, his arms at his side.

Two white men stepped forward and reached out for him. Williamson recognized them as Davis and Chandler, the ones Rastus Turner had described. One of them was short and wore a dirty gray rebel uniform; he had a sickly toothless grin on his face and a few wisps of blond hairs combed over his nearly bald head. The other was taller, with beady eyes and a dark beard; he had a Confederate officer's cap perched cockeyed on his head, a rusty crossed-swords emblem pinned to the front of it. Both of the men carried sidearms in flap holsters, and the taller one had a short sword tucked into a dented scabbard, but none of these weapons were ready for use.

Williamson could see an elderly jailer standing outside the cell, clutching an oversized ring of keys. There didn't seem to be any other men nearby, but he wanted to be sure before he made his move.

"C'mon," said the short man with the toothless grin. "Git on outa here. Yew got an appointment ta keep, up the hill." He shoved Williamson's left shoulder, but the blow had as little effect as if it were delivered against solid rock. The smile faded from Toothless' face. "G'wan. *Git!*" he roared.

The tall man with the beady eyes reached out for Williamson's right arm. "This niggah won't be nearly so much trouble once he's been branded," Beady Eyes laughed, "an' castrated."

Williamson made his move.

His fluid judo motions, practiced over long hours on the tumbling mats, came to him reflexively. Diving for Beady Eyes' knees, he bent the man double and sent him sprawling into Toothless. Toothless reached for his flap holster, but Williamson dealt a crushing blow to the man's right arm, forcing his elbow backward to the breaking point. Beady Eyes drew his short sword but, with a fearsome judo kick Williamson forced the point of the wide blade harmlessly deep into the wall. Then

Williamson was out the cell door, running fast and barefoot over dusty flat rock, even before the startled old jailer could raise his voice.

Behind Williamson, black powder pistols detonated with reverberant thunder and Confederate minié balls ricocheted noisily among the boulders, kicking up sparks and spitting shards of gravel. Angry shouts echoed through the cavern as other men ran to aid his pursuers, eager for the thrill of the hunt. He tumbled over a gap in an embankment and crouched low behind a boulder, taking a moment to assess the situation and examine his options. His chest heaved, his breath rasping in his throat and his pulse pounding like a runaway jackhammer. Then, as his hand groped out to feel the edge of the boulder, he felt the cold circle of a pistol muzzle press into the back of his neck and heard the distinct four tiny clicks of the hammer being cocked back on a Colt revolver.

"Don't move," said a stern voice behind him. A *female* voice.

"Tamara?" he gasped in disbelief.

The pistol was withdrawn from his neck. "Rudy!" Grier stage-whispered. "C'mon. Let's get out of here!"

He smiled and shook his head. "You know the way?"

"I found my way down in here," she said firmly, "and you can damn sure bet I'll find my way out." She lowered the hammer on her Colt Python and handed the gun butt-fist to him. "Now take this and cover me."

"How will I ever thank you?" Williamson chuckled.

"We'll discuss that over champagne and bed-springs," said Grier tersely. Another Confederate bullet bounced off the rocks, just over her head. "That is," she added, "if we can get outa here with all our parts."

"Sister," whispered Williamson to himself, scrambling to follow her up the rocky path, "if you only knew. . . ."

* * *

They reached the surface after nearly a half hour of running, shooting, and ducking bullets. The clean, cool night air tasted like wine after the stifling mushroom-choked hell of the cavern below, but there was no time to stop and enjoy it. Williamson sent Grier running to her squad car radio to summon backup assistance, while he made a dash for the Civil War reenactors' campfire.

"Fellahs," he said. "Do you remember me?"

They looked up, haggard faces nodding. "You're the one who that lady cop was looking for," answered one of them.

"Yes," Williamson said, "I am. And right now, she and I both need your help." He pointed at their cannon. "Do you folks know how to *use* that thing?"

The sirens of the backup units were already sounding through the park as the first wave of Confederates emerged from the tunnel. A dozen ragged men, including Toothless and Beady Eyes, dashed straight toward the brave group of Union Army reenactors, who were crouched low on the left and right of their artillery piece. The men in gray, brandishing muskets and bayonets, let loose a fearful series of rebel yells.

"Fire!" called Williamson.

The cannon thundered, leaping backward on its wheels as it spat smoke and belched flame. The projectile struck the ground a few yards ahead of the tunnel entrance, blowing great chunks of the park's once-immaculate lawn into the air. Most of the Confederates tumbled to the ground at the impact. Williamson took out Toothless with Grier's Colt Python. The reenactors charged forward with bayonets gleaming, ready to seize prisoners for the greater glory of General Grant and President Lincoln. A few of the rebels threw their hands in the air, but several others, including Beady Eyes, slipped back into the tunnel.

The four Metro Atlanta Police backup units jumped the curb and screeched to a halt by the Cyclorama, rotating lights still flashing as the sounds of their sirens died out. Blue-uniformed officers climbed out quickly, buckling the chin straps of their eggshell-white helmets and jacking the pumps of their riot shotguns. Kennedy scurried ahead of the group, awkwardly fastening his bullet proof vest. "Williamson! Grier!" he called out. He gestured at the Confederate prisoners being herded at bayonet point by the Union reenactors. "Who *are* these people?"

"I don't know," said the Yankee sergeant, interrupting, "but I'll tell you one thing, they've sure got the buttons wrong."

Williamson smiled. " 'Late Conflict,' " he quipped.

Kennedy's forehead creased. "Williamson, do you mind explaining what's—"

Gunfire crashed.

Everyone turned—and drew their breath in short.

Assembled around the entrance of the tunnel was an entire field unit of Confederate cavalry. Dozens of albino horses stood flicking their tails as their riders, grim men in gray, fingered the handles of their rusty sabers and unsnapped the flaps of their holsters. Behind them was a row of rebel infantrymen, their number increasing rapidly as more armed men streamed from the tunnel to take up positions to the left and right.

A white-bearded officer, with a peacock plume in the band of his hat, sat on a dappled gray mare at the head of the column. He held up a smoking pistol in one hand as he surveyed the array of squad cars, armed policeman, and Yankee reenactors lined up around the Cyclorama. Then he turned, looking from Beady Eyes on his left to the nervous young bugler on his right, and shouted out a command that had not been heard over this history-laden field for more than a century: *"Charge!"*

The rebel's bugle call blasted out as the riders spurred their mounts and thundered forward, swords flashing in the moonlight and revolvers blasting plumes of sulfurous gunsmoke.

The startled policemen didn't wait for any orders from either Williamson or Kennedy. They immediately returned fire, riot shotguns coughing lead and ejecting hot casings as fast as they could work the pumps. The Union Army reenactors opened up with their period weapons and managed to score another lethal hit with a cannonball. Glass shattered in squad car windows and bullets ricocheted crazily, denting fenders. Horses fell screaming to the ground. Men cried out in pain. Bayonets punctured flesh, and the ground ran red.

There were only two more live rounds in the Python when Williamson saw Beady Eyes make a break from the group and take cover in the open rear door of the Cyclorama. He chased after the man anyway. Williamson had a score to settle. Ducking gunfire and stray horses, he made his way through the confusion to the doorway, and went inside.

In the dark stillness of the museum, Williamson stalked his quarry. Footsteps echoed loudly through the air-conditioned marble corridors, but he could follow Beady Eyes by the man's foul scent alone. Up the stairs, down another hall, and into the main exhibit area he ran, getting closer.

The lights went on unexpectedly, and Williamson found himself in the center of the Cyclorama itself. All around him was the giant motionless mural of the Battle of Atlanta, its foreground filled with three-dimensional mannequins wearing the uniforms of the blue and the gray, frozen forever in one bloody instant of history. Then tape-recorded shots rang out and preprogrammed flashing lights began to wink on and off. The motor-driven theater cars began to move, their seats empty, Williamson hopped into one of them and crouched low.

Beady Eyes was in here somewhere. Somehow the fool had unwittingly flipped the switches and started the show, all for an unwilling audience of one. Which meant, Williamson concluded, that Beady Eyes must be—in the control booth!

Glancing up, he saw his quarry's gray hat ducking low behind a row of red levers and a panel of blinking buttons. Williamson raised the Python and fired. The reaction was immediate; Beady Eyes stood up and raised a black powder pistol, firing twice. Williamson took his last shot, and planted a .357 bullet squarely in the rebel's thigh.

Blasted off balance, Beady Eyes slumped against the speed controls. His uninjured leg whipped out frantically, his boot snagging on the edge of a passing theater car. Metal gears ground noisily as Beady Eyes' body was stretched like a rubber band between the control booth and the car. With a frantic scream, the desperate Confederate raked his free hand over the control panel, pressing every button at once. The theater cars' gears engaged once again—and instantly tore him apart.

Beady Eyes' shredded torso fell down into the diorama at the base of the mural, where it landed in a heap of dummy Confederate corpses and was impaled on a prop sword. His severed leg, still attached to the moving theater car, smeared streaks of red in constant circles until Williamson switched off the machinery.

Grier and Kennedy arrived with a phalanx of cops behind them, just in time to see Williamson step down from the control booth. "What happened?" asked Grier.

Williamson shrugged. "He got the buttons wrong."

Kennedy shook his head. "Who *were* those lunatics out there? Don't they know the Civil War is over?"

Williamson took a deep breath and wiped the sweat from his glistening black forehead.

"Yes, it is," he said, "*now*."

THE MORNING OF AUGUST 18TH

by Ed Gorman

With a thunder of engines, they came. . . .

I happened to be in town that hot morning, getting some parts for the old red Ford tractor I just won't give up on, when I saw the first of them pull into the Bob's DX across the street. Bob didn't want their kind of business, but he wasn't about to say anything. Nobody was.

The biker's name was Randy. He had one of those big Harleys with handlebars so wide he looked like he was wrestling it instead of driving it. Black leather pants he wore and a clean white T-shirt with a rebel flag on the back. His blond hair rippled down to the middle of his back. The black eye patch gave him the edge of menace he wanted.

If he noticed me, he didn't let on. He was just looking at scenery and I was part of it. He flipped his cigarette dangerously close to the gas pumps and then stalked inside to the shade and the soda machine and the smells of car oil and Hershey bars. Bob, who was on the drive talking to Earle Haskins, raced over to pick up the smoking cigarette the way a parent would race after a toddler who was walking toward a river.

He ground out the butt and then made a big disgusted pantomime face to Earle.

It was August 18th, the same day it always was when the bikers pulled into town. Randy always came first, and alone.

And all the same things were going to happen, too. Paul Rice, the Chief of our six-man police department, was going to get shot in the shoulder; Amy, the cute little hip-switching waitress who works over at the truck stop, was going to get raped; and old man Stevenson was going to have a fatal stroke when six bikers roared their choppers through his prize-winning flower garden.

This is what they did every single time, and it wasn't going to be any different today.

But I'd be lying if I told you that those were the things uppermost on my mind.

No, what I was worried about was my family. It was always the same for us, too, and when I thought about it I felt ashamed that there was absolutely nothing I could do about it.

I don't know if you've ever read the Book of Job but you should because it's the truest part of the whole Bible, a part I discovered by myself in church one Sunday when I got bored with the sermon and started looking for my own sort of truth. And there it was in Job, a guy who asked the kind of hard questions that ministers don't like you to ask. Job was wondering, and wondering real loud, why things had to be the way they were, and why we were never permitted to understand any of it.

> But he is unchangeable and who can turn
> him?
> What he desires, that he does.

Job 23.13

Over lunch I told Cassie, my wife, about the first biker arriving. She had been just about to take a spoonful of Campbell's vegetable soup (even on hot days, we tend to eat soup for lunch) but then returned spoon and soup to her bowl. She looked at me with sweet brown eyes that had turned suddenly sad.

"I don't know if I can go through it all again," she said quietly.

"We always say that. But we get through it."

"It gets harder every time. Especially—you know, Susan." She paused for a long moment then said: "We need to tell her the truth now."

I tried a smile, but I doubt it was convincing. "Meaning, *I* should tell her."

"You said you would."

The smile again. "Yes, but only after you seduced me and made me make all sorts of wild promises."

"I'm glad I still have that sort of effect on you."

I took her hand. I felt so much tenderness, I wanted to cry. It was going to happen all over again, and there was no way I could stop it.

"I'll talk to her," I said.

She took her hand away. Went back to her soup. After two spoonfuls, she looked up and said, "She heard him again."

"In the woods?"

"Uh-huh."

"Could she make any of it out?"

She shook her shining fine red hair. "Just the voice. As usual, it scared her. She had a nightmare again last night. Didn't you hear her?"

"I guess all the work I was doing on the back acres must've wore me out."

"She needs to be told, John."

"I know. I just wonder if she'll believe it. I mean, it took *us* a long time to believe it. I mean, the more you understand it, the crazier it gets."

This time it was Cassie's hand seeking mine. "You'll need to take her to the grave up on the hill. She spends a lot of time up there, you know."

"I know," I said, finishing off my soup. "Too much time, actually."

I stood up, gave her a husbandly kiss on the cheek, and went off looking for my daughter, who had eaten and returned to play before I'd come back from town.

Took me ten minutes to find Susan who, it turned out, was down at the creek saying good-bye to the frog she'd captured in a Mason jar a few days earlier. She'd decided it wasn't fair to keep him in captivity.

She was just waving good-bye when I reached her, and when she turned to look up at me—the green frog was already springing from smooth hot rock to smooth hot rock—she had tears in her eyes.

She was ten and probably too old to pick up and hug and carry on with the way I did, but I thought, *what the hell*. She was my daughter and I loved her more than sunshine, and if I wanted to treat her like a small child sometimes, what was the harm? Her eyes had the grace and wisdom of her mother, and her mouth the wry-sad humor Cassie said she found in mine. In her white blouse and jeans, she smelled of sunlight and heat and summer.

"Do you think he'll be all right?" she asked when she was sitting on my forearm the way she'd sit on a swing seat.

"He'll be fine."

"Where will he stay tonight?"

"In a motel."

She giggled. "He will not. Frogs don't have motels."

"They most certainly do."

"Huh-uh."

We walked a ways.

"I had a nightmare again."

"That's what Mommy said."

"I heard him in the woods yesterday. That's what I had the nightmare about."

"Daddy needs to tell you some things, hon."

"What things?"

I was angling across soybeans to the hill where the gravestones were.

"Is it about him? The man in the woods."

"Yes."

"He scares me."

I wanted to say that he scared me, too, but it wouldn't have been right. We walked on.

The gravestone is large and made of pink granite and on its face it reads:

THE GULAGER FAMILY

James	Cassie	Susan
1931–1967	1932–1967	1957–1967

One with the wind and The Lord

The gravestone rests beneath an oak whose limbs seem to reach out to the wide green valley and the blue, blue river below. Our little town has a water tower and a red brick library and three white churches, each with an exultant steeple.

When I set Cassie down, she walked over to the gravestone and stared at her name. She did that a lot, came up here and stared at her name on the gravestone.

"I want to tell you about the man in the woods, hon," I said.

I wasn't sure she heard. She couldn't take her eyes from her name.

"He's a director. He's making this movie called 'Hells Angels Hellions' and he makes us keep doing it over and over again until he's happy with what he's got."

Her eyes looked up. "Those men on those motorcycles, they're going to come back again, aren't they?"

"Yes, hon. I'm afraid they are."

"They're going to kill me and Mommy again, aren't they?"

That was the thing. We experienced all the pain and terror and suffering of dying—and yet we came back.

I looked away momentarily. Tears were hot in my eyes.

The same all over again. Again and again and again. Retake after retake after retake.

The biker gang, preceded by the biker named Randy, would come to town, sack it, and then on their way out of town stop by our farmhouse where my family and I would put up a long and bloody battle until I saw Susan and Cassie die in the fire that engulfed the house. I would run through the house trying to save them and when I came screaming out of the house, on fire myself, the bikers would shoot me and kill me.

This is all I knew about the picture. I mean, somehow the gravestone is in the final scenes of the movie, but I'm not exactly sure how those scenes go.

"I'm going to have fire on me again, aren't I, Daddy?"

I picked her up and walked to the edge of the hill and looked out over the valley.

"How come this is happening to us, Daddy?"

"I'm not sure, hon."

And I wasn't. Neither Susan nor I had any memories of life past a few weeks back, a few weeks always leading to August 18th over and over and over again.

We wouldn't even have known about the director except one day when Susan and I were in the woods, we heard him. He was giving some people instructions about getting ready for the farm scene with the Gulagers. Us.

The funny thing was, we could never see him. We ran all through the woods all day long trying to see him, but he was never more than a disembodied voice.

"It hurts, Daddy, when the fire's on me. I'm so scared when I can't find you and Mommy, and it hurts so much."

I was going to say something, but then I heard the roar of them as they rounded the last bend just outside of town.

Far below now, I saw them.

The bikers.

August 18th.

The cries of my daughter and wife.

"I'm scared, Daddy. I want to go somewhere and hide."

But there was no place to hide. No place at all.

Then the gunshots cracked the silence, echoing off the valley.

August 18th.

All over again.

THE THING FROM LOVERS' LANE

by Nancy A. Collins

It roamed by night ...
to slake its monstrous thirst for beauty!

"Is that us, or is it really that foggy out there?" Carol Anne giggled, pointing to the Chevy's steamed-over windows.

"I'd say it's fifty-fifty," Billy replied, wiping clear a spot on the windshield with the heel of his palm. To the casual observer, the world beyond the hood of the car seemed to have disappeared. "Boy, that fog crept up pretty fast, didn't it?"

Carol Anne plucked a lipstick cylinder from her purse and angled the rearview mirror so she could fix her makeup. "What do you mean 'fast'? We've been parked out here for over an hour!"

"Are you suggesting that it's time I took you home?"

Carol Anne dropped the lipstick back into her purse. "Of course not! I'm just saying that, y'know, time flies when you're, y'know, having fun."

Billy grinned crookedly, smoothing back his blond ducktail. "So, that's what you call it, huh?" His grin grew bigger as he reached across the front seat. "C'mere, sweetie-pie; y'wanna have some more fun?"

Carol Anne blushed and giggled again as she wrig-

gled against Billy's leather jacket. She liked the way it
smelled in the close heat of the car—like something
alive. But even as she responded to his caresses, she
really *did* think it was time to go home. She wasn't
afraid of what might happen—they'd gone all the way
once before, after all. No, she was afraid of screwing
up her alibi. She told her parents she was going to the
double feature at the Bijou with Phyllis Tarkington.
The movie let out at midnight, and that meant she had
to be home by twelve-thirty, or else her folks would
get worried or, worse yet, suspicious.

Her father didn't approve of boys like Billy. Billy
emulated tough guys like Marlon Brando and James
Dean and liked Elvis and was into hot-rodding. Billy
smoked cigarettes and drank Iron City Beer. None of
which were things that went over big with Mr.
Fairweather. Which suited Carol Anne just fine.

All her life her parents had been on her about how
she was their "little angel" and how important it was
for her to always be on her "best behavior." It was important to be pretty. Important to be nice. Important to
be popular. They were so happy when she became a
cheerleader. They were even happier when she was
voted Homecoming Queen. As if being the Homecoming Queen of a nowheresville like Misty Valley really
meant anything!

Daddy was always coming home late, too tired to do
anything but watch the Dumont and bitch about Eisen-
hower. On the weekends he shut himself away in his
office and drank martinis, except for when he was out
mowing the lawn or mucking out the rain gutters. Mom
spent most of her time getting tranquilizers from her
doctor, playing bridge, and harassing Daddy for new
kitchen appliances. The more electric the better. Last
month he got a new electric dryer to replace the old
gas-powered one. Carol Anne guessed that appliance

buying was what passed for sex between her parents nowadays.

Aside from getting excited over her making the cheerleader squad and being the Homecoming Queen, her parents didn't seem that interested in what was going on with her life, except to remind her to be a "good girl." If they found out that she was out parking with Billy Mahan, they'd really flip! But she wasn't in the mood to deal with Mom's hysterics and Daddy's bluster. Tonight wouldn't be a good night for them to find out about Billy.

Then again, it wasn't exactly like they were necking on the park bench next to the band shell. Lovers' Lane was really an old logging road on the side of Goat Hill, which overlooked Misty Valley. On a clear night, you could look out and see the entire valley spread out, with the lights of the town reflected in the Miskatonic River, which wound through the center of the village like a dark ribbon. But tonight wasn't one of the clear nights, that much was certain. Misty Valley was definitely living up to its name.

Suddenly there was a sound from outside and the whole car shook as if someone had jumped on the rear bumper.

"What th' hell—?" Billy twisted around to glare out the back window of the car. It was fogged over.

Carol Anne sat up quickly, rearranging her clothes as best she could. Her lipstick was smeared. "Billy, what was that?"

"Some dumbass is messin' with us, that's what!" he snapped. "I bet it's that dickweed, Schaumberger!" He opened the driver's door, peering into the heavy mist that surrounded the car. "I know that was you, Markie!" he yelled into the night. "You don't fool me!"

There was movement nearby, and the sound of

someone pushing through the woods, away from where the car was parked.

"You better run, Schaumberger! 'Cause when I catch you, I'm gonna kick your butt over your eyebrows!" Billy shouted, and set off in the direction of the noise.

"Billy! Don't!" Carol Anne cried out, grabbing at his sleeve, but it was too late. As she watched Billy disappear into the surrounding fog, tendrils of mist crept into the car. She shuddered and yanked the door closed behind him, hammering the lock down with her fist.

After crashing headlong fifty feet into the woods, Billy saw the tree just before he hit it. One minute he was running through the fog, threatening to tear Markie Schaumberger a new asshole, the next he was sitting on his butt, his nose bleeding and lip swelling up like a balloon. Hell, it almost seemed as if the damned thing leaped in front of him! He was definitely going to make Schaumberger eat his jockstrap this time!

As he sat on the ground, gingerly fingering his swollen lip, it suddenly dawned on Billy that whoever interrupted his makeout session with Carol Anne, it sure wasn't Schaumberger. Markie would never let an opportunity as ripe as this one go without his patented hee-haw laugh. In fact, the surrounding woods were ominously quiet, except for the sound of the fog dripping from the trees.

He slowly got to his feet, suddenly uncertain of his bearings. He knew he couldn't be far from the car—but he was now completely turned around. He'd never parked this far down Lovers' Lane before. In fact, most of the kids never parked down here. Billy wasn't exactly sure why. Maybe it was posted or something. Normally he wouldn't have come here, except Carol

Anne was afraid of their being together getting back to her parents.

There was a sound off to the left—or was it the right? Billy spun around like a child playing Blind Man's Bluff. He'd completely forgotten about his split lip and bloody nose. He was thinking about what had jostled his car. And how it might not have been human, after all. He remembered his old man telling him about how he used to hunt bear up in the hills before the Second World War. Sure, his old man was a lush, and the war was fourteen years ago. . . .

There was a smell—a rank, animal stench—and Billy could feel whatever was in the mist. It was big and it wasn't human. And then it was on him, and there was nothing but darkness and the stink of wet fur.

Carol Anne fidgeted and pulled her letter-jacket tighter. She peered out the windshield, but all she could see was gray nothing. She couldn't even play the radio, since Billy had taken the keys with him. She frowned and drummed her heels against the floor of the car. She wondered if he'd caught up with Markie Schaumberger and if he was kicking the little creep's butt. Probably not, though.

No doubt they were having a good laugh at her expense out there. Billy was probably telling Markie how much he'd managed to get off her. And once Markie knew something, it was all over school! Damn Billy!

Muttering under her breath, Carol Anne got out of the car. She cupped her hands to her mouth and shouted: *"Billy! Billy, where are you?"*

Silence.

"Billy! I know you're out there! Answer me!"

Still no response.

"Damn it, Billy! This isn't funny! I want to go home!"

Carol Anne's anger faded, to be replaced by concern. Something was wrong. Billy might be immature, but he wasn't an utter jerk. He wouldn't leave her stranded. Something must have happened. Maybe he fell down and hit his head on something. What if he got lost and fell down the side of the hill?

Carol Anne moved in the direction Billy had gone. "Billy? Billy—are you okay? Billy?"

There was the sound of something moving in the mist. Something coming her way. But whatever it was, it wasn't Billy. For one thing, it was too big. And, for another, it smelled funny. Carol Anne was too scared to scream. She wondered if it was a bear. Then she saw it.

Old Gooney was having beans for dinner.

Old Gooney always had beans for dinner. And he cooked them the exact same way each time. He cut open the top of the can and stuck it in the fire until he could see the bean juice bubble, then pulled the can out with a pair of tongs he scavenged from the town dump. When the beans cooled down, he'd eat them with an old tin spoon some hunter left behind a couple of deer-seasons ago.

Old Gooney didn't hold with people much. Never had, even as a young man. He grew up on Goat Hill, born in the three-room farmhouse his ancestors built two hundred years ago. It never had electricity or running water.

His folks kept to themselves pretty much, too, so when they died, Old Gooney didn't see any need to change his ways. So he kept living in the old farmhouse, until five years ago, when he got drunk and set the place on fire. Since then, he'd been living out of the old chicken coop. He slept inside the shack, but did all his cooking outside. On nights like this, he usually kept the fire burning all night long, not daring to go to sleep until dawn broke over the valley. You never knew what might be abroad on nights like this.

Something in the woods roared. It startled Old Gooney so bad he dropped his can of pork-and-beans. Old Gooney got to his feet, clutching Pappy's squirrel rifle to his chest. He rarely spotted the thing that roared in the woods, but he knew its name. He'd glimpsed traces of its passage every now and again, as had Pappy, and Grandpa, and Great-Grand before him.

"The Goat's loose in the wood!" Old Gooney whispered aloud.

Then he heard the scream.

Old Gooney's heart stopped beating for half a minute, then kicked back into gear at twice its previous speed. He was no longer standing in front of the chicken coop. He was cowering inside a farmhouse that no longer existed. It was thirty years ago and he was listening to the screams of a woman trapped in the fog. But this time he had to try and stop it.

He found the girl not a quarter-mile away, near the old logging road. She was lying facedown on the ground, covered in mud and dead leaves. Her poodle skirt, with its layers of petticoats, was torn to shreds, as if made of tissue paper. At first he thought she was dead. When he rolled her over onto her back, he realized she was still breathing. The insides of her thighs were smeared with a mixture of mud and other things, and Old Gooney took off his jacket to cover her shame.

The girl was in a bad way, but she wasn't dead. He got back to his feet. He'd have to fetch the pickup and bring her into town. Normally he only went into town once a month, to cash in all the sody bottles he collected along the roadsides. He didn't have much use for folks, but he wasn't going to let some poor little gal die by herself on Goat Hill. Not this time.

As he was preparing to leave to get the truck, Old Gooney saw something moving in the mist. Something familiar. He pointed his squirrel rifle at the thing, his face twisted into a knot of hate.

"You git away from here! Git, or I'll blow you so full of holes you'll look like a lace curtain!"

The thing in the mist grunted, whether in assent or amusement, and was gone.

Sheriff Mayhew received a frantic telephone call around one from Maynard and Blanche Fairweather, reporting their daughter missing. He had a bad feeling about that one. His years as an infantry soldier in Korea and a police officer in the States had fostered a sixth sense for impending tragedy. Misty Valley was no Pork Chop Hill, but it wasn't your average little town; that much he'd learned in the five years since he'd taken the job. There was something strange about the whole area that he could never really put his finger on. He'd heard wild stories, no doubt inflamed by hard drink and country bumpkin superstition so dense you couldn't drive a nail through it, but if even a fraction of what the locals gossiped was true—well, at least he wasn't the sheriff of Dunwich or Innsmouth.

His suspicions concerning the Fairweather girl were confirmed when he got the call from Doc Wagner an hour later, reporting that the old hermit that lived on Goat Hill had delivered her to the Municipal Hospital, and that she appeared to be the victim of a rape.

When he got to the hospital, the Fairweathers were already in the lobby. Blanche was in hysterics and Maynard was standing there, holding her up by the elbows.

"My baby! My baby!" Blanche Fairweather blubbered. "How could this happen? *How?*"

"You're gonna catch the bastard who did this to my little girl, aren't you, Jim?" Maynard asked, although he made it sound more like a threat.

"I'm going to do my damnedest, Maynard. Excuse me, but I need to speak to the doc."

Doc Wagner was still in the emergency room, talking in low tones with a nurse. Carol Anne Fairweather lay unconscious on the examination table, covered by a clean sheet. Her eyes and mouth were bruised, but she seemed otherwise unharmed. Doc Wagner looked up from the clipboard.

"The Fairweathers are outside, Doc. I think someone ought to see to Blanche."

Wagner nodded his understanding. "Betty, why don't you administer Mrs. Fairweather a mild sedative?" he said, motioning with his clipboard. "I need to speak with Sheriff Mayhew."

Mayhew waited until the nurse left the room before turning to face the doctor. "So—what have we got here, Doc?"

"To tell you the truth—I don't really know."

"What do you mean? Was she raped or not?"

Wagner sighed as he scratched the back of his head. "Well, sexual intercourse *did* take place. . . ."

"Then it's rape. Judging from the bruises, the girl *was* assaulted, am I right?"

"It's just—well, it's just that this is completely unlike anything I've seen before."

"What do you mean?"

"It's the amount of semen, Jim. Judging from what I've found, there must have been at least ten of them. Possibly more. But there's no sign of the physical trauma a multiple rape inevitably produces."

"What about the girl? Will she pull through?"

Wagner shrugged. "Her vital signs are all very strong. Her unconsciousness is more the result of emotional shock than physical damage."

"Who brought her in?"

"Old Gooney, believe it or not."

"Gooney? That old recluse that lives up on Goat Hill? How'd he find *her?*"

"Apparently she was on his property. Lovers' Lane isn't too far from his place."

"Is he still hanging around?"

"I had Betty fix him up with a cup of coffee and a sandwich. He should still be in the staff lounge."

Mayhew could smell Old Gooney the moment he opened the door. The hermit was sitting at the break table, clutching his coffee in one hand and a half-eaten sandwich in the other. His face was seamed by wrinkles and dirt, his chin covered by whiskers the color of chewing tobacco. He wore several layers of tattered castoffs and a discarded hunter's cap that made him look like a demented Elmer Fudd.

"Mr. McGoohan—?"

The hermit scowled. "Pappy was Mr. McGoohan. Everybody calls me Gooney. You'd know that, sonny, if you was from here."

"I've been here five years, Mr.— I mean, Gooney."

"Five years!" Old Gooney snorted his derision. "Nobody's from here unless they got three generations buried in Forest Glen!"

"Gooney, the doc tells me you're the one who brought in the girl."

The hermit's rheumy eyes glistened for a second and he stopped chewing his sandwich. "I heard her screamin', out in the woods. When I got to where she were—she was like she was."

"Gooney—did you see anything?"

Gooney nodded his head soberly, his eyes fixed on something inside his head. "I sure did. I see what did it to her."

Mayhew leaned forward anxiously, no longer mindful of the old man's stink. "Who was it, Gooney? Who did you see?"

Old Gooney shook his head. "Weren't no 'who.' It were a *what*."

Mayhew rolled his eyes. Great, his one eyewitness was not only an old coot, he was crazy as well. He felt his patience begin to melt. He took a deep breath and tried to keep the anger out of his voice. "Come on, Gooney, you don't have to be afraid of some young punks coming after you! I'll see that you're protected."

"You're damn right I'm scared! But it ain't of no hoodlums! I know what I seen, and it weren't no man!"

Mayhew straightened up and wearily massaged his eyes. "Okay. Whatever you say, old-timer. But I'll need you to show me and my deputies where you found the girl."

"It'll have to wait until dawn, Sheriff," Old Gooney explained. "My ol' pick 'em-up truck ain't got but one headlight workin', and that's stuck on high-beam. The fog's too thick t'try and make it back up the hill tonight. Besides, I wouldn't go back out there even if you drove me!"

"Why's that?"

"Don't you know nothin', boy? The Goat's in the woods tonight!"

They found the Chevy parked on the side of the road just after dawn. They found the owner not long after. He was lying unconscious in the woods, with a large bump on the back of his head, a split upper lip, and a bloody nose. It was hard to say whether he'd been knocked unconscious or simply lost his footing in the dark.

Mayhew spat when he rolled the boy over. Billy Mahan. What the hell was a girl like Carol Anne Fairweather doing out on Lovers' Lane with Billy Mahan?

The boy groaned and his eyelids fluttered open as

Mayhew nudged him with the toe of his boot. "C'mon, Mahan! Get your ass up!"

Billy sat up slowly, massaging the back of his neck. "Ohhhh! My head! Where am I?" His eyes widened and he looked around anxiously. "Carol Anne! Where's Carol Anne?"

"She's in the hospital, Mahan."

Billy staggered to his feet. "Hospital? What's she doing in the hospital? What happened to her?"

"That's what we'd like to know, Mahan. Your girlfriend was attacked last night."

Billy eyed the surrounding woods and shuddered. "There was—there was something in the mist. It was looking inside the car at us. I thought it was, you know, some of the guys, trying to scare us. I followed it into the woods—"

"You left the girl sitting in the car by herself?" Mayhew shook his head in disgust.

"I–I thought it was friends—" Billy swallowed hard, trying to keep himself from breaking into tears. This was bad. Real bad.

"Maybe it was. Maybe your friends were waiting to have themselves some fun. Was that it, Mahan? Was that your game? Were you supposed to lure Carol Anne out here, so you and your no-good punk friends could have some 'fun'?"

Billy turned and stared at the sheriff. "What are you saying, Mayhew?"

"I'm saying I'm arresting you for the rape of Carol Anne Fairweather, punk," Mayhew snarled.

Billy sat hunched over in the back of the squad car, his manacled wrists attached to an eyebolt screwed into the floor between his feet. The car didn't have protective mesh separating the front and back seats, so this was how Mayhew transported his more dangerous prisoners. Mayhew sat next to Billy, a drawn pistol aimed at the boy's midsection, while his deputy served as chauffeur.

The deputy passed the radio receiver to Mayhew. "It's for you. Harlan says Doc Wagner just called."

Mayhew shifted his grip on his service revolver as he took the mike. "Yeah, Harlan. What is it?"

"Doc says the Fairweather girl finally woke up."

"Is she able to talk?"

"Doc says she tried to kill herself. Stuck herself with a knife. He says he needs you over there pronto."

Mayhew stared through the window of the Intensive Care Unit at Carol Anne Fairweather. The room was no bigger than a broom closet, and most of it was taken up by the hospital bed and the respirator beside it. Carol Anne looked even worse than before, only this time her hands were bound to the metal railing on the sides of the bed with pieces of soft cloth.

Doc Wagner shook his head and turned away from the view. "Damnedest thing I ever saw, Jim! We were in the examination room—the girl wasn't conscious more than a minute or two, I swear! Next thing I know she's screaming at the top of her lungs 'It's in me! It's in me!' and somehow snatches up a scalpel and starts stabbing herself in the belly, like she was trying to cut herself wide open!

"I don't have the facilities necessary to help her here. I called an old medical school chum of mine over at Arkham. He's agreed to admit her to the university's Medical Center for me. There's an ambulance on its way to pick her up."

"Did she say anything before she went under, Doc? Anything about who attacked her?"

"She wasn't making much sense, Jim. But from what little I was able to understand, the Mahan boy wasn't the one responsible."

"*Somebody's* responsible, damn it! And if it's not him, then he probably knows who is!"

"Jim—just because the boy greases his hair back, wears a leather jacket, and likes to drag race doesn't make him a criminal."

"Maybe not. But raping a girl does."

They held Billy for two days without officially charging him. On the third day he was released after Sheriff Mayhew received a phone call from Doc Wagner, who had traveled to Arkham to check on Carol Anne's condition. She had regained consciousness and spoken to him at length, all the while insisting that Billy was not the one responsible. An important piece of physical evidence also helped clear Billy of the rape charges. Doc Wagner had taken a smear of the rapist's semen and analyzed it in the Miskatonic University's laboratories, in hope of discovering just how many attackers there were and what their blood types might be. Billy didn't know what the exact results were, but they completely exonerated him.

So, on Tuesday afternoon, Billy found himself walking down Main Street in the direction of the house he shared with his father. The cops had towed his Chevy to the impound yard, next to the Miskatonic River Bridge, and he needed his dad's signature to get it out, since he was under age.

As he headed home, he could feel the eyes of the town on him, following his every move. As he walked down the sidewalk, merchants stared out at him from the shadowed doorways of their stores, like cavemen fearfully watching the passage of a dangerous animal. As he neared Hank Emerson's barbershop, a woman grabbed her toddler by the arm and hurried across the street, glancing over her shoulder at him as if he were a pursuing bear.

He'd never been very popular in Misty Valley. His

family had always been fairly low on the town's peck-
ing order—his dad was the village boozer and his
mom, before she split three years ago with a traveling
salesman, had held the position of the drunkard's slat-
ternly wife.

Billy had cultivated the rebel outsider image as a
way to deal with the embarrassment and stigma of being white trash. He'd always told himself he was bigger than Misty Valley. Destined for better things. He
didn't care if the bastards who lived in Misty Valley
liked him or not.

The fact that Misty Valley's precious, perfect Homecoming Queen had picked *him* to give it up to had
made him feel like he'd managed to pull one over on
the whole stinking township. But now he no longer had
what few friends he'd managed to cultivate, since
Mayhew had dragged them all in for questioning.
Nothing had come of it, except the destruction of Billy's friendship with Markie Schaumberger.

Billy was drawn from his reverie by the sound of
tires squealing and the next thing he knew a large,
fleshy man with a florid face and receding hairline was
charging at him, screaming obscenities at the top of his
lungs.

"You filthy hoodlum bastard! I'll kill you! I'll
fucking *kill* you!"

Before Billy could react, the fleshy man smashed his
fist into his face, bloodying his nose. Billy staggered
backward, too surprised to do more than blink in confusion.

"Maynard! Stop! Stop it, Maynard!" A middle-aged
woman threw open the passenger door of the Buick
that was in the middle of the street. Billy recognized
enough of Carol Anne in Blanche Fairweather's face to
figure out who the fleshy man was.

"You ruined my daughter, you lousy stinking *punk!*"

Maynard Fairweather shrieked, aiming another blow at Billy's face. "My princess! My baby girl!"

Billy stepped out of the way of the swing and grabbed the older man's arm, twisting it behind him. Fairweather's face suddenly went white with pain.

"I didn't *do* anything to her, Mr. Fairweather!" Billy said from between his teeth. "You got the right to hit me that one time, 'cause I did something stupid and I wasn't there to save her when I shoulda been. But I didn't *hurt* her! Why would I? I *love* Carol Anne! And she loves *me!*" Billy wasn't exactly sure if that last part was true or not, but it might make Carol Anne's old man less likely to try and kill him on the street again.

"You're lying! Carol Anne would never have gone out with someone like you!" Fairweather spat, his breath redolent of vodka martinis. "My daughter's a *good girl!*"

"Maynard, you're *embarrassing* me!" Blanche Fairweather hissed. She was looking around nervously, no doubt keenly aware of every eye in Misty Valley being focused on them. "Stop this fighting right this minute!"

Billy pushed Fairweather away from him with a single shove. Fairweather staggered a few steps then landed heavily on his well-padded butt.

Billy shook a finger at Fairweather, whose wife was clucking over the grass stains on his slacks. "There's only one drunk asshole who's ever kicked my ass, and that was my old man! And the last time he tried it, I cleaned his clock! You try and take a swing at me again, square-nuts, I'm gonna forget you're Carol Anne's pop and smear you but good—dig?"

With that, Billy stormed off in the direction of home. His old man better be at least half-sober when he got there, because the lush was going to spring his wheels even if it meant he had to drag him down to the impound yard by his short hairs.

Billy had been driving with no particular place to go for the better part of two hours, trying to figure out what had happened to him and Carol Anne that night. While he was stuck in the jail, he'd overheard the sheriff talking to the deputies and the doctor about the old hermit, the one called Gooney. Apparently he'd seen whoever it was that attacked Carol Anne. Or at least claimed he did. In any case, the old man's refusal to finger Billy was another reason they'd been forced to cut him loose.

Old Gooney knew something, of this Billy was certain. But what?

Maybe it was up to him to find out.

He followed the old logging road up Goat Hill. It was getting late, but Billy doubted that Lovers' Lane would be seeing much action for some time to come. After what had happened to Carol Anne, the kids in town were too scared to park there for their "inspiration."

It took him a while, but he finally found the rutted turnoff that led to what was left of the McGoohan farm. The pastures had been allowed to go fallow, although he could make out a few low walls made of natural stone that once marked off the fields. The farmhouse itself was a burned-out husk, the roof collapsed on itself. There was a ramshackle pickup truck parked next to what looked like a chicken coop. The outside of the coop was covered by dozens of old license plates scavenged from derelict cars. Sitting in front of the shack, tending a small campfire ringed by whitewashed stones, was the filthiest old man Billy had ever laid eyes on.

The hermit didn't move to greet Billy when he left

his car, but neither did he reach for the ancient .22 leaning against the shack.

"You Gooney?"

"Yep. Who might you be, young 'un?"

"Billy. Billy *Mahan*."

Old Gooney grunted and nodded. "You're the one who was out here with that lit'l gal. See the sheriff let you go. I told that damn fool you weren't the one to blame. I'm fixin' dinner, boy. Only got one can of beans."

"Uh—that's okay. I already ate."

"Good. 'Cause I weren't offerin' you none."

Billy hunkered down next to the fire, opposite Old Gooney. The old man smelled like he hadn't seen soapy water in a season or two. Underneath the pungent reek of body odor was the smell of squeeze. Billy's dad drank it every now and then, when he didn't have the money for store-bought alcohol.

"How come they didn't believe you when you told them I wasn't the one?"

Old Gooney cackled, exposing a mouth that was mostly wrinkled gum, except for a couple of teeth jutting sideways, like the tusks of a wild animal. "Cause I'm crazy as a bedbug, sonny! Can't you tell?"

"Maybe you just *look* crazy."

Old Gooney stopped laughing and gave Billy a strange look. It encouraged the boy enough to keep on talking.

"I mean, somebody like you, living alone out here, you must see a lot of things most folks don't know about. . . ."

"That's the Lord's Truth," Old Gooney muttered, pulling his moth-eaten jacket tight against his shoulders.

"Why don't you tell me what it was you saw—or thought you saw—that night? The sheriff might not have believed you—but I will. Something tells me you and I—maybe we saw the same thing."

Old Gooney sat there for a long moment, sucking on what remained of his teeth, staring into the fire. When he finally spoke, it sounded more like he was clearing his throat than talking.

"Goats."

"Beg pardon?"

"I said *goats*. That's what we used to raise out here. McGoohans always been goatherds, since the day they come over from Scotland, back in the 1750s. Guess we was goatherds over there, too. That's why this place is called Goat Hill.

"This here's a real strange patch of country, boy. Right strange. Even though I ain't never been so far as to Aylesbury, much less Arkham, I know that for a fact. There's something about the countryside here-abouts—something about it that draws evil to it. Misty Valley ain't had the troubles like some of the other townships—such as Dunwich or Innsmouth. But maybe its time is comin' round at last.

"My granny used to go on about such things all the time. About how some of the early settlers carried on with the Indians that was here before 'em. They used to dance round nekkid under the full moon on top of The Devil's Hop-Yard, or pastures, like The Grove, calling down gods—or demons that called themselves gods—doing things no Christian would dream of.

"Granny would go on at length about it—but then, she was a Whateley. The Whateleys was turned that way, you know—no, I reckon you wouldn't. That was a while back, and most folks around here have made sure to forget about what happened over in Dunwich.

"Anyways, Granny's first cousin was involved in that mess. Folks called him a wizard, and I reckon he was, in his way. In any case, he got hisself mixed up with things older an' meaner'n the Snake in the Garden. But that don't have anything to do with what happened to your girlfriend—not directly, anyway.

"As I was sayin', there's always been strange things afoot in the Miskatonic Valley. Always will be, I suppose. When I was a boy, I used to walk the pasture with Pappy. He was always lookin' for breaks in the walls and keepin' an eye out for wild dogs and the occasional wolf or bear that might be after his herd—oh, yes, and panthers, too. Every now and then—especially after one of the heavy fogs—we'd come across goats that'd been attacked.

"Most times it was a bear or a panther had got 'em. But sometimes . . . Sometimes we'd find a billy torn to shreds, like someone had yanked its legs off, one by one. And the nannies—sometimes the nannies would be dead, but just as often they'd be alive, bleedin' outta their hindquarters. Whenever we'd find a nanny goat that way, my pappy would take his rifle and put the poor thing outta its misery.

"At first I thought he was doin' it out of kindness, on account of the animal being all ripped up inside. But one day he told me mercy had nothin' to do with it. He killed the nannies for fear of 'the thousand-and-first.' When I asked him what that meant, he warned me never to allow 'the Goat's seed to grow.' Which I thought was fair strange, seein' as how we was goatherds. But it wasn't until later that I realized he weren't talkin' about no ordinary goat.

"It happened back in '28. Shortly before the Horror over in Dunwich. Folks never knew the truth of what happened out here that day, and after what became of Wilbur Whateley and his twin brother, folks were more than ready to forget what happened that season. I weren't but sixteen. No older than you."

Billy grunted and tried to hide his surprise. Old Gooney was a year younger than his own father.

"It was getting on dusk. Me and Pappy was walkin'

the herd back from the north forty, when the fog came up sudden. I could tell by the way Pappy got anxious that it weren't no natural thing. As we got close to the house, there was this scream—"

Old Gooney closed his eyes and grimaced, no doubt still hearing the echoes. He produced a glass milk bottle filled with squeeze and took a healthy swig. When he opened his eyes again, they seemed to burn in the flickering light from the campfire.

"Pappy set out for the house at a dead run, me on his heels. When we got there, Maw was nowhere to be found. Everything was in its place and there was no sign of a struggle. Then there was another, louder scream. It came from the woods. Pappy grabbed up his rifle and told me to stay put. I told him no, I was gonna go with him to help Maw.

"To my surprise, he hauled off and punched me full in the mouth! Knocked out two of my front teeth! He seemed more scared than mad, though. He said 'I told you to stay put, and I meant it! The Goat's in the woods, boy!' And then he was gone. That was the last I saw Pappy alive.

"I didn't witness what happened that night—I didn't have to. I heard my Maw scream Pappy's name. I heard the gunshots. I heard whatever it was Pappy was shootin' at give out a roar so powerful it was as if all Creation had been given throat. Then I heard Pappy scream. I was scared piss-yeller. I spent the whole night burnin' the lamp and prayin' behind locked doors and shuttered windows.

"I found them come the dawn. They weren't more than a stone's throw from the door yard, as it were. Apparently, Maw had gone to the edge of the wood to pick some wild mushrooms for dinner. Pappy always had a hankering for them things. Pappy looked like one of his billy goats, tore limb from limb and scattered about like a scarecrow. Maw was a different story, though.

"Her dress was nothing but tatters, her face was all bruised, and both her legs was broke, but she was alive. I reckon she was in what they call shock. She lay there in the mud, all bloody and nekkid, moaning Pappy's name over and over. I tell you, no boy should ever see his mama in such a state. . . .

"As I was standing there, starin' at what was left of my folks, I hear this noise from the woods. I look up and I *see* it. I see the thing that done it. It stood taller'n a man, and it was dark and hairy all over, the eyes shining red like a deer's caught in a headlight. The dew was shinin' on its coat, and it smelt just like a wet dog. Only it weren't no dog."

"What was it? What did you see, Gooney?"

Old Gooney shook his head and his mouth bowed into a fierce rictus, as if he was uncertain whether to laugh, cry, or vomit. "I seen the *Goat*, boy! Shub-Niggurath: the Father of Nightmares; the Black Goat of the Wood; He of a Thousand Young; the Lord of the Grove! *That's* what I seen! And the shaggy bastard gives me this look like I ain't worth worryin' over, an' disappears back into the forest.

"I look down and see Pappy's rifle lying right at my feet, along with some ammunition. I pick it up and all the while I'm loading the rifle, I'm rememberin' them nanny goats. And how Pappy told me the thousand-and-first must never be born. And I recalled how Granny used to go on just before she died, the whip-poorwills calling outside her window, about the Old Ones and how their time was coming round again. I kept thinkin' about them things and thinkin' about them, so I wouldn't have to think about what I was about to do.

"I buried my folks in the north pasture, where it's sunny most the time. I told the folks in town they'd died of the influenza. Most everyone believed it. If anyone was suspicious, what went on over in Dunwich ended up drawing their attention away from me. I kept up the farm the best I could, but I got to drinkin' and I could never bring myself to take a wife, knowin' what I know about Goat Hill.

"The livestock finally died out in '36—too many of the billies was gettin' killed, and the nannies were as liable to end up bein' shot as drop a kid, and I had neither the money or inclination to replace 'em. So I made do by leasin' parcels of land to the lumber companies, but that petered out a few years back. Now all them loggin' roads is good for is for kids to come up and smooch in their cars."

Old Gooney spat into the fire. The flames flared brighter for a moment, then died back down. "If you'd parked down the road a piece, it would never have bothered you. Just like it's never bothered any of the other young'uns who park there. The stone walls keep it in, y'know. That's why Pappy was so keen on keepin' them up. It's the only thing I still bother with, round here. Don't know who'll see to it once I'm gone.

"I'm the last, you know. The last of the McGoohans. The last of the goatkeepers of Goat Hill. You're right lucky, you know that, boy? I know you might not feel that way, but you are. It decided not to kill you, for some reason. Maybe because you didn't attack it, tryin' to save your mate. The girl, though—that's another story. Luck's turned its face from her.

"I should have killed her when I found her. I should have. But I couldn't bring myself to do it. Not again." The old hermit began to cry, the tears trickling down his cheeks, cutting trails through the dirt and grime. "It's up to you, boy. It's up to you to see that the thousand-and-first ain't born. It's up to you to see that the Goat don't roam the woods beyond this cursed valley."

Billy left Old Gooney to his bottle of squeeze and his can of pork and beans. As he headed back in the direction of Misty Valley, he looked into the rearview mirror one last time. The old man was still squatting in front of his shack, muttering to himself about Black Goats and the return of forgotten gods.

Old Gooney felt better after he got the beans in him. He wasn't sure if it was the food that made him feel different or if it was talking to the boy. He'd never told a living soul about what had happened to his folks. He hadn't known such inner peace in thirty-one years.

He smiled and took another pull on the squeeze. Although it was a touch cool and the mist was already starting to rise, it looked to be a nice night for sitting out under the stars. Then he noticed the whippoorwills. Judging from their calls, the woods had to be full to overflowing with them. He remembered what his Granny had said about the whippoorwills calling to the souls of the damned, and how they escorted the dead to hell.

There was something moving in the woods, and it sure wasn't a whippoorwill. Old Gooney reached for his rifle and got to his feet rather unsteadily. He'd finished more than half the squeeze since the boy left. He peered into the shadows beyond the meager ring of light cast by his fire.

"I didn't tell him nothing!" he shouted at the darkness. "There's nothing he can do to you—nobody will believe him!"

The something in the dark moved closer, and the smell of animal threatened to overpower even Old Gooney's potent stench. He took an involuntary step backward. His hands trembled as he lifted the rifle.

"I've served you! I served you as my Pappy served you! And his before him! Is this how you repay us—by

rapin' our wives and daughters? By murderin' our fa-
thers and sons?"

Old Gooney fired the rifle, but the thing swatted him
aside as if he was no more than a stinging gnat. He
landed in the cookfire, his clothes igniting with a dry
cough. His voice rose to a scream, the words a mixture
of English and some strange, unholy language unheard
since the days of the witch-hunts: *"Ia! Ia! Shubb-
Niggurath fhtagn!"*

But before Old Gooney could finish, his seven-times
great-grandfather brought a cloven hoof down on his
head, crushing it like an overripe melon.

The whippoorwills took flight.

The sheriff showed up at Billy's house the next day
and arrested him for the murder of Silas McGoohan,
better known as Old Gooney. According to Mayhew,
Billy had gone out there to silence the old man for fear
of him "telling the truth" about what happened to
Carol Anne. There was absolutely no proof, except for
his tire tracks at the scene of the crime, and after Billy's public fisticuffs with Maynard Fairweather, the
town was ready to believe him capable of anything—
including stomping a helpless old coot to a bloody
pulp and setting him and his shack on fire.

The hearing was exceptionally quick and the decision to try Billy as an adult was protested by only two
people—his public defense attorney and his father. Billy's trial was scheduled for later that year. The judge
refused to set bail, fearing Billy would flee the juris-
diction, and he was forced to spend the three months
preceding the trial in the jail over in Aylesbury.

As for Carol Anne, the weeks following her attack
proved to be equally unpleasant. After she recovered
from her stab wounds, she was transferred from the
Medical Center to the Arkham Institute for the Men-

tally Ill, where she was placed under round-the-clock supervision for the first month of her stay.

Despite repeated visits by her parents, Sheriff Mayhew, and Doctor Wagner, Carol Anne refused to talk about what happened that night, except to deny that Billy was involved. During her second month at the Institute, it was discovered that Carol Anne was pregnant. Despite pleas from all concerned, she refused to terminate, even though Doc Wagner had secured permission from the state for a therapeutic abortion. She was convinced the child belonged to Billy, and Doc Wagner, when pressed, confessed he seriously doubted the child to be the product of the rape.

Carol Anne was released into the care of her parents the week after Billy was found guilty of murder in the first degree and sentenced to die in the electric chair. Her parents watched her closely, but outside of the occasional nightmare and a suddenly acquired phobia concerning fog, she seemed her old self again. Except for the pregnancy, of course.

Mrs. Fairweather frowned at her husband, who was massaging his lower jaw as if trying to force his facial muscles into something besides a grimace. They sat opposite each other at the dinner table, with Carol Anne forming the final point of the triangle. Taking a deep breath to steady herself, Mrs. Fairweather pushed a color brochure across the table toward her daughter.

"Are you quite sure that's what you want to do, dear? I mean, you didn't even *look* at the pamphlet. I mean, the home and its grounds look quite lovely, and I'm sure the staff will be oh so nice to you, dear. . . ."

Carol Anne shook her head firmly and wadded up the brochure for the Miskatonic County Home for Young Mothers without looking at it. "I'm not putting my baby up for adoption, Mom, and that's final!"

Mrs. Fairweather shifted about uncomfortably.

"That's all well and good for you to say *now,* sweetie. But what about *school?* Principal Strickland says that having a girl in—well, in your condition, is bad for morale. Carol Anne—you're the Homecoming Queen! What kind of standard are you holding up to the other girls? If you keep the baby, I'm afraid you won't be allowed back into class come the new school year!"

"I don't care! I'm *not* giving up my baby!"

Mr. Fairweather's face went from bright red to purple as he slammed his fist onto the table, making his wife jump. "Damn it, Carol Anne! We've put up with this foolishness long enough! You stalled the doctors until it was too late, and now you're backing out of your agreement with *us!* We told you we would bring you home and not press charges against that lousy Mahan kid if you agreed to put the baby up for adoption!"

Mrs. Fairweather leaned forward and grasped her daughter's clenched fist. "Carol Anne—please, listen to reason! You keep insisting that Billy is the father. But what if he's *not?* Do you want that kind of reminder staring you in the face every day for the rest of your life? And what about the child? How do think he'll feel, growing up with people whispering behind his back. It'll be bad enough that his mother is unmarried—but to have that on top of it? Carol Anne—what will people *think?*"

Carol Anne tore herself away from her mother and stood at the end of the table, her voice trembling. "I don't *care* what anyone thinks! And despite what you and Daddy think, I know what's good for both me *and* my baby! And for the last time—Billy *is* the father! He *has* to be!"

"But, Carol Anne! Princess . . ."

"You don't understand, Daddy! You've never *understood!* All you care about is what the neighbors think and what they're gossiping about you at their stupid bridge parties!" Carol Anne sobbed, clutching her swollen belly the way she used to hug her teddy bear. "The only person who *really* cared about me was Billy—and now he's going to die, because of something he didn't even *do!*"

Before the Fairweathers could respond to their daughter's outburst, she turned and fled to her room, slamming the door shut behind her.

The prison where Billy was sent to wait out his time before his execution could be carried out was on the outskirts of Arkham. Although confined to Death Row, Billy soon learned he had special privileges denied the rest of the prison population, one of which was unrestricted access to the library. He'd been thinking about a lot of things since the night he spoke to Old Gooney. Although he'd never been one for books, there wasn't a hell of a lot to do on Death Row, especially since his father—the useless boozer—had managed to kill himself by burning down the house during a drunken bender shortly after the sentencing.

The prison library, as it turned out, was quite extensive and had a rather esoteric selection of books. Perhaps Miskatonic University being nearby had something to do with it. Billy soon found himself poring over books detailing the dark and arcane history of the surrounding countryside, some of which dated back as far as three centuries. While the accounts chronicled in the various texts were far from graphic, what they hinted about reminded Billy of what Old Gooney had rambled on about the night he was killed. Stuff about witches and sacrifices and things that lived in the wild spots that watched and waited. And the more he read, the more he worried about Carol Anne.

The week before his rendezvous with the electric chair, Billy wrote a letter to her, begging for one last meeting. He wanted to tell her good-bye and ask her forgiveness for "not being there when you needed me most."

Carol Anne showed the letter to her parents and pleaded with them. They *had* to let her go. They just *had* to. At first they were against it, but after conferring with Doc Wagner, who feared a relapse into suicidal depression, they grudgingly agreed to drive her to Arkham so she and Billy could see each other one last time.

They arrived within an hour of Billy's execution. Although it was highly irregular to do so, Carol Anne was allowed into the prisoner's cell unsupervised. Billy was sitting at a small metal desk that was built into the wall. He was busy writing something, and there were books piled next to his elbow, all of them bearing the stamp of the prison library. Billy's last meal—consisting of fried chicken, mashed potatoes, cornbread, and strawberry ice cream—sat untouched on a tray next to the single cot, the gravy and the ice cream running into one another.

"B–billy?" Carol Anne's voice was little more than a whisper.

He turned in his chair and looked at her. It was the first time they'd laid eyes on each other since that night on Lover's Lane, eight-and-a-half months ago.

Billy's hair was no longer greased into a ducktail—the prison barber had been by earlier that day and shaved his skull in preparation for the electrodes. His leather jacket and pegged jeans had been replaced by institutional denim.

Carol Anne was no longer the nubile cheerleader, her figure obliterated by her distended belly and maternity dress.

"Hi. The warden said I could only talk to you for a minute or two."

Billy got up, nodding silently. His eyes were focused on the mound of her belly. "How long?"

"Doc Wagner says the baby should be due a couple of weeks from now—a month at the most." She stepped forward, pointing her belly at him. "Feel it, Billy. Feel your baby."

Billy shook his head. "No. It's not *mine*."

Carol Anne's face crumpled inward. "You can't mean that, Billy."

"Like hell I don't! It *wants* you to think I'm the father! That way it's *safe* for it to be born!"

Carol Anne took a hesitant step backward, the look of hurt on her face replaced by fear. "Billy—you're talking crazy. You're talking like the baby is controlling me!"

"Not the baby—its *father!*"

"Billy—why are you looking at me that way?"

"I'm sorry, Carol Anne."

"Sorry?"

"Sorry I wasn't there to save you. But maybe it's not too late. Maybe I can still save you. Maybe I can save the world, too."

"Billy? What are you talking about? Billy—?"

The guards unlocked the door at the sound of the scream. They found Billy Mahan standing over Carol Anne Fairweather's battered body. Although by all accounts they had been alone for less that two minutes, the prisoner had used the time to pound the girl's head into a pulp, having hammered her skull against the edge of the toilet in the corner of the cell.

The prisoner was dragged off to the chair laughing and crying and shrieking something about goats being loose in the woods, the blood and brains of his former girlfriend congealing on his clothes. If the governor possessed any doubts concerning the execution of the troubled delinquent, this certainly erased them. Billy met his fate at the hands of the Massachusetts penal system at exactly midnight.

A huge number of whippoorwills—the largest mass sighting in the Arkham Audubon Society's records—was later reported to have taken flight at exactly 12:01.

"We are gathered here today in the sight of God to bid farewell to Carol Anne Fairweather. . . ."

Maynard Fairweather stood at his daughter's grave and wondered where they went wrong. The minister's words turned into droning as he lifted his eyes from the hole in the ground and scanned the assembled mourners.

There were quite a few of them—most were Carol Anne's schoolmates. Unused to the concept of mortality, they looked more scared for themselves than grieved for their friend. Doc Wagner was there, of course. He kept sneaking looks in Blanche's direction, no doubt checking to see how she was holding up. Sheriff Mayhew was also in attendance, looking uncomfortable in his dress uniform. The rest of the faces were unfamiliar to him—belonging to Blanche's bridge club biddies, or, worse, simple curiosity seekers. Come to get a look at the coffin of the Girl From Lovers' Lane. The one who was raped and then murdered, her brains hammered into suet by her juvenile delinquent boyfriend. The one her parents didn't even know about until it was too late.

Unable to bear the speculation in their eyes, Maynard lifted his gaze higher, scanning the surrounding headstones and vaults of Forest Glen Cemetery. Many of the monuments dated back before the Revolution. His eye wandered to the woodlands that ringed the graveyard and continued up the side of Goat Hill, then was arrested by an unfamiliar sight.

At first he was at a loss to place what seemed so odd—then he realized that the hillside facing the town was in the process of being cleared. He vaguely remembered hearing something about the old hermit's farm being bought by some land developer out of Boston. Something about a housing development—Shepherd's Meadow Estates. Even as he stared at the hill, he could see a tiny bulldozer knocking down what looked like a stone wall.

Thinking about Goat Hill made him think about Lovers' Lane, which made him think of Carol Anne again. Maynard lowered his eyes, blinking back the tears. He reached out blindly, groping for his wife's hand at his side, but couldn't find it. Then he remembered her hands were full. He glanced at Blanche from the corner of his eye. He was really proud of how she was taking it. She'd even stopped taking those damn pills of hers. She told him that they'd made a lot of mistakes with Carol Anne. Mistakes they couldn't afford to repeat, now that they'd been given a second chance. Maynard wiped his tears on his cuff and reached over to pull back the edge of the blue blanket his wife held cradled to her breast.

Carol Anne had lingered on life support for twenty hours at the Miskatonic University Medical Center. She'd remained alive just long enough for an emergency caesarean to be performed. Doc Wagner was amazed. "It's like Nature itself bent the rules so this baby could be born." Despite the trauma associated with its delivery and being premature, Carol Anne's baby was an otherwise healthy boy.

Maynard's grandson—as yet still unnamed—yawned and regarded him silently with an eye the color of cigarette smoke. Although both grandparents had searched the child's face for signs of their daughter, it appeared he took after his father. Whoever that may have been.

Doc Wagner had insisted that the child could not have been conceived as a result of the rape. He claimed that the sperm samples he'd had analyzed weren't human. Which was complete and utter hog-wash. After hearing that, Maynard was convinced that Wagner was addicted to the same pills he was so quick to prescribe to all the housewives in his care.

After the casket was lowered into the ground, Sheriff Mayhew came forward. He coughed nervously as he shook Fairweather's hand.

"I'm real sorry about all this, Maynard. Uh, I hear you and Blanche are moving to Boston."

"I put in for a transfer. There are too many memo-ries here, Jim. Blanche and I thought we'd be better off somewhere else, what with the baby and all. . . ."

"Can't say I blame you."

"Doc Wagner tells me some girl got attacked over in Dunwich the other night. That true, Jim?"

Mayhew's face twitched when he spoke. "You heard right. One of the Bishop gals got herself raped."

"And—?"

"Looks like it was the same fella. Or fellas. Look, Maynard—I better get goin'. Good luck in Boston, okay?"

Blanche Fairweather joined her husband as they walked back to the car. "What did Jim Mayhew have to say?"

"Nothing. He was just wishing us luck on the move, that's all."

"It was a nice service, don't you think? I mean, I thought it was sweet that Carol Anne's little school friends came, don't you?"

"Yes, dear."

"And the baby was so good during the whole thing! Why, he didn't cry once!" She smiled down at her grandson. "You were a good wittle boy, weren't you, lamby-pie?"

"Blanche, we're going to have to give the boy a name. We can't keep calling him 'lamby-pie.'" May-nard sighed as he opened the car door for his wife.

"I know, honey. It's just that Carol Anne never really brought up any names while she was expecting. She said if it was a boy, she'd name it after his father. But I don't want to name him after a murderer."

"Billy wasn't his father, Blanche."

"I guess not—" Mrs. Fairweather froze as she was about to get into the car, frowning in the direction of the nearby woods.

"What's the matter?" Maynard asked.

Blanche shook her head as if to clear it. "Nothing. Must have been my eyes playing tricks on me. I could have sworn I saw something moving over there. As if someone was watching us from the trees."

Blanche Fairweather tightened her grip on her grandson as the car pulled away. She didn't dare look back in the direction of her daughter's grave, for fear of discovering what she'd glimpsed had not been an illusion after all. The baby gurgled, distracting her from her train of thought.

She smiled down at him indulgently. He was going to make a handsome man, of that she was certain, although he did seem a tad swarthy. But then, women always responded favorably to the dark, Mediterranean types.

And from the sheltering shadows, the Black Goat of the Wood lifted a hand in silent farewell as his thousand-and-first get, its time come round at last, sped off into the world of mortals, to begin his father's work.

JUNGLE J.D.

by Steve Rasnic Tem

*Born in a concrete world . . .
trapped in a green hell!*

You can keep on mockin', but I can't stop rockin' . . .

Tony couldn't believe his luck. Here he had himself a *bad* girl. Joy, the baddest girl he'd ever known, and not only was she *with* him, but she was with him in a stolen Chevy making it ninety miles an hour cross-country on Route 66, and how's that for some kind of rock'n' roll legendary-type road trip? Halfway between Las Vegas, New Mexico, and Santa Fe now, give or take a few tumbleweeds. The sky wide open for dreams. It was like some kind of goddamned movie! The gang was going to shit, if he ever saw the gang again. Maybe he'd send them a picture postcard, with one of them hot dog stands shaped just like a coney on it, send it to Carson's Drugstore so they all could read it. Cool, man.

"Long as nobody got hurt." That's what his grandma woulda told him. Long as nobody got hurt—like that was the answer for everything. And maybe it was. But sometimes the answers run out, Grandma, and people—Well, you know people *do* get hurt. And deep down, Tony knew he much preferred it be the other guy what got hurt.

Tony turned his head once again to moon over Joy, and he was so excited, and it felt like maybe his head went a little too far, and he liked the feeling, so then it was like his head was spinning around like a record, but unevenly, so that every song played had a roughness to it, his head playing some angry song like Link Wray's "Rumble" over and over again. He could still see Joy through his dizziness: sitting all pretty in her yellow capri pants and pink sweater, wearing his black leather jacket—*his*—even though he'd only had it about a week he didn't mind—she just looked too cool sitting there with her pink-framed shades puffing on another cigarette and moving her butt slow with the rock of the car, making that crisp vinyl snapping sound in that rollin' rhythm like they were maybe doing it on his grandma's bedsprings.

'Course they *hadn't* done it yet even though she was so damned hot she was too cool, in charge like, but they *would* do it, Tony knew, he could tell by the way she kept her tongue in his mouth longer than any bad girl ever had before.

Tony had been in love four times in his life for sure, but this time it was the best, the very best, the coolest, the wildest. Lots better than when he was in love with plain Jane Atkins, and her daddy had to drive them places, and she didn't like it that he smoked, said it made him taste bad, not that there was *that* much tasting going on what with her old man hanging around all the time. And miles better than the Thompson twins— when they slapped you, well, you knew you'd been slapped.

"Goddamn!" Tony shouted out the window, then howled just like Wolfman Jack, just like Lon Chaney Jr. having an orgasm. He turned to Joy to catch her cool reaction and she smiled this thin, cool smile at him and blew a smoke ring. Goddamn, he wished he could blow smoke rings like Joy.

And that was about the time *it* happened.

The *its* in Tony's life were always different, and always big. The last *it* was when he decided to blast out of New Jersey and head west, taking Joy with him and using whatever transportation he could find, having it somewhere in the back of his head that they would make it to California somehow and the Beach.

It was old man Perkins' car he took, who'd just happened to have put a new tune on the vehicle, and was sitting there at the time drinking a brew with just the happiest look on his face. Tony had had to knock that smile off him when Perkins tried to stop him from taking the car. That was too bad, really it was, because Tony much preferred nobody getting hurt. That was his one rule, which was saying a lot, given how Tony felt about rules. But even that rule was a preference, because above all else Tony wasn't going to be stopped. It was only natural, the law of the jungle and everything. Ungawa! A man's gotta do what a man's gotta do. He wondered if he could wrap his mouth around Joy's pink and slippery tongue and still maintain a steady ninety miles per. Hell, nothing ventured nothing gained.

But right then Tony thought about his grandma, and that took a little bit of the fire out of him. Hell, she'd raised him and bailed him, and that had to count for something. Maybe at least she'd have a good funeral to attend someday, let her be the center of attention for once, everybody feeling sorry for this old lady who'd been saddled with this J.D. from hell when his own momma, her daughter, died on that sleezoid boyfriend's motorcycle. Anybody could have been the daddy, and that meant no daddy at all which was just fine with old Tone. Tony had left that sweet old grandmother of his all alone in their apartment. She was practically blind and she could hardly walk, so he knew it wasn't a very nice thing to do. But what else could a fellow do? A guy just couldn't be thinking about his grandmother all the time. It was like living with dead people.

Which he almost was, a couple of times, maybe three. He had a round scar the size of one of Joy's smoke rings on his forehead from that last fight with the Seventh Street Slashers. He'd open his eyes sometimes while he and Joy were kissing and he'd catch her with her eyes open, staring at *it*. Bad girls kept their eyes open when they kissed—he'd concluded that a long time ago.

Tony kind of wondered sometimes if maybe that scar was one reason he and Joy hadn't done it yet, her being grossed out or something, when he realized he was right in the middle of another big *it* because the goddamned car was rolling over and over and Joy had this funny look on her face—still cool—but her mouth was wide open but no sounds were coming out, just smoke ring after smoke ring.

It was then Tony realized what tune was playing on the radio. "Runaway," by Del Shannon, one of his absolutest favorites, but he had a feeling he might miss the end of the song. Things were spinning pretty good now, and there were little green alien types, like huge frogs, clinging to the windshield even as the car turned over and over: little green men looking in on him and Joy.

Tony woke up hot and wet like he had his head stuck to Carson's fry grill. Meat was popping and sizzling, smelly enough to make his mouth water.

He opened his eyes and salt sweat washed down from his forehead and everything went blurry. Then he remembered what had just happened and he tasted some of the stuff at the corners of his mouth expecting blood, but it was sweat like he thought, but a little heavier than he'd expected, almost like oil. He wiped the crap out of his eyes with the back of his hand.

Green surrounded him, bent down and hugged him, smothering him in tits and hair all green. He breathed it in and tried to lick it in and out of his mouth, unable to get enough. Then the green cleared a little and he could see more: the Chevy's radiator steaming and hissing, lying on top of a dead hippo whose meat was roasting in the shape of that very same radiator. Roast hippo meat wasn't a bad smell, but it was too early in the morning to be thinking about hippo burgers, so pretty soon his belly was spinning just like the car. Which there was no other sign of. But then he realized "Runaway" was still playing, although a much rougher version than he'd ever heard before, like they'd overlaid a new track with a lot of fuzz pedal in it. He looked up to find where the sound track for this dream was coming from: there was the radio, just the radio, all lit up but with no visible source of electrical power, sitting in the lower branches of a big palm tree. Now playing the opening to "Surf City."

"Here we come," Tony mumbled, "Sweet Buddy Holly." Then he threw up.

Tony looked up into a sky full of green and hair. He could hear his grandmother crying in the distance. He could hear the preacher man speaking to a milling crowd he could damn well hear but could not see.

"He hath lived fast. He hath died young. He hath delivered unto us a good-lookin' corpse."

Tony opened his eyes wide. The preacher was looking down from heaven right at him, and he looked like an ape. He *was* an ape. Then there were other ape heads right up there beside the first one: a row of smiling, goofball coconuts.

"Ah, jeez . . ."

One of the apes covered Tony's face with a leathery palm and pushed him back against the ground. Then they were dragging him faster and faster through the jungle, his head bouncing off fallen trees, rocks, and hardened lion crap. Tony had visions of being nurtured and raised by these apes, learning their ape language, becoming skilled in their jungle ways, being part of a jungle gang that roamed and hunted and killed, that did pretty much whatever they pleased. Then they came to a sudden stop before a hillside, and headed back to the trees, leaving Tony there with his head spinning. An animal looking something like a cross between a dog and a very sick house cat stuck his head out of a hole in the embankment. Then there was his twin brother, and another, another still, until the hole was filled with about a dozen of those identical ugly animal heads. One of them squirmed out of the hole, came over to Tony, sniffed him, then raised his leg and pissed on him. Then he yipped to his brothers—they all came out and pissed on him, and then they snared his clothes with their teeth and commenced dragging him through the jungle at breakneck speed again.

That entire day Tony was passed in similar ways to the tiger clan, the elephant clan, even the goddamned wildebeest clan, but he wasn't kept anywhere longer than a few sniffs and a lot of good peeing. By sunset he was bone-sore and stank to high heaven, and he'd pretty much given up on the idea of becoming intimate with any clever jungle ways.

That's when his last potential adoptive jungle family—a ten-yard-wide black mass of no-nonsense army ants—deposited him face first in front of a small jungle dwelling—a jigsaw puzzle of branches, fronds, and mud. Tony shook the jungle debris off and climbed unsteadily to his feet. A few broken sticks had been stuck to a door crudely fashioned from some salvaged crates.

A small bald head appeared in a hole in the hut wall. "Vot iss this?" the head asked him.

Tony looked at the door again with sudden understanding. The handful of broken sticks formed a swastika.

Over the next several weeks Tony was schooled in the clever jungle ways of the expatriated Nazis. They weren't such bad guys, really, although maybe just a bit intense. They liked injecting him with strange things or feeding him indescribable crap and seeing how he reacted. Mostly he reacted by throwing up.

After a while they let him inject the blacks they kept in a large pen in a nearby jungle clearing. That wasn't too bad, kind of interesting, really. The stuff he injected the blacks with must have been a lot stronger than the stuff the Nazis used on him because the blacks would scream for a long time after he injected them, roll their eyes, and stick their swollen tongues out sometimes until they bit their tongues in two or choked, sometimes both. It was actually kind of funny, sometimes, if they jumped around rubbing their balls or crapping all over themselves, say, or they screamed over and over until it was like this loud, crazy song. Now and then he'd feel a little nervous about being alone in that pen with all those crazy, naked blacks, what with just the hypo to protect him, and what with them knowing what he'd been doing to their buddies. But the Nazis had armed guards just outside the fence carrying these huge tommy guns, and guard dogs with heads the size of watermelons. When the dogs crouched by the fence and growled, showing their long, swordlike teeth, even the bravest of the blacks moved to the center of the compound. Tony figured these dogs were some kind of special Nazi jungle breed—he'd never seen anything like them in any of the pet stores in New Jersey.

He never could figure why the Nazis were injecting the blacks with all that crap, but then he figured it wasn't any of his business either. His grandma always told him, "People have their reasons." That was her other big-time saying. "Long as nobody got hurt." Yeah. But blacks don't count. Even grandma would've agreed with that. It was too bad really—Tony *loved* their music. It wasn't fair, but it was the way it was. It was nature, and half of them living in the jungle like they did, the other half in some filth-hole of a city somewhere, they *had* to know that.

After a few months the Nazis must have given up on the blacks, though—figurin' they'd never change—and they started injecting stuff into Tony again. Or maybe it had more to do with the fact that most of the blacks they had penned up were dead by then, except for a couple of near-giants, Jo Jo and Kang, who had always been a pain to mess with.

Or maybe they were done with their *animal* tests, and now they were ready for the *real* thing. Ungawa.

Actually, Tony didn't mind particularly. Life in the jungle had proved to be a lot less interesting than in the Tarzan movies. It was hot, it was steamy, and other than poisoning the blacks or playing poker with the Nazis there wasn't much to do. He'd tried to swim the local river once, but what with the alligators, hippos, and eels it was a lot more crowded than your average Jersey pool, and almost as nasty.

He tried making friends with some of the local animals. "We're of one blood," he'd say as a surefire junglecratic opener. "I am a cub of the . . . the Nazi clan. And you?"

But they either ignored him, shit on him, or tried to eat him.

So he let the Nazis shoot him up with practically everything in their mad scientist pharmacy, as well as with whatever they could find crawling around on the jungle floor that could be jammed into their giant Germanic steel Mixmaster.

And some of it wasn't all that bad. After one particularly good jolt, Tony decided that the lead Nazi, a guy named Fritz, looked pretty good in leather. Tony's leather jacket, in fact.

And as they say only in the movies, that brought him to his senses.

"Joy! What have you done with my Joy?"

"Ya, ya. Der jungle be a sad place sometime. Iss not Fritz's fault, however."

Tony was staring right at Fritz when the Nazi's head disappeared into a cloud of blood. The rest of the Nazi's body stood upright a moment, long enough for the mist to form its first blood drops on Tony's leather jacket, before it toppled forward, revealing the two giant blacks, Jo Jo and Kang, massive bloodstained stones clutched in each of their massive hands.

Tony's bowels suddenly filled with wet, jungle heat. But he couldn't move.

Jo Jo dropped his stones, which bounced unnoticed off his foot and a knee. He reached over and stripped the jacket off the Nazi's back with a single offhand gesture. He brought the jacket up to his nose, sniffing loudly with nostrils that looked like bowling ball holes. "Hmmmm . . . white jungle princess," he declared.

"Joy? You can find Joy?"

The giant Jo Jo slipped his arms into the jacket, apparently oblivious to the numerous splits he was creating throughout the leather. "We take you . . . her place."

"Ju ju!" Kang shouted excitedly, jumping up and down, feet thundering on the jungle floor.

Leave it to a black to get even his best friend's name wrong, Tony thought, but he nodded and smiled anyway. After all, the guy *was* humongous.

Jo Jo slapped Kang across the face and the giant immediately stopped his gibbering. Then the two of them headed away from the Nazi compound with strides so long Tony choked on his spit trying to keep up.

Tony heard the drums starting up shortly after they lost sight of the Nazi huts. Kang started squalling, "Ju ju! Ju ju!" again, and Jo Jo had to slap some calm into him yet again. Actually, Tony kind of liked the accompaniment. He thought it was kind of Bill Haley, and what better omen than that?

A few things happened along the way, but something always happened when you had to take a long jungle road trip. Jo Jo jumped into the river and roiled around with a croc for awhile, but it was a little like watching some fat broad in a bad porno flick making it with the black stud, so Tony lost interest pretty quickly. Kang kept running away and Jo Jo kept dragging him back, until finally the lions got Kang which was kind of a good thing since Jo Jo seemed to be getting pretty pissed off at the way Kang kept mispronouncing his name.

The distant drums never let up, though, and Tony was getting pretty tired of that, and now that they were in the swamp country the mosquitoes were about the size of Fender guitars and just as mean. Things kept sliding over Tony's shoes down in the mud, and more than a couple of times Jo Jo had to pull something off him, but Tony couldn't see much detail down there in the swampy dark.

Then finally they were out, and they were in this sunny place, and there was a car radio up in every

bright yellow and pink palm tree, and each radio was
playing a different Beach Boys tune, "Surfin' " and
"Surfin' Safari" and "Surfin' U.S.A." and "Surfer
Girl" all blending together into this crazy, hypnotic
cacophonic medley that made Jo Jo gyrate and kick up
the sand and made Tony desperate to follow his every
single move, which he could not possibly do, what
with being a white trash punk from Jersey.

Then he saw Joy, still wearing those cool shades of
hers and blowing smoke rings, in the teeniest leopard
skin bikini he'd ever seen, sitting up on what was left
of the stolen Chevy, which looked pretty swell up on
blocks on the beach glistening.

But before he could say anything to her the giant
black Jo Jo bounded over to her and gave her the long-
est, deepest, wettest soul kiss Tony could imagine outside a nightmare. And Joy sure wasn't resisting any.

"Ah, jeez, Joy! You *are* a *bad* girl!" Tony shouted.
And then he saw all the beautiful little brown-yellow
babies with the curly hair playing around the front seat
of the Chevy. "A *bad*, *bad* girl!" And Joy just winked,
and blew this huge smoke ring, even with Jo Jo's huge
tongue in her mouth.

About that time these big planes roared overhead,
bigger than anything Tony had ever seen outside a science fiction movie, and these men came zooming by
with jets on their backs just like the Rocketmen, and
Joy and Jo Jo were waving at them and their little
brood of mixed bloods were jumping up and down
with all this natural athletic ability they'd obviously in-
herited from their daddy.

"Ah, jeez, so *bad!*" Tony shouted, as the Nazi sub-
marine came up out of the shallow waters. The hatch
opened, and there were all the Nazi jungle clan, his
clan, and they were fighting off the apes and lions and
crocs trying to board the sub, with the Rocketmen
coming up fast behind.

Tony didn't have much choice. He dived into the ocean, spitting up saltwater as he swam toward the Nazis and their special jungle ways, and a past where he belonged.

THE BLOOD ON SATAN'S HARLEY

by Gary Jonas

*A hellrider of the apocalypse,
he burned rubber on that blackest patch of highway
where demons dwell!*

Joe Crane roared into Onkawa, Oklahoma like a pissed-off demon bent on destruction. His Harley growled as he downshifted and moved through the sparse traffic. Who was this mysterious vigilante he'd heard so much about? How many bikers had the bastard offed?

Joe parked his hog at the diner and looked up and down Main Street. It was the last day of October and the air was beginning to bite like a junkyard dog. Across the street was a video store advertising Halloween specials on horror movies. Next to that was a hardware store. Two old men sat on a bench glaring at him, but Joe didn't give a shit. He was used to the stares he attracted.

He was a big man with long brown hair and steel-blue eyes. A former linebacker for the Oakland Raiders, he'd given up football when they moved the team to L.A., a city he hated. Now he roamed the highways of America, living free and easy.

As Joe approached the diner, an old woman darted around the corner and clutched at the sleeve of his leather jacket. "You seek revenge," she said. Her voice sounded like fingernails scraping a blackboard.

Joe looked at her and raised an eyebrow. Her eyes were solid white. She didn't face him as she whispered, only gazed sightlessly at the street.

"The man you seek rides the highway after midnight, slaying all who dare to ride motorcycles into his domain."

"That's right," Joe said. "I'm here to kill him!"

"He is already dead. He lost a battle on that highway. His head was severed by a biker like yourself. He will not rest until his head is returned to his body."

Joe rolled his eyes. "Shit, lady, I saw that TV show. Headless biker, my ass."

"Don't ignore the legend, Joe! Heed my warning!"

"Lady, I'm not your guide dog, so you'd better get out of my way," Joe said and pushed through the glass door into the diner.

The old broad was fucked in the head. But how did she know his name? Maybe she was an old football fan; he ran into one every now and then. But this woman was blind. Joe had never done the suit-and-tie color commentator bit, and he sure as hell hadn't done much talking on the football field.

Damn. He didn't have time to worry about it. A middle-aged woman stood behind the counter. "We're closed," she said. Her name badge said *Marge*.

Joe grinned. "What if I said *open sesame?*"

"We don't want no trouble," Marge whispered.

"Any trouble," Joe corrected. "And if you'll toss a thick steak on the grill, you won't have any. I like it so rare that when I cut into it, it screams. Got it?"

Marge glared at him for a moment, then nodded and pulled a steak out of the refrigerator. Joe took a seat at the counter. There were two other customers in the diner. A woman Joe might have found attractive if he'd been drinking a lot, and a twelve-year-old boy—

obviously the woman's son. The boy said something about "that man" and his mother whispered at the kid to shut up. Joe grinned and slipped off his leather jacket and removed his dark shades, tucking them into his shirt pocket. He adjusted his shoulder holster and waited for his steak.

Before it arrived, the sheriff entered the diner. The first thing the man's eyes focused on was Joe's .38. "You got a permit to carry a weapon?" asked the sheriff.

Joe slapped his gun permit on the counter. "Right here."

The sheriff picked it up and shook his head. "This ain't from Oklahoma, sir."

Joe shrugged.

The sheriff took a deep breath. "I'd appreciate it if you'd keep the weapon out of sight, sir. Folks in this town don't cotton to strangers."

"I've noticed," Joe said. "In fact, that's why I'm here."

The sheriff sighed. "Don't tell me you're after the vigilante."

"The bastard killed a friend of mine and I'm willing to bet he's not in jail."

The sheriff rubbed his eyes. "No one knows who the vigilante is. Leastwise, they ain't saying. I've tried to catch him, but I've had no luck. Son of a bitch killed a policeman from Tulsa. We're after him, all right."

Joe kind of liked the sheriff. He seemed like a decent man who didn't pass judgment. Joe'd had trouble with lawmen before, but instinct told him that this man was different. "Well, Sheriff, I'll find him. You can bet your badge on that."

The sheriff sat down on the stool next to Joe and leaned in. He whispered, "What you're about to hear? I never said it. Understood?"

Joe nodded.

"This vigilante fella. We figure he's a biker like you. Rides a Harley and kills anyone who rides a motorcycle down his lonely stretch of highway between midnight and five a.m. Cuts off their heads. Including cops. We've been after him for almost a year, but the bastard's got the luck of the devil. At midnight. On Halloween night. With a bitch-harem of black cats crossin' his path."

The sheriff shook his head. "We tried sending a cop on a bike—the Tulsa cop I mentioned. The vigilante chopped off his head and left it on the doorstep at the police station. No one else volunteered to ride down that road."

"Figures," Joe said, thinking back to the old lady. What if the killer really was dead? That would explain why Karl died—he sure as hell wouldn't lose to a *living* man. Maybe the sheriff was dead-solid right with that *luck of the devil* line. Joe shrugged; he'd seen a lot of weird shit on the road. He'd be ready for anything.

"You're planning on going out there, ain't you?"

Joe nodded.

"You and me," the sheriff said, "we never talked."

"Never even seen you before," Joe said.

The sheriff left the diner and Marge set a huge steak on the counter before Joe. When he cut into it, the blood stained the plate red.

The night air held its breath as Joe raced down the highway. He felt the vigilante's presence before he saw him. Clad in black leather from neck to toe, the vigilante blended into the darkness as if it owned him. Joe knew it wasn't a trick of the light or an acid flashback. The rider who followed him had no head. From time to time as Joe glanced back, it looked as if blood were spurting from the dead man's neck.

Joe smiled as he gunned his Harley along the treacherous winding curves of Highway 10. At each curve he leaned so far that an observer would have thought he was laying the bike down. Joe loved this kind of ride. It reminded him that he was still alive. If you didn't flirt with death from time to time, you could forget how wonderful life was. Joe lived his life on the edge where each breath could be his precious last.

"Come on, you Sleepy Hollow reject!" Joe called over his shoulder. "Come and get me!" *Like you got Karl.*

The only sound was the roar of Joe's Harley. The vigilante's hog whispered along the road like a ghost. The headless rider leaned forward as if to cut down on wind resistance and surged ahead, gaining ground.

Joe smiled, keeping an eye on him in the rearview.

The rider suddenly sat up straight and produced a sword from within his jacket. The blade reflected moonlight. Even from a single glance in his rearview, Joe could tell the blade was stained with the blood of many bikers.

The road arced around a bend and the guardrail was broken before a steep embankment. Joe swung his Harley around and screeched to a halt facing back the way he'd come. He pulled his .38 and waited until his pursuer whipped around the curve.

"Kiss your ass good-bye," Joe said and squeezed off three shots into the headless rider's chest.

The rider flew off the back of his jet black Harley. The bike itself soared off the road and crashed down the embankment. The rider landed on his back and slid off the road, but caught himself on the shoulder, clutching at dirt and rocks and grass until he stopped. His sword lay in the middle of the road.

"Shit," Joe said. He'd hoped the rider would follow the bike. But what the hell, maybe this turn of events would buy him an adrenaline rush worth remembering.

The vigilante climbed to his feet. A dozen black cats, their eyes glowing neon green, weaved a path around the dead man's heavy black boots. Joe raised the .38 and pulled the trigger. The headless figure jerked back, momentarily scattering the cats, but then continued forward. Joe shot him again with the same effect.

He shoved the .38 back in his shoulder holster and twisted the gas, jerking the handlebars to the right so the back tire swung around. Demon cats screamed under heavy rubber tread and went flying every which way in a shower of blood and fur, and then Joe's hog knocked the headless killer on his ass.

Joe parked the Harley on the shoulder and climbed off. The dead man stood and moved toward Joe, who smiled. He hadn't had a good fight in a long time. Back when he'd played football, he'd been ejected from the game numerous times for fighting.

This time he could be ejected from life.

"Bring it on, pal," Joe said.

The headless man rushed forward. Joe punched him in the stomach, but the dead man grabbed him around the waist and lifted him off the ground. Joe tried to twist free, but the vigilante smashed him to the ground, knocking the wind out of him. Joe rolled to his feet, trying to catch his breath, the stink of brimstone filling his lungs. He spun around with a back spin kick, but the vigilante blocked it and punched him in the face.

The pain felt good. Joe tasted blood and grinned. They traded blows. Joe kicked the headless man in the balls, to no effect. The vigilante slammed his fists into Joe's chin time and again, the blows landing with jackhammer force. Joe fell back and shook his head clear. This wasn't as much fun as fighting a live man, Joe decided. Getting hit wasn't so bad, but you liked to be able to hurt your opponent. Dead men felt no pain.

Joe guided the fight onto the highway. The vigilante landed a solid blow to Joe's eye. Blood blurred his vision. He let the dead biker hit him with a solid uppercut that knocked him off his feet. When he hit the road, he reached out and clutched the vigilante's fallen sword.

Joe rose, holding the sword like a samurai warrior. When the headless man reached for him, Joe chopped the vigilante's arm off. Then he dropped low and cut the demon's legs out from under him. Then he sliced off the other arm. He thought about keeping a trophy, but decided against it. He tossed the sword over the embankment, then picked up the torso of his opponent.

The old lady had said the vigilante wouldn't rest until his head was reattached to his body. *Good,* Joe thought. For killing Karl, he'd never get that rest. But Joe decided to make sure the bastard couldn't kill anyone else. He threw the torso into the sweet bye and bye.

"Let's see you pull yourself together now, asshole," Joe said. He picked up the legs and arms and carried them to his bike. The fingers of the dead man still wriggled, clutching at air. Joe started the Harley and screeched off down the highway. A mile down the road he hurled the dead man's left leg into the high grass along the shoulder. A couple miles farther along, he stopped at a bridge and tossed the man's right leg into the river, watching for a moment as the water carried the gruesome trophy out of sight. After another couple miles, he threw the left arm into the woods. He stopped a few miles farther and tossed the right arm, fingers still clenching and unclenching, into a ditch.

Joe thought about his buddy who'd died on that lonely highway. Now that his killer had been dealt with, Joe was sure that Karl was free to roam the highways of the night on a sleek black ghost Harley. Maybe someday, Joe would meet up with him and they'd shoot the shit about the good ol' days when the drugs were cheap and the women were easy.

Smiling at the thought, Joe rode into the night, sure in the knowledge that somewhere up ahead there'd be a diner with a surly waitress and a thick steak that would cook up bloody and rare.

I WAS A TEENAGE BOYCRAZY BLOB

by Nina Kiriki Hoffman

Growing ... growing ...
a test-tube terror with a hunger that knew no bounds!

Sometimes don't you just want to eat everything? Not because you're hungry, but because it's annoying you, and if you absorb it you might be able to control it, or at least make it shut up?

My sixteenth year was like that.

All the good-looking girls, the ones with hair long enough to tie back into ponytails, the ones who wore circle skirts and little sweaters that their Peter Pan collars lay down flat over, they all had cute boyfriends and swell social lives.

I, Patty LeFevre, had two girlfriends who were losers and lowlifes like me, and we knew a few boys—Mooch, Vic, Tony—who would whistle at us if they were in a moving car and we were on the sidewalk, but as for face-to-face conversation, forget it. These were the kind of boys who would know more about your shoes than your face because that's where they would be staring. These were the kind of boys who had trouble getting two words or more out of their mouth in a straight string. These were the kind of boys, in short, who were a perfect match for the kind of girls Rita, Cathy, and I were. We all kind of resented that.

I mean, so Buddy Holly wrote some cool songs and sang them okay. Wouldn't you rather be seen with Elvis?

So it was Saturday night, date night, and people with dates were out in cars or at the movies or at the Foster's Freeze or at that abandoned house in the woods that Buck Nilson had found and set up like a dance club or someplace else that was so cool we didn't even know about it.

It was Saturday night, and Cathy, Rita, and I were at the Carnegie Library, the way we were every Saturday night. Not to read, of course. To plot and plan.

"Maybe I should just cut it all off," Rita said, pulling her thick frizzy black hair back to try to make it disappear.

"You would look like a clown," said Cathy, who didn't mince words. She had long limp dishwater blonde hair that was so fine it made a ponytail about a pencil thick, and lay like a rat's tail flat on her back. She wore it down instead, which wasn't much better. And she had thick glasses which made her eyes look giant and not quite human. When she really looked at you, you felt like you were under a microscope.

"Cutting off all your hair would be pretty drastic," I said, trying to tone Cathy down, the way I always did. "There must be a reasonable alternative."

"My mom keeps telling me to just braid it," Rita said, "but that makes me look like a ten-year-old. You don't think Yvonne ever has this problem, do you?"

Yvonne had thick bleached blonde hair that pulled back into a ponytail any pony would be proud to claim.

"No," Cathy and I said together. Yvonne never had any problems that we could see.

"Maybe if I wore a brighter color of lipstick nobody would notice my hair," said Rita.

"That'll never work," said Cathy. "It's too easy. We're never going to get boyfriends without a lot of hard work, so we might as well concentrate on developing our strengths. Let's have an update on Project: Manhunt. Have you made any progress with project The-Way-to-a-Man's-Heart, Rita?"

Rita's face screwed up. She was supposed to be discovering the ultimate cookie recipe. "No," she whispered.

"Why not?"

"After I burned that last batch so bad, Mom won't let me in the kitchen anymore. She had to buy new baking sheets."

Cathy adjusted her glasses and glared at Rita. "Well, that's not very resourceful of you. You could have asked me or Patty if you could cook at one of our houses."

"I have homework," Rita whispered.

"Oh, please," said Cathy. "Tomorrow afternoon, you come over to my house and start baking. Patty, have you come up with a science project yet?"

"Yeah, I have this idea about chemically treating cellulose viscose in the post-spinneret acid solution to create a stronger polymer for—"

"Good, good," said Cathy. "Keep an eye on those scientific boys. Even though they look like jerks now, they might make good money later. Try to get them to think about dating." Then she frowned. "What happened to your idea to research special perfumes that attract male animals to females?"

I shook my head. "Professor Brandon wouldn't approve that study," I said. "But he did give me a key to the lab so I can work after school unsupervised."

"Wow," she said. Her eyes narrowed behind her glasses. "There's got to be a way we can use that. Could you run both projects at once?"

I blanked. "I don't know. Maybe." That would mean spending a lot of time in the lab—maybe missing dinner. Which might be a good idea; I wasn't sure. I had considered keeping careful notes about what Cathy and Rita and I ate and then measuring our weights and trying to figure out why they stayed small while I got bigger and bigger, when as far as I could tell, I wasn't eating any more than they were, but I knew Cathy would never approve a project like that. Without her cooperation, I couldn't do it. I glanced out the window. If I were picking my own projects to do, they wouldn't involve making fancy cloth or special perfume. I would rather study fossils or explore jungles or cook up some really terrific rocket fuel.

Out in the parking lot, Vic and Mooch and Tony were leaning on Mooch's powder-blue convertible and staring up at the window I was looking out of. I'd been noticing them there the past couple of weeks. Maybe they had plans, too.

"And how about your project, Cathy?" I asked. "Any new insights from Project: Ear-to-the-Door?"

"Milton hasn't brought any basketball players by the house since last week," said Cathy.

"You could be resourceful. You could sneak into the locker rooms and listen from there."

"Don't be ridiculous, Patty."

I shrugged.

"They would kill me if they caught me," Cathy said.

"Oh, well," I said. I thought her project of listening in on her brother and his friends took a lot less effort than Rita's and mine, but things with Cathy were never quite fair. That was the price we paid for hanging out with her and sucking up her ideas. Before Cathy came to Rolling Rock High, Rita and I had been loser low-lifes with no plans at all.

I worked late in the lab every night that week, telling my parents that I would eat a nice dinner of cheese and crackers after I got home. It would have cheered me up if they had worried about me breaking curfew, but they knew I never had dates; they never waited up for me or asked me uncomfortable questions the next morning. I was too tired to eat by the time I got home every night, and by breakfast time I was feeling too ill to eat much more than oatmeal. Lunch was, of course, cafeteria food. I was all for sucking up gelatin with a straw, but a lot of the other food left me cold, especially the every-Friday offering of breaded fish plywood.

By Friday night I was feeling weak and woozy from fumes and lack of food. That night I was running the pheromone experiment on one lab table and cooking up a vat of viscose under the safety hood while mixing up my acid bath on the other table. I was pretty sure I was close to a breakthrough on the pheromone experiment. I had tried a little of Batch Six at lunch that afternoon and saw guys who never gave me a second look—football players, the class president—turn around as I walked by. After actually seeing me, they turned away again, but I thought this was a good start. And Vic—well, old Vic had definitely drooled *while* staring at me.

I didn't think my weakened physical state would affect my experiments. When I looked over my notes every morning, they seemed just as precise and detailed as ever, and the time notations showed that I had been alert all the hours I was in the lab. But I was short on sleep that night, and short on stamina, and there was this really irritating electrical storm going on. The most irritating thing about it was that every time the thunder boomed I jerked awake and realized for a second that I had been sleepwalking through my procedures, but I couldn't stay awake long enough to shut down all my work and get myself out of the lab.

Finally a bolt of lightning hit somewhere on campus. The electricity went out, although the bunsen burners kept flaming. I thought I'd better turn them off before anything else happened, but as I headed toward the ta-

ble with my pheromone experiment I tripped over my
viscose vat. It splashed all over my feet and legs. It
burned! Falling, I grabbed for the nearest thing, which
turned out to be the acid bath solution. As I pitched
forward, I felt it burn into my skin. I was still reaching,
and I managed to knock over my pheromone experiment, too. I barely had time to feel upset about all the
work I was losing before my head hit the cement floor.

Waking up was a new and different experience. I
couldn't figure out how to open my eyes. I kept trying
to lift my eyelids, but I didn't seem to have any eyelids. And then again, I was . . . *tasting* more things than
I ever had before. It felt like my skin had turned into
a giant tongue. I tasted air and cement and chemical
fumes and dust and skin flakes and some other stuff
that I somehow knew what it was but I didn't feel like
admitting that I knew. Suffice it to say humans and
other animals excrete and exfoliate and otherwise ex-
own a lot of various fluids and solids, and I knew what
they all were without ever having been aware of them
in this particular tasty way before.

What was worse: I wanted more. More of, like, everything.

It didn't take me too long to figure out how to move.
While I was tasting the floor, I was feeling it with my
underside, too, and I realized that if I sort of thought
myself in one direction or another, I moved across new
stretches of floor, and what was my underside turned
into my upper side, and topside turned to bottom. Also
I could gather myself up tight or spread out thin. Everything tasted terrific, even stuff my brain, such as it
was, identified as disgusting.

I didn't realize I could hear until the school bell
went off. Sound was a different experience, too—it
pressed against my skin. I didn't have ears, but I un-

derstood what I was hearing, even though I was hearing it in a new way.

I waited to see if I would hear or somehow sense the onrush of activity the bell usually signaled, students racing up and down the halls, doors slamming, talk and shouts, but I heard nothing like that. Was I actually deaf as well as blind? How come I could hear the bell, then?

Saturday. Of course, it was Saturday. The school bell must be on automatic. It couldn't tell a school day from a weekend or a holiday.

I rolled toward where the door had been, or at least where I thought it had been. I found the crack under it, so I gathered myself together and reached up for the doorknob. I pressed myself around it. Golly, it tasted good. So many different hands had grabbed it since it was last cleaned. For a minute I couldn't think about anything but the taste, but then I absorbed everything tasty and remembered that I was trying to open the door.

I couldn't seem to get a grip on the handle, though. I knew I had some sort of muscular structure—after all, I could move—but grip wasn't in my behavior repertoire. I spread out to think about it.

There was the crack under the door. I pushed part of myself under it, waiting until the rest of me was too big to get through, but that didn't happen. Eventually all of me had slid out under the door. Cool! I licked off the outside doorknob and flowed down the hall.

Something poked me. I stopped and gathered myself into a near-sphere. It poked me again. It tasted pretty good, and I could also taste in the air an intensification of human particles. What was happening? I flowed up around the poking thing and discovered—

Oh, man alive, I don't really want to talk about this next part, but I'm a scientist. I can't shy away from the facts even when I don't like them.

Okay. Okay. It was a human hand. In fact it was Swen the janitor's hand. I flowed up, over, and around it and tasted ambrosia, nectar, the most delicious thing I'd ever eaten, squared. I hadn't realized how hungry I had gotten, all those days and nights without proper nutrition. I engulfed the hand. I flowed up the arm. Swen struggled and screamed and tried to get loose from me, but I was so in love with all his molecules— though his clothes didn't interest me—that I just kept grabbing more and more of him, phagocytosing and pinocytosing for all I was worth. Yum! Even his struggles improved his bouquet. What a guy.

What a guy. The best meal I had ever eaten. And I was still kind of hungry . . . and outside there were a lot of other guys, I just knew it.

As I flowed down the hall toward the stairwell, I realized that I had grown. For an instant I wished I could hold a pen and see to write something, because keeping track of the changes I was undergoing would have been true to the scientific method. Oh, well. I had other fish to fry.

I found the door of the building—I still seemed to have my good sense of direction—and oozed out under it. It occurred to me that whatever I looked like would probably seem strange to people who saw me on the street. People. Yum. I wondered if they would approach me, maybe poke me with a stick or a broom handle the way Swen had, or if they would run away. I would have to experiment.

So it was Saturday morning. Where would everybody be? Shooting hoops, maybe, cruising around, maybe, sleeping in after a wild Friday night. Chances were that people who got up early would be at the Foster's Freeze, two blocks away from the high school, having curly fries for breakfast instead of hot cereal or eggs.

I thought about Freez-E, the Foster's Freeze mascot,

a little ice cream cone with a goofy face on it and a
loop of soft ice cream curl at the top standing in for
hair. I had always been suspicious of talking food,
dancing food, food with faces, and more and more often food had been talking/singing/dancing on television
commercials. What were advertisers thinking? People
wanted to eat things they could converse with? What
next, talking toilets?

But my perspective had undergone a severe shift. I
was anxious to eat any talking, singing, dancing thing
with a face I could get my—well, my whatever on. I
oozed, flowed, crept, leaped, slid, glided along the
sidewalk, straining whatever senses I had for signs of
life.

Car engines revved not far off. A dog barked. Birds
sang. I oozed over sidewalk and used chewing gum
and cigarette butts and drips from ice cream and all
kinds of other interesting tastes. I scraped across bottle
caps; they didn't hurt me. I reached out and tasted
some grass beside the sidewalk. Yuck. Not my cup of
tea. Which was a pity.

"Hey!" someone yelled. I didn't recognize the voice.
It sounded female. "What in heaven's name—" and the
impact of feet hitting earth, moving away from me
rather than toward me. I wondered if I should follow.
I thought about Mooch's powder-blue convertible,
about Mooch and Vic and Tony, who suddenly seemed
like the most desirable people in the world. I didn't
need them to string two words together or to look at
my face. All I needed was for them to be themselves,
their own delicious selves. If anybody was going to be
at the Foster's Freeze this early in the morning, it
would be those three, hoping that somebody more interesting would show up so they could edge near
enough to *feel* like they were doing something.

I oozed on. I had to drop down off the curb and
cross a street. I could hardly look both ways. I won-

dered what would happen to me if a car ran over me. Would I just get thin in places and then be able to regroup? Or was my brain in danger of being hit? My brain was now capable of being thin enough to slip under a door. Somehow I didn't feel threatened.

Water was running along the street, right near the curb. I could hear the repetitive sound of a rainbird somewhere nearby. The flowing water tugged at me, whispering that we were twins and it would show me a really cool place to go. Substantially weird—how could water have a voice? For a minute part of me formed a dam, but the water just built up and flowed over me, heading toward lower ground. What cool stuff. I felt poetically attracted to it. Then I thought, *Hey, what's the story here? I'm not a beatnik. Bring on the boys.*

So I made it across the street and up the opposite curb. I was cruising now.

Sirens and cars approached, probably together. I wondered if I should hide, and then thought, *Yeah, right!* How could I find a hiding place without eyes? And what could anybody do to me, anyway? It might be interesting to find out.

Cars screeched up to the curb and their engines stopped. Doors slammed. "What the—" said more than one male voice. I slowed and drew myself up into a sphere again, angling toward them. *Yes, my pretties, my little appetizers, come closer,* I thought, and I could hear them coming.

"What's that smell?" whispered somebody.

"Barbecuing steak?"

"The best pipe tobacco in the whole world?"

"Just-mowed grass on a baseball diamond right before the game?"

"Twelve-year-old single malt scotch?"

"Chocolate chip cookies hot out of the oven," said somebody else, putting a hand flat against me. I savored him, making myself take my time. I loved everything about this guy.

He didn't start screaming until a couple of minutes later, and by then I had a grip on two or three of the others.

Bullets didn't seem to affect me at all, I noticed absentmindedly; I was paying much more attention to my taste treats. Their panic enhanced their flavor. Somebody tried to set me on fire, but that didn't work either. Actually, it felt rather nice. A woman turned a hose on me. I was too busy to listen to water words.

I tasted and savored and devoured and engulfed. All the screaming around me just made things sweeter. And in the end, nothing stopped me from resuming my journey toward the Foster's Freeze.

"What is it? Where did it come from? What is it doing? What does it want? Did you know it already killed three people? All that was left behind was their clothes and shoes. Do something! Burn it! Poison it! Shock it! Bomb it! Chop it into little pieces!"

I was temporarily sated. I was serene. I oozed on.

Somebody did manage to run over me with a car. I gathered myself together and continued. Someone poured acid on me. It tasted all right. Somebody dropped a grenade on me. The explosion was quite tasty, all those excited gases trying to spread outward. Air raid sirens went off, fire engine sirens went off, cop car sirens went off. Radios talked in excited voices about menaces to mankind. People ran back and forth just outside the range of my reach. Guns threw bullets at me; they went right on through and I closed up the holes they left behind. Somebody shot a missile at me, but it did the same thing. *Can't shoot a cloud,* I thought. *If I were being scientific, how would I stop me?* I wondered. I couldn't think of a way offhand.

They had evacuated the Foster's Freeze by the time I got there, which depressed me. I went inside anyway and oozed up into the rotating pie display. I had never been able to eat all the pies I wanted. The Foster's Freeze had all kinds: blueberry, cherry, banana creme, coconut creme, chocolate, lemon meringue, rhubarb, mince, and custard. I ate them all. Somehow they just couldn't compete with the tastes of all the other things I had been eating lately.

I went after a half-eaten hamburger somebody had left on a table. It tasted okay, but it still wasn't nectar or ambrosia. I stuck a pseudopod down into somebody's leftover milk shake. Yikes! Rather than me absorbing it, it moved all around my pseudopod and hurt me somehow.

Ice cream: dangerous. I made a mental note.

I fled out into the sunlight. Boy, did it feel good. There was still a lot of people noise, and the taste of fear and panic in the air. I sat on the pavement and let the sun thaw out my pseudopod and wondered what to do next.

Maybe it was time to get down to business. I thought about boys again, and begin wishing some would show up. *Come to me, come to me. I am everything you've ever dreamed of.*

"Mooch!" yelled a girl's voice.

Cathy!

"What's the matter with you, Tony?" cried Rita's voice. "We just came to look! Get back here. That thing is dangerous!"

Boys, I am your dream. I can fulfill all your desires. I can make you feel really good. Come closer, my dear entrees.

"Vic, no!" yelled Cathy. "Can't you hear me? Stop!"

They were coming to me, boys I hadn't really dreamed of, boys I'd almost let into my mind as possibilities. You could dream about Buck Nilson or Todd Baker. You could fantasize about those guys ever noticing you and saying something heart-throbby, like, "What beautiful eyes you have," or, "I love you."

Or you could be realistic. Scientific. Admit that you'd never find anybody better than Vic or Mooch or Tony to love, and start thinking about how to convince Vic or Mooch or Tony of the same thing. It was hard to be scientific around Cathy, who had grand dreams, but I had been working my way toward it when this whole thing happened.

I could taste their approach in the air. All three of them. *Yes,* I thought. *I'll give you what you really want. Anything you really want. Come to me.*

A fragment of my mind separated from the rest. *Patty, what on Earth are you doing?* it said. *You're killing people! Goodness gracious, you're even contemplating killing people you sort of like, not enemies like the ones we had in World War II, or the Russkies with their stupid Sputnik. Thou shalt not kill, Patty. Thou shalt not kill!*

Be quiet, I thought, *who cares. Nobody ever cared about me while I was . . . me. Why should I care about them?*

Care about them because they're human beings. Anyway, how can you tell if they ever cared about you? Did you ask them?

How come Cathy and Rita are hanging out with Mooch and Tony? How come nobody asked me?

Well, you weren't exactly easy to reach last night, or any night this week.

They knew where I was.

Give them the benefit of the doubt, said this annoying mind fragment.

I could taste Vic; he was the closest. I could almost taste his whole substance even though he hadn't touched me yet. Brylcream and zit medicine and shaving lotion, skin and bone and blood, ketchup on his breath, sex on his mind, soap on his skin. A total nirvana of a snack.

I wanted him *so much.*

At that moment somebody turned fire hoses on all of us—maybe they wanted to wake up the boys or maybe they wanted to wash me away. I could have resisted. I could have grabbed the boys before the water drove me away. I reached out a pseudopod toward Vic, but then I retracted it. I listened to the water instead.

Come, come, shatter, re-form, come with us, it said as it hit me hard. *Flow, travel, seek!*

I let it take me. I joined with it.

We sought. We sought our way down storm drains where we joined with other water and all sorts of tasty things that water had brought with it from its explorations all over. I spread myself out along the sewer ways. I absorbed all kinds of tasty tidbits, including an occasional rat. I sought and explored and spread and survived.

All in all, I kind of like it here. Occasionally I reach up for a truly heavenly treat, but only occasionally.

My most difficult challenge is that Vic went into sewer work when he graduated from high school. He comes down here sometimes, smelling like himself, but smelling all grown up, and I keep wanting him.

So far, I've managed to restrain myself.

BULLETS CAN'T STOP IT

by Wayne Allen Sallee

*A towering terror ... beyond reason, beyond
imagination!*

Believe you me, what happened at the drive-in that
night was something else. I wish I could retell the story
with sound effects that would fit our terror, though that
might actually make it something more humorous, like
in *Invasion of The Saucer-Men*. Now that was like a
cartoon, with a harp being played while Frank
Gorshin's character was being knocked flat by his
buddy. Yeah, just visualize in your head the things we
came up against in that one hour. If you saw the movie,
even once, well then you could get a pretty good picture. And—get this segue here—to start *this* particular
picture off right, I'll run down the cast of characters:
There was myself, Aubrey Maddox, and I guess I'm
the skinniest of the bunch, and my best buddy Johnny
Coronette, and a neighbor girl of his, Gloria Talbot.
Johnny knew even more about old 1950s monster movies than I did, and that surprised me when I first met
him because he certainly had a decent physique and
probably should have been hitting the big screen at the
Colony or Marquette with a different girl every weekend instead of hanging around with the likes of me.

Gloria was younger than the two of us, and Johnny

had brought her along to get a scare out of her. See, the drive-in was one of those virtual reality thrill machines where your favorite movie scenes get programmed through head goggles and isometric gloves. Johnny could rattle off every movie Richard Denning ever acted in from *Creature From The Black Lagoon* to *Black Scorpion,* and my first adult dream (if you could call it that) was about stealing Cynthia Patrick away from John Agar because he was too afraid to fight *The Mole People,* with a background song called "You're Gonna Lose That Girl" from The Beatles' HELP! album. I've often wondered how many people dream with background music. Gloria was born between the assassinations of the two Kennedys, so she was going to be in for a treat, as Johnny said along the way. I mean, Gloria's formative years were spent at the Jerry Lewis Cinamerica watching Charlton Heston movies against her will and/or better judgment.

We all had ideas of what movies we wanted to morph together once we got to the drive-in in Manteno, though it was mostly Johnny talking nonstop as the Camaro sputtered along the Tri-State, the windshield wipers slapping back and forth across our vision. First big rainstorm of the summer hits on Friday night. Par for the course in Chicago. But the weather wasn't going to stop us from getting to the Bullets Can't Stop It Drive-In in rural Manteno, an hour south of the city.

And aside from the weather providing proper atmosphere, like being spooked by Henry Mancini's theme for *Creature Features* back in the seventies, strains of a piano over Dwight Frye in all his grinning madness, we had been saving our money for the better part of a month to hit the drive-in. The price was based on similar so-called thrill rides at the Disney complex in Japan and the virtual reality games along Navy Pier. Fifty dollars for thirty minutes, fright (okay, *excite-*

ment) guaranteed. The drive-in idea had coincidentally been developed by one of the Japanese cybers, Jay Osigu, and was backed by the Wimberger Corporation.

The Van Nuys-based Wimbergers had first tried out their Virtreal Graphics™ in Arizona and Missouri, for the cowboy and gangster buffs. Kansas City has the highest mob concentration outside of New York City, and the St. Valentine's Massacre Theater propelled the corporation into the big time, making them "the goods," as Johnny Coronette put it when he first read about the drive-in's impending opening.

Manteno, Illinois, is forty miles southeast of Chicago, and is best known for being the onetime site of the state mental institution. A common line as we were growing up was, "You see that guy? He looks like he just came from Manteno." Things like that. Now the town held the Mavros printing plant, several farms, a Fatty Pig BBQ, and the Bullets Can't Stop It Drive-In.

Our destination was actually a theater, but each individual parlor, or sensor cage, was made to be perceived as a drive-in good ol' Hicksburg, U.S.A. on a summer night, except you weren't in cars, you just had the biggest freaking screen imaginable, one that would make Grant Williams look like anything but *The Incredible Shrinking Man*.

Johnny was a wealth of ideas for morphing combinations of films together. He thought of putting Elvis instead of Landon in *I Was A Teen-Age Werewolf*. We both had Gloria snuffling laughter with our snarls and sneers. "Ah'm a wolf, ya gotta believe me 'n lock me up, man," and "Ah got sompin on mah lip, oh, is' jus' muscle tissue, mah boy, mah boy." Then I mentioned how it was too bad we couldn't get other films besides monster titles into the computer, an example being *Oceans Eleven* and *Attack of The Crab Monsters*. In that one, the crabs took over the voices of their victims, and wouldn't it be great to see cheesy-looking crabs talking with the voices of Sammy Davis Jr. and Peter Lawford? Johnny thought of mixing *Seven Brides For Seven Brothers* with *Dracula's Daughters*. Man, we had Gloria in tears, Johnny just grinning away like the night was ours.

Which was the whole point of the drive-in.

The parlors were immersive, that is, set up with the goggles and gloves, everything attaching the patron to the computer simulate. It was set up for volume business, so there could be up to five people in each room, or *film*, at each interval.

Move them in and out, fast as possible. Clear the program and let the next group have their fun. But the drive-in was nearly empty that night, probably because of the rain. (I'd hate to think it was due to Barry Manilow's one-night set at the World Music Theater in Tinley Park.) Also, the Famous Monsters convention was coming up for Labor Day and most people with our cinematic sensibilities could easily have been saving up for that.

But I'd like to think it was the rain, because of what happened later. It was *exactly* the type of plot device you'd see in a B-movie from the fifties. Due to the inclement weather, we passed right by a foreboding clue as to what was to come later, Devery Truax's old beater GTO, parked in Fatty Pig's lot, the faded tan of the car against the lime green brick of the restaurant like some hideous color scheme for a bed and breakfast overlooking the Cal-Sag Channel.

I only realized it later, that the car had been there, when I was putting all this together. Devery Truax's car with the faded RAT FINK bumper sticker and the glow-in-the-dark Frankenstein on the dashboard. Truax was a punk from the word go, looked about as tough and talked with the same kind of mock intimidation as John Ashley in *High School Caesar*.

He also had it bad for Gloria Talbot. Hell, who wouldn't? Shoulder-length auburn hair, thin comet trails for eyebrows that waggled with amusement, and eyes that were the color of charcoal smoldering inside emerald green glass. A gal like this hanging around two four-eyed goons like me and Johnny, who knew?

Truax had also brought two others with him that night: Del Teach, this gangly computer geek who looked like his parents had been involved with atomic projects and hadn't properly protected themselves, and Clement Wing. The latter fellow was this borderline autistic from down the block I lived on.

Wing's father had been a Chicago cop same as mine, and there were many summers when our dads were working third shift and slept in the afternoons, I had to take Clem somewhere and keep him occupied on days when his father really needed to sleep. More often than not, I'd take Clem to play pinball games or go to the Ford City Cinema on Wednesdays, when you could get in for a dollar matinee by showing a Pepsi-Cola bottle cap. Clem was thin with hair the color of dirt. He had five o'clock shadow by the time he was fifteen. Forget my lame joke about Del Teach; the real mystery was Clement Wing.

The doctors never did pin down exactly what was wrong with him; eventually he was diagnosed autistic at the age of five. If he had been born ten years later, there might have been a better medical understanding of his situation, but he, like myself and Johnny Coronette, were products of the waning months of the 1950s.

I knew I was constructing an armchair diagnosis, at best. Clem was able to talk lucidly, though he chose to remain silent most of the time. But he could certainly be eloquent. Earlier that summer, I was watching *The Killer Shrews* on Channel Eleven's *MOONLIGHT MADNESS* when my hound dog, Rusty Wells, born the week Elvis Presley died, looked at me the way dogs do when they know it is time. I carried her onto the back porch as she shuddered her last and sat through the morning to keep the crows away from her still form.

Clement saw me the following week and said how maybe Rusty was peeing on her way to heaven, burning the grass so I'd be able to find my way that much easier when my time comes. Autistic? Hell, then I'm a sadomasochist. Or something. You see my point at the absurdity of how Clement Wing was perceived in this world.

His parents were content with the doctor's diagnosis, the way a ghetto family will deny on the ten o'clock news the fact that their eleven-year-old son shot dead an honors student on the next block over, that their boy was not involved in some gang initiation.

In its own way, the "world" Clem lived in made it easier for him to get by. Before Johnny Coronette got some meat on his bones and buffed out a little, we'd both been antagonized by Devery Truax and his goon squad.

They would go after Clement Wing, as well, but he would stand up to them.

Actually, I always thought it was because he didn't know how to be afraid.

We pulled up near Druktenis Road, close to the south end of the lot, spooky woods beyond the Camaro's headlights. The drive-in off to the right, pastel blue and pink neon, the only thing missing was a soda shoppe. Johnny was still going two-forty on the possibilities to be had. I said how next they ought to morph television shows of the past, have a big immersive cage and call it "Tonight's Episode." Or combine TV *and* film, make a show starring David Janssen as *The Amazing Colossal Fugitive*. Gloria laughed at that one, because her mom watched the black and white reruns on a cable station out of New York.

Johnny, not one to be upped, said that they could do similar morphing with the recent remake with Harrison Ford. Turn Sam Gerard, Kimble's nemesis, into the rampaging behemoth. You could see (and hear) it now: Tommy Lee Jones towering over Harrison Ford, bellowing, "Richard, do you want to get *stomped?*"

More gales of laughter.

Fade out to the next scene, the interior of the drive-in. POV, mine.

We paid our money to one of the tellers. The place was nearly deserted, although a crowd of balding, gray-bearded guys were lined up by the Hondo Suite, where all the Japanese monster movies could be morphed. I'd bet every one of them would fight whichever monster to successfully win the love of Emi and Yumi Ito, those six-inch princesses from Infant Island, The Alilenas. One of the men even looked like an old Raymond Burr, in an odd sort of way.

It was while we were cracking wise about the *Gajira* guys that Devery Truax must have come in, because we certainly would have suspected something was up, particularly if we saw the two lackeys, unwitting or witless, that he had in tow.

We talked some trash as we stood in line for our turn in the Bug-Eyed Monster Room, waiting for the usher to explain the programming to us. There were poster headings on each wall, like banners, and Gloria read them out as Johnny and I took turns guessing which movies the blurbs belonged to.

A Savage Giant on a Blood-Red Rampage. The Biggest Thing Since Creation. Mightiest Double Bill In The Universe.

Spewed From Intergalactic Space . . .

Flying Saucers Attack . . .

Clawing Up From The Depths Of The Earth . . .

Johnny won, of course, by guessing that *The Two Most Hellish Horror Hits That Ever Turned Blood To Ice* were *The Screaming Skull* and *Terror From The Year 5000*.

Like we were betting real money.

Then the usher came by and handed us our equipment and explained the program. We would each have thirty minutes in the same room and be outfitted with goggles which fit snugly over our heads (and, thankfully, glasses). The programming board itself fit over our forearms like compact shields. The small boxes were made by a German company, *Fassl GMBH,* and weighed no more than a Sony Walkman. A long rubber tube connected the Virtreal Ops™ to the gloves we wore.

The gloves looked more like black matinee gloves or those Isotoner gloves you always get at Christmastime from some obscure relative. They were lined with veins and bladders, and compressed air was pumped through during the action. The gloves also recorded galvanic responses, that is, our heartbeats and pulse rates.

The computer wire-frames covered certain parameters, commonly referred to as "flock of seagulls," random sensors and velcro diodes that would interface the sensory feedback. The program display was comparable to a list of selections on an ATM machine. Films to choose from for morphing purposes were listed alphabetically, by subject, and by actor/actress. For example:

ATOMIC MONSTER   APE   AGAR, JOHN

There were also optional settings for effects like The Tingler and music (à la the Del-Aires surf music from *The Horror Of Party Beach*). Plus, you could choose backgrounds and/or stages that included the Downing-

ton Diner from *The Blob,* Belton High School from *I
Was A Teen-Age Frankenstein,* or even the Tivoli Theater from *Village of The Giants.*

We each made our selections, the lights went down.
And all hell broke loose.

This part I found out from Johnny afterward, while
I was in my hospital bed:

Devery Truax had bribed a now-unemployed usher
to let him and his two companions inside our sensor
cage. The week before, Del Teach had stolen a Virtreal
Ops board from the drive-in, (he had *also* stolen the
money he had used to pay to get *into* the drive-in, but
that's a different story). He spent a week screwing
around with it, turning it into something, well, something *evil.*

And poor Clement Wing was the unwitting vessel.
Evidently, Devery had something on the kid, what
amounted to blackmail. Maybe he was threatened with
having his parents told that he was looking in Gloria's
bedroom window or something. The rigged board and
attachments were hooked up to my autistic neighbor
and the switches turned on.

Once activated, it overrode our individual programs.

The simplicity of what Devery Truax and Del Teach
had done was this, they had plugged Clement Wing ef-
fectively into a computer that was "fright guaranteed."

Clement Wing who had never showed fear in all the
years I've known him.

Through all the mental battles we fought.

Through all the films we had seen.

This is how it spilled out. And I mean that quite literally. Everything, every single freaking Bug-Eyed
Monster (and then some) imaginable spilled into our
immersive, collective subconscious, sluicing into

our mental receptors as if we were standing in Smallville U.S.A. under a liquid sky.

At the time that Clement's device overrode the mainframe of the room—and it only *happened* in our particular suite—Johnny had already set himself up as the hero in *The Day The World Ended,* saving Lori Nelson *and* Richard Denning from telepathic, cannibalistic, four-armed mutant buglike creatures, but Gloria and myself were still deciding. (I had been giving serious thought to "fulfilling" my childhood dream of actually winning Cynthia Patrick away from John Agar without ever having to sing that insipid Beatles tune.)

But what I saw (not then knowing we all shared the same "screen," as it turned out), was the three of us in the same film, just the way Del Teach had programmed it. We were in an empty parking lot, drive-in speakers and jacks in even rows around us. The large screen in front of us was blank because it was still daylight, and there were the muted hums of cars on an interstate behind us, making a ribbon across a horizon the color of torn plums.

The floor of the sensor cage had been transformed into the gravel of an actual drive-in, with rows cleared by the travel of the patrons' cars. There was the detritus of said patrons around me. Our positions were exactly as they had been during "real time," moments before; Gloria was standing between the two of us. I could see that she and Johnny were wearing the goggles and gloves, so I assume I was, as well. No special costumes, considering the fact that we had all materialized into a common arena as if we were characters in one of those mutant comics, and had been inexplicably transported to an antimatter universe to fight The Thing That Shouldn't Exist or something like that.

A desolate wind blew as a red sun slowly set above the treetops beyond the screen. An Oh! Henry Mega-Size wrapper twisted around my ankle, then skittered away. I could smell Gloria Talbot's Tabu perfume and buttered popcorn.

I glanced over to the woods above the hill, the front-age road to the expressway, assumedly, and did a double take. I could've sworn I was looking at the sil-houette of Alec Rebar, *The Incredible Melting Man,* shambling down the incline with dangling arms and bell-bottom hospital-issued whites. The image made me think of a live-action Saturday show from my youth, *H. R. Puf-N-Stuf.* Don't ask me why—I even thought that back in 1978 when the movie was on a double bill with *Saturday Night Fever.* I still thought I was the only one seeing this until I heard Johnny through my head-set, asking where the hell was Richard Denning?

Suddenly, as if with the setting sun, everything went to black and white; the sky, the trees, the big screen. Even the pink and blue neon. Shadows were now ev-erywhere, draping across the lot, elongating the speak-ers, the ones dangling now resembling bloated spiders.

It happened all at once. If I had smoked some mar-ijuana as I had been viewing *Altered States,* I might have started to take it all in stride. It wasn't just bugs. (Our specific room was going to be bugs. Only bugs, the creepy-crawly kind. Or, at worst, bug-eyed creepies like the bloated-headed thingies in *Invasion of The Saucer-Men.*) Not behemoths, not sea serpents, cer-tainly not blobs and flying brains.

But that's exactly what we got. The three of us alone, against the hordes of fifties films. Where the hell was Nestor Paiva when you needed him?

There was a playground in front of the drive-in screen, and this was where the giant, hairy tarantula began its slow, ominous crawl, coming into sight over the teeter-totter and then the twirly-bird. I was watch-ing *that* when I felt things scurrying over my feet. It wasn't candy wrappers this time, it was those mousy killer shrews, gnawing at my ankles. I jumped away, oddly thinking of my dog Rusty and feeling like momentarily weeping.

From out of the screen itself, giant grasshoppers from *The Beginning Of The End* began climbing downward to ground level. I started looking for my friends. Johnny was a few feet away, dodging a familiar gelatinous hunk of goop. Nope. Sadly, Steve McQueen was nowhere around with a fire extinguisher from the concession stand.

And Gloria was jumping up and down because the earth around her was being sucked in. I immediately thought of those damn mole people. She screamed then and I saw a transparent floating brain, from the planet Arous, natch. It was hovering there, deciding when to make a move, I suppose. Maybe it was waiting for its cue.

I even saw shooting stars and flying saucers in that monochrome sky of Midwestern stars. Would we have to wait for the computer to run its program through, or for security to be called? I couldn't even tell if our thirty minutes were anywhere near being expended.

Oh, and there were sounds, don't get me wrong. Not just of the three of us struggling, with Gloria not screaming, to her benefit, let me set the record straight. We heard, well, *I* did, the chitinous, whirring sounds of what I could only guess to be the giant ants of *Them,* just beyond the horizon (or even in the sewers). And I heard an unseen voice saying, "You think I'm the freak, well, let me tell you. I'm not the freak, *you're* the freaks. I'm not growing, you're shrinking!" The male voice started laughing, but then stopped abruptly as if startled.

And I saw why, just as everything became a brilliant Technicolor. Just as everything started dawning on me.

The cars on the Interstate, silent through all this, had stalled, the occupants looking out their windows.

Pointing at the horizon. The bugs and monsters moving away, not just from us, but just *away*.

The drive-in screen was being shredded from behind, beyond our field of vision. I looked at Johnny and Gloria, and they stared back at me helplessly. Frankly, none of us knew what the hell to expect next.

There was a blur of blue and shiny black coming into view as the screen tumbled and the dust from the gravel cleared. *Oh, Jesus,* I thought.

The newest "monster" was Buddy Love, the latter half of the Jekyll/Hyde-like creature created by Jerry Lewis' character—damned if I could recall his name—in *The Nutty Professor.* But . . . why? All these other films were familiar to me, I had seen them with . . . Clement Wing. I had also seen *The Nutty Professor, Three On A Couch,* the list of Pepsi matinee movies went on.

And I understood. I concentrated and recalled standing in front of the sensor cage. Had I imagined hearing Devery Truax, Del Teach, and Clement Wing? Had this whole program been jury-rigged?

This scene was Clement's consciousness finally taking over. Suave and cool Buddy Love, replete in his slicked-back hair and blue lounge jacket with the black lapels. The swagger and the way with the ladies he would never have in his life.

Poor Clem. Devery, that motherless . . .

I concentrated harder, figured will power might work. Clem had always been close with me. I shut my eyes, my last image being Johnny and Gloria, thoroughly confounded at this hundred-foot Jerry Lewis thing.

All I saw was the gray behind my eyelids, and I blocked out all sound, whispering to Clement to please stop this. I made myself envision Buddy Love's transformation in reverse, turning him into a celluloid parody of Clement Wing, with uneven buck teeth and mussed hair the color of dirt. I felt light-headed.

Gloria finally let out a gasp.

She had her hand to her mouth as she saw me there in the hospital bed. Johnny was there beside her. I was found unconscious in the sensor cage after the computer shut down, they tell me, and now I'm at Silver Cross Hospital in Joliet.

Then the doctor tells me it is time for me to rest and he gives me a shot of blissful Demerol. Like I said, fright guaranteed. Clement Wing was not afraid until he saw himself the way everyone else saw him, as a nutty professor. He wasn't scared by ants, grasshoppers, brains with spinal cords attached, or giant sea serpents. He was—for a time—an automaton, and bullets couldn't stop it.

Truax and Teach are out on bail, poor Clem's in psychiatric counseling.

My parents told me I'd been contacted by an independent film company regarding possible film rights after our ordeal made the wire services.

I suppose it is something to bring up with Johnny and Gloria, but frankly I don't think I'm up for any kind of a sequel.

This story is for Kurt & Amy in L.A. and Jeff, Andrew, Harry and Diana in Chicago. Here's to late night viewing.

RACE WITH THE DEVIL

by Randy Fox

He was a be-bop-a-loser ...
until she gave him woman love!

The pain was gone. Gene hadn't opened his eyes yet, but the absence of pain was an overwhelming feeling all its own. He had grown so used to it—the knifelike spike in his stomach, the ever-present agony in his left leg—that he could hardly move in its absence.

He slowly opened his eyes and was blinded by the sunlight filtering through the leaves above him. The sounds and smells of the meadow flooded his senses. He squinted against the bright light, and a shadow fell over him.

"Well, it's about time," said the shadow's owner. Gene's eyes adjusted to the light, and he saw a tall, buxom woman towering over him like a giantess. She was wearing black leather pants, a white shirt, and a black leather jacket. She had long brown hair, sharp—almost cruel—eyes, and full lips that seemed to naturally shape themselves into a snarl. The kind of kitten that could give you that woman love, but also the kind you sure didn't want to cross.

"Got an eyeful yet, stud?" she said.

"Is this heaven?" Gene asked. "Am I dead?"

"Do I look like an angel?" she replied.

"But I remember a hospital, and the blood. . . ."

"That was a long time ago, baby," she said. "I don't know why it took you so long to get here. All I know is that we're gonna be late. You don't wanna keep the gang waiting." Reaching out, she pulled him to his feet and then walked from the tree to the Harley that was parked a short distance away. She slapped the seat of the bike. "C'mon already."

Gene followed her hesitantly, with neither the pain nor limp he was used to. He wasn't sure if he was more astonished by where he was, or how strong he felt. "But how did I get here?" he asked the woman.

She chuckled. "You done been sleeping under that tree for too long. Now get this straight. Your name's Gene, my name's Allison, and we're gonna be late if you don't get on the bike like nowsville, baby."

Gene swung one leg over the bike and sat down. Allison hopped onto the seat behind him. He started the bike, and they rolled out of the field and onto the road.

"This all seems so strange," he said. "I've got all these memories that just don't make sense anymore."

Allison laughed in his ear. "You're just real gone, aren't you, dad?"

The bike roared down the road. Gene seemed to know exactly where they needed to go. They drove for a couple of miles and topped a hill. Below them was the dirt drag strip. The gang was already there.

There were about ten people standing around a pink '56 Thunderbird and a couple of motorcycles. The gang was half guys and half girls, all of them dressed like Gene and Allison.

Gene guided the cycle up to the car, Allison's arms tight around his waist. The gang cheered their approach. Some of the members looked a little old to be in a gang, but Gene wasn't exactly a kid either. "Say, mama, 'bout time you showed up," a dirty-blond-haired guy complained through a puffy smirk. He was leaning against the fender of the car with his arms crossed.

"Don't lose your head, Vic," Allison said as she hopped off the bike.

Vic grimaced at her. "Why you, I oughta," he mumbled.

A tall thin guy who could've passed for Gene's brother grabbed Vic's arm. "Cool it, man. Don't be a rat fink. We ain't here to fight each other. Gene's gonna show them Els a thing or two."

"Ron's right, baby," Allison said. "That is, if they got enough guts to show up."

A roar came from over the hill to the left, and the gang turned to see a fleet of hot rods heading their way. Gene felt like he recognized the leader of the Els, but his thoughts were still so jumbled that he couldn't be sure. The cat was driving a gold Caddy convertible. His black hair was slicked back in a ducktail, and his full lips curled up in a one-sided snarl as his eyes met Gene's.

The Caddy pulled up beside the T-Bird. The hot rod gang surrounded Gene's bunch and revved their engines, filling the air with the sound of hammering pistons. Their leader stood up in his seat and looked around at the cars. Grinning viciously at Gene, he snapped his arm down and the sound of the engines cut off abruptly, like a needle being pulled from a record.

The leader's cold stare drilled into Gene. "You ready to race, catman?"

Gene didn't know what to say at first. He still didn't know what was going on, but it all seemed right for some reason. "If you're ready to lose," he answered.

The Els leader chuckled a fake laugh as he looked around at his gang. They joined him, laughing nervously.

Michael slapped Gene on the back. "You guys won't

be laughin' so hard when we blow that Caddy off the
road!" Michael was a pretty hep cat, but he could be a
real animal when he lost his temper.

The leader of the Els snapped his arm down again,
cutting off the ensuing laughter. "Let's git it."

The scene exploded into a flurry of activity. Gang
members moved the cars and motorcycles out of the
way. Gene jumped into the T-Bird and cranked it. The
engine roared to life. He was reaching down to pop
the hand brake when a blond-haired guy from his gang
slapped him on the back.

"Win this race so we can go home," he said.

Instantly, Gene recognized the guy's face. "Eddie?"
he said, "But you're . . ."

"No time for the summertime blues now, man. You
gotta beat this cat." Eddie walked away. Gene stared at
him until Allison stepped forward and eclipsed his
view.

"Win this one for me," she said. Then she leaned
over and planted a hard, wet kiss on Gene's mouth.
Moving away, she winked at him. "We know who's the
real king."

Gene glanced at the leader of the Els, who was grinning condescendingly. Gene ignored him and looked
straight ahead. Natalie stood in front of the cars with
her arms spread wide, a handkerchief in one hand. She
smiled at Gene and brought her arms down.

The T-Bird leaped forward like a great beast on the
attack. A cloud of dust and smoke blossomed from behind the two cars. Gene glanced to his right and saw
the leader of the Els grinning at him.

Gene ended the stare down with a jerk of his head.
He couldn't let this cat psych him out. He had to keep
his eyes on the road. He was going to win this race.

It was then that he heard the voice echoing in his
head. *Loser! Cripple! Has-Been! Second rate is all you
ever have been or will be!*

"No!" Gene said, keeping his eyes fixed on the road in front of him.

One hit was all you could ever manage. Just a drunken old dead cripple at thirty-six with a rotten gut. Nobody misses you. Say your name and people just say, "Who?" Just give it up, daddy-o.

"You're wrong!" Gene screamed. He jerked his head to the side and saw the leader of the Els laughing at him. The familiar pain began to shoot through his left leg and a burning sensation scorched his stomach. The gold Caddy started to pull ahead. Gene floored it, and the T-Bird exploded forward. Gene jumped into the lead.

The Caddy dropped back and then started to gain again. The leader's face was set with grim determination. The cars roared on down the line. The Caddy was about half a car-length back when it slammed into the T-Bird's side.

Gene fought with the wheel to keep control. *Give it up, loser,* the voice said. Gene didn't answer it this time. The Caddy slammed into him again, and both cars weaved as Gene and the leader struggled for control.

The Caddy inched up until it was almost even. Gene glanced over and saw the smug look on the devil's face. He whipped the wheel around and crashed the front of the T-Bird into the Caddy. For a split second, Gene saw the panic on the leader of the Els face, and then the Caddy veered off and spun out of control. In his rearview mirror, Gene saw the car head up the embankment and then flip over and over.

Gene hit his brakes, and the T-Bird spun to a stop. The Caddy had come to rest on one side, halfway up the embankment. Gene could see the members of both gangs rushing to their cars and bikes at the other end of the drag strip, but the leader of the Els was nowhere in sight. Gene jumped out of the car and ran toward the wreck.

He got to the Caddy just before the others reached it. Running up the embankment, he saw the leader of the Els struggling from the wreck.

"You okay, man?" Gene asked. He reached for the leader's shoulder as the other gang members came running up the hill behind him.

"Get away from me!" the leader of the Els hissed. He turned suddenly and hit Gene hard in the chest, knocking him down the embankment.

Gene rolled through the dirt to the bottom and pulled himself up. The leader of the Els was still by his car. "You loser!" he shouted. "Don't you know who I am? I'm The King! I *always* win the race. I *always* get the girl. You're nothin' but a lousy imitation! Have you got a jet plane? Have you got a mansion? Have you got your own stamp?"

Gene didn't answer. He was too busy staring, because the leader of the Els had changed. He was now dressed in an Army private's uniform, and his hair had shortened to a crew cut. The Caddy behind him had become an olive-drab jeep.

"I could have any woman I want!" the leader yelled. "All you've got is a bottle you can drag your stupid old crippled ass inside of."

This time Gene saw the change come over the leader. His body blurred and flowed into another shape before Gene's eyes. The guy was now a clean-cut, square version of his earlier self, dressed in a red silk shirt and a white sport coat. "How many movies were you in?" the leader shouted. "I was a star! I won all the fights!"

He then started singing a medley of stupid songs about goop, and shrimp boats, and bossa nova babies. Before he could finish, he shifted again and grew into a fat, flabby man wearing a white jumpsuit that looked like it had been stolen from a circus. His long bushy sideburns stood out from his round jowls like weeds. He babbled on about his momma in a drugged-out voice before collapsing onto his enormous rear end.

The leader of the Els lay still in the dirt. The car behind him creaked horribly, twisting into the shape of a hearse.

Tearing his eyes away from the nightmare in front of him, Gene stumbled into Vic.

"Watch it, soldier!" Vic shouted. Gene stared at his buddy in disbelief. Vic was dressed in dirty army fatigues and was carrying a machine gun.

"What's happening, Vic?" Gene asked.

"Shape up, dogface!" Vic barked. "We've all got our parts to play; how else are you going to eat?" Vic began to change rapidly, shifting from soldier, to gangster, to baseball player, and on through a mixed bag of appearances. "You can't let your pride get in the way," he continued. He paused suddenly, becoming an old, tired-looking man in a wrinkled dirty suit. He looked up, and panic filled his eyes. "Sweet Jesus! It's comin' down!" he screamed.

"Don't listen to him." Michael grabbed Gene's arm and pulled him to one side. Michael looked normal enough, except for being older, but Gene had never seen him this calm, especially in a crazy situation like this. "I'm a *real* angel now, did you know that?" Michael said, and then he stumbled away from Gene singing a hymn.

Gene shivered. All around, the gang members, both male and female, were shifting and changing, melting into different clothes and appearances. Some were changing into the walking wounded like Vic, but most were becoming straight-backed, clean-cut squares who prattled on about their Kiwanas Club meetings or PTA bake sales. Gene's mind reeled.

And then he saw Eddie.

He was a walking corpse. Blood covered his body from the deep cuts and open wounds. One side of his face looked like it had been scraped away. "I never shoulda got in that car . . . I never shoulda got in that car . . ." Eddie croaked over and over as he dragged himself toward Gene.

Gene watched him approach, and suddenly a flood of hidden memories washed over him. The missed chances, the car wrecks, the failed marriages, the drugs and booze, and most of all the incredible pain. He doubled over as he felt the change starting to flow through his own body.

NO! he thought, pulling himself up from the dirt. *I never gave up! I made a lot of mistakes, but I never gave up!*

Gene made a break for the Harley, but the pain in his leg and the brace that suddenly ensnared it slowed him down. All around, the former gang members closed in on him. Michael was leading the pack, spouting off about the importance of good family values in entertainment. The other guys were reciting the statistics of their investments plans, while the girls were exchanging recipes.

But they couldn't move very fast, and Gene made it to the bike one step ahead of them. Allison was leaning against it, her features twisted, fighting against the changes that were threatening to consume her.

Gene reached out and pulled her onto the bike. "We've got to get out of here," he shouted, and she collapsed against his shoulder. He stomped the starter, and the bike roared to life. The pack had surrounded them, but Gene popped the clutch and the bike tore through the crowd. A hail of pocket protectors and Tupperware flew up behind the Harley as Gene plowed on.

They left the mob behind, the bike roaring away from the drag strip. The meadow was the only place

Gene could think of to go. Everything had started there. Maybe he could end it there, too.

As the bike flew down the road, Gene began to cough. Blood seeped from his mouth and drooled down his chin. The burning in his stomach felt nearly volcanic, but he refused to stop.

Gene parked the bike underneath the big tree, in the same spot where he'd opened his eyes just a short time ago. The tree was now leafless and dead. Gene helped Allison off the bike. She collapsed into the dead grass underneath the tree.

Gene was shocked by her appearance. Her thin skin was ghastly pale, and it clung to her bones. She looked up at Gene through deep, sunken eyes and spoke softly. "They've been poisoning me," she said, and then mumbled on about the conspiracies against her.

Hot tears burned Gene's eyes. It wasn't fair. He couldn't lose it all again, not like this. He steeled himself, and he felt his body begin to change. "I'm not going to lose this one," Gene whispered, staring deep into Allison's eyes. "And I'm not going to lose *you.*"

Suddenly, Gene's old Gibson was hanging from his shoulder. He gripped the neck of the guitar with his left hand and realized that *this* was his last chance. He strummed the opening chords and began to sing. He sang about wanting alot alot-a lovin' and wanting alot alot-a huggin', and about a girl he was gonna get. *Uh-huh. You bet.* The song came from inside him, from the place where he had hidden all the pain and frustration. All of his doubts and fears poured into the song and were released by the only part of him that had always been safe from the pain, his music. It swelled outward with an intensity that could be nothing else but rock 'n' roll, and it swept across the meadow and rang through the leaves of the tree. He was blind to the world as he poured his soul into the music.

Gene finished the song and opened his eyes. The

meadow was once again rich and lush, and bright green leaves covered the tree. Allison was sitting on the Harley, giving him a look that only a cool kitten like her could dish out. She scooted back on the seat and made room for him. He got on and started the bike.

"Still think you're in heaven, baby?" Allison shouted over the rumble of the bike's engine.

"I don't know," Gene said. "I never really believed there was such a place."

She laughed as the bike rolled on, raising a cloud of dust. "You should know by now, honey," Allison said. "There's always a second feature."

THE GOOD, THE BAD, AND THE DANGED

by Adam-Troy Castro

With six-guns thundering . . .
they ride the brimstone trail!

We figures we's home free when we loses that posse
near MacKenna's Canyon, but then that windstorm
comes up, straight outa the ground it feels like,
swirlin' all the dust and grit so thick we cain't tell the
difference 'tween up and down and sideways. Big
Red, he's wounded already, he dies the first night.
Poor One-Eye gets separated from us one night after
that. On the third night, somethin' the size of a loco-
motive swoops outa the sky all silent-like and plucks
poor Mississippi Blue outa his saddle without even
gettin' a rise outa his horse. By which point them of us
what's left—just me and Snake and Deke and the
Kid—is purty much in agreement 'bout two things:
first, that this ain't no ordinary sandstorm, and second, that we sure as spit ain't in any territories we
know. Not even in Mexico.

So when the wind starts dyin' down and we hears
that piano music up ahead it don't matter none that our
recent troubles up north done put us offa towns. We
sees all the houses low and squat against the night, and
the lanterns burnin' in the windows, and to us it looks
like heaven. By the time we rides up the main street,

which is deserted 'ceptin for us, me and Snake and Deke and the Kid can breathe the way human beans is supposed to breathe. Snake gets his breath and wonders, "Ain't there noplace a civilized man can go to get a drink in this here town?"

"And a bath," says the Kid, who always set great stock in bathin' regular. His mama's influence, I reckon. "I don't wash up soon, I's likely to die of embarrassment."

Deke, who don't get jokes, says, "Do people really die of that?"

And the Kid, who makes a righteous LOT of jokes, says, "Sure, Deke, sure they does. Just check it out next time you shoot somebody. It ain't the bullet what kills them. The bullet HURTS, but it ain't fatal. Look in the eyes, and you'll see: they die cause you made 'em feel silly."

Deke says, "I guess that makes at least as much sense as the bleedin' theory."

The main drinkin' establishment is 'bout four or five houses down the main street. We hitches the horses by the water trough, more'n a bit spooked by the way there ain't nobody else around: no horses, no people, just a mess'a tumbleweeds bouncin' back and forth acrost the dirt.

Me and Snake and the Kid goes inside, leavin' Deke as lookout, and sees that the saloon ain't exactly the jumpin'est place we ever stumbled into either. They's only five folks in here: the bartender, who looks to be ninety years old, the piano player, who could be the bartender's granpappy, the local whore, who's too purty to be workin' a dump like this, and two depressed old geezers playin' cards. Only the whore looks up to see who we are. They's a strange expression on her face—not saucy and invitin' the way a proper whore's supposed to look, but scared. I gets the idea she done wore that face long as she been here. It don't make me feel too good 'bout bein' here mysef.

The bartender is washin' a glass which has probably been collectin' dirt since before Mrs. Lincoln dragged her husband to that damnfool play. He says, "What."

Just like that. *What.*

I's not in any mood to care. "We want four rooms in the closest thing you got to a hotel, and a stable to put our horses in, and somethin' to eat, and somethin' to drink so we can wash the taste'a sand from our mouths, and do you think you can help us with all that without makin' it sound like we's ruinin' your whole day?"

The bartender looks at me, and then at Deke, and then at the Kid, and then his eyes get all round and bulgin', like we's just about the dumbest specimens he ever seen.

"FOUR rooms?"

"Yeah. Four."

"But there's only—you left a man in the street alone?"

I says, "There a problem with that?"

"Jeezus, you best hurry up and get that sorry bastard in here—"

We doesn't get a chance to ask the fella what bee just raised a welt on his backside, cause just 'bout then, the horses outside start screamin'. Deke's yellin', too, but it ain't the way he yells when there's shootin' goin on. When there's shootin' goin' on, he yells whee and whoopee and yahoo like there ain't no better fun to be found on God's Green Earth. But now he's yellin' like an old lady trapped in a burnin' house, and it sure as hell ain't no sound we ever expected to hear him make.

Me and Snake and the Kid, we draws our guns and runs to the door to help him. Snake and the Kid gets there just before I does, and when they sees what's goin' on out there they stop in mid-step like their feet been nailed to the wood. I bumps into Snake's back and almost knock him over. The Kid says, "Jesus!" and sinks to his knees, which is kinda funny, 'cause I thought he gave up religion when I first took him from his mama.

And Snake, who I once seen charge a thirty-man posse with two bullets in his gut and none in his gun, and then actually *get away* 'cause the folks in the posse figured any man makin' a charge that blood simple had to have fifty even crazier friends behind him, backin' him up, well, Snake just faints dead away. . . .

And now that they's both outa my line a'sight, I looks through the saloon doors still swingin' open and shut from Snake and the Kid bangin' into them, and every time they swing open I sees what's happenin' in the street.

Deke and the horses are bein' eaten alive by tumbleweeds.

Two of the dang things is attached to the side'a my horse, and burrowin' their way into its skin, and sprayin' its blood all over the street. Three are hard at work on the other horses, and four others are playin' with Deke, battin' him back and forth between them like a ball. They done already taken a few pieces outta him, but he's still fightin'; even as I watch, he manages to lift his bloody right arm long enough to shoot one of 'em.

It don't do no good, though, 'cause tumbleweeds ain't even remotely inconvenienced by bullets. They's fulla holes already.

I push my way out the swingin' doors, figurin' on findin' some way to help him even so, but I don't get no farther than four or five steps before I sees it's too late anyhow. One of 'em done grabbed hold of Deke's back and started spinnin' like a wagon wheel, carvin' out big red pieces'a skin and flesh. Another bounces by and rips his shootin' arm clean off. Then they takes his other arm and then they takes his eyes and with 'em they takes mosta his face, and still he don't fall—he just staggers round in the street, like a drunk too bone crazy to die, screamin' dirty names at the bastards even as they eat him up alive.

One of the tumbleweeds, figurin' it's finished with the meal it's made of my best horse, bounces up and lands at my feet. I 'spect to be a dead man then. But it don't take a bite or nothin'. It just sets there a second, admirin' my boots, before bouncin' off, to join the rest of the gang dismemberin' Deke.

I knows then what I gots to do. And I does it ... I takes aim and I pulls the trigger and I puts a big fat bullet through the head'a a man been ridin' with me for twenty years.

There turns out to be a heap more brain than anybody who ever knew Deke woulda ever guessed.

He falls—

—but he don't hit the ground, 'cause all of a sudden he and the horses ain't there no more.

And I goes back inside, where the cardplayers done finished draggin' Snake into a corner. The bartender, who's standin' by the door all pale and sweatylike, says: "He's gone to Boot Hill."

I grabs the man by his collar and pulls him close and says, "That's right. And less'n you tell me just what the hell's goin' on here, you's followin' him."

He swallows, but don't quite manage to say nothin'. So naturally, just to put some fear'a God into him, I starts draggin' him toward the swingin' doors.

Somewheres behind me, the whore says, "Put him down."

Now, as I done already made clear more'n once, I's

been 'round quite a bit in my time, and I been to all
different kinda towns, and though I never up until now
been to the kind of town where the tumbleweeds et
people, I's purty much figured out the way towns
work. And if they's one thing I know it's that whores
don't just haul off and give orders, the way this one
here just done, 'lessin they's already pointin' a loaded
weapon.

I turns. And she's packin', awright. Snake's gun.
She's pointin' it straight at my face, and her hands
ain't shakin' even a little bit, and I knows deep in my
gut that she can shoot real fine, and that if I say
anythin' stupid, I's gonna have some daylight shinin'
right through me.

I drops the barkeep, and faces her, hands up.

She lowers the gun a mite. "Pick a chair."

I look at the Kid, who's back on his feet, lookin'
pale as he did the day I first introduced him to hard
liquor. He also looks kinda ashamed'a backin' down
from the door the way he done, and he gives me a look
that says he'll make up for it soon's I need him to. I
gives him a relaxin' look, tellin' him not to worry
about it, and turns back to the whore, and picks a chair
and sets down in it so she can 'splain it all to me.

She says, "The tumbleweeds weren't our idea. They
were His."

She's got a strange kinda accent, which I cain't place
'til I realize it's education talkin'. "Who?"

"Marshal Kane."

Which don't impress me no way. "I eats marshals
for breakfast and farts 'em out for lunch."

"That was a wonderful performance. You deserve an
Oscar. But you've never met a lawman like this one.
He's . . . well, we haven't figured out what He is, because we don't seem to have a word for it . . . but human's definitely not it. All we know is that He can do
just about anything He sets His mind to doing . . . and

that somehow, in whatever hell he came from, He picked up a twisted liking for Westerns. If He wants a showdown with you, you're already dead. But if He wants you to play townspeople, you're going to have to play by His rules, and by His script. You can't know the kind of things He'll do to you if you don't."

I says, "Try me."

She don't flinch. "We're all damned here."

I looks at the Kid and the Kid looks at me and between us we look plenty scared. As for Snake, he's just beginnin' to wake up, and he looks purty upset to find out that what happened to Deke weren't no dream he could just wish away by blinkin' a few times. I don't blame him, but I ain't rid herd over them boys for so long by turnin' weepy the first time things got rough. "Well, Marshal Kane's had it easy. He ain't had to deal with me yet."

She snorts. "Yeah, right. Like you're something He hasn't whipped a thousand times already."

"Maybe I is."

"I'll believe that when I see you outdraw him."

I shrugs. "Ain't nothin' this side a' hell I can't outdraw."

Nobody says nothin' to that. And for a spell I reckon I done convinced them I got the situation under control, but that spell just lasts and lasts, and as I look from face to face I don't see none of them appearin' all too impressed. I's about to get a rise outa them by sayin' I's lookin' forward to shovin' the lawman's head up his rosy white ass when the whore takes pity on me and says, "Evening, Marshal."

Now *that* impresses me, 'cause up 'til now there ain't been a lawman anywhere could keep his vest free'a bullet holes tryin' to sneak up on me from behind.

Unfortunately, what I sees when I shifts my chair to look impresses me even more.

'Cuz I cain't for the life'a me figure out how he fit through the door.

He seems to be about six foot higher than the ceilin', even though the ceilin' don't look like it's bulgin' any to accommodate him. He's all a-shadow, like he's blockin' some bright light shinin' behind Him. But there ain't no bright light behind Him; I can look right past Him—hell, through Him—and sees there's nothin' but the saloon doors swingin' open and shut behind Him. I cain't make out His face, but there's definitely a tin star on His chest, and His eyes . . .

. . . His eyes . . .

. . . well, lookee here. Me and my boys once rode into a settler's camp where all the people was dead from a poisoned water hole. It looked like any other water. But lookin' at it, and knowin' what it done, made us feel cold and funny . . . like it was alive and hated us and wanted us to jump down and drink it. I cain't look at this marshal's eyes without thinkin'a the way the sun sparkled on that there water hole.

The marshal nods at the whore. "Evening, Janey." Then He looks at me, and I feels my knees turn to Mississippi mud. "And you. I heard what you said."

"Good for you, Marshal. I done said it loud enough."

"Have you come to make trouble in my town?"

I says, "Me? Hell, no. I'm a peaceable man."

He sneers at that, and I gets a glimpse inside His mouth, and there's somethin' other than a tongue in there. Somethin' alive, and furry, and tryin like hell to fight its way out. "You can't fool me, Rico. I've been following your work for a long time. You might even say I'm an admirer. That last big shootout—in Harmony, six months ago? The one in the abandoned church? That wasn't just a gunfight. That was . . . Art."

"Yeah?" I plucks an open bottle of whiskey from the

table, pretendin' to drink. "That's plenty generous of you, Marshal. I always thought I was purty sloppy that day."

The marshal looks embarrassed, like some little boy I just told to get lost. "Well, maybe you were. I don't know all that much about art." Then He smiles, and His grin turns wider than His face, and His teeth grow as big and as sharp as railroad spikes. "But I do know what I like. . . ."

I gots to give Him this much: in all my years I only seen one other man draw that fast—a stone-cold killer named Frank, who rode with my boys for a spell before he got a railroad job and got hisself killed by that harmonica player down in Sweetwater. Folks used to say Frank could outdraw a sneeze. But even on his best day, Frank never been half as fast as me. And before the marshal's hand's even halfway to His holster, I done already dropped the whiskey bottle, drawn my guns, and shot Him twice in the chest.

You want to call shootouts art, that one was it. That one ought to be in one of them museums or somethin'. Hell, I thinks I even impressed Snake and the Kid with that one.

But though I thinks I surprised the marshal, too, I don't actually bother Him none, 'cause my shots just go through Him without even leavin' holes. and when _He_ finishes drawin', His hands come up empty, cocked into the shape of the pretend-guns kids make playin' cowboys and Indians.

He points one of them fingers at me and says, "Bang."

There ain't no noise other than that, but I fall down yellin', 'cuz I gots a bullet hole in my left shoulder. I knocks over a chair on the way down, too busy thinkin' 'bout how much this is gonna start hurtin' in a second to even worry about how He done that. He says "Bang," again, and the floor next to my ear splinters, wood chips cuttin' pieces in the side'a my face. I rolls away just before the third "Bang" can get me in the leg.

Somewhere in there the Kid pumps a coupla more rounds into the marshal's chest, but them two turns out to be as useless as the last two, so they ain't even worth the mention.

At 'bout the same time, Snake makes one of his famous damnfool charges. He makes a flyin' run which starts from the far corner and takes him acrost the top of three tables, and whoopin' and hollerin' like a buzzard come down to take a rabbit, plows headfirst into the marshal's gut. No, not into the marshal's gut—it's worse than that. He goes halfway *through* the marshal's gut, sinkin' right into it like it's some mud too wet to even raise a splash. And there he sticks. Snake's legs swing down and kick against the barroom floor, tryin' to push him the rest of the way through, but whatever the lawman's made of done already hardened around him, so there ain't nothin' left for him but drownin' in the flesh of the law.

I shoots the marshal in the head. Not 'cause I think it's gonna do any good, but 'cause I cain't thinka nothin' else to do.

The Kid fires again, yellin', *"What the hell you made of?"*

The marshal, He opens His mouth to answer, but Snake's done got his feet flat against the floor, and is usin' the last'a his strength to push the lawman back. Ain't none of us in the room really thinks Snake still knows what he's pushin', but as it happens he's just strong enough to knock the marshal backward through the swingin' doors. On His way out the marshal trips, and falls flat on His ass in the street, with Snake's legs flailin' in the air above Him. As the doors swing shut, I can see them tumbleweeds poppin' in from all directions to join the fight. Two land on the soles of Snake's boots and start whirrin' away, carvin' them down to the bloody bone even as I watch.

I's 'bout halfway to my feet, with notions'a runnin' out into the street and shootin' that there marshal a few more times, just in case He does got somethin inside Him that bleeds . . . when Janey's hand closes round my wrist.

I turns to look at her.

She says, "Hey, Quick-Draw McGraw! Marshal Kane's just playing with him, that's all. If you want to live more than thirty seconds longer than your friend, you'll follow me NOW."

I ain't never run out on none'a my boys before, but she makes sense, and I ain't lived to my respectable age by throwin' good blood after bad. "KID!"

The Kid's standin' at the swingin' doors, tryin' to figure out just when the whole blamed world went crazy on him. "WHAT?"

"WE'S CLEARIN' OUT! GET A MOVE ON!"

You gots to give the Kid credit for havin' more guts than brains—for a second there he looks about to argue. But then he says somethin' his mama wouldn'ta been too happy 'bout and follows us out. We runs out the back, with Janey in front leadin' the way, the Kid behind us coverin' our backs, and me holdin' my right hand over the impossible hole in my left arm. It's too dark to see much, but far as I can seen there ain't none of them tumbleweeds around right now. Not in this direction.

There's this little worn-out path in the dirt, that you wouldn't notice if you ain't already known it's there—and when I looks ahead to see where it's headin' I see this terrible black shape sittin' dark and mean in the distance. Just lookin' I knows what kind of place it is.

"That the local Boot Hill?"

"Yeah," Janey says. "That's what it is."

"That where we's headin'?"

"Let's hope not."

She leads us along, past the wooden fencin' that backs up all the houses on Main Street, and into this wide-open place that's as black as the Panhandle on a starless night. I cain't hardly make her out, even though she's just a couple steps aheada me, and I gots what they call uncommonly good eyes. Movin' so fast that me and the Kid has troubles just keepin' up with her, she takes us down into a dried riverbed, and then up the other side, and then down this whole 'nother path that takes us closer to that low black hill. And then, just as I was think'a askin' if she's just runnin' around blindly or has somethin' resemblin' a plan in that purty little head of hers, she just skips over this half-buried boulder and leads us along a gully on the other side. "Come on," she says, crawlin' into a place where the stone hangs low over the ground. I starts to say that there cain't possibly be room for all three of us in there, but by then she's already all the way in, so me and the Kid just shrugs at each other, sinks to our bellies, and follows her.

Turns out there's a purty tolerable cave in there— once we climb down, it's more'n big enough for the three of us, and so deep I only has to stoop a little bit to stand up. Leastways we thinks it's a cave, 'til Janey strikes a match and lights a lantern hangin' from a railroad spike stuck into the wall. Then we sees that the cave's all square, with walls shored up with timber, and enough supplies for a long winter.

The Kid's pale, like all the blood done already drained outa him. But Janey's face just seems to float in that flickerin' blackness, and she looks dang comfortable there, like that's the way she's used to folks seein' her.

I grins. "Purty respectable hideout, Janey."

"Thanks. About two years ago a bunch of us snuck out of town and dug it out one shovelful at a time, so we could use it whenever the marshal got cross at somebody. Sometimes if you wait Him out a while, He changes His mind and you can show your face in town again."

"How long's a while?" the Kid asks.

"My husband Brock was down here for four months before he strolled back into town looking for the marshal's forgiveness." Her face turns grim. "It wasn't long enough. The marshal started hanging Brock in the town square the next day."

"*Started* hangin' him?"

"Yeah. You don't want to see that. The way the marshal does it, it takes about two weeks to die."

Me and the Kid spends the next couple a seconds digestin' that. Then the Kid says somethin' that makes me awful proud of him. "Well, I don't care if that marshal's the devil hisself. I ain't hidin' in here for no four months."

"Me neither," I says. "If we're gonna get killed, I'd just face the marshal down and get all the bother over with."

Kinda put off by that, Janey takes a bottle of whiskey and some strips of cloth from a little metal box. "Let me see that arm."

I obliges, and while she tends to my wound she starts mutterin' to herself. "I can't *believe* the macho bullshit I keep getting from you Old West idiots . . . you're just like Him. You *all* think God gave you a Morricone sound track."

It's about the tenth thing she's said what don't make any sense, but before I can say anythin' the Kid beats me to it. "Ma'am?"

"What?"

"You ain't really from around here, are you?"

She stops cleanin' my wound long enough to glare. "No shit, Sherlock."

"Was it a sandstorm for you, too?"

"No. It was a fog. About four years ago, our time. Brock and I were driving down the Pacific Coast Highway—you don't know where that is, probably; most people I meet here don't—and Brock was talking about this new Spielberg script he just read, and how there was a part in it I was right for, and this pea-soup fog just popped up and surrounded us, and the next thing we knew we were in the middle of the desert, driving into this town. Where He was waiting for us." She lets out this sound that could be a laugh and could be a cry, then covers it up with a grunt as she ties my bandage tight. "He was just setting up the town then. We were the first: His choices to play the Town Drunk and the Town Whore. I still don't know why He picked us, when everybody else who rides into town seems to actually come from your time. I think . . . it's because Brock made a Western once. A really bad one. And Marshal Kane takes things like that personally."

I flexes my left arm. I probably won't get much use out of it for a while, but then I always done my best shootin' with my right. "Why you helpin' us?"

"You outdrew Him."

"Didn't do me no good."

Janey's eyes burn bright. "It doesn't matter. I've seen Him bring hundreds of you people here, sometimes one at a time, sometimes ten at a time, and you're all armed to the teeth, and you all shoot it out with Him, and you all end up buried in Boot Hill. But I don't want to spend my life living out a B-movie for His amusement. And if anybody has a chance of finding out how to send that bastard back to hell, it's you."

Me and the Kid sets there quietly, takin' that all in. We don't say what's on both our minds—that reputations are a real pain in the ass. You spends your life buildin' 'em, gettin' 'em all shiny and clean, but in the end they ain't good for nothin' but fillin' your days and nights with one stupid challenge after another. It woulda been nice to try to get our hands on some fresh horses and skedaddle out of here ... but even if we still seriously thunk the Marshal woulda let us go, we cain't even consider it now that she done gone ahead and said that.

I says, "You gonna have any trouble gettin' back to town?"

"Nothing I can't handle."

"Then find your marshal and give Him a message for me. Tell Him Rico said He's a lowlife snake with chicken piss for blood and buffalo crap for brains. Tell Him I said his mama's the ugliest two-dollar whore in Laredo and His daddy's the crater what gets made whenever an Alabama drunk passes out in horseshit. Tell Him I said the only reason I didn't kill Him dead the first time I seen Him is that I felt sorry for all the fleas who'd have to find another mangy dog to live on. And finally, tell Him that if I ain't made it clear enough for Him, which is possible, Him being so bone stupid and all, then He should come see me in half an hour at—" I mentions the first close place what comes to mind, "—the top of Boot Hill, where I'll be perfectly happy to take my time tattooin' it on His big yellow belly. You got that?"

I figures she's gonna say I done lost my mind. Then she smiles. "Mind if I add a few lines to that? Strasberg called me a genius at improv."

"Janey," I says, figurin' it ain't gonna screw me worse than I's already screwed, "have yourself a real hootenany."

"Get the bastard nice and steamed," the Kid puts in.

"Thanks," she says. And then before she leaves she leans forward and kisses me on the cheek. "Be careful."

Which don't make sense no way. What's she tellin'

me to be careful for? If I was interested in bein' careful I wouldn't be ridin' with folks like Snake and Deke. I wouldn't be wanted in six territories. And I especially wouldn't be sendin' the marshal no message like that. That ain't *Bein' Careful,* 'lessen there's some definition I missed in school. Tellin' me to *Be Careful* now is just dead-bone stupid.

Then I remembers that she done snookered me into doin' all the hard work, and I figures she ain't all that stupid at all.

Women.

The Kid waits till she's gone. "Okay. What's the plan?"

"We goes to the top of Boot Hill, and we waits for Him to show up."

The Kid nods eagerly. "And?"

"There ain't no *And,* Kid. There's just us goin' to Boot Hill, and waitin' for Him."

Now, the Kid's 'bout one of the best gunfighters I ever seen, but he's still a young'un, and capable of not understandin' things the first time you 'splain 'em to him. "THAT'S IT? YOU TELLS HER TO SAY ALL THAT—TO *HIM*—AND YOU SAY THAT'S ALL YOU GOT FIGURED OUT?"

"Yep. If I tell Him to meet us somewheres in half an hour, we gots at least half an hour to come up with a plan."

"Like not showin' up," the Kid suggests.

I doesn't even bother to answer that. There are some things that just ain't done.

We waits for a spell, just to give Janey enough time to get back with our message, then crawls out of her hidin' place, takin' the lantern with us so we can see where we's goin. Almost as soon as we sees what it's really like up there, we wishes we left the light back in the cave. 'Cuz this is the kind of place what's better off left in the dark. The lights of town is far behind us, now—farther away then I remembers walkin'—and 'ceptin' for the pointy iron fence surroundin' the top of Boot Hill and the little red schoolhouse just a little ways from the top everythin' around us comes pony express from hell. For instance, just a stone's throw from us, somethin' that looks like a rattler is suckin' the yolk from somethin' that looks like a egg ... but they both has human faces, and the rattler don't look any happier 'bout his breakfast than the egg does. It hurts my head just to think 'bout that one.

As we come up to the iron gate of Boot Hill, the Kid calls me by a name I ain't heard him use in ten years: "Pap?"

I don't think nothin' I seen today surprised me as much as hearin' him call me that. "What?"

" 'Member what you told me when you gave me that choice between ridin' with you and stayin' on the farm with Ma? That whatever I chose, you didn't want me bendin' your ear with regrets?"

"Yeah. I 'member."

"Well ..." he says. And stops. "I guess I don't got nothin' to say then."

I says nothin' to that, but I understands it. 'Cuz I's also spent the last coupla hours figurin' as how the outlaw trade ain't nearly as fun as it used to be.

We walks through the gate to Boot Hill, which at first I got trouble recognizin' as a graveyard. There ain't no headstones 'splainin' who's dead and how they got kilt, just hundreds of wigglin' upside-down L-shapes planted two-by-two in the dirt. I cain't figure out just what they is 'til I moseys close enough to a couple.

"Boot Hill," the Kid whispers.

That it is. Whoever these poor sodbusters was, they was all buried straight up-and-down, with their heads pointin' down and their boots stickin' out of the dirt. From the way they's a-wrigglin' I don't think they's all too happy 'bout spendin' all of eternity this way. Now that we's close enough I can hear this low moanin' that sounds like it's comin from a hundred mouths at once ... and it's all comin' from underground. ...

"I hear Deke," the Kid says. "and ... and Snake!"

I listens, and dang if the Kid ain't right. Deke and Snake are 'round here somewheres pissin' and moanin' just like the rest of them. "Yeah, I hears 'em, too."

"B–but ... Pap ... that doesn't make sense! How can they be here when they ain't even been dead long enough for a funeral?"

I 'members seein' Deke's body fade away soon as it hit the ground that last time, and reckons I now know where it went. Must be awful convenient, that trick— what with not havin' to employ an undertaker and all.

I thinks about it some more, and after a spell I figures that this marshal ain't so much playin' this lawman game by brand new rules as makin' all the old rules stretch out of shape to suit Him. There's a difference. And to win this gunfight I just needs to make them rules work for me 'steada Him.

The Kid's starin' at me. "Pap?"

I says, "Go look for Snake. Lemme know when you sees him."

"Deke, too?"

"Deke don't got a throwin' knife hid in his boot. Hurry!"

We starts runnin' up and down the grave sites, lookin' at the boots stickin' up out of the ground. They's all sorts of pairs, some shiny and new like they's just been bought by some dude purtyin' hisself up for a dance, some all wore out with half-rotted feet visible through the holes in the soles. There's a coupla pairs of Indian moccasins, too, and one feller with a club foot, and another with a peg leg, and a few who ain't wearin' nothin' but socks.

The Kid lets out a holler. "Over here!"

I runs over. Sure enough, there's Snake's boots, stickin' up out of the ground, and the handle of his throwin' knife is still in its sheath just the way it's sposed to be. I pulls it outta the boot, and feels its sharp edge with the tip of my finger, and thanks Snake for not losin' it. 'Cuz right now it's the only thing I got sharp enough to do what I needs done.

The Kid says, "Think we's gonna end up buried like them?"

"If we is," I says, meanin' it, " 'taint gonna be that sorry son of a bitch who buries us. *That* sorry son of a bitch is dead. Git your ass by the front gate and watch out for Him. Slow Him down if you can."

"SLOW HIM DOWN?"

"I'm countin' on you, Kid. I's gonna need a few minutes."

Lookin' pale, but game, the Kid nods and runs to the gate. I sets right down on the dirt, flips open my weapon, and workin' by the light of the lantern, starts unloadin' the rounds, one by one.

I does what I needs to do purty quickly, all told, but it seems to take 'bout a million years, 'cause just as I gets started this music starts wellin' up all 'round us. Ain't like any music I ever heard in any saloon I ever been in. This stuff sounds like they's 'bout ten million guitars backin' up the wailin' of ten million women, and there's this drumbeat behind it tryin' to imitate the hoofbeats of a horse. I knows it means the marshal is comin', and that makes me so nervous I ruin the first bullet and have to throw it away so I can commence with the next one.

I's 'bout finished that when I looks up and sees a cloud of smoke formin' right at the front gate. It's big as a mountain, seems like, and darker than any night I ever seen. Even as I watches, the smoke starts pullin' together in the shape of a man. I shudders and looks down and slips the finished bullet into the slot.

That's One.

The marshall hollers, "RICO!"

I doesn't answer Him 'cause I ain't finished. I just starts on another bullet and fixes it up as fast as I can, hopin' He don't find the Kid 'fore I's done.

Two.

"RICO!" the marshal hollers again. "I'M HERE, RICO! YOU CALLED ME OUT, NOW SHOW YOURSELF!"

Right in the middle of the "yourself" the Kid's gun fires. Glass shatters, and somethin' goes FWOOMP. Since I feels the heat even from here, I knows what I's gonna see even before I ups and looks at it.

The Kid's done pulled off the same trick he pulled 'gainst a bounty hunter named Josey a couple years back. Josey had us all pinned down with nothin' but the one bullet in the Kid's gun, and rather than hope Josey stuck his head up long enough to give us a clear shot the Kid just used that bullet to shatter a lantern thrown into the air over Josey's head. The burnin' kerosene all came rainin' down on top of Josey and Josey came runnin' out from behind that rock yellin' and hollerin' and slappin' at the flames dancing up and down his ass. By the time he dove into the crick to put hisself out, the fella was in such bad shape that we just let him be, 'steada killin' him, since his bounty huntin' days was over anyhows.

The Kid's given the marshal a taste of that same medicine, and this time his aim's even better: the kerosene's splattered all over the marshal's chest and shoulders, and the fire's startin' to catch on His arms.

Trouble is, the marshal ain't flailin' 'bout and screamin' the way Josey done.

Nope.

The marshal actually seems to like it.

He just stands there, grinnin' like it's all a big joke, and lettin' the fire spread 'til He's wrapped in it.

Janey's right behind him, yellin' her pretty head off: "RICO, YOU DUMB HICK! DON'T YOU THINK WE ALREADY TRIED FIRE?"

I finishes off the third bullet and slips it into the chamber. That's Three.

Hurryin' now, 'cuz I doesn't know how much time the Kid's got left, I forces myself to look down and concentrate on what I'm doin. But I hears some of what comes next: the gunshots and the roarin' of the fire and the Kid cursin' every time one of his bullets don't do nothin' and Janey cursin' with words even the Kid don't know. Just as I slips in the fourth bullet another gun fires and I realize Janey's gotten into the act, shootin' useless bullets into the marshal just to slow Him down in case I do decide to show up and join the fun.

That does it. I woulda been more comfortable with six shots, but with a woman at stake. I's gonna have to make do with four.

I flicks the revolver shut and stands up. "COMIN'!"

The marshal's head turns, and even through the flames I can see His squinty eyes and His big fat grin. The fires are dyin' down, now, mostly for lack of anythin' to burn, but they's still dancin' on His head and on His shoulders and they looks mighty comfortable there, like that's where they feels they belongs anyhow.

Janey stands behind Him, all black from the smoke, and cryin' like she don't know if she'll ever be able to stop, and despite what she's wearin' she don't look like a whore anymore: more like a little girl who's been taken away from her mama and don't know if she'll ever be able to find her way back home again.

I looks at the Kid, who's standin' off to one side, and ain't surprised to find out he's got the same look on his face. He misses his mama bad. And it ain't just today; lookin' at him I reckons he's felt that way a long, long time.

I's gonna have to make sure he gets a chance to see her.

I turns toward the marshal and starts walkin'.

Marshal Kane puts His hands on His hips. "So you've finally decided to come out and fight like a man, have you?"

"You gots an awful strange notion of fightin' like a man, mister."

He shrugs. Basically admittin' that I's right 'bout that, but makin' it clear it don't make no difference either way.

When I's at proper shootout distance, somethin' tugs at my feet, and I look down to see what it is. Hands. Cold as the grave, and brown with dirt. They's come straight outa the ground and grabbed me by both ankles, just tight enough so I knows they won't let me duck and roll like I done at the saloon. This here shootout's gonna take place from a standin' position.

"So you don't run," the marshal says nastily.

"How do I know *you* won't run?"

Another pair of hands comes up outta the ground and grabs the marshal by *His* ankles. They gets a nice firm grip, too, though for all I knows, they won't slow the marshal down any more'n a face full of burning kerosene done.

I grins at Him. "You set a lotta stock in bein' fair, don't you, Marshal? In playin' by the rules, even when you don't let nobody know what them rules are?"

He nods. "I'm a straight-shooter, pilgrim."

"That's what I was hopin'," I says.

And we does it.

And just as we both goes for our holsters the dang music wells up again, comin' from all sides it feels like, and even though we's both movin fast as anybody in any gunfight ever moved, time slows down so it takes forever anyways. I sees Janey dartin' out of the way and the Kid pressin' his belly 'gainst the dirt and the marshal's hand closin' around the empty space in His holster and His fingers curlin' into the shape of a gun and my own real gun comin' up to point at His chest, and it seems to take 'bout a million years for all this to happen, every second a' that million years filled with those dang guitars and the choir of heavenly women singin' "Oooo-wooo." I has time to see, that for once I's just a bit too slow. I been outdrawn. Not by much. He's gonna be up and firin' just a heartbeat before me.

He says, "Bang."

And once again, somethin' cuts a hole in me, rippin' right through my side. It ain't a killin' shot—the marshal wants His fun. Still, it almost knocks me over—and though I manages to stay standin', I cain't seem to straighten up or point my own weapon where I needs it to be.

The marshal laughs all sarcastic like. "Mother of Mercy, is this the end of Rico?"

I points somewhere in the vicinity of his chest, not knowin' if I's gonna be anywhere near close enough, and fires.

Time slows down again, this time so much that I can follow the round speedin' between me and Him. I sees that it ain't gonna hit near the chest. It's gonna be a gutshot, of the sort that takes days killin' you. The marshal watches it come, lookin' bored. He makes faces at it, sayin' hurry up, I don't have time for this.

The bullet inches into His belly.

And His eyes go all wide, and He tries to take a step back, and the hands holdin' Him by the ankles don't let Him, and He grabs for His stomach and brings up fingers all covered with blood, and He looks at me, wearin' the face of a man who up 'til now ain't known what fear was like and just had it forcibly 'splained to him.

The Kid yells, "PAP!"

Janey shrieks, "I DON'T BELIEVE IT! YOU GOT HIM!"

I don't rightly believe it myself. But I sure is glad to know it.

The marshal fumbles for His holster, like He 'spects to find a real gun there. But He's movin' a lot slower than me now, and this time my shot don't move slow at all. Oh, no. This time it hits Him right away, blowin' the pointin' finger right off His right hand so He cain't make a gun with it no more. He screams, and starts bawlin', and I finds myself feelin' sorry for Him, and wonderin' whether I should just let Him go.

The feelin' goes away quick, though.

'Cuz almost as soon as I thunk it the marshal starts changin' all over, so He don't even look like He's sposed to pass for human. His head starts meltin' into His shoulders and His arms start flappin' like they ain't got bones in 'em and this great big mouth filled with rows and rows and rows of fangs opens in the middle of His chest and SOMETHIN' that looks like a face starts hollerin' at me from the back of His throat, and the Kid starts doin' his Jesus, Mary, and Joseph act again and Janey starts yellin' "KILL IT! KILL IT!" and rather than argue with them and continue lookin' at somethin so dad-blamed ugly, I just obliges—firin' my last shot right into that sucker's big yap.

It's the best shot I's ever fired, bar none.

The face in the back of the marshal's throat stops yellin', and the thing that was the marshal just falls down Dead.

And just sinks into the ground.

For a second I thinks He's gonna come walkin' back through that gate, laughin' at me for bein' stupid enough to think I won, but no: He's dead awright. I know that 'cause the holes He made in me ain't hurtin' no more. They ain't even there no more. A second later Boot Hill ain't a graveyard no more—it's just a mound'a dirt in the middle of a desert, with nothin' buried in it but more dirt and maybe a rock or two.

Janey's still here, but not by much—I can see the stars shinin through her. And though I knows some of what she's sayin' 'cause it's what I'd be sayin' if I was in her place, she ain't makin' a sound.

I find myself hopin' she gets that Spielberg part she's right for. Whatever that means. I says, "My pleasure, ma'am."

And then she's gone.

I's aware that the Kid's starin', hopin' that I 'splain it 'fore he gets around to askin' me, but I cain't be bothered with that yet. I moseys over to the edge of the hill so I can take a looksee. The schoolhouse ain't down there. The town ain't neither. There's just desert. Which suits me fine. I ain't never had much use for towns, and after tonight I thinks I got even less.

"Pap?" says the Kid. All timid like, like I ain't heard him sound for a while.

"Don't worry about it. We's gonna visit your mama."

"No, it ain't that. I . . . I gots to know."

I takes out the last bullet and hands it to him. "Don't drop it, Kid. I's gonna want to keep this one."

He stares at it, soundin' out the letters I scratched in the metal. "Kay Ay Enn Eee." It takes him a second to sound it out. He ain't never been much of a reader. "KANE." Another second. And then his eyes go all wide. "That's IT? That's how you done it?"

"Don't be ignorant, Kid. I did it the same way I always do it—by outshootin' the bastard. 'Course, I out-shot Him in the saloon, too. But the second time the bullets had His name on them."

I adjusts my hat and starts down the hill, to start the long walk acrost the desert.

I think I goes 'bout a mile 'fore the Kid catches up.

THE SLOBBERING TONGUE THAT ATE THE FRIGHTFULLY HUGE WOMAN

by Robert Devereaux

*She was amazing. . . . She was colossal . . .
but size isn't everything!*

Sally Holmes was married to a swell guy. She liked working in the lab. Holding clipboards and making notes for Doctor Baxter while hiding her beauty behind glasses and a tight bun was her idea of fun. She did it well.

And she gave her husband John a nice home. Soon, if they could figure out where children came from, there'd be pattering feet to feed. John was a good man. They'd been childhood sweethearts. Now John was a police lieutenant. She didn't understand his work. Heck, truth be told, she barely understood her own. But all Sally had to do was to poise her fountain pen smartly above her clipboard and act as if she were saying clever things, and Doctor Baxter was more than pleased to keep her around.

The one thing Sally liked about Doctor Baxter, other than her paycheck, was his way with words. He was a blob in pretty much every respect, balding, sags of flesh stuck on his face like sneezed boogers on a mirror. But when he spoke, his labials, his fricatives, his palatals, his urps of intelligence, the way his moist pink tongue oystered in his mouth—all of those oral sorts of things made Sally go all soft and squoozy inside.

For months he'd been working on something top secret, putting in so many hours he might as well have camped out at the institute. He let no one into his inner lab. But the notes he dictated tantalized her. He overworked his staff, but Sally didn't mind (she knew that *John* did). It just meant more toward their nest egg, more smart repartee over the clipboard, and more of that clever tongue.

When Doctor Baxter invited her that evening into his inner lab, just him and her around, Sally had no inkling that anything more than science was on his mind. He held the unsealed door for her, and she stepped in, sniffing a barnyard stench she'd caught wind of before.

John lay there in his pajamas, wanting his wife next to him. It felt so great to hug her, pajamas to pajamas, and give her a pristine little kiss good night. And every so often—once every few months if he was lucky— she'd be open to cuddling in the dark, to undoing certain strategic snaps and letting him shoot an icky mess inside her while she lay there so calm and sweet and receptive. He'd give his standard "Sorry" in her ear, then roll off her, shame in him, yes, but feeling glad too that she hid her disgust so well.

It proved she loved him.

Still, he sensed there was something missing in their marriage. As Sally flitted about the kitchen or Hoovered the rugs or knelt to dust the baseboards, John felt as if there were a crack in her smile—almost as if, God forbid, a first wrinkle were appearing in that smooth peach-infant face of hers.

His wife needed reassurance.

Oh, heck. He'd drop in at the lab. Yes, yes. He'd dare to be different. Flinging the covers back, he leaped out of bed. Would he put on the clothing he'd tossed into the hamper? No. New ones. He wouldn't sweat too much in them and he could wear them again tomorrow.

Sally'd be thrilled to see him. A sweet surprise.

Baxter anticipated her amazement.

"Oh, my!" she ejaculated, her fetching shoulder blades flexing like coy airplane struts under that white coat she plumped out so well in front.

"You've never seen a ten-foot cock before?" The bird was indeed awesome there in its cage, its magnificent head turned in quirk, one squint-eye wide as a saucer. Too bad he hadn't chosen a hen for his experiments. She would've made one heck of a meal, and there were other interesting avenues (so to speak) that might have been explored. He was tired of cleaning up after Giganto here, and tired of feeding him. Damn rooster was due for death.

"Goodness, Doctor Baxter," Sally exclaimed. "What've you been up to?"

"See that?" he said, pointing to the bell jar on the table, with its throbbing pink crystal. "I concocted that substance. I call it gargantium. It makes organic matter grow. Don't ever disturb that glass container, or there's no telling what will happen."

"I won't." She shook her pretty little head so that her radiant tresses primped and fluffed like in a shampoo commercial; no, wait, he was imagining that. Her bun held her hair tight, severe, puckered like a clenched rectum.

Baxter stepped in front of her. "But that's not why I invited you into my inner lab."

"It isn't?"

"No." He eased the carving knife from his cavernous coat pocket. "I'd like you to undress for me, Sally—nice and slow, nice and sexy, one button, one snap at a time."

Sally blanched fetchingly. "I can't do that."

He placed the blade against her neck. "You can," he insisted, "and you will. But first, undo that god-awful, fershlugginer bun. Let your Prellity down, sweet-cakes."

Tears welled up as she reached to free her hair. Her breasts rose with the motion. Doctor Baxter fixed on them with those ugly eyes of his. He was a loathsome lunk of a man. Except for his tongue. Poor thing seemed shanghaied into saying awful things, but some-how that didn't diminish its beauty.

The magnitude of her anger startled her.

Sally'd never been angry about anything in her life, not one blessed thing.

But even as her fingers worked the buttons and tears gathered in her eyes, she was angry about this. Her an-ger was hot and solid, coming deep from her insides but hiding itself as it grew. He couldn't detect it. But she could surely feel it. And soon, but she feared not soon enough, it would lash out at the scientist Sally had trusted to be good but who was very bad indeed.

"Not fast enough," he said. His free hand shot forth and yanked her lapel to one side, so that her white satin slip showed from her right shoulder strap down to where it cupped in lacy fullness her huge right breast. Where his brutish paw touched her, her flesh ached.

She looked at the knife in his hand, the sharp blade, the brown rippled wood of its handle. She wanted so badly to wrest it away from him, to use it on him.

"Faster!" he said, drool dripping from his lips. You never knew about people. You just never knew.

John adored being a police lieutenant. All the boys in blue—nice, decent Christian fellas—loved and re-spected you. You got to wear stylish suits with paper cut creases ironed into the legs. They snugged your badge into a real nice soft-leather case that felt as cozy as suede when you whipped it from your inside coat pocket and held it up for a citizen's eyes.

He maneuvered the Plymouth along the quiet streets, a bouquet of long-stemmed roses lying beside him.

A lanky young man was walking an Airedale. John hit his horn lightly, waved, took the return wave. The dog's no-nonsense yap filled the air with glee. Life was good. Life was very good. Life was very very very good.

But it could be better.

He could assure Sally that he loved her, that there'd never be for him any woman in the world but her. That was what a wife wanted to hear. For John, there'd only always been Sally. No one else. And there never *would* be anyone else. Never never never.

He hummed a sprightly tune.

There was Baxter Enterprises ahead. The guard at the gate grinned at him. He lifted the flowers, said, "For my sweet honey," and the mustachioed geezer in uniform nodded and waved him through. "Say hello to the missus for me," the guard shouted, shrinking in the rearview mirror.

"I will," yelled John. He rolled up the window, the corners of his mouth hurting from his smiles, and pressed on toward the main building.

Baxter had his way with her. Though smart and snappy as always, Miss Holmes was passive like a good dolly ought to be. On the floor, upon the air mattress he forced her into blowing up, he felt all her secret places, he tasted her, he lay his bulky frame on her and forced his manhood inside her. The air was thick with bird smell, tainted by hints of formaldehyde from the embryos jarred on the table above them.

So enthralled did he become and so passive and almost not-there was his victim that he lost track of his carving knife. And suddenly there was a tugging at his hand, and an emptiness there. Then his shoulder caught fire, a jag of outrage sinking thickly inside. His secretary wiggled like a bazillion panicked eels out from under him as the pain erupted, a swift deep cramp in his upper torso.

He screamed, not continuous but blips—sharp, barked, like a wounded mutt. Her face flared and bloomed. *Shrew,* he thought. *Termagant.* That's what she had turned into. She gripped the knife handle and yanked it out. He felt somehow as if his lungs followed it, and yet it was a hurt he needed from her. She had repented. She would help him to a hospital, stanch his blood, bandage him, make him all better, hold him, kiss him, dump her dorky boy in blue.

The she docked him. She fisted his shaft, razored a chill below, pressed it in, cutting through no-resistance, through sponge cake, burrowing and spreading a volcano of agony. Her first thrust had enervated him. He could only make faint shows of protest as she unmanned him. Suddenly he could no longer feel the squeeze, although he saw the purple flesh blanch in her fingers, saw her pry his member away, felt his groin skin peel up, a gigantic splinter of pain, toward his navel.

His thing thwapped on the floor where she tossed it.

He rocked and screamed, energy draining from between his legs. His attacker—*he'd* been the attacker; now *she* was—bounded up, clattered in his tools above, came back with a bone saw.

And then—Oh, God—she severed his hands.

Rage drove her on. This monster had touched her in all her secret places. Now she was dismantling him, all his offending parts off and away. That's the way it had to be, Sally's crazed mind told her.

His resistance was all in his voice. The bone saw

snagged on the air mattress, which burbled its air away through washes of blood. But the vile hand snapped off, cracking and tearing like an uncooked lobster claw. The other, as his stump feebly brushed her back with sticky protest, proved even easier.

Time for his tongue.

She'd brought back a bull castrator—why he had one, she didn't stop to ask. But her bloody hands tore at his jaws and jammed the instrument deep down into his throat, watching the tongue slither in snug where a pizzle would ordinarily go. Then she clamped shut, freshets of blood upshooting, spraying her breasts with hot gore. And out the quivering, tantalizing, tormenting sucker came.

Though it, too, had violated her, she didn't toss the tongue to the floor as she'd done with his hands and his manhood. She rose, unlidded the first jar she saw, took out the chick embryo, and dropped in the tongue, lifting the jar, hugging its chill to her breasts.

She was aimlessly meandering, slowly, randomly, her face a veil of tears, wounded tears, tears of rage.

Sally's foot struck something. She glanced down at it, Baxter's right hand. The things it had done! Still with the jar hugged to her chest, she bent down, snatched the odious thing up and hurled it away from her.

The bell jar rang from the impact, lifted, tottered, and fell with a decisive clatter to the tabletop, rolling off and shattering on the floor. The pink crystal pulsed and hummed. Its light filled the air. The sound it made rose, higher, higher, like a menacing theremin.

And then the explosion came, pink goop in the air, on her flesh, down her throat. It coated her arms where they hugged the jar, radiating there, pulsing. Sally wanted to scream, but she choked on the stuff, and felt it strangely warm all over her.

* * *

Just as John killed the Plymouth, he felt a *whumph* in the air. It was a subtle pop, but all his antennae of love and protection immediately sprang up and out.

Sally was in danger.

Without remembering how he'd done it, he was suddenly outside the car, his hands on the closed pinging car door. It felt as if it took forever, but he raced to the entrance and plowed through, down corridor upon corridor to Sally's lab. "Sally!" he yelled. "Sally! Sally! Sally!"

No one.

But John took in the door to the inner lab, its edge blasted and pulsing pink from lights within. He dashed to it, yanked it open.

His wife was facing away from him, naked and sobbing. On the floor lay Doctor Baxter, parts of him missing, him nearly dead but not quite so. A gigantic rooster stood in a cage in the far corner, stinking the place up.

John approached his naked wife. There was yucky pink stuff in her hair, all over her body, on the jar her hands gripped so tight. The residue of some pink substance lay like shards of shattered icicle on a far table.

"Honey?" he said. "Are you okay?"

Her face was slabbed in tears.

She looked down, noticed what she was holding, set it with other jars like it on the table beside her.

She turned to him, held out her hands, but then raised them as he approached. "I . . . I'm all goopy."

"Here." He looked around wildly, saw some linen on a shelf. "I'll get you a towel."

He got her a towel.

Doctor Baxter, gurgling, died. "He attacked me," she said. John nodded. His wife was one savage biddy. But, by God, she'd had good reason. There was cleanup needing to be done, here and in their lives. But he vowed, by his love for her, to see things through to the end.

Baxter woofed his last breath. His mouth, his groin, his wrist stumps felt as if God, frowning from on high, had snapped bear traps on them and salted his wounds, skewering his celestial disapproval in like sharp smoldering stakes that glowed white hot, turning, twisting, searing, never a dull moment in his tormented body.

Then suddenly the pain, pricklike, was cut off.

He was somewhere else. Somewhere cool and moist and cloying. He couldn't see. He couldn't hear. But he felt himself alive and whole, if uprooted. And he could taste—oh, yes, he could. Yucky tasting stuff; unpalatable, though he had no palate.

But something most succulent lay close by, something he had tasted recently and could still, in sensual memory, recall with wicked delight. He pulsed. He surged. But this new body, if that's what it was—limbless, but mere limb—would take some getting used to, to make it motile, to seek out and taste that recalled succulence once more.

A light shone, warm and pink (now how could he sense, being blind, colors?), a finger's reach from him. It felt like sunlight on seedlings. He sensed arousal, the shift of flexible flesh, an overpowering urge to grow.

In bed that night, after the police procedurals had swept through her, Sally tossed and turned. An extra long bath had helped, steaming there, quite out of it, till the water grew cool. But she still felt Doctor Baxter's vile acts clinging to her—that and the glowing pink goop, the gargantium the explosion had drenched her with.

At midnight, she woke in a sweat.

John was snoring beside her, big long snuffly snorts that made him less than appealing. His exhalations stank like sodden cigars, like burnt toast threaded with maggoty shreds of pork.

When Sally shifted to turn him on his side, away from her, her pajamas clung tight. The button strained at her breasts, alternating left-and-right-facing vees of fabric. Her hips drew the cloth taut as snapped sheets. Breathing was difficult. Had she put on a pair of John's pajamas by mistake? Nope. The monogram, a red SAH, was hers.

John snorted awake.

"You okay?" he mumbled.

"Yes," she said. "Go back to sleep."

She tried to do the same. Funny. Her pajama bottoms used to cover her ankles. Now they'd started to creep up her calves, clinging there like wet wraps of sea-weed.

She dismissed it, tried to find sleep. But Baxter's words of warning and the image of a ten-foot cock refused to leave her mind.

John feigned sleep. But it wouldn't come. In the moonlight seeping in their window, he let his glisten-ing eyes open. His wife lay upon her back, dozing fit-fully. It was a warm night. The covers slanted at her waist.

My God, he thought, *her breasts are mammoth.*

Sally was so beautiful. It tore him up inside that she'd endured the nightmare of being violated by Doc-tor Baxter. The warped deviant deserved to have his . . . but then John remembered. Baxter *had* had his . . . ! And by Sally's dear hand.

He propped himself slowly on one crooked arm, head in hand, and beheld her. Sweet face. Wanton hair, down now, rioting like rainbows on her pillow. Some-how, there seemed *more* of her tonight. He loved her so. He wished there were some way he could undo her pain.

Undo her buttons.

Her breasts were so huge. Pregnant women, he'd been told, got that way. Maybe they'd have a child after all. But he doubted that. They plumped there under the strain of cotton, huge soft cantaloupe mounds that would one day droop and sag like ugly sacks of pudding, but didn't now. They cantilevered, as magic as flying buttresses in their firmness, their heft, their suspension.

One day, maybe, Sally would let him see them naked.

But that day, he knew, lay far in the future. His wife was no slut. And she'd been through a personal hell that would take time and patience to heal.

The bastard (oops, he amended it to "bad man") ought to have his. . . .

Ah, yes. Small favors.

Baxter felt in-tight. Jar-shaped. He had to get out before the confinement squeezed him to death. He'd never felt so helpless. Then he realized, with a virtual smack to his nonexistent forehead, that he was all muscle.

He contracted, tensed. Waited until he felt cramped again. Then, abruptly, he flexed.

And suddenly he was free!

Sensing sharpness, he gingerly moved over fragments so as not to cut himself. He tasted wood, fell, thwapped to newly mopped linoleum tile. Licking the ammoniac tang of Mr. Clean, he pulsed and throbbed toward freedom.

A pressure halted him. He smelled the black stink of Cat's Paw shoe polish. Swooping across leather, he found flesh, flesh that shook, jittered. Panicked hands batted at him. But he clung tight, wrapping about an ankle. His spittle turned the flesh soft and absorbable. He took the stuff in, the blood, the bone, lapping up thighmeat as his victim fell, scream-vibes egging him on.

It felt positively erotic to sate himself.

Like lava, he smacked up the body inside the clothes, tasted groin slit, hair, belly, breasts. A female cop, was his guess as he gobbled. And alone, based on the help she didn't get. His tonguebody thinned and imbibed, slapping like a wave, receding, drawing sandflesh, sandbone, after it, trails of bloodbubble foaming behind.

When nothing remained but cop suit, he ambled on.

Sally, by the dresser, held her glasses confusedly in her hand. The arms had snapped when she tried to put them on. But strangely she could see fine without them.

"Listen," John said to her. "I'll take the day off. I've got time. We'll go to the beach."

"You think that would help?" Nothing would help.

"It's worth a try."

After a time, she relented. Her husband seemed to be standing in a hole, but he was solid and reassuring. It was a blessing to be in his care. When she took her one-piece into the bathroom to change, it wouldn't fit.

So they got in the car and went to Macy's.

For some reason a white bikini, one of those new and daring suits, seemed right. When she looked at herself in the dressing room mirror, Anita Ekberg came to mind. Milk bottles. *My, my,* she thought, *I am filling out.*

She could scarcely pull her clothing over it, the red checkered shirt, the slacks. Was it time to diet? No. She wasn't fatter. Just larger. Hmmm.

"Let's go," she said, taking John's arm.

On the drive to the beach, she brooded on gargantium.

* * *

Jones Beach was crowded that day. *Must be lots of folks on vacation,* John thought. They strolled along the shore, his wife's statuesque body—and since when had she become statuesque?—drawing stares. There was no hope of finding seclusion, but between beachfronts, they found a bit more room to spread out the pea-green army blanket.

At a distance, an unchaperoned bunch of teens played jungle music, tinny, from a tiny transistor radio.

Sally tucked her hair into a bathing cap, white with plastic flowers daisied on it. John frolicked with her in the waves, splashing her, being splashed. For the moment, everything seemed normal again.

Back on the blanket, her body glistened with droplets as she lay down. Sleek curvy back. Wondrous front. What a full voluptuous woman his wife was. Odd. In the store, her bikini had fit fine. Now the flesh strained at it and he fancied he could see the cloth tugging, thinning.

"Jeepers, this suit is tight," she said.

John looked over at the teens. They were jiggling to the radio noise. Disgusting. America was in trouble.

He heard Sally prepare a sneeze.

When he turned to her, the sneeze blew into her hand and her suit exploded off her. For a second in the bright sunlight, his wife was bare-ass naked.

She took the Lord's name in vain.

Then she grabbed a towel, two towels, and sat there rocking, crying, lamenting, "What's *happening* to me?"

Baxter tasted dirt, gravel, cinders, dog doo, hawked gobs of spit. He preferred the lady cop. He craved more female flesh, and one dainty dish in particular. When he picked up the tracks of his former secretary, he'd be hot on that cutie's trail, no question.

But in the meantime, he slithered along the edge of

downtown North Allville. Somehow his senses of taste and touch were so acute, he could grope along an internal map of the town. He had ghost visions, ghost hearings, faint white whispered things, that corresponded to what was out there.

A malt shop near the railroad tracks.

He sniffed females, lots of them.

The air jittered with passion sounds. He could feel the floor shaking as he slid through the open door. There were seven of them, smelling like high school cheerleader types. With his tip, he eased the door closed, locked it, turned the OPEN sign to CLOSED.

High giggles knifed the air.

Ponytails twirled, hips gyroed in long poodle skirts. Then he attacked, and the giggles turned to screams.

He sucked up girlflesh, swelled, grew. This was the life. Blood, bone, bile, chocolate malts half-digested in smooth taut burst tummies.

Much better than dog doo.

But nowhere near as delectable as sweet Sally Holmes.

Weeks passed. The evidence of Sally's transformation had become so clear that, the day after the beach fiasco, she fled. Nearly seven feet. She was growing and growing fast. As she left, she had to duck through the front door to avoid braining herself.

She kept to the woods during the day, moving at night in a direction that called to her. To clothe herself, she stole sheets off lines, pinning them together with wooden clothespins. She raided gardens, wishing she had money to pay the good people she stole from.

Her mind was expanding, too. Her rage. And, God help her, her libido. She'd never been so horny and so angry, and her thoughts had never ranged so widely over being and nothingness, the meaning of life, and the silly putterings of the diminutive creatures she es-

pied from where she hid. Whole passages of Plato and
Aristotle she had slid over in school now came back,
making sense. She embraced what was right in them,
tossed what was wrong.

When she was thirty feet tall, she began not to care
who saw her move at night. At forty feet, she bared her
breasts, feeling nightbreeze and sunlight tauten the
huge nipples. At fifty feet, she started to tease the little
people, gripping cars and jiggling them, lifting them by
the roofs so swiftly that sometimes—like painfully in-
ept special effects—it seemed she lifted the landscape
along with it. She wrecked upright structures. Steeples,
radio towers, anything lofty she tore off, feeling en-
raged and good and sweaty. During the day, she sought
out bowllike depressions, cool, lush, comforting, to
sleep in.

She had no idea what place instinct drew her toward,
but it was good, very good indeed. Of that she was
sure.

John fixed upon the U.S. map the sergeant was
pointing to. The country was going crazy. His wife,
breasts bare as a harlot's, had grown huge and was destroying property left and right. Rumors of a giant
tongue circulated, and whole villages' populations disappearing. The only thing left behind? A trail of
bloody saliva.

"Mrs. Holmes was spotted here *(thwap),* here
(thwap), and here (big *thwap*)," the man said. He was
square-jawed and steely-eyed. "You men notice where
she's headed?"

Everyone grumbled a yes like they were in church
with their heads bowed muttering amen.

"That's right," he said. "The Grand Canyon. We can
let her be, then zoom in with helicopters, pick her off."

"Hold on," said John. "That's my wife you're talking about."

"Don't be a chump for love," said the sergeant. "We have a public nuisance on our hands. And I aim to wash it off. With steel slugs of civic soap."

"Have you no heart, man?"

"I have a duty to all Americans. That, uber alles."

Everyone grumbled, "Yeah, yeah."'

John grabbed the pointer. "Listen, men, I know Sally as well as anyone. I can reason with her, persuade her to stop destroying erect edifices."

"She's a monster!"

"She's my *wife!!!!!*"

He put it so strongly, the other cops relented.

The sergeant rested a hand on John's shoulder. John knew he wasn't a bad man. Just a jerk.

"Time to get *you* to the Grand Canyon," he said.

And it was.

Baxter loomed at the edges of the drive-in. The film splashed up there, from his honed sensors, he supposed was some dark and scary thing. Good. Made it easier for him to claim victims. Black night, black screen, black cover.

He liked the juicy females, the ones the crew cut boys liquefied with their fingers, squirming out of clothing as easily as out of their virginity.

In the back row a Dodge rocked. He could tell it was a Dodge because his tip traced the chrome letters. Baxter tasted unwashed car, skimmed through the window crack, and dove for the couple in the backseat. He hated boy-taste, but (just as he'd saved the best for last over dinner as a boy) he absorbed the boyfriend first, while he muffled the screams of the half-dressed dolly. Then he turned his all to savoring dessert.

She was mere appetizer, a speared shrimp.

Sally Holmes' sweetness lay on the wind, and Baxter's drool slathered his pathway toward her. In his future, he sensed a deep wide all-engulfing hole.

* * *

Sally recognized it, of course. She and John on their honeymoon had spent time here, had gone down on donkeys.

The Grand Canyon.

Then it had felt like love.

Now it felt like home.

Oblivious to the gaping miniatures scurrying about at her feet, she unpinned the diaperlike loincloth whose taut clutch vexed her, dropped it, and started her long descent to the bottom where the river was.

One weird-eyed maniac feasted his eyes on her, as she lowered her nude body over the rim. She jiggled her boobs at him, then took a deep breath and blew him, midst debris and rubble, back toward the panicked masses. Lustily, she laughed. Then the rim rose above her skull and she was on her way, night's gravid moon lighting rock and brush along the trail.

The local police tracked her with binoculars and with telescopes, relaying her whereabouts to John at the lowest point of the canyon.

When he came upon her, she was reclining, buck naked, near the river. She was obscene. She was beautiful. His shame, under his pants, grew hard. His wife's hand was on her womanhood, stirring it like she stirred cake batter in her Betty Crocker apron. Her deep throaty moans echoed in the vast rocky gorge.

"Sally," he shouted. She didn't hear him. He yelled her name over and over until he grew hoarse.

Then she noticed him. A look of desire burned in her eyes. "John," she intoned, a deep throbbing need there.

"My dear darling," he mourned, "they say there may be an antidote, they say—"

She grabbed him, not hard, but firm as one might grab a kitten or gerbil. "Fuck antidotes," she said in rumbles of husky thunder. "I *like* being big."

He chided her for her crude language, but she merely laughed, booming, like the genie in *The Thief of Baghdad*.

Then she brought him within whiffing distance of her womanhood. He recognized the morning-after manhood stink (but writ large and overpowering) before his bath.

"Make like a statue," she ordered. "Rigidify."

Before he could ask her why, he found *out* why.

Like a diver just before splitting the silent water, he took a breath. That saved him. Into warm gooshy hugs of pudding was he thrust, splooshing about in smooth dark pulsings that brought cows' udders to mind. It was divine and it was terrifying. Just when he knew his lungs would burst, Sally unencunted him, frotting his forehead against a ruddy nub (what *was* that thing?), above which curled riots of coarse straw abruptly thatched. Then—and by the grace of God he could sense when, so he could gulp a goopy breath—she'd plunge him back inside her, twisting him and turning him like an agitator in a washing machine, like an orange half being brutally juiced.

But abruptly he was out, laid on the ground, chilling in the night air. He blinked his stuck eyelids open. And saw—oh, God, he wanted to shit—a gigantic tongue throbbing not six feet away, bloated, bloody, spilling icky rivulets of drool down its unclean sides.

Baxter cared not a lick for the jerk. He'd served as—what did whores call it?—a *dildo* for Baxter's bitch.

But now the bitch had Baxter to satisfy her.

And satisfy her he would.

Tasting more sandstone powder as he rolled on, Baxter leaned against her massive thigh, slurped at her perineum, caught her spillage where it dripped, slowly slalomed his tip up the swollen slit of her excitation toward her sweet hillock of delight.

But she seized him, shoved him in. She embraced him like any animal, and he embraced the opportunity to thrust as deep as he could, elongating, conforming himself to her inner shape, vibrating, throbbing, shuddering, as he moved inward. A tiny bit of him, where she had disembodied him, jazzed at her womanhood. But the rest was inside, not yet releasing his devouring fluid. Time enough, in orgasm, to make her die. He filled her, pulsating against her walls, sweeping beyond the cervix into the uterus itself, filling it like a plump-passioned fetus, poised to wail in ecstasy like a sweaty trumpeter nailing a string of high notes.

She was coming.

And—oh, God—she was *squeezing*.

He flexed, but it did no good. She was crushing him. He tried to release the killing fluid. Got some out, felt the beginnings of meld.

But it was too tight. Too fugging tight.

Trapped.

He fluttered.

He died.

Sally tightened in orgasm. Boulders shook loose at her screams. Her husband, with his hands up to his ears, looked like a drooled-upon letter T.

But the golden tongue she'd had to have was releasing venom, was stuck inside, even as she shuddered in ecstasy. It stung her center. She felt the life squeezed off there first, even as her final orgasm played out. The hurt bled outward from her womb, attacking kidneys, pancreas, islets of Lagerhans, on and on.

Lights winked out all over her body.

"I'm dying," she gasped.

"Oh, no," said the pipsqueak. "Honey, that can't be."

She tried to expel the inert tongue like unfertilized tissue, tried to yank it out. No go. It stuck there like a wasp's barb, sinking its killing force deeper with every breath.

Her lungs felt the slash of cut glass. Her heart.

"Good-bye, John," she gasped.

"I'll never forget you," he screamed. "Nobody will."

The thing that had killed her pooched out of her like a melting strawberry popsicle, dripping crimson gush along her buttocks and onto the earth. It looked like a wilted poinsettia clasped in a clutching infant's hand.

At the height of the terrible display, she had glowed pink: the same pink as in the lab that fateful day. John had felt a warmth beyond embarrassment along his front but mostly in his manhood.

"Bury me deep." Sally's eyes grew fuzzy.

John did a hasty calculation. "I'll bury you *well*," he said. He was hard. To his astonishment he didn't feel any shame. Not only was he hard. He was thick and long, much longer, much thicker than ever in his life. He felt the blunt bludgeon through his trousers. A fucking spade handle stood there.

Crude language had suddenly become okay. In fact it was a decided turn-on. His bulb-head throbbed.

Thoughts of conjunction soared in his head. Thoughts of people watching him score with lots of chicks, sticking his tool in places it had never dreamt of going before.

"Kiss me, John."

He approached her lips, thinking to peck them. Then she inhaled suddenly and he was a hot dog snug in two soggy bun-halves. But a moment later, her death, huge and final and thick with shadows, flooded out upon a slow exhalation and he fell, body-kissed, cock-kissed, to the earth.

Still erect, he picked himself up.

Sally had left him memories.

He patted his pants.

And she'd left him *this*.

And *this* would guide him henceforth on his solitary way.

PLAN 10 FROM INNER SPACE

by Karl Edward Wagner

From the tomb of the past they came . . .
a hellborn army bent on atomic destruction!

One of the stranger films of the 1950s—or probably ever—was Roger Corman's *Plan 10 from Inner Space*. Impressed by the films of Edward D. Wood, Jr., Corman was inspired by the success and critical acclaim of *Plan 9 from Outer Space* to produce a similar sci-fi opus, but on a much lower budget.

Two happy events coincided: Corman found a film lab with partial reels of film which it would sell for scrap. A starstruck pizza delivery boy named Karl Edward Wagner came by just after the film was delivered and, while Corman was calculating the tip, boldly announced that he was really a struggling scriptwriter. Corman invited Wagner in and, over a few beers and the pizza, he outlined his ideas.

Wagner phoned back to Pizza-A-Go-Go to say he'd just quit, then brought in the undelivered pizzas while Corman sent out for two cases of Coors. By morning, they had brainstormed the entire story treatment, much of it written by Wagner on pizza cartons and empty beer cases. This may explain some of the plot inconsistencies, but probably not all.

Telling Wagner to have the shooting script ready by

Tuesday, Corman obtained the needed $15,000 backing from a major tobacco company. He then assembled a cast entirely made up of extras, which accounts for the brief appearances of all the characters. Johnny Decade was played by a James Dean stand-in who needed work. Corman shaved expenses further by using stock footage found here and there and incorporating it into an already confused script. The film was shot in two days, mostly at Denton High School and the old Denton Cemetery. Props were minimal, special effects marginal. Two actors walked out after the first day and were written out of the script. Johnny Decade's fight scenes were actually performed by a young Bruce Lee with peroxided hair.

Only a few prints were ever made, and these received poor distribution on a double-bill with *Invasion of the Surf Mutants*. Critical reviews were mixed. Recently the film has become a cult favorite on videocassette rentals. Discouraged by his lack of success in Hollywood, Wagner emigrated to London and found work as a fry cook at a fish and chip shop in the East End. His several scripts for *East Enders* have been scathingly rejected, although he still keeps at it.

The original story treatment for *Plan 10 from Inner Space* was long believed lost, until Wagner discovered his carbon copies, cobbled together with script revisions, some of it reproduced from pizza cartons, and reassembled the mess. While possibly derivative of various sources, Wagner nonetheless anticipated a number of coming film motifs—some might say anachronisms in 1959—including the segment where dinosaurs in the shape of lizards with horns and other bits attached menace a tourist park. Unfortunately, this scene would have put the film $250 over budget and was scrapped. Wagner used this section of the manuscript to wrap three orders of cod and chips and cannot remember what he had written. He does claim that another extraordinary scene was sent off with an order of halibut, rock eel, chips and saveloys, but one must question his memory, as well as his insistence that Elvis comes in every night and that Corman stiffed him for the beer and pizza.

(From *Drive-Thru Fiction* by Kent Allard. Used by permission of the author.)

Elroy's little deuce coupe rumbled onto the cemetery lane. He made a turn onto a well-known side lane, looked about, then cut off the engine. He slicked back his ducktail.

"I thought you were taking me home," protested Betty Jane White. "Why are we stopping here?"

"It's only nine o'clock." Elroy reached under the seat and pulled out two beers, swiped from his parents' refrigerator. "You don't have to be home until ten. I thought we'd just sit and watch the stars. Want a cigarette?" He drew a pack from the rolled sleeve of his T-shirt.

"I don't drink," said Betty Jane. "But I'll have a smoke." She felt very daring. "Look! There's a falling star!"

Elroy was wearing a church key on a chain around his neck. He cracked open both cans of Bud and handed her one. "Come on. Don't be so square."

Half a cigarette and two sips later, Betty Jane was feeling the effects. She was a cheerleader at Denton High: very pretty in a blonde ponytail, white Angora sweater and a poodle skirt. She and Elroy had been to the sock-hop at the high school gym. This was their first date, and friends had warned her about Elroy.

By the time she had finished the beer, Betty Jane was very drunk, and Elroy had his hand inside her sweater—massaging her breasts, still encased by her cone-shaped bra, He put his other hand on her knee, moved his hand higher.

"Stop!" Betty Jane tore away from his kiss. "What do you think you're doing!"

"Well, if you don't know, I'll show you."

"No! You'll just take me home! Now! I'm a nice girl!"

"Put out, or walk out, sweet thing."

"I'll tell my father about this!"

"He'll wonder what you were doing parked in a cemetery, drunk. I'll tell the boys in shop class."

Betty Jane pulled away from him, opened the car door, and strode angrily away into the darkness. Elroy was laughing. Once she reached the main road, she could find a public phone and call Dad. Bill's Burger Mart wasn't too far.

She was wearing high heels, and her feet were sore from dancing. Betty Jane paused against a tombstone to massage her ankles.

Suddenly there was a bright light overhead. Betty Jane looked up in alarm, then screamed. She started to run, but her high heels caught in the grass, and she tripped and fell. Lying there, she continued screaming, looking into the sky.

Elroy was on his second beer. He chuckled as he heard her distant screams. She'd be running back, begging for a ride. He lit a cigarette.

The sky turned bright. Elroy's first thought was cops with a spotlight, and then he saw a gigantic shadow beneath the light. Something like a giant spider with huge pincers. Elroy was screaming now. He tried to start his car. It wouldn't start. The shadow loomed over him as he screamed.

The two detectives climbed out of their Nash and surveyed the crime scene.

"What do you make of it, Joe?" asked Sergeant Bill Munday of his partner Joe Cannon.

"Hard to say, Bill. This hot rod looks like it was torn

apart by a giant can opener. And look at those beer cans. Could be those teenagers were drag racing. High on beer, came through here too fast and flipped over."

It was the next morning. Munday and Cannon had been called in from homicide when the smashed hot rod and parts of a body were found.

"Hot rod belongs to some juvenile delinquent named Elroy Longstreet. We should be able to get a positive identification from that hand over there. He had a record."

Sergeant Munday consulted his notebook. "Last seen leaving one of those rock and roll dances at Denton High in the company of one Betty Jane White, cheerleader. No sign of her. Reported missing by her parents. No sign of her body. Nothing at the hospitals."

"She may have been thrown clear," said Cannon. "We'll have to search the entire cemetery. Could be the same pack of dogs that tore this punk apart dragged her off. I can't think of anything else."

Sergeant Munday examined some deep tears into the sod. "What do you make of these, Joe?"

"I can't say, Bill. Maybe done when the hot rod rolled over."

"Well, Joe. It looks like it's going to be another long hard one." They got back into their Ford and drove away.

"Bring in the Earth-girl prisoner, so that I may inspect her," ordered Oberführer Elsie von Kampf, privately spoken of as She Werewolf of the SS. She was a tall blonde woman, very striking in her jackboots, black uniform, monocle, and riding crop.

Betty Jane, her hands tied behind her, was quickly dragged in by two burly SS guards. She was frightened, but defiant. "Whoever you are, you'll never get away with this! My father is a lawyer!"

"We happen to know that he is a nuclear physicist at the Denton Research Laboratory."

"What?"

"Remove her handcuffs."

Betty Jane held out her hands in front of her. A surly guard unlocked her wrists.

"Remove her Angora sweater. And her poodle skirt. And her petticoats!"

Betty Jane screamed and struggled to no avail against the brutish SS guards. "You'll pay for this! I'm a cheerleader at Denton High!"

In a moment Betty Jane was stripped down to her white cone-shaped bra and panty-girdle and beige stockings. Flicking her riding crop, Elsie walked about her, studying Betty Jane closely. She playfully tugged at Betty Jane's blonde ponytail.

"Yes. Good Aryan stock. We'll save her for breeding purposes once she has been correctly indoctrinated. A simple cheerleader! One with connections with the CIA! Do you take us for fools!"

"You Nazi monster!" Betty Jane broke away, but the sullen guards caught her in an instant.

"Tie her to that whipping post," Elsie ordered. "A little discipline is in order. Then we'll place her in the cell with the other Earth-girls awaiting the mind-control implants. Soon this so-called Betty Jane will tell us everything we wish to know."

Betty Jane struggled against her bonds as Elsie smacked her repeatedly. She was collapsing, when:

Suddenly the door burst open. An SS officer rushed in. "Herr Oberführer! The giant spider-grab has escaped!"

"It must be captured at once and restored to our control device!" Elsie shouted. "Throw this Earth-girl into the dungeon! She'll talk soon. And it's *Fräulein* Oberführer, you *Dummkopf!*"

* * *

Johnny Decade tooled his maroon chopped and channeled 1950 Mercury into the Denton High parking lot. He got out, turned up the collar on his red nylon James Dean jacket, combed his James Dean hair, then lit a cigarette, leaning back against the Merc and looking cool. It was already five minutes past the first bell, so another five wouldn't matter.

Two men in cheap suits climbed out of a Chevy and approached him. They flashed badges. The fat one said: "I'm Sergeant Munday. This is my partner, Detective Cannon. Our boss is Captain Crawford. It's a clear day here just now, but showers are expected by afternoon. We're from homicide."

Johnny Decade drew on his cigarette, blew smoke on their badges. "Look. I'll pay those parking tickets."

"This is a whole lot more serious, son." Cannon, slender and balding, pulled out his notebook. "We understand that you were quite friendly with one Miss Betty Jane White."

"Sure. We were going steady. Then she dumped me for that greaseball Elroy Longstreet."

"I assume you read the papers," said Munday. "That is, if you can read."

"My folks got a TV. So what?"

"Then you know that Elroy Longstreet was brutally killed and that Betty Jane, last seen with him, is missing." Cannon read from his notes.

"Sure. I told her the guy was a creep."

Sergeant Munday scowled. "You're taking this pretty lightly for a guy whose steady girl might be lying in pieces somewhere."

Johnny Decade tossed away his cigarette. "That's because I'm a cynical rebellious teenager. I don't know nothing about the other night. I skipped the sock-hop and stayed home doing homework. Ask my parents. Now, if you aren't going to arrest me, I'm late for study hall."

"We'll be watching you, punk!" Munday called after him.

"Do you think he knows anything, Bill?" Cannon asked.

"Too early to say, Joe. Too early to say. It's just that the boys at the lab claim that those marks on the ground were made by a giant lobster, and they're flying in a scientist and his assistant from Oak Ridge. Until then, Johnny Decade is our only lead."

They got back into the Nash and returned to headquarters.

Munday and Cannon were waiting at the airport when the Lockheed Constellation landed. As the passengers exited from the DC-3's ramp, a stunning blonde in a tight-waisted Christian Dior New Look dress and pert hat was backing down the flimsy stairs, assisting an elderly gentleman in an outdated white linen suit and a much worn Panama hat. Her seams were straight as she struggled to keep balance on her gray kid pumps.

"Look at the gams on that doll!" Cannon whistled.

"I think that's Professor Northrop the dame is helping. Let's go."

As Munday and Cannon moved forward, the girl caught her stiletto heel on the ladder. Sergeant Munday ran to her just in time to catch her in his arms. She was a most pleasant armful. Munday was on duty. He set her down and gave a hand to the elderly gentleman.

"Professor Northrop, I presume?"

"Yes. That's correct."

"I'm Sergeant Bill Munday and this is my partner Detective Joe Cannon. We're here to escort you to our criminal investigation laboratory. Where is your assistant?"

Professor Northrop beamed and chuckled. "Why,

you've already made her acquaintance in a most timely fashion. This is my daughter, Lee."

"Thank you for rescuing me just now," said Lee, extending a gloved hand. Her handshake was firm.

"But I thought . . ." stammered Munday. "I mean, we were expecting . . ."

"You mean you didn't think a girl could also be a scientist?" Lee gave him a cold look.

Professor Northrop hastened along. "My daughter has often assisted me in my research. She received her first Ph.D. at age fourteen and has earned two more since. Now let's stop wasting time. Our country may be in danger!"

Cannon wiped his brow and replaced his hat. He whistled softly. "Well, what do you know. Beauty and brains. And cold as ice. What a waste!"

They climbed into the bathtub Nash and sped away.

There were five of them waiting for him beside his Merc when Johnny Decade came out of detention hall: Biff, Tab, Rock, Hud, and Jet—five of the toughest hoods at Denton High. Their steadies were watching from a safe distance behind a 1951 Ford. Henry J. Biff, the gang leader, was toying with his switchblade on Johnny's right rear tire.

"I wouldn't do that," Johnny warned quietly.

"True, Daddy-O," said Biff. "But only because I want to keep the blade nice and sharp when I cut up your pretty face. Faggot."

There was a round of laughter.

Johnny Decade sighed. "Look. I don't want any more trouble. What's this all about?"

"Elroy and Betty Jane." Biff flipped his switchblade from hand to hand. "Someone chopped Elroy into stew meat and kidnapped Betty Jane. We all reckon it was you."

"Say, what? Betty Jane and I were going steady."

"Because you're an intellectual, which means you're a dirty Commie and a pansy. You probably have her tied up somewhere."

"No. I'm a disturbed and alienated teenager, barely able to control my inner rage."

Biff came toward him, glancing back to his fellow hoods. "You all heard him admit it. Now let's make him tell us where he's got Betty Jane."

Johnny Decade broke Biff's arm with a half-crescent kick, sending the switchblade flying. Tab had a baseball bat, but Johnny's full-crescent kick shattered that and Tab's shoulder. Rock and Hud rushed him, swinging chains. Johnny somersaulted over them, changed to Southern Praying mantis style, made several grunts, and left them groaning on the blacktop. Jet was drawing his zip gun when Johnny's flying kick caved in his sternum.

"Anyone else want to play?" Johnny Decade wiped his nose, assuming a Drunken Monkey stance. "No? Then I'll go find Betty Jane on my own."

Biff was holding his broken wrist. "You don't fight fair with that judo stuff! You haven't heard the last of us! My brother Spam is a member of the Denton Hell's Angels!"

"Ha!" sneered Johnny Decade. He leaped into his Merc and peeled out as the girls watched in awe.

"Yes," said Professor Northrop, adjusting his thick glasses. "There can be no doubt about it. Don't you agree, Lee?"

They were studying large plaster casts of the strange tracks found at the scene of Elroy Longstreet's smashed hot rod. Munday and Cannon stood by, along with General Wheelright, who had just flown in by military jet from Washington.

"Yes, Father. There can be no doubt." Lee examined the plaster casts closely. "Only, it's impossible!"

"Nevertheless," pronounced Professor Northrop, "these impressions were made by the feet of a giant spider-crab—*not* a giant lobster as originally conjectured. Note the typical pincer prints at the end of each leg. Such a creature must weigh ten tons or more. It could crack open a Sherman tank as easily as we shell a peanut."

"But creatures such as these have been extinct for millions of years!" General Wheelright protested.

Professor Northrop readjusted his glasses. "We cannot ignore scientific evidence. Dr. Northrop, your opinion?"

Lee furrowed her brow and shifted her legs as she sat down, exposing a lot of knee. "Such creatures once inhabited the Antarctic continent. Could it be that atomic testing may have melted the ice that preserved them? But how could one have suddenly appeared here? General?"

"This is strictly hush-hush," warned General Wheelright. "However, there have been numerous reports of UFO sightings near Denton. The army doesn't wish to cause alarm among the citizens, but we just might be dealing with very modern aliens here, not some ice-age monster lobster."

Captain Crawford had been listening to all of this in disbelief. Nonetheless, an Army general and a team of scientists . . . "Bill," he ordered, shaking his head, "you and Joe get a Geiger counter and go check out that cemetery for any signs of radiation. If there are aliens and flying saucers about, that should prove it. Oh, and be careful."

Lee stretched prettily. "Well, Father and I have had a long flight. I think we'll go to our hotel and get some rest. By the way, doesn't the famous flying saucer authority, Dr. Jack Lindstrom, live here in Denton?"

"He does," said Captain Crawford. "But the man is a beatnik kook. Not worth contacting."

Lee adjusted her skirt. "Maybe. Maybe not."

"Bring in the Earth-girl!"

Still in her underwear, Betty Jane was led in shackles before Oberführer Elsie von Kampf, She Werewolf of the SS.

"Please," Betty Jane begged, "may I have my Angora sweater back? It's freezing in here."

"All in good time," said Elsie pitilessly. She sniffed Betty Jane's sweater and rubbed it against her face. "You are beneath the North Pole and must endure the cold. You are Aryan. Creature comforts are nothing to you, Betty Jane White—or shall I call you Betty Jane *Weiss!*"

"No!"

Elsie cracked her riding crop across her cheek. "You Earth-people are stupid! Do you think we are not aware that you are the daughter of the famous nuclear scientist, Professor Edelweiss Weiss!"

"No!"

Elsie whacked her other cheek. "We are wasting time! Take her to the indoctrination room and prepare her!"

Brutal SS guards dragged the screaming girl into another room, where behind a translucent screen brutal SS nurses undressed her, slinging her undergarments atop the screen. In a moment Betty Jane was strapped onto a laboratory table, with only a scant two bands of sheet to hide her nakedness. She struggled, but to no avail.

Oberführer von Kampf leered down at her. "Very pretty. Prepare the mind-control implant!"

A brutish SS nurse brought out a metal ovoid, no

larger than a big jelly bean, with eight metal prongs. It resembled a spider with an SS insignia on its back.

Betty Jane screamed.

"Move her ponytail to the left, Gretchen," ordered Elsie, moving closer with the device.

"My left or your left?"

"Just do it! And hold her head!"

Betty Jane struggled, but in an instant she felt a sharp pain penetrating the base of her skull. And then there was only a misty numbness.

"Now she is ready for indoctrination," said Elsie sadistically. "Lead her into *his* presence!"

Moving as in a dream, still clad only in her bra and panties, Betty Jane let them pull her into another room. It was a laboratory of some sort, with lots of laboratory equipment and flashing lights from several humming banks of instruments.

"Strap the Earth-girl to the chair," Elsie commanded. "Tightly! Make certain that her head is firmly secured. I myself will attach the cosmotrode!"

Betty Jane struggled weakly as Oberführer von Kampf lowered a helmet not unlike a hair dryer over her head, then connected some wires.

Elsie stepped back and replaced a cigarette into her long cigarette holder. She blew smoke into her captive's face. "Now you shall see, stupid Earth-girl!"

The She Werewolf of the SS whipped back a curtain.

Betty Jane screamed.

Floating in a bubbling tank was the body of Adolf Hitler, fully uniformed, his arm raised in a salute. His eyes were open and stared into Betty Jane's.

Betty Jane screamed and struggled against the straps that held her.

"Useless to scream, Liebchen," sneered Elsie. "No one here to come to your aid! We are in a base far beneath the South Pole. Just before Berlin fell to the Untermensch, the Luftwaffe successfully developed

what you stupid Earth-people call the flying saucer.
The SS used these to establish a secret base here beneath the Arctic ice, and at the last instant succeeded
in rescuing der Führer from his bunker. Nazi science
has preserved him in a deathless state of cryogenic
animation until we are prepared to strike back and establish the Fourth Reich! Ha ha!"

"You're mad!" spat Betty Jane, too stunned to follow it all.

"You'll soon sing a different tune." Smiling evilly,
Elsie attached several additional wires between Betty
Jane and Adolf Hitler, then grinned sinisterly as she
flicked a number of electrical switches. "Sing now, my
Liebchen! Ha ha ha!"

Betty Jane's scantily clad body jerked and jumped
against the straps holding her to the chair. The control
device affixed to the back of her neck vibrated with
white heat. Betty Jane screamed. Suddenly she
slumped over, her head still clamped into the electronic
helmet.

The She Werewolf of the SS studied the gauges and
flashing lights on the instrument panels, then adjusted
several dials. Satisfied, she examined Betty Jane's
unconscious body, cut off the power switches, and removed the helmet.

She held the Angora sweater to her face, then ordered Gretchen: "See that the Earth-girl is properly
attired when she is next brought before me."

Sergeant Bill Munday and Detective Joe Cannon
were exploring the old cemetery. Munday waved about
the Geiger counter, while Cannon carried the flashlight.

"Sure is dark tonight, Bill," said Cannon. "Look!
There's a shooting star! Looks like it fell close by."

"The public doesn't pay us to be stargazers," Munday reminded him tersely. "We're here to look for evidence."

Munday paused. "Hey! Listen to this Geiger counter! She's going a mile a minute!"

Cannon put down his flashlight, drew out his notebook, and began to take notes. "Count on the counter's rising."

Suddenly they were both engulfed in a bright light. "What's that!" shouted Munday, drawing his revolver.

Cannon made a note. "It's a flying saucer!" He put away his notepad and drew his revolver.

Suddenly a hideous shadow fell over them. The shadow resembled a giant lobster.

Both detectives cowered back in terror, emptying their automatics into the sky. Futilely.

Screams echoed into the night.

Oberführer Elsie von Kampf, She Werewolf of the SS, flicked her riding crop and adjusted her monocle. "Bring in the Earth-girl!"

Betty Jane marched into the command room. She was clad in a tight SS uniform, complete from cap to black miniskirt and knee-length high-heeled boots. She saluted: "Heil Hitler!"

"Heil Hitler!" Elsie returned. She fitted a cigarette into her long black cigarette holder. "Do you understand your mission, Fräulein Obersturmführer Weiss?"

"Alles in Ordnung, Herr Oberführer!"

"Fräulein," Elsie corrected, flicking her riding crop.

"Alles in Ordnung, *Fräulein* Oberführer! I will lead the other Earth-girls back to the planet's surface in a flying saucer, seek out and abduct a certain Professor Edelweiss Weiss, and return with him to our Antarctic base. Here we will interrogate him and learn the secret of his pluto-neutronium ray."

"Depart at once!" Elsie commanded. "Sieg Heil!"

"Sieg Heil!" Betty Jane marched away, followed by half a dozen similarly clad Earth-girls.

Ignoring the bright lights in the interrogation room, Johnny Decade coolly lit a cigarette. Captain Crawford slapped it from his mouth.

"Detectives Munday and Cannon have been found macerated!" Crawford barked.

"Found doing what?"

"Chopped into hamburger! What do you know about it, kid?"

"Nothing." Johnny Decade retrieved his cigarette. "I was home all night watching TV and waiting for a call from Betty Jane. Just ask my folks if you don't believe me."

"So you know where Betty Jane is!" grated Crawford.

"Maybe. Maybe not. I'm an alienated and misunderstood youth."

"You talk tough. We'll see how tough you really are." Crawford wiped his balding forehead. "All right, boys. Give him the works!"

Just as the pair of brutal cops closed in on Johnny Decade, the door opened. A tall muscular man in a blue suit strode into the room. He flashed a badge. "Agent John Mayer. FBI. We're taking over this investigation. Come along, Mr. Decade."

"But I've got three unsolved murders and a disappearance on my hands," Crawford protested. "This young hoodlum knows something—and I'll make him talk if we have to beat him into silly putty!"

Agent Mayer drew up sharply. "Do you love your country, Captain Crawford?" He opened his notebook.

"Yes. Of course." Crawford wiped his forehead.

"Then you won't interfere with a federal investigation. Will you?" Mayer grinned. "By the way, we know all about that waitress at Bill's Burger Mart. And we have photographs."

"I love my country." Crawford mopped his brow. "Anything I can do to assist . . ."

"We'll let you know. Come with me, Johnny."

Johnny Decade followed Agent Mayer from the room. "Hey Daddy-O! Thanks for getting me off the hook. I've been in hot water with these squares ever since I got my first speeding ticket when I was thirteen."

"Can the wise lip," said Mayer, walking briskly.

"So, why is the FBI taking an interest in me?" Johnny questioned. "No one else ever has."

"Except, perhaps, Betty Jane White?"

"So what?"

Agent John Mayer pushed Johnny Decade against the outside doorway. "Listen up, punk! A few hours ago Professor Edelweiss Weiss, a noted atomic scientist, was abducted from his laboratory by an attack force of girls in SS uniforms. According to his housekeeper, their leader was Betty Jane *Weiss!* You know her as Betty Jane *White!* They departed in a flying saucer. You and Betty Jane were going steady—it's all in our files, so don't try to deny it. What *else* do you know about her connections with the CIA, the SS, and UFOs!"

"I don't know anything! Betty Jane is a cheerleader at Denton High. That's all."

Agent Mayer looked Johnny straight in the eye. "Young man! You may be a hood and antisocial, but do you want to see Americans goosestepping under the Nazi flag! Do you want SS flying saucers controlling this entire planet!"

Johnny Decade lit a cigarette. His hands shook. "All right. Everyone thought he was crazy. I didn't. Now I know he was right all along. I'll take you to my former science teacher, Dr. Lindstrom."

"Jack Lindstrom?" Mayer consulted his notebook. "He's a fired and washed-out drunken kook. Thoroughly disgraced and discredited."

"Maybe so." Johnny Decade drew on his cigarette. "But Dr. Lindstrom is the world's foremost authority on Nazi experimental aircraft. Could be he's the last hope for the free world. I know where to find him. And I'm going to help you, Agent Mayer. But only for Betty Jane. It's a frame. A cheerleader would never turn against her country."

"That's true," said Agent Mayer, making a note.

Johnny Decade tooled his chopped and channeled Merc into the driveway of Dr. Lindstrom's secluded residence in one of Denton's canyons. It was a ranch-style house with an adjacent laboratory that had once been a two-car garage. A yellow and green Edsel convertible was parked beside an aging Buick.

Agent Mayer consulted his notebook. "The convertible was leased by Professor Northrop. He and his lovely daughter have preceded us."

Johnny Decade lit a cigarette. "You feds seem to know everything."

"It's our business to know everything about everybody. Let's go."

No one answered until after several rings. Finally, Lee Northrop opened the front door. She looked ravishing in a pink and charcoal gray dress with matching hat. "Yes?"

"FBI." Agent Mayer flashed his badge. "We're here to speak with Dr. Lindstrom."

"He and my father are in the laboratory," said Lee, swishing her skirt as she let them in. "Follow me."

Her high heels clicked against the hardwood floor. Johnny Decade watched her legs while he combed his hair. Beautiful, but cold as ice.

In the laboratory, Professor Northrop and Dr. Lindstrom were wearing white lab coats and examining a series of grotesque plaster casts. They looked up as the others entered.

"Agent John Mayer. FBI." Mayer flashed his badge. "I'd like to have a few questions answered."

Dr. Lindstrom straightened from his study of the plaster casts and shook hands. "Johnny Decade. Working for the FBI. I always knew there was much good beneath that cynical pose."

Johnny Decade lit a cigarette. "I'm just the driver."

"Same old Johnny," Dr. Lindstrom chuckled. He was a man of about thirty-something, tall, blond, powerfully built. Lee had been watching him out of the corner of her eye.

"Well, we are scientists here. There are many questions we would like to find answers to. Professor Northrop?"

Professor Northrop went to the blackboard, picked up a pointer, and pulled down a rolled-up drawing. "This is a drawing of a giant crab-spider, long believed to be extinct. Frozen remains have been recently discovered in the polar ice. A terrible monster, larger than an elephant, capable of ripping apart a brick building with those terrible pinchers. Note the similarity of its clawed feet to those prints found near the smashed hot rod."

Professor Northrop drew down another drawing. "This is a drawing of a giant sea scorpion, also believed to be extinct for millions of years. It was the size of a school bus. Again, remains have recently been discovered near the North Pole. Note the similarity of its legs to the casts of the marks found in the old cemetery where those two detectives were macerated. And this," he unrolled another drawing, "is a giant lobster, larger than a killer whale. Once again, believed to be extinct, but its footprints match those cast from footprints where Professor Weiss was abducted. I believe that three of your agents were devoured trying to stop it."

"That's top secret!" snapped Agent Mayer. "How do you know about this?"

"We are scientists," said Lee, serving up coffee. "It is our profession to learn everything about everything."

Professor Northrup helped himself to one of Lee's brownies. "Dr. Lindstrom will explain further."

Lindstrom squared his shoulders. "For what I am about to show you and for my theories, I was laughed at and fired from my position as science teacher at Denton High. I think that laughter will soon stop."

He rolled down a screen and switched on a slide projector. "This photo was taken by the OSS in 1942. It was our first warning that the Nazis were developing flying saucers in addition to the V1, V2, and V3 weapons."

It was a blurry photograph of something resembling a hubcap, floating in midair. Swastikas were dimly visible on the object.

"These are later photographs taken during the close of the war. You can see the advances in design. In another year, the Nazis might well have *won* the war." Dr. Lindstrom flipped slide after slide through the projector.

"As the war ended, the Nazis destroyed all production factories as well as all records of their flying saucers. They didn't want any evidence falling into the hands of the Allies. And yet, these photographs you're now observing were all taken during the last two years. Note the SS markings. And note that these saucers show even further development from earlier prototypes."

Agent Mayer scowled. "The FBI has known of these Nazi flying saucers since the first sightings. None were ever captured during the war. We had assumed that the

Nazis had destroyed them all. Then we learned of these recent findings. How can you explain that, Doctor?"

Dr. Lindstrom turned off the projector, turned on the lights, and pulled down a map of Antarctica, pointing at a strange black circle close to the South Pole. "Scientific research has proven that there is a vast world of caverns here at the South Pole. The Nazis established a secret flying saucer base in the waning days of the war. After the Allied victory, the SS moved all saucers and factories into this subterranean sanctuary, waiting for the right time to strike back at the Free World."

"And here is your proof!" declared Professor Northrup. "Based upon our observations, my daughter and I are convinced that these giant monsters have been revived from the polar ice and fitted with control devices. These monsters will obey the diabolical commands of their Nazi masters. Earth will be helpless against fleets of flying saucers armed with the pluto-neutronium ray and filled with behemoths that time forgot!"

"I'll phone Washington at once!" said Agent Mayer.

Johnny Decade lit a cigarette, wondering if he'd ever see Betty Jane again.

Oberführer Elsie von Kampf, She Werewolf of the SS, was in a rage. She strode along the ranks of her miniskirted SS girls, switching each of them with her riding crop. "Fools! Earth-girls are so stupid! And you especially, Obersturmführer Weiss! How could you abduct your father and omit to steal the radium capsules necessary to power the pluto-neutronium ray!"

Betty Jane stood at attention. "My orders were to abduct my father. I was only obeying those orders, Herr Oberführer."

"*Fräulein* Oberführer!" Again, Elsie smacked Betty Jane across her tightly leatherclad bottom. "This time I personally will lead the mission to seize the radium capsules. And then your father will assemble the pluto-neutronium ray for *our* purposes. Is that not so, Rottenführer Weiss?"

"Ja wohl!" said Professor Edelweiss Weiss. He was attired in full SS uniform, and an SS mind-control spider glinted from the base of his shaven skull. "Sieg Heil!"

"Heil Hitler!" Elsie saluted. "Now we go to complete the final step in the conquest of Earth!"

Agent Mayer hung up the phone. "The Army will be here in a matter of hours. General Wheelright is taking command."

"Not enough time for that!" snapped Dr. Lindstrom, examining a map. "According to our calculations, Professor Weiss must have hidden the radium capsules necessary to energize his pluto-neutronium ray in the old Denton Cemetery, the very spot where all the recent saucer sightings occurred. Those Nazi fiends will return to search for them at any minute. It's up to us!"

"I'll have Captain Crawford bring in all available police!" Agent Mayer dialed furiously.

"It may not be enough to stop them!" warned Northrup. "Remember, they have prehistoric monsters under their control!"

Johnny Decade lit a cigarette. "You guys go on ahead. I think I can find us some more help, and fast."

"I'll get the Geiger counter," said Dr. Lindstrom. "Lee, you'd better wait here. Bake another batch of brownies. We'll be hungry when we return."

Lee pouted. "You forget that I'm a scientist."

"Have it your way, sister. Let's move out!"

Johnny Decade skidded into the parking lot of Bill's Burger Mart, a popular hangout for Denton's teenagers. Hot rods and choppers were parked all around. Johnny tossed away his cigarette and lit another.

Instantly, a burly giant in Hell's Angels gear approached him—his cohorts close behind. "You just saved me the trouble of looking for you, Johnny. You broke my kid brother's arm. Now I'm gonna break both of yours."

"No time for that now, Spam," said Johnny, lighting a cigarette. "Betty Jane's life is in danger! We have to move fast to save her!"

Spam looked puzzled. "Say what?" He scratched his graying beard.

"There's a Nazi flying saucer over at the old cemetery. SS spies are searching for Betty Jane's father's radium capsules. They're certain to have Betty Jane and the professor along to aid them in their search. The Army has been called in, but they won't be here soon enough. Only us teenagers can stop those Nazi devils!"

Spam considered the situation. "Well, it sounds fantastic, but lately me and the boys *have* noticed some funny lights over at the old cemetery."

Johnny pressed on. "Don't you see! If the Nazis get their hands on those radium capsules, they can rule the Earth! I may be cynical and alienated, but I won't let my kid sister be eaten by a giant crab monster from the Arctic! And that's what we're up against! Now are you going to fight or turn chicken?"

"Let's rumble!" Spam roared. "Come on, you hot rodders, too! Betty Jane is in danger!"

"I need to stop by the Denton Hardware Store," said Johnny. "We'll break in and take all the dynamite my rod can carry. We'll need it against these space monsters!"

"Break-ins are us!" shouted Spam, leaping onto his chopper. "Let's go, like *nowsville!*"

"Best watch your step," warned Dr. Lindstrom, steadying Lee as she stumbled in the old cemetery.

"I can take care of myself, Dr. Lindstrom," Lee said archly.

"Please call me Jack."

"All right, Jack. Now turn on that Geiger counter."

Lee was carrying a flashlight. Agent Mayer and Professor Northrop were searching another part of the cemetery. "Sure is dark here at night," said Lee, clinging to Jack's muscular arm.

Suddenly a bright light shone down upon them. Jack dragged Lee behind a large tombstone.

"It's a Nazi flying saucer, all right!" Jack whispered. "I don't think they've seen us. We'll hide in that crypt over there!"

The light moved away as they crept toward the crypt. Lee's high heels caught in the turf, and she fell, looking over her shoulder as the bright light swept toward them once more. Jack rushed back, swept Lee into his arms, and bore her into the crypt.

"Look!" whispered Lee. "It's the Weiss family crypt!"

"Of course!" blurted Jack. "And the Geiger counter is going crazy! We should have guessed! The radium capsules are hidden here!"

"Then the Nazis will be here in an instant!"

"They'll not take those capsules without a fight," said Jack, drawing his revolver steadfastly.

Outside, Professor Northrop and Agent Mayer saw the blinding light hovering overhead. Soon it was joined by a hideous shadow rather like a giant crab-spider. The policemen opened fire with Tommyguns and tear gas. Two of the cops screamed and vanished from view, then the shadow crumpled to the ground.

"Ugly brute," commented Agent Mayer, reloading his automatic. "I hope there aren't many more lurking about." He glanced at the colossal corpse. "Just what is it, Professor?"

"Some member of the spider-crab family, no doubt," said Northrop. "Long extinct. Heaven knows what else these Nazis have in store for us."

"Here comes more company!" barked Agent Mayer. "Make every bullet count!"

A group of SS stormtroopers were slowly striding toward them, crossing the cemetery with arms outstretched, eyes blank, faces expressionless.

"Let 'em have it!" ordered Agent Mayer, aiming his automatic.

The policemen fired a hail of bullets, but to no avail. The SS stormtroopers kept on coming.

"Great heavens!" swore Agent Mayer. "Bullets can't stop them!"

"They're SS zombies!" shouted Northrop. "We're doomed!"

Suddenly the cemetery was filled with choppers and hot rods.

"It's Johnny Decade and the teenagers!" Agent Mayer shouted.

"Keep your headlights focused on the Nazi zombies!" ordered Professor Northrop. "The brutes can't stand the light!"

The SS zombies began to stagger under the cascade of bright light streaming onto the cemetery grass.

"Let's go, kids!" shouted Spam, flourishing a chain. "We'll finish off these Krauts!"

He turned to Johnny Decade. "Hey, aren't you coming?"

Johnny lit a cigarette. "No, Spam ... I got a date with Betty Jane."

Inside her flying saucer, Oberführer Elsie von Kampf was furious as she glanced at her television screen. "Those teenagers are destroying our master plan!"

She switched her riding crop. "You! Rottenführer

Weiss! Take Obersturmführer Weiss with you and recover the radium capsules at once! Do not fail! Heil Hitler!"

"Heil Hitler!" Obeying orders, the two marched away.

Elsie switched on her saucer's monitor screen. Dinosaurs battled on a barren and bleak landscape. The She Werewolf of the SS watched intently. "Yes! This is what we will unleash upon you stupid Earth-people if you do not submit! Thousands of these behemoths are frozen beneath the Antarctic ice! Without complete surrender, we shall destroy the entire surface world! Ha ha ha!"

She placed a cigarette in her cigarette holder. "Scharführer Gretchen! The instant these fools have returned with the radium capsules, release the rest of the monsters! We'll prove to these Earth-men that resistance is futile, then we'll send in the dinosaurs!"

Johnny Decade dashed toward the Weiss family crypt, playing the crazy hunch that he might find Betty Jane there.

He guessed right. Inside the crypt, Lee was screaming from the floor, having tripped in her high heels and fallen. Dr. Lindstrom was battling with Professor Weiss, while Betty Jane stalked purposefully toward Lee, her fingers outstretched to claw the scientist's face.

"Quick!" shouted Dr. Lindstrom. "Remove the SS mind-control devices from their necks!"

Johnny Decade saw the glint of a metal spider spearing the flesh just above Professor Weiss' collar. Leaping forward, he dislodged it with a half-crescent kick. Professor Weiss staggered, then slumped to the crypt floor.

An instant later, Johnny was struggling with Betty Jane, holding her arms as she tried to scratch out his eyes. Lee's screams rang against the walls of the crypt. Dr. Lindstrom quickly reached beneath Betty Jane's ponytail and removed the mind-control device. Betty Jane slumped into Johnny's arms.

"Is she. . . ?"

"She'll be coming around in a moment," reassured Dr. Lindstrom. He helped Lee to her feet and embraced her.

Betty Jane's eyelids fluttered, then she held her hand to her forehead. "Oh, Johnny! What happened? Has this all just been a bad dream?"

"A very *real* nightmare, Liebchen." Professor Weiss picked himself up from the crypt floor. "One which will grow worse! When we do not return soon with the radium capsules, Oberführer Elsie von Kampf will release the rest of the monsters. They will wipe out all resistance, while the She Werewolf of the SS obtains the capsules. Once powered, the pluto-neutronium ray can instantly melt down any city on this planet!"

Johnny Decade lit a cigarette. "I've got a cure for monsters. Professor and Betty Jane, can you lead me to that flying saucer?"

"Certainly, Johnny. But we'll have to hurry!" Betty Jane exclaimed. "Dad, you wait here."

A minute later the two were in Johnny Decade's chopped and channeled Merc and tooling across the cemetery grass.

"There it is!" shouted Betty Jane, pointing. "Hidden beside that grove of trees!"

Johnny saw a glowing light coming from what resembled a pair of hubcaps welded together.

"Better get out now, baby. There's enough dynamite in this car to level Los Angeles. I'm going to give it to those Nazis. Right down the throat."

"But Johnny!"

"I'll jump at the last second. Don't worry about me.

You just get out and give me a cheerleader smile and a wave and a jump for luck as I peel out. Hurry! Earth is running out of time!"

Betty Jane stood beside the Merc as Johnny Decade gunned his engine. As she did her cheerleader stunt, Johnny popped the clutch and peeled out across the lawn. Betty Jane's high-heeled jackboots caught in the sod, and she stumbled and fell.

Racing through the darkness, Johnny could see the flying saucer looming in front of him. He lit a cigarette, perhaps his last one. With the glowing light almost blinding him, he aimed the Mercury straight for the saucer, fumbled with the door handle.

It was stuck.

Suddenly it came open. Johnny leaped from his hot rod and rolled across the grass, stunned. The Merc continued its last run, and seconds later the sky lit up with a monstrous explosion.

The Army medic finished listening to Johnny Decade's chest. "You're in fine shape, son. Just a little dazed by that blast."

"That was one brave thing you did, son," said General Wheelright, gazing at the burning crater where the flying saucer had been. "When you finish high school, I'll make certain that the Army has a place for you."

"What now, General?" asked Professor Weiss.

General Wheelright put down his binoculars. "Well, now that Dr. Lindstrom has located the Nazi flying saucer base beneath Antarctica, we'll just send over a few B-36's and drop a few hydrogen bombs down their rat hole. Think that will take care of those monsters, Professor Northrop?"

"It certainly will!" Professor Northrop was smiling as his daughter and Dr. Lindstrom strolled away for a kiss.

A sergeant came forward and saluted General Wheelright.

"Anything get out of there, Sergeant?"

"No, sir. We did find a girl wearing a white Angora sweater and a poodle skirt walking about in a daze. Apparently she was with those bikers, because she rode off with them."

"Well, let's wrap this up." General Wheelright lit a cigar. "Wait here, kids. I'll have a jeep take you home. Doctors, I'll need you for debriefing."

"That girl in the white Angora sweater and poodle skirt," Betty Jane said, once they were alone. "I was wearing that same outfit when I was captured. Do you suppose Elsie. . . ?"

"Not a chance," said Johnny Decade, hugging her. "I'll buy you a new Angora sweater tomorrow."

After their kiss, Betty Jane said breathlessly, "Oh, Johnny! You saved my life! You saved the world! And you sacrificed your hot rod! What can I ever do to repay you?"

"Well, there is something I've been meaning to ask you." Johnny Decade lit a cigarette, a wistful twinkle in his eye. "Could you pick out an Angora sweater for me to wear, too?"

ABOUT THE WRITERS

JAY R. BONANSINGA has written articles for everyone's favorite culture vulture publication, *FilmFax*. His novel *The Black Mariah* has been optioned for the screen, and he's scheduled to make his bow as writer/director of *ManSlayer,* a martial arts/dark fantasy.

EDWARD BRYANT has twice won the Nebula Award for best short story. His book reviews appear in *Locus* and *Cemetery Dance,* and his acting credits include *The Laughing Dead* and *Ill Met by Moonlight.* Ed has also notched time on the ol' experience-meter as a stirrup buckle maker and a radio talk-show host.

ADAM-TROY CASTRO has one of the most original imaginations in weird fiction, a fact illustrated by such stories as "Clearance to Land" *(Pulphouse)* and "Miracle Drug," which was featured in his collection, *Lost in Booth Nine.*

NANCY A. COLLINS is the author of *Wild Blood* and *Paint it Black.* She is best known as the creator of Sonja Blue, a vampire whose recent appearances include *A Dozen Black Roses* and a comics adaptation of *Sunglasses After Dark.*

ROBERT DEVEREAUX is the author of *Deadweight* and *Walking Wounded.* His current projects include a fantasy novel based on Wagner's *Die Meistersinger.*

RANDY FOX grew up in Kentucky, just down the road from the Jesse James Drive-In. His stories have appeared in *Hardboiled* and *More Phobias.* He's working on a rockabilly mystery novel.

ED GORMAN has published several suspense novels and three collections of stories. *Million* called him "one of the world's great storytellers."

NINA KIRIKI HOFFMAN has the most melodious name in dark fantasy (if you don't believe us, try singing it to the tune of the Hawaiian Christmas classic, "Mele Kalikimaka"). Her novels include the Stoker-Award winning *The Thread That Binds the Bones* and *The Silent Strength of Stones*.

GARY JONAS writes tales of fantasy, suspense, and horror, and pens book reviews for *Cemetery Dance* and *The Iguana Informer*.

REX MILLER is the author of ten novels, including the paperback bestseller *Slob*. Perhaps he's best known as the creator of "Chaingang" Bunkowski, a man-mountain psychopath who'd put the shiver to Leatherface's spine.

SEAN A. MOORE is the author of *Conan the Hunter* and *Conan and the Shaman's Curse*. An avid épée fencer, he lives in Boulder, Colorado with wife Raven and their dog, cat, and parrot.

GREGORY NICOLL serves on the Foreign Films committee of Joe Bob Briggs' Drive-In Board of Experts. An indefatigable writer of short fiction, he has notched three appearances in *The Year's Best Horror Stories*.

DAN PEREZ is an alumnus of Houston's long-lost Thunderbird Drive-In Theater, where he saw *Old Yeller* and *A Fistful of Dollars*. His credits include *Amazing Stories*, *Cemetery Dance*, and *Xanadu 3*.

WAYNE ALLEN SALLEE is currently researching a biography of fifties film favorite John Agar. A collection of Wayne's stories, *With Wounds Still Wet*, was published in 1995.

STEVE RASNIC TEM has written more than 200 short stories. Recently he switched gears and edited *High Fantastic*, an anthology of Colorado fantasy, sf, and horror.

TIA TRAVIS plays bass guitar in a hillbilly/surf band called Curse of Horseflesh. Her stories have appeared in *Shock Rock II*, *Northern Frights III*, *Fear Itself*, and *Young Blood*, and she recently completed her first novel.

Shortly before his death, award-winning writer, publisher, and anthologist KARL EDWARD WAGNER joked about writing a sequel to his drive-in contribution featuring Mexican wrestlers, go-go dancers, beach parties, and robots. The editors wish that Karl would have had the chance to tell that tale, and we mourn his untimely passing.

ABOUT THE EDITORS

NORMAN PARTRIDGE has sold more than fifty short stories, plus several comic book scripts. His Roadkill Press collection, *Mr. Fox and Other Feral Tales,* won the Bram Stoker Award and was a finalist for the World Fantasy Award. Stephen King called Partridge's first novel, *Slippin' into Darkness,* "a five-star book."

Partridge is a lifelong fan of drive-in movies. As a youth, he saw a double-bill featuring *The Music Man* and *Planet of the Apes* at a drive-in somewhere in Los Angeles, and he has nightmares about trombone-playing gorillas to this day.

Veteran anthologist MARTIN H. GREENBERG is the winner of the Ellery Queen Award for lifetime achievement in mystery editing and the Milford Award for lifetime achievement in science fiction editing—the only editor to receive both honors.